The sun slipped behind the ridge. The canyon darkened. A new wind rose from below, cool, dry, and strange. It didn't whip or gust. It climbed smooth and deliberate, brushing past their cheeks like breath.

Martin turned, suddenly alert. The hair on his arms lifted. Something whispered in that wind, not a word exactly, but a shape of one. Syllables barely formed, curling around his ear like it belonged to a voice he should remember.

"de nashaaaaaa . . ."

Martin stepped back from the edge quickly. "You feel that? Did you hear that?" he asked.

"de nashaa?" asked Brian, "What the hell is that?"

Neither Martin nor Mr. West answered. Mr. West was intently staring down into the canyon, not blinking.

A Davis Mountains Ghost Story

Kyle Vernon

A DAVIS MOUNTAIN GHOST STORY

<u>Other Books By Kyle Vernon</u>

Digby the Church Mouse: Saving Home

Digby Saves His Home (2nd Edition)

<u>Other Books Edited By Kyle Vernon</u>

Sail Ho! by Sir James Bisset (2nd Edition)

Tramps and Ladies by Sir James Bisset (2nd Edition)

Commodore by Sir James Bisset (2nd Edition)

If you enjoy the book, please tell a friend.

This story, including all names, characters, and incidents portrayed, is **fictitious**. No identification with actual persons (living or deceased) is intended. The 220th Cavalry Regiment depicted in this work is entirely fictitious. It is not based on any real military unit, nor is it intended to represent one, past or present, within the United States Armed Forces or the military of any other nation. Any resemblance to actual regiments, battalions, service members, or historical events is purely coincidental. This fictional unit has been created solely for narrative purposes and should not be interpreted as a commentary on, or criticism of, any real-world military organization or personnel.

This disclaimer also applies to the Apache and the Apache Nation. In no way does this book accurately portray Native Americans or their rich and vibrant cultures, nor should it be considered an authority on their customs, rights, or traditions. The use of the Apache language in this book is generated through *polytranslator.com* and is constrained by its accuracy.

While many of the locations referenced in this work, such as Fort Davis, Fort Davis National Historic Site, Alpine, Balmorhea, and the surrounding West Texas region, are real places, the events, characters, and institutions portrayed within are entirely fictional. This includes depictions of the Fort Davis Independent School District, Sul Ross University, and Balmorhea Independent School District, which are used fictitiously for narrative purposes. Any resemblance to actual persons, living or dead, or to real events is purely coincidental. No part of this story should be interpreted as a reflection of the policies, actions, or personnel of any real-world school district, university, or community.

PREFACE

In my own way, this ghost story is a tribute to many of the great men I encountered as a Boy Scout growing up in the 1970s and 80s. Some of my fondest memories come from the stories told around a campfire…tales that sent our young imaginations running wild. More than once, we screamed bloody murder and nearly lost control of bodily functions when the adult telling the story suddenly came hurtling across the campfire, shrieking a blood-curdling howl. We always laughed afterward. Only in recent years have I come to realize how unique that experience truly was.

Electronic devices pale in comparison to a campfire story on a warm summer night, under a million stars dancing across the sky, with perhaps a few coyotes nearby singing their own tales to the moon.

In many ways, this story is a salute truly earned and well deserved, to those men who shared stories, their stories, with me. Storytelling and face-to-face interaction are vital elements of human experience. Sadly, that essential need is denied, one child at a time, as they are handed a device to keep them quiet. Electrons make terrible mentors. We must recognize this truth: we need each other more than we need to interact with a device. All that we are stands to be lost if we forget our humanity.

Dedicated in loving memory to:

Joseph Wayne Word	**Marvin D. Eastman**
(1926 – 2012)	(1923 – 2007)
My Stepfather	My Scoutmaster

Between these men and so many others on my trail to Eagle, I thank you for being there when I needed you.

And to **Buffalo Trails Scout Ranch**: Only my teen years on staff were spent there, but the memories last a lifetime.

Other Disclaimers

Some portions of this novel were refined with the assistance of AI, particularly for proofreading, structural editing, and enhancing atmospheric detail. All final creative decisions, narrative arcs, and content were written by the author.

This story was inspired by a newspaper article published in the *Midland Reporter-Telegram* in the early 1980s. I have plotted and planned this novel intermittently since then. Only after discovering the existence of the Confederate sniper rifle, and the unique ammunition it used, did the story arc finally come together into the form presented here.

The Confederate sniper rifle mentioned in this story is based on a real historical artifact and serves solely as a plot device. It is not intended to carry any broader symbolic or political meaning.

Chapter Flourishes

Throughout this novel, you will notice a symbol appearing at the beginning of each chapter. This image changes across the story, beginning as the Native American symbol for 'cloud' and gradually building, chapter by chapter, into the symbol for 'storm.' This transformation mirrors the rising tension of the story, as the haunting presence in the Davis Mountains grows stronger with each passing event.

Unless otherwise noted, each flourish also contains a photograph I personally took in the Davis Mountains in June 2025. These images, drawn from real places, serve as small windows into the land where the story unfolds. They are intended to share the beauty and scenery with readers unfamiliar with this unique region. Locations of photographs may be found in the addendum.

The flourish designs are inspired by Native American symbols. Their inclusion here is done with deep respect for Native American artistry, iconography, and the cultural traditions they represent. While symbolic, these images are not used to depict or appropriate sacred meanings. Rather, they serve as atmospheric accents, honoring the connection between land, story, and memory.

This creative choice is meant as a tribute, not a literal interpretation, and I sincerely hope it enriches your experience of *A Davis Mountains Ghost Story*.

Contents

Chapter 1
First Heat

The heat shimmered across the highway, a wavering ribbon of black threading through the red rock mountains of West Texas. It was the long kind of summer heat, the kind that stretches from sunup to sundown for months without mercy. By early August it had become a brutal, omnipresent force. The scrubby mountains ringed the land, their dark red cliffs etched against a sky so blue it looked scalded. They bore the heat like old kings, still unbothered, shaped by fire long ago. They drew in the sun's weight and held it deep in their bones. Plants that could afford to drop their leaves had done so. The rest simply endured, suffering daily from the relentless heat. A few, especially those near the blistering pavement, skipped the wait for fall and withered to nothing. The highway stretched ahead, a black stripe with brown trim, framed by the sun-scorched cliffs.

The right turn signal blinked, though no one was around to see it. The older-model Dodge Ram veered off the main highway and onto a narrow strip of Ranch Road. Martin hadn't seen another car since Balmorhea State Park, fifteen minutes back, a tree-lined oasis known more for its spring-fed pool than its traffic. As he made the turn, his eyes jumped to the truck's water temperature gauge. It was habit now, but still necessary. The needle was edging too close to the red. A quick glance at the other digital readout confirmed why the truck was struggling. It was 104°F, the hottest temperature outside since the trip began.

He took the first low water crossing at a decent pace, but the next two sent the contents of the three big boxes riding beside him shifting and bumping. This was the fourth move in as many years, but this one was supposed to be for several years, at least. College was behind him, and his marriage was just beginning, early days, but promising for the long run.

A soft ding sounded from the dash. The temp gauge had pushed into the red. He eased off the gas and let the truck roll to the shoulder, guiding it with one hand while the other rolled down the windows, killed the A/C, and cranked the heat all the way up. Hot air from outside mixed with the even hotter air blowing from the vents. It was stifling. Sweat started to bead across his forehead, almost instantly.

Even though he had less than two miles to go, the new house was still out of sight, tucked around a tight bend and hidden behind a prominent ridge. He already knew there was no cell service out here; on a previous trip hauling furniture, the call with Lindsay had dropped the moment he left the flats and started climbing out of Balmorhea. He glanced at the outside temp, now reading 105°F, and wondered how long he'd be stuck. Twenty minutes? An hour? At that temperature, maybe until sundown, unless he could speed things up.

He looked over at the seat beside him, crammed with a chaotic mess of boxes and leftover apartment junk. Closest to the passenger door was a brand new weed sprayer, still in its box. He'd picked it up on clearance a few days earlier, thinking it might come in handy. Now it just might. If he filled it with some of the emergency water he carried for the radiator and misted the coils, it could cool things down faster.

Martin was mid-spray, fine droplets hissing as they hit the hot metal, when he finally heard tires on gravel. His friend Brian had rolled up almost silently in his much newer dark green Chevy crew cab. The passenger window slid down, revealing Brian's spitting gap and toothy grin.

Tall, broad across the chest, and already sunburned along the bridge of his nose, Brian leaned toward the window with that same mischievous glint in his brown eyes Martin had known since college.

"I'm so glad to see you're handling the radiator weed problem. Heard it's a bad year for 'em," he said, laughing, "How long you been here?"

"Long enough to roast my ass," Martin replied, not missing a beat. He was wiry and trim, with short-cropped dark hair and a sweat-darkened T-shirt clinging to his back. "Forget the grill, we'll just wave what we want cooked in the air for a few minutes."

Brian squinted at the faint wisps of steam curling up from the truck's hood, then nudged his cap back as he eyed Martin's setup.

"Now that you're raking in that big teacher money, maybe it's time to retire this relic," he said, nodding at the Dodge.

He paused a beat, choosing his next words carefully. There was a flicker of envy in his tone, but he didn't want it to sound like bitterness.

"I mean, it's not like you've got a house payment. Your father-in-law set y'all up right. A whole section of land, an honest-to-God square mile of Texas, and a house on top of it."

Martin angled the nozzle left and was rewarded with a sharper hiss from under the hood. Progress.

"It's not like he handed us the land. And the house is nothing fancy. It's a repossessed manufactured home." Martin said, adjusting the sprayer nozzle. "The land it sits on is the biggest mess of catclaw acacia, mesquite, and scrub oak I've ever seen. When I finally get to turn those goats loose, thanks again for the gift, they're going to stand in the trailer doorway, look me dead in the eye like, 'You assholes want us to eat what?' and never take a single step outside."

They both laughed, picturing goats with attitudes and zero work ethic. Of course, they knew goats would eat just about anything. Eventually.

Brian leaned an arm on the doorframe. His tan was baked in from years of working outdoors, and his forearms were crisscrossed with faded scars from barbed wire, fencing jobs, and youthful stupidity.

"What's the story on this place, anyway? I mean, I know it's smack between the two school districts you and Lindsay are teaching at, but your father-in-law said it's been in your family for decades. How'd one of the most successful landmen in Texas end up with this biological trainwreck? No balance, just ugly."

Martin paused to work the pump on the sprayer, the water stream thickening in response. He didn't answer right away.

"He didn't buy it, that's for sure," he said finally as he stood up from pumping. "His great-uncle, a man named Herbert, talked a guy down from jumping off a building the day the stock market crashed in '29. A few years later, that same guy gave him this land as a thank you when they met up again. They served together on a Merchant Marine ship during the war."

Brian worked his lips to whistle low but only blew air out instead.

"Yeah. His great-uncle never married, no kids, so he willed it to my new father-in-law. Mr. West," Martin was never comfortable with calling him Dad, "Not every day a six-year-old inherits a square-mile of Texas. I think he tried selling it a couple times, but no one bit. When Lindsay got hired at Fort Davis ISD and I got picked up by Balmorhea ISD, he jumped into action. Got a well drilled, found the home, and had it hauled in. I think he called in a few favors from some oilfield buddies to get it all done. I know he picked up the solar panels and battery at auction three days before our wedding."

Martin lifted the weed sprayer and checked the water level. It was low, but it looked like the job was done. The needle on the truck's temp gauge had dropped back into safe territory. Brian watched for a moment, then seemed to remember why he'd shown up in the first place. Five hungry people were waiting just a couple of miles away. He was the one hauling steaks and groceries.

"All right, I'd better get moving. I drew the short straw and got sent to town for supplies. Your new father-in-law shoved two hundred dollars at me and told me to spend it all on food. The first meal at your place is going to be a feast! How soon do you think you'll get there?" asked Brian.

Martin stepped closer to the open window, the sprayer still in hand. "I think she's good to go now. I'll be right behind you. Oh, hey, don't be surprised when you try to give him the change from the store and he tells you to keep it. He does that to me all the time."

Brian tipped his cap, slid the gear shift down, and rolled forward a few feet before hitting the gas. Martin watched his former employer turned friend and best man disappear down the road and around the bend, dust rising behind it.

Martin half-placed, half-dropped the sprayer onto the passenger-side floorboard and clicked his seatbelt on. The outside temp now read 105°F, but the radiator had cooled off, more than enough to finish the drive. He put the truck in gear and pulled back onto the road.

Chapter 2
The First Supper

He smiled as the house came into view a few minutes later. It was the only structure for miles, just a double-wide sitting low and long on the land. Its white metal roof reflected the sun in a dull shimmer, and the light gray siding with dark brown trim gave it a kind of understated permanence. No lawn to speak of, just scattered shrubs, mostly shaved down to stubs nearest the house, and a patchwork of greyish loam that passed for soil. It wasn't hard to notice some shrub remains looked paler green than others, already the result of the traffic parade and numerous tires rolling over them the last few days. The largest brush, by far, was a squattish desert willow that had volunteered to grow long before the house was built and brought in.

Besides Brian's truck, four other vehicles were clustered near the house: a white Jeep Wrangler and three pickups, a couple hitched to trailers. The home sat a good two hundred feet off the road, with tire tracks packed into the dusty approach.

Martin couldn't see it from this angle, but there was a small metal barn located about thirty feet off the southwest corner, and behind that, row after row of solar panels feeding into the largest battery he'd ever laid eyes on. There were bigger, sure, but this one took up as much space as the six-burner grill parked on the patio. It powered everything, the house and the 500-foot-deep water well behind it. He'd been told the well alone had cost nearly twice as much as the house, but that was about all his new father-in-law had shared. Martin hadn't worked up the nerve to ask what the whole setup really cost. Wedding gift or not, it was hard not to feel the weight of it.

Just a few minutes behind Brian, Martin climbed the three metal steps and opened the front door. A welcome rush of cool, moist air spilled out to greet him, brushing against his sunbaked skin like a blessing. The evaporative cooler was running strong, which meant the plastic water line had finally been hooked up to the big black tank out back. That was the kind of thing his father-in-law handled without fanfare, just one more quiet victory in the long list of prep work he'd overseen. Like a battlefield general with a clipboard, he'd coordinated a small army of workmen to get the place livable. After the blast furnace Martin had just driven through, he was deeply grateful to have the man on his side.

Inside, Lindsay met him with a tight hug, her arms wrapping around his back, the swell of her baby bump pressing into his stomach. She jumped back almost immediately, laughing.

"Jeez, you're boiling. Did the radiator give out again?"

Martin ran a hand across the back of his neck. "Yeah, just past the turn. I had to mist it down with water. Didn't Brian say anything?"

"Nope. He flew through here and went straight out back with the steaks. Dad has already got them on the grill."

He gave a tired grin, then took a moment to look at her properly. She'd just turned twenty-three, her sandy blonde hair pulled into a loose braid that hung over one shoulder. Still tall and athletic from her volleyball days, she carried herself with that same calm confidence that had stopped him cold the first night they met, back at that mixer her sorority hosted, where he was working as the DJ. He'd been running sound, manning the DJ table on a borrowed setup, thinking more about keeping the playlist going and the party hopping than impressing anyone. Then she walked up with a plastic cup in hand, leaned over the table, and asked him why he looked so worried. That was it. No games, no fluff. Just her. He explained to her, in detail between running the board, that one of his amps had failed and the one he borrowed from the music shop wasn't working correctly, or correctly enough for his comfort.

She was still like that. Sharp, focused, grounded, and now she was carrying a ring on her finger and their first child.

As they passed through the living room, Lindsay paused and tilted her head toward the hallway. "You see that nail by the corner?"

Martin glanced over. "Yeah?"

"That's where I hung my dreamcatcher. The one I made in college art class, sophomore year."

"The purple and bone colored one?" asked Martin.

She nodded. "I've hung it there three times. Nail, screw, even a large cup hook for good measure. Every time, I walk through here a few hours later and find it on the floor again."

Martin raised an eyebrow. "Could be vibration from the door, maybe?"

"I thought that too. But it's not dropping when the door slams or anything obvious. It's just... not staying. Like something keeps knocking it down, but nobody hears it," Lindsay spoke with a casual hand lifted towards the location.

"So, what do you think? The house is bad juju?"

"Maybe. Or maybe it doesn't want protection hanging there, I designed it after one I saw on the internet. One promising protection," she said, half-joking, but her tone faltered. "Anyway, I gave up. It's leaning against the couch now; I pitched a few bent nails and my last shred of college pride," she ended the conversation and changed the topic, "Apartment all cleared out?" she asked.

"Yeah. But it wasn't the 'quick trip' I imagined. We accidentally left a few boxes behind in the bathroom and closet; those last-minute ones always feel heavier. Loaded those boxes into the truck, the entire bed and most of the front seat are stuffed full. I vacuumed again and handed the keys to my replacement. She's probably moving in as we speak. I forgot to ask about the pet deposit."

"I'm sure they'll send it."

Martin gave a skeptical look. "Not if they remember Dumpsy. Where's that orange menace, anyway?"

He glanced around the living room. The house still smelled faintly of paint and cardboard. At just over 1,600 square feet, the double-wide wasn't anything fancy, but coming from an apartment half the size, it felt massive. Laminate floors throughout, cool air blowing from the vents, a proper kitchen, and three full bedrooms. One was already turning into a nursery, the master still crowded with boxes and a bed frame, and the third sat completely empty, waiting for a reason to matter.

Or a visitor.

****

Dumpsy was a force majeure in their relationship, an uninvited, unforgettable little chaos agent. Disguised as a flea-bitten, scrawny kitten, he'd appeared like fate one evening while they were walking together through the sunken gardens off Abe Street. If their relationship was a brick wall built of shared experiences and lengthy conversations, Dumpsy was the mortar that locked much of it in place.

It was on their fourth date that they spotted him. They noticed him just after sunset, mewling softly near the path, his ribs visible through a patchy coat. Starving and desperate, he approached people as they passed, begging for scraps or a scrap of kindness. But it was the couple walking just ahead, barely fifty feet in front, that changed everything. Not only did they shoo the kitten away, but the man also hurled a beer bottle in the kitten's direction.

The sound of it shattering against a stone snapped the air. Lindsay gasped, hands flying to her mouth. Martin froze. The couple in front moved on, oblivious to the shock they had dispensed. Then, without a word, Martin rushed toward the trembling ball of fur that had darted beneath a bush, yowling in fear while the other couple laughed and walked away.

It took teamwork and patience. Lindsay sprinted back to the truck for leftovers from dinner, while Martin knelt nearby, speaking in calm tones and coaxing. Slowly, cautiously, the kitten crept out, until Lindsay swept him up in her arms like he'd always belonged there.

Instead of a movie, the night turned into an emergency vet visit, Martin driving with one eye on the road and the another watching Lindsay and the little bundle she cradled. They left the clinic with more than a check-up; they picked up food, a litter box, toys, and supplies from a late-night supermarket. It didn't even need to be debated. Since Lindsay still lived in the dorms, they decided the kitten, clearly dumped, would move in with Martin at the manager's

apartment he rented at the Blue Mountain Apartments. He'd tell the owner later.

From that night on, there was no more "casually dating." Lindsay came by every day, often bringing treats or supplies, sometimes just sitting on the floor with Dumpsy asleep in her lap while she talked about her day. He wasn't just a pet. He was a fixture, a tether, a little orange matchmaker who had clawed his way straight into both their hearts.

****

Looking around the new house, Martin and Lindsay eventually found Dumpsy, now nearly two years old, dozing atop a stack of half-unpacked boxes in the guest room. Only the tip of his orange tail moved, flicking lazily every few seconds in acknowledgment of their presence. His head didn't even lift.

Lindsay smiled as she gently rubbed the cat's back. "He's been like this since yesterday," she said. "Rode out here with me in the Jeep. You'd think he'd hate it, but he was calm, like weirdly calm. Stoic, even. Barely made a sound the whole three and a half hours." She shook her head and laughed. "Waltzed through the place like it had always been his. I think he likes sleeping near the floor vents. Spent most of yesterday sprawled across one, and that was before we had water getting to the cooler."

Martin chuckled and let the image settle in, a pampered, heat-averse Dumpsy stretched across a vent like a lazy dragon.

A door creaked open down the hall. Mrs. West stepped out of the guest bedroom, brushing her hands on her jeans. "Do either of you smell fireworks?" she asked.

Martin turned. "Fireworks?"

"Or gunpowder. Like someone fired off a couple rounds in the hallway."

Lindsay wrinkled her nose and sniffed. "I don't smell anything."

"It was faint, but sharp. I was unpacking a box and caught a whiff of it, burnt, metallic. I thought maybe something scorched in the wiring.

"Martin glanced toward the cooler outside a nearby window. "Could be the new straw pads settling in. They give off some strange odors until they soak a bit."

Mrs. West gave a thoughtful frown. "Maybe. Just caught me off guard."

She waved it off and headed past them and toward the kitchen, but her shoulders were a little tighter than before.

They stepped outside a few minutes later into what passed for their backyard, all 640 acres of it. Like the front, the land had been cleared of most of the ever encroaching catclaw, but out back there was something more: a proper concrete patio, twenty feet by thirty, covered with a taut black mesh that gave just enough shade while still letting filtered sunlight through. Rain could still come through it, but slowly, preferring to run off over soaking through.

The sun was easing down into the western sky now, low but not yet angled enough to throw light beneath the mesh canopy. Martin stepped off the short stairway and smelled the scent of sizzling meat from the grill. With the heat he had just endured still fresh on his mind, it gave him a fresh appreciation for what the steaks were enduring.

His father-in-law stood beside the cooker like a man born to the task, spatula in hand and attention focused. He was telling Brian, who was seated closest to him, all about the problems the driller had with the property's water well.

"…busted a piston rod the moment the bit touched the ground. That took too long to repair, so he brought out his second rig the next day, but that one had water in the fuel line, which took two hours to fix. And if that wasn't enough, he lost a cone off his new drill bit at 300 feet," he stated matter-of-factly. "It cost him a lot of time."

"Unlucky, sounds like." Brain replied as he sipped his beer.

"He said as much, but with a lot more choice words thrown in," finished Mr. West.

A large, white expanded-metal table with a half-dozen mismatched chairs was arranged in a casual semicircle between the back door and the grill, which sat just off the patio's edge on the farthest side from the entrance. The entire patio area was much cooler than the surrounding landscape thanks to a series of water misters attached to each patio upright. Just like the evaporative cooler filling the new house with cool air, the outside air around the back patio was much more tolerable. It looked like the kind of setup that would grow over time, guests added, chairs swapped, stories told.

Beyond the grill, maybe forty feet farther out, stood the white metal barn. It was large enough, in theory, to take both Martin's Dodge and Lindsay's Jeep if needed, though the doors might not shut completely once they were inside. That was mostly due to the massive house battery stored at the back of the structure, a matte gray box the size of a commercial freezer. Martin had been told there were larger ones, but this was the biggest he'd ever seen up close. It could power the house, the 500' well, and then some.

The barn itself sat on a freshly poured concrete pad, Martin noticed it looked about the same age as the back patio. Less than two weeks old, easy. He noted it was smooth. Whoever poured it floated it well.

Next to the barn was a tall, dark black plastic water tank, at least eight feet high and as wide around as a rolled bale of hay. It had likely come surplus from some Permian Basin oilfield storage lot, overkill, sure, but dependable. Martin remembered from earlier conversations that it held 1,200 gallons and would soon be filled by the deep well nearby. Between that and the solar rig, the house could run self-contained for weeks. Maybe even longer. And it would be more than enough to support the fifty goats he kept imagining out here, his solution to the catclaw infestation. That, or a flamethrower.

Located a distance off the northwest corner stood a second modest metal barn for the livestock. He and Mr. West had picked the spot deliberately, far enough to muffle animal noise and avoid the worst of the smell from the goats that would soon be arriving. Especially with the prevailing wind coming out of the southwest. That way, the evaporative air conditioner wouldn't draw goat stink straight into the house. Like the barn with the battery inside the structure itself wasn't much to look at, but it was modern with a concrete floor and steel beams strong enough to survive winds from any storm, save maybe for a tornado.

Stepping off the back patio Martin noticed a couple of additional trucks and an SUV parked around the back side of the house. One of them belonged to his father-in-law, hitched to the same trailer they'd used during last deer season. The old 4x4 Gator UTV was still strapped to it, far from new, but in solid shape. It had performed like a champ on the family's leased land up in the northern Panhandle. Steep hills and muddy creeks proved not to be much of a challenge, even if both were located with feet of each other. Piled

in front were enough railroad ties for tomorrow's goat corral project being built at the second barn.

****

That trip to go deer hunting had been something special. The West family and Martin had bonded in a way only shared campfires and early mornings in blinds could make possible. Everyone except Lindsay's youngest sister, Elise, had managed to tag a deer. She'd lined up on a fine-looking buck with her .257 Weatherby Magnum but missed it clean. In the few seconds she worked the bolt for a second shot, the deer had vanished into a patch of high scrub. Still, five deer between six people made for one of the happiest and most laughter-filled Thanksgivings Martin could remember. Not only did Martin's 8-point buck wind up on the wall, but Mr. West also gave Martin a "gently used" Browning 30.06 with a scope at the end of the hunt.

****

Dinner that late afternoon on the back patio carried that same easy rhythm. Everyone dug into grilled steaks and cold sides served with a healthy portion of laughter as they swapped stories from the big move.

Best man Brian shared how he'd earned a warning from a DPS trooper after getting clocked at 85 mph outside Rankin. Fortunately, the trooper had graduated from the same high school Brian had attended a decade earlier. They ended up spending more time trading stories about teachers than discussing the ticket.

Mrs. West talked about how a stray piece of twine jammed in her SUV's trunk latch kept triggering warning lights, forcing her to pull over several times before figuring it out. Lindsay had convoyed with her two sisters, stopping at nearly every convenience store between San Angelo and Balmorhea. Elise, the youngest, had spent most of the drive DJ'ing from her jeep, queuing up road trip playlists and insisting that every gas station snack be "audited for morale." The group call they'd kept going the entire drive proved to be a brilliant idea, especially when they passed Brian on the roadside mid-ticket.

Martin had been the last to arrive. He'd stayed behind to walk the new apartment manager through her duties. She seemed confident until the conversation turned to pool maintenance. He'd gone over the pH testing and chlorine adjustments in detail but confessed to the dinner table that he'd called the property owner afterward with a warning. "You might want to keep a close eye on her, chlorine's not her strong suit," he said with a sheepish grin, but he knew she would learn like he did.

As the sun slipped lower in the west and dessert plates clinked with forks and second helpings of pie, Mr. West finally broke his quiet streak.

"Martin," he said, setting down his glass, "seeing as this land's about to be managed for the first time in who knows how long, I figured I'd loan you the Gator until deer season. Same goes for the truck I used to bring it down with. I'll ride back with the Missus."

Martin blinked, stunned, and leaned back into his chair. "Wow. That . . . would be great," he said, still processing.

Mr. West wasn't finished.

"With our first grandkid coming, my wife and I both figured you could use something a little more dependable," he said. Then, a

pause. "Also . . . I've got a deep, dark secret I need to share, with all of you."

All conversation stopped. Eyes darted around the table. Even Mrs. West lowered her glass and stared, her expression unreadable.

He chuckled softly at the weight of their reactions, "I know, I know. Sounds dramatic. But here it is: I'm a Landman. I've spent most of my life walking, mapping, photographing, and negotiating over everything from five-thousand-acre oil leases to crooked fence lines behind someone's trailer. I've seen and done just about everything there is to do with land…"

He paused, then added, "Except this place. My own property."

He looked out across the back acreage, where the land rolled gently away toward the distant ridgeline. "I've never once plotted this land. Never walked the full perimeter. Never marked the corners. Not even once. I pay the taxes and nothing else."

He pushed his chair back, stood up, and clapped his hands together.

"So, after we're done stuffing ourselves, let's break out the GPS, grab the field kit, load the Gator, and go find the corners of this old square mile. We may be the first owners to walk here since the 1930s, and I'm not sure the man that gave it to my great uncle ever stepped on it either."

Whatever tension had crept into the air vanished in an instant.

"I know one corner's up on the ridge in front the house," he said, waving toward the horizon, "and the other three are either south or off that way." He gestured broadly toward the sun, now about three hours from disappearing behind the mountains. "One of them, maybe, somewhere down in that arroyo bottom. Might be a good hike, but the satellite photo looks like it may be off a cliff."

.

Chapter 3
Marking the Corners

Every inch of land felt older than it looked. With Mr. West at the wheel, Martin riding shotgun, and Brian perched in the back with the stakes and gear rattling beside him, they set off once the Gator was down off the trailer. Only the materials for the goat corral remained on the trailer. The first marker they planned to place was the northeast corner, easiest to reach since the house sat near the eastern edge of the square laid out on the old plat map that was digitized and being shown on a laptop sitting near Mr. West.

They headed back down the Ranch road, rolling toward the wide bend just east of the house. As they drove, Mr. West explained the easement tied to the road itself, his voice low and steady over the rumble of tires in dirt.

"FM easement's narrow here. You can see it's been widened over time, but our fence line still holds. There's about 150 feet of that ridge up ahead that's barely on the property."

The Gator left the pavement with an unsettling bounce, and Mr. West handled the rough terrain with practiced ease. He sat straight-backed, lean in build, his iron-gray hair tucked under a weather-stained cap. His skin, darkened by years in the oil patch, was weathered and creased, more from sun and wind than age. He wore a faded long-sleeved pearl-snap shirt, the kind that made you think he hadn't bought new clothes since the second Bush administration.

In no time, they found themselves parked atop a high ridge where the land began to fall away in layers. The bend in the highway lay just to the north, gleaming faintly in the sun. Mr. West killed the engine and stepped out, adjusting his hat against the glare.

"This is the highest point on the whole place," he said, kicking the dry soil lightly with his boot heel. "Lines based on an old railroad survey from the late 1800s. Runs due south to that fence over there, right past that pipeline easement. See that booster station? That's where the other corner, the southeast property stake goes."

While Mr. West hammered a thick pine stake, the first of the four, into the rocky ground, its top wrapped in fluttering white engineering tape, Martin and Brian took in the view.

To the south and southwest, the Davis Mountains rose in layers, rugged, ancient, and sun scorched. The range was a mass of deep red cliffs, steep slopes, and jagged ridgelines, as if some lumbering giant had chiseled them from the Earth. Scattered stands of live oak clung to the hillsides, gnarled and weather-beaten, while the remaining cover was a tapestry of dry brown grass and stubborn scrub, all baked into stillness by the summer heat.

****

Martin had learned early that West Texans didn't give compliments so much as they offered comparisons. And Brian's grandfather, a leathery man with a voice like crushed gravel, had once muttered that "the only thing more stubborn than a goat was a West Texan trying to make a living off 'em." Everyone laughed and agreed, but Martin had filed it away as a kind of truth.

The Millrick ranch had stood outside San Angelo since before statehood, at least that's how Brian told it, and it had held on through bad markets, dry spells, and more than one half-baked cousin who tried to run things sideways. Goats and mohair in the early days of the Millrick Ranch paid the bills, but everything hung in the balance of capricious rainfall patterns, the hallmark of west Texas weather. When the market was up, the rain failed. When the tanks were full, the bottom dropped out of prices. It was a see-saw operation with a shifting center of gravity.

Then oil came. Not in geysers, not enough to make headlines, but steady. A few pumps in the west pasture started paying the bills. And decades later, wind turbines joined them, marching across the far ridges like strange white sentinels. Income layered onto income, and suddenly the ranch wasn't scraping. It was standing solid, but not tall; dependable, because each industry added another dice in the roll.

But goats remained, more for the ranch's tax permit than necessity. This allowed the ranch's land to be valued based on its agricultural productivity rather than its market value.

Martin had first shown up there as a skinny undergrad with a buzz cut and a notebook. He was looking for summer work, and they were looking for help during lambing season. A scrawled HELP WANTED note on the Angelo State student union board led him to call twice. Brian remembered that. He'd told Martin later,

"Nobody calls twice unless they're desperate or serious. You didn't sound desperate."

Most college kids just wanted beer money. Martin showed up asking about parasite load and hoof rot. Within two weeks, he could trim hooves, pull kids, and identify half the herd by name. Brian's dad, a man of few praises, had once muttered, "That boy's either got a plan or a hole he's trying to fill."

Martin came back that summer, took shifts in the worst heat and rode along to biology classes in the fall when his truck was being repaired. They became friends somewhere in that blur of work and lectures, sweat and textbooks. It was during those long drives to the University's research plots that Martin had first talked about Lindsay, this smart and athletic woman he was seeing. It was about the time he was securing Brian's services as a best man that he told him about the land her father had offered them out in the Davis Mountains.

When Martin called later to ask if Brian still sold goats, the answer came before the question finished. Of course he did.

And now here they were, standing on the edge of a new 640 acre mess. Brian, who used to be just an employer and then a classmate, was the first person Martin wanted to call friend after his arrival in San Angelo from Temple.

It wasn't just the goats anymore, they were friends.

Brian pulled out his phone, checked the screen, and gave a short laugh. "Hey, we've got a signal up here."

Martin checked his own. Sure enough, a couple of bars.

"Clear line-of-sight," Mr. West said, standing upright again. "From up here, you'll have eyes on Highway 17. Every morning you'll turn left to head to Balmorhea, Martin, and Lindsay will turn right for Fort Davis. Not a bad commute, really. Twenty miles. Long but pretty. Traffic certainly won't be an issue."

Martin stepped beside his father-in-law, squinting out toward the hazy horizon where the earth folded into layered shades of red, gold, and purple. Mr. West raised a finger and began pointing to the skyline.

"That one there, that's Star Mountain. This ridge we're on is part of it. I only know this from the satellite image."

His hand shifted southward. "That sharper one is Big Aguja Mountain. Further over, see that broad mound? Campers from the Boy Scout camp call it Central Peak, but on the maps, it's listed as Black Mountain."

The nearly silhouetted peaks loomed in the distance like old memories, imposing, weathered, and still. Martin took a slow breath, the dry air sharp in his nose. This wasn't the kind of place you owned even if a piece of paper stashed somewhere said you did. It was the kind of place you learned to live with, patiently, respectfully. The land didn't bend easily. It endured.

"Men, we're racing sunset here. The next stake is a breeze, but the west side of the lot is probably going to be as tough as it is rugged. Let's get a move on," said the older man. They climbed into the Gator and set off back to the road leaving the stake with the engineer's tape fluttering in a soft breeze behind them.

The Gator's tires hummed softly as they rolled back onto the Ranch road, the ridge now behind them. Dust kicked up behind the wheels, caught in the slanting light of the westward sun. Mr. West drove with one hand on the wheel, the other resting lightly on his knee, calm as ever. Martin sat beside him; a topo map displayed on the PC his father-in-law had placed there. Mr. West didn't need to look at anything but the road as they drove toward the distant pump station. Brian bounced slightly in the back with the gear, holding on to the roll bar and taking in the long views.

The Gator bumped over a shallow ridge, its suspension creaking under the weight of three adults and a steel toolbox rattling in the

back. Dust on the road peeled up behind them in slow, lazy curls, indicating that vehicular traffic on this Ranch road was practically nonexistent. Martin leaned forward in his seat, squinting into the distance as they crested a rise and the land fell away in folds of scrub and scattered oak.

Brian sat up straight, chewing on a toothpick like it owed him money. "Man," he said, "this property's got a weird mix of cover, especially the west side off the road. Y'all notice how thick the acacia is? And the scrub oaks are twisted to the point they're kinky."

Mr. West kept one hand steady on the wheel, the other resting on the gearshift. "That's Pleistocene outwash, son. Big Aguja spilled half the mountains through here back when mammoths roamed. It's sandy, loose stuff. It never really developed the way bottomland soil does. Another ice age or twenty thousand years and it might be decent."

Brian nodded. "Makes sense. I figured this was floodplain material, but the term my professors used was a 'high bench' if there is a drop off to the west. But the brush density's odd. Too clustered for natural regeneration. It's like the land's been holding its breath for a hundred years and just started exhaling acacia."

Martin raised an eyebrow. "That bad?"

"Not bad, just . . . unusual. Acacia this thick usually means something got disrupted. Fire cycle, grazing pattern, overgrazing, hell, maybe just time and neglect. But if y'all clear it, mulch it, and keep it on a cycle, this soil's got potential. Even if it is on the raw side."

Martin looked up from the handheld GPS unit in her lap. "What about irrigation? That water well, how did it test?"

Mr. West cracked a smile. "Fifty gallons a minute. Results came in just last week."

Brian let out a low whistle. "That's a gift. You could run pecans on that, if the soil has the zinc. But smart money says after the acacia is gone, you can put in a vineyard first then nut trees, something with shallow roots and a drip system. Just don't go thinking about pivoting irrigation. Fifty is nice, but not enough for a pivot."

He gestured broadly at the ridgeline to the east. "You've got elevation, water, and wild soil. If you're willing to wrestle with the brush, you could turn this place into something special."

Martin gave a half-laugh, looking out across the land. "You make it sound like this land's been waiting."

Brian didn't answer right away. He narrowed his eyes toward a knot of scrub oak, where the shadows clung a little too tightly for the late afternoon sun.

"Maybe it has," he said quietly. "Just not sure what for. My professors back at Angelo State would have fits if they saw this, there's too much brush."

They were headed southeast now, following the road before veering off toward the flatland next to the road. The ridge had gotten only taller in this section of the trip as they went further south, but it had also moved further to the east leaving a widening flat expanse between.

"You ever think about selling this place?" Martin asked, loud enough to cut over the wind and the rumble of the engine.

Mr. West glanced sideways, his face unreadable beneath the brim of his hat. "Almost did," he said. "Twice, actually. Had buyers sniffing around just last year."

"Then why not?" Martin asked.

The older man slowed and leaned slightly into the turn as they turned left off the pavement and followed a faint, dusty two-track toward a distant line of catclaw and creosote about fifty yard behind the pump assembly.

"Well, because of what's under us right now," he said, rapping a knuckle on the side rail. "This stretch of the Davis Mountains sits

right above the southern extension of the Delaware Basin. Not a lot of folks know that."

Brian perked up in the back. "Wait, the Delaware basin? I thought that it was way out by Pecos and northwest of there. Ya know, by the Delaware Mountains."

"It is. But the basin dips under these mountains too. Shallow at first, then deeper. And while these hills are all rhyolite, igneous, solid stuff from an eruption about sixteen million years ago, the basin beneath is a different story. Shale layers, ancient seabed, fossilized pressure cookers. There's a better-than-decent chance there's gas down there. Maybe a lot. Some of the wells south of here near Alpine spew out millions of cubic feet a day. Which is what is in that pipeline next to us right now. I know the owner, they carry a lot of Transon Oil."

Brian blinked. "There were volcanoes in Texas?"

Mr. West laughed. "Oh, sure. Most of the Trans-Pecos was volcanic at one time. All this," he motioned to the slopes and crags around them, "this is what's left of a five or six caldera's worth of ash and tuff eruptions. These mountains aren't eroded ranges like the Rockies. They're the cooled remnants of fire."

Brian let out a low whistle. "I thought Texas was mostly flat and full of cows. Nobody told me we had volcanoes under cattle ranches."

"We don't advertise, and they're extinct," Martin said with a grin.

Mr. West nodded. "Most people don't see this part of the state unless they're lost or looking for stars. But geologists know. And so do energy folks. There's interest in these deeper pockets. Quiet interest."

He eased off the gas as the road narrowed, the Gator bouncing slightly as they crossed a shallow dip lined with gravel and the familiar brown sun-dried grass.

"So why not sell when they came calling?" Martin asked.

Mr. West took a moment to answer. "Because I still hold the mineral rights. I may have no use for 'em now, but one day, maybe you or Lindsay will. Or your kid."

He looked out over the land, the light now lengthening across the flats, painting everything gold and rust.

"They offered good money, but it wasn't worth giving up what might be down there. And once you sell mineral rights, it's impossible to get them back. This is Texas and it isn't wise to let rights like that go. I'll pay the property taxes and keep this land."

Martin nodded slowly. He'd always figured the land had simply been forgotten about all these years, but this was something more. Something strategic.

"You think there's enough to drill?"

"Too expensive to drill since the price of gas is too low, but give it ten, fifteen years," Mr. West said. "Horizontal drilling and fracking have changed the game. All it takes is one new well somewhere nearby and suddenly the math changes."

Brian whistled again. "Man. I just thought we were out here staking land for goats and stories. Didn't realize we were riding over a giant gas vault."

Mr. West chuckled, easing the Gator to a slow stop.

"Well, the goats are still part of it," he said. "This land's gotta look like it's lived on, managed. It keeps the tax folks satisfied, and it keeps any claims clean. But yeah, part of why I wanted to walk the corners is to make sure we're still clear on all the lines. If the ground ever does become more valuable, I want to know where we stand. Literally."

As the motor noise died away a lone mockingbird sang from a nearby prickly pear. Not the wild song of care abandoned because spring had arrived, but more of a sing a bit and wait a bit. "This is close. Let's get out and put the second stake right about where that fence corner is. Your neighbor has fenced in his property."

Martin grabbed the map and the GPS. Brian pulled a stake of the pile of three along with the small handheld sledge, too big to be a hammer, too small to be backbreaking when you swung it. Together, they stepped off the Gator and into the brittle hush of early evening.

The second stake went in with hardly any effort, just a few minutes of checking coordinates, a couple swings of the sledge, and it was done. As they stood over it, all three men turned and looked back toward the distant ridge where the first stake had gone in.

Even straining their eyes, there was no sign of it now. Without binoculars, or maybe even a telescope, it was impossible to see. Martin was struck by how deceptive the land had been. He imagined the plot much smaller than this. Until this realization the section seemed manageable. In person, it was immense. And now he realized just how much of it sat across the road from the house.

With time slipping, they moved quickly. A neighbor's well-maintained fence ran along the southern boundary, making travel easier. The Gator rattled westward, kicking up dust as it passed through narrow lanes in the brush, the ever-present catclaw acacia swiping at them like pickpockets in a crowd. Thorns scratched along the paint and clawed at sleeves. Every few feet, something thudded or scraped against the Gator's frame.

At the third stake was a surprise.

They coasted the Gator to a stop and climbed out, boots crunching dry gravel as they approached the location marked by the GPS. Where they were standing was relatively flat, much like the location of the second stake. It was easy enough to drive the third stake into the soil, but ten feet beyond the marked location, the land simply ended. What opened before them was massive.

The cliff dropped straight down, easily sixty feet. Below, a wide arroyo twisted across the landscape, its bottom strewn with sunbaked rock and shadowed crevices. On the far side, nearly half a mile away, the land rose again, as if the canyon had been carved out with a dull axe.

"Say 'Hello' to Big Aguja Draw, boys. Deep enough to cut through the Star Mountain Rhyolite and into the limestone basement rocks. A ghostly white stripe in a land covered in red."

Martin noticed the canyon wasn't entirely white, a fair amount of the predominant lava was scattered randomly about in various sized boulders, many of those were jagged, but some of the boulders were rounded showing the result of a long journey from upstream. Red drops on a field of white.

Martin stepped carefully to the edge and scanned the horizon. To the north, the canyon deepened and bent slightly east, snaking back into their property. Somewhere down there, in the tangled heart of that channel, was where the fourth corner stake would go.

Mr. West frowned, peering down and shielding his eyes from the low sun.

"If the third stake is here…," intoned Mr. West as he pointed at the PC screen, "then the fourth stake is a doozy. This cliff here at stake three pales in comparison to what we're going to find there. We'll skirt the cliff's edge and try to find where the north fence line intersects with the canyon, but I don't think we're placing that last stake today. Unless one of you brought rappelling gear I don't know about," he said with a dry chuckle. "I'm not even sure how to get down there. We might have to approach from the south or see if the folks up north will let us follow the wash upstream."

They loaded back in and pushed north, the Gator creeping now, the terrain worsening with every yard. Catclaw lashed at them like angry hands. Even Mr. West had to raise his arm more than once to keep from catching a thorn to the face.

"This brush is something else," Martin muttered, wiping sweat from his forehead.

"It's trying to kill us," Brian added, swatting away another branch. "I vote we rename this location something more honest. Like Masochist Flats."

"That's a bit dramatic," Martin said, ducking under a branch.

"Not dramatic at all. We're all bleeding while swerving around in brush thick enough to hide a murder in."

They all laughed, until a fresh branch tore through Martin's sleeve and lashed Brian across the shoulder. The laughter died quickly, replaced by a shared hiss of pain as blood welled up from the fresh scratches.

"I knew this leg would be rough," Mr. West said as the Gator bounced over the terrain, "but this… this is brutal." His voice had shifted, no longer bemused. He was starting to wonder how much abuse the Gator could really take.

Finally, they reached the northern boundary fence, marked by a tired strand of barbed wire and a weathered cedar post. They stopped, cut the motor, and stepped out, but a quick look told them everything they needed to know. Getting to the last corner would be no easier on foot. The brush was too thick, and the canyon too close. They walked carefully toward the edge, shirts catching and tearing on unseen thorns. A few birds nearby chirped their evening songs of the day.

Mr. West pulled out the GPS and narrowed his eyes. "We're about fifty feet off," he said, pointing straight out over nothing. "And a hundred feet above. We're officially not doing the fourth stake today."

The three men stepped forward, boots crunching over sun-bleached stone. The land fell away without warning, dropping into a sudden gash of earth so deep it seemed to swallow light. Layers of canyon wall faded into darkness, the floor far below already touched by early evening shadow.

"Are those... bones?" Brian asked, voice quiet, but not from awe.

Even in the fading light, the remains were unmistakable with scattered pale shapes littering the slope below the cliff. Animal skulls of all types appeared. Some ribs were located together, and some scattered about. Legs were bent at wrong angles or completely missing. Some bones were little more than fragments; others looked recent. Among them were a few darker forms, still furred, slumped and bloated.

"That's a lot of bones," Mr. West muttered. "And not all old ones, either. Grab the binoculars from the glove box."

Martin turned, pushing back through the thorned acacia, which clawed at his shirt and raked his arm hard enough to draw blood. He barely felt it. The Gator's door creaked, its sound sharp in the hush, and when he returned with the binoculars, the silence had deepened. The birds were gone.

Mr. West scanned first, then passed the binoculars to Martin with a grim expression.

"Equal opportunity killer," he said. "I see deer. Javelina. Maybe even an antelope or two. All of them are right here. Why?"

Martin brought the glass to his eyes. The magnified view struck him like a punch. A deer carcass lay awkwardly across a broken stone, its ribs torn open. Nearby, a javelina sow, stiff-legged in death. Three small piglets neatly beside her, untouched by scavengers.

"Javelina don't jump off cliffs," he said. "They don't line up to die."

Brian rubbed at a fresh gouge on his forearm. "Maybe something spooked them and the fence herded them. Forced them too close. Maybe they panicked."

He took the binoculars and panned slowly. "Fifteen... sixteen skulls. Just deer. Not counting everything else."

The sun slipped behind the ridge. The canyon darkened. A new wind rose from below, cool, dry, and strange. It didn't whip or gust. It climbed smooth and deliberate, brushing past their cheeks like breath.

Martin turned, suddenly alert. The hair on his arms lifted. Something whispered in that wind, not a word exactly, but a shape of one. Syllables barely formed, curling around his ear like it belonged to a voice he should remember.

"de nashaaaaaa . . ."

Martin stepped back from the edge quickly. "You feel that? Did you hear that?" he asked.

"de nashaa?" asked Brian, "What the hell is that?"

Neither Martin nor Mr. West answered. Mr. West was intently staring down into the canyon, not blinking.

Brian gave a nervous chuckle. "Weird acoustics," he muttered. "Canyon playing tricks with sound."

Martin could see that Brian wasn't just unsettled. He was spooked.

The wind whispered again, more distinct this time. Not in any language Martin knew. But the rhythm of it chilled him, ancient and intimate, like something said not to the ear, but to the soul.

He looked once more at the boneyard below. So many animals had fallen in the same spot, as if drawn to it. It was as if something had called to them.

The air was heavy now, thick with dust and something else, something unseen but coiled tight around the stones below. The laughter from earlier was long gone. Even the UTV behind them had gone silent, its engine ticking stopped.

Aware that one wrong step could be deadly, Martin stepped back until he could turn around safely. Something was wrong with this place, he felt. Not just death, not just misfortune. The land remembered something. The land wanted something.

The Gator's engine rumbled to life with a tired cough as the three men climbed back in, shirts torn, arms scratched, dust thick in their noses. The canyon and its strange graveyard of bones faded behind them as Mr. West turned the Gator east. The sun was gone now, and darkness was closing in fast. The Belt of Venus was already climbing high in the east.

Martin sat up front with the PC perched across his lap, GPS sitting on his right thigh. He held the smaller GPS unit in his right hand unless he had to defend his face from the vicious onslaught of catclaw, then he'd just pick it up to keep it from bouncing off his leg, even though he'd rather close the laptop and use it as a shield. Brian rode in back, perched beside the stakes and battered gear, his knees rhythmically bumping the unyielding plastic back of Mr. West's seat. With each bounce, an ache was setting in a little deeper.

The going was slow. The trail, if it could even be called that, was more suggestion than path. Catclaw acacia scraped at them in waves, slashing at the side and clawing at exposed skin. In the fading light, the brush didn't even look like vegetation anymore, it looked alive. Reaching. Grasping. Refusing to let go.

"Fifteen deer skulls, all of them close together," Brian said, finally breaking the silence. "That's not just some weird accident. That's… eerie."

Martin nodded slowly. "They weren't all fresh. Some had been there for years, I'd guess. But the sow and her piglets, those were recent."

Mr. West eased the Gator up and over a small rise, the vehicle rocking gently. "Even if it's over time, they're all dying in the same place. That's what's strange. You don't see that. Not without a cause."

"Could it be locoweed?" Brian asked. "You know, *locoweed?* I lost some of my goats to it in high school. Animals that eat it go nuts. It must taste good, too, because my goats would seek it out if they

were dumb enough to try it the first time. Tremors, confusion, bad coordination. They just… run themselves into trouble. They want it, but it kills them. In my rangeland science class, I learned it's got selenium in it. That stuff makes holes in their brains."

Martin looked back over his shoulder. "I thought that was more of a livestock problem, cows, sheep. You think it affects wild game too? Even Javelina and Deer?"

Brian shrugged. "Maybe. If it's blooming nearby and they're desperate enough, sure. It screws with the nervous system, doesn't it?"

"Locoism," Mr. West added, almost absently. "Yeah, it'll make cattle stagger, drool, even forget how to eat. I saw it once, back in the '90s, a small herd of goats eating that stuff off the shoulder of a ranch road I was on. Looked like they were on ice skates."

Martin grinned but didn't laugh. "Still doesn't explain why they all went off the same cliff. You'd think after the first two or three, the herd would learn."

"Unless they weren't thinking straight," Brian countered.

Mr. West tapped the steering wheel with his index finger, thinking. "Could be a factor, sure. But I don't remember seeing any patches of locoweed. Not along that ridge or anywhere else on this property. Then again, I wasn't exactly looking for it."

Martin rubbed the back of his neck, absently feeling the sting of a fresh catclaw scratch. "Maybe it's the fence. Not just the placement, but what it does. You've got animals moving fast, being chased, maybe by a mountain lion or coyote. They hit that fence line, turn west, and instinct tells them to follow it to the edge. But the land just drops out from under them before they realize what's ahead," he paused, "By then, it's too late to stop."

Brian frowned. "So, you're saying it's not the land that's killing them, it's the design. A funnel."

Martin nodded. "It doesn't take a lot of pressure to make a bad decision when you're scared."

The Gator lurched as it rolled over a buried root, then dipped into a shallow wash before bouncing up the other side.

Mr. West slowed to a crawl. "It's the first theory that makes sense. The fence forces a direction. The predator adds urgency. And that rise, hell, it's gentle enough that it doesn't even look like a cliff until you're right at the edge."

"Designed by accident," Brian said quietly. "A perfect death trap."

They crept forward another hundred feet. The brush tightened around them. Even the purple had drained from the sky now. A clot of clouds loomed above the nearby mountains, changing from light gray to black as they stopped reflecting the last of the sun. The scrub oak ahead wasn't as thick as the catclaw, but the thicker branches hung lower and struck harder.

Then, *crack.*

A sharp noise rang out from the Gator's front end, followed by a pop and a dull clunk. Mr. West hit the brakes.

Martin was already climbing out and shaking his cell phone to turn on the flashlight. "Headlight's out," he called, circling around. "A branch got under the housing. Snapped the lens and tore the wiring loose. We're running half-blind now."

Mr. West grunted. "Perfect."

The remaining headlight threw narrow shadows ahead, making the catclaw look like twisted arms reaching out of the earth. Martin stood for a moment, scanning the landscape. The moon had taken command of the southeastern sky, gibbous, white, and sharp-edged. It cast a ghostly sheen across the brush and distant hills, just enough light to make the shadows seem deeper.

"Let's get moving. I'd like to be home before Lindsay starts to worry."

Chapter 4
Silence and Soil

Late light filtered through the catclaw, turning the shadows gold and the silence sharp. The trail back felt rougher than before, as if the land had grown less welcoming. Between the thorns, the twisted brush, and the silence clinging to the arroyo behind them, Martin couldn't shake the sense that something old and unseen had stirred. The Gator crawled forward again. With one headlight out, their world shrank to a pale cone of visibility. Each branch that scraped the body sounded louder now. Every bounce felt sharper.

Martin leaned forward; arms crossed. "You know what bothered me the most?" he said quietly. "It was the silence."

"The canyon?" Brian asked.

"Yeah. No buzzards. No coyotes. Not even flies. Just skeletons and whispers. Just bones and a weird feeling breeze."

"I noticed that too," Mr. West said. "It felt… sterile."

"Like something's keeping the scavengers away," Martin murmured.

The Gator groaned over another rut. A branch dragged along the side panel with a shriek.

"Okay, now you're creeping me out," Brian said from the back. "Let's just stake that corner next weekend and forget the rest. Concrete it if we need to and never go back."

The vehicle jolted again, harder this time, and all three men shifted in their seats.

"Was that metal?" Brian asked.

Mr. West gave the wheel a short turn. "Frame hit a buried rock. No damage, just my patience wearing thin."

They popped out of another steep dip, and finally, the lights of the house came into view, white from the inside, but the outside ones were dimmer and pointed toward the ground.

"Those outside lights look odd?" Martin asked.

"Yeah. The foreman I hired to drill the well told me the exterior lights needed to be pointed down. I thought he was kidding me at first, but there is a world class observatory nearby."

The Gator galumphed out of the brush and onto the mowed patch behind the house.

Lindsay stood on the back patio, arms folded loosely over her belly, her silhouette framed by the glow of the glass door. Dumpsy pressed against the glass beside her, clearly aware that dinner time was approaching.

Relief settled over the men like a thin blanket.

As they rolled into the yard and parked near the livestock barn, Mr. West finally exhaled.

"Well. One more stake to go," he said, powering down the Gator. "We'll figure out how to reach the arroyo bottom later. I'll see if I can track down a number for the landowners to the north. If we can follow the wash upstream, maybe we can get the Gator down there. The benches on the sides looked drivable."

Martin climbed out, stretching. He looked westward, toward the place they'd just come from. The canyon was out there still, maybe half a mile off, but it felt bigger now than when they'd stood at its edge. Deeper. Older.

What bothered him wasn't just the silence or the bones, but the feeling the land didn't want them there. It was the sense that the land hadn't wanted them there.

Lindsay was waiting for him on the patio as Martin stepped up, brushing catclaw and dust while picking the thorns from his sleeves. Her arms were still folded, but her posture softened as he got close.

"My sisters headed back to San Angelo," she said. "Didn't want to drive too late. Mom said she and Dad are going to get a room in Fort Davis for the night. She's inside trying to get the dishwasher sorted now. How did it go out there?"

Martin was about to answer when Brian stepped out of the darkness and into the soft glow of the patio light, his sleeves streaked with dirt and thin lines of blood. Mr. West followed a step behind, wiping his hands with a rag that had long since lost its color.

The mood shifted from unsettling to something quieter, more reflective. It was the kind of exhaustion that left room for memory.

Lindsay shifted her weight. "So y'all don't look so good. How did it go out there?"

"We found bones," Martin said. "A lot of them. Just… stacked up in this little arroyo like they'd been gathering there for years."

He exhaled slowly, still processing what they'd seen. "Not scattered. Not chewed. No sign of predators or weathering. Some were sun-bleached, others still yellowed with age. Whole skeletons, just lying on top of each other like they went there to die," he swallowed. "and the way it felt standing there . . . it wasn't right. Like the land didn't want us there. Even the shadows felt heavy."

He glanced toward the edge of the dark. "It looked peaceful at first, but it wasn't. It felt… chosen. Like something had called them there."

Chapter 5
Questions in the Dark

As Brian adjusted his hat he was vaguely aware of the stinging sensations on his neck and scalp. "Three stakes and a mystery," Brian offered, his voice a little too serious to be joking.

Lindsay raised an eyebrow. "Mystery?"

Martin nodded. "Yeah. There's a cliff, pretty big one, out on the western edge of the property, just like your father predicted from the satellite photo. We found animal skeletons. A lot of them. Deer, javelina, maybe even some antelope."

"But all in the same spot," Brian added, almost cutting in.

Lindsay blinked. "Huh?"

"I didn't take any pictures," Martin said, frowning. "Should've. No signal out there, but the camera still works. It was just… strange. Like a mass grave, right at the edge of the canyon. The skeletons were grouped together like something drove them off. We're guessing they ran along the fence line and didn't realize the land dropped out from under them."

Lindsay looked toward the darkness behind them; the direction of the canyon now hidden in the night. "That's unsettling."

"Yeah," Martin said, glancing over his shoulder. "We're still not sure what to make of it."

"Well," she said, holding the door open, "let's get inside and talk about it. We finally got the dining room table put together and found five of the six chairs. The sixth's probably off somewhere with Dumpsy fur all over it."

Brian gave a tired grin and stepped up closer. "I'd love to stay and be the talk of the town, but I've got land of my own to work back in San Angelo. It's three and a half hours, four if my new DPS buddy decides to meet up again, but I would get more than a warning this time, I bet."

They laughed, and farewells were traded. Lindsay skipped the handshakes and gave Brian a full hug, her pats on his back raising tiny dust clouds.

Brian bounced down the steps and disappeared into the night, the sound of his truck door slamming and the engine growling to life marking his exit.

Mr. West lingered just a moment longer.

"I'm gonna grab your mom and head to the motel," Mr. West said, stretching his back as he stepped off the patio. "Y'all get some rest. Don't forget, Lindsay's got that first OB-GYN appointment with her new doctor in Alpine tomorrow. Your mother's driving. I'll be back in the morning to help with the corral."

Another round of handshakes and hugs followed, along with Mrs. West coming down the back steps to join her husband and inform the assembled crowd that the dishes were being washed. His boots crunched softly across the gravel as they vanished into the dark.

Under a sky filled with more stars than either one of them could remember, they watched Lindsay's parents drive off in the SUV. Mr. West's truck and trailer remained parked nearby and it dimly reflected the light from the house's exterior lights.

It seemed quieter after both her parents were gone. Settled, in a way.

Inside, the air was cool and dry. The dining room table stood proudly in the center of the space, recently assembled, one screw still resting in a plastic bag that Martin was sure wasn't extra. Lindsay leaned in the doorway, watching him with a tired smile.

"Weird day," she said.

Martin nodded. "Yeah. And it's not over yet."

She gestured toward the kitchen. "Come get some water. Then tell me more about the cliff."

Martin hesitated near the doorway. Something about the canyon still clung to him, not fear, exactly, but the sense they'd brushed against something older than they were meant to. Something that didn't want to be understood.

He followed her in, the screen door sighing shut behind him.

Later, seated at the dining table, Martin traced the wood grain with his fingers for a few seconds while waiting for the glass of water, then finally spoke when it arrived.

"It didn't feel right, Linz."

43

She set her glass down and leaned forward. "The bone pile?"

He nodded. "Yeah. I mean, I've seen dead animals before. Scavenged carcasses, even full-on coyote kills. But this? This wasn't that. It wasn't random. It looked like something had neatly gathered them. Just bones."

"Could it have been flooding?" she asked. "Something washing them into that spot?"

Martin shook his head slowly. "No. We're uphill from the wash. And there wasn't any sign of debris. No branches or erosion channels. Just that clearing, and all those bones like they'd been placed."

Lindsay frowned, folding her arms loosely across her chest. "You think someone did it?"

He looked up at her, then down again. "I don't know. Maybe. But if they did, it wasn't recent. Some of those skeletons had been there for a while. But others… weren't. It's like something's been calling them in, year after year. And we're only just now catching on."

The room went quiet for a moment. The hum of the refrigerator, the tick of cooling metal on the stove, mundane sounds, but distant somehow, like they belonged to a different kind of night.

"I didn't like standing there," Martin added. "It felt… heavy. Like the air had weight. Like we were trespassing in a place the land wanted forgotten."

Lindsay reached over and touched his hand. "You think it's connected to the land?"

"I don't know," he said. "But it's bothering me."

He took another sip of water, eyes on the dark window above the sink.

"Lindsay… I know we've talked about this before, but I still can't figure out why your dad's being so generous, with everything. The house, the well, the land. We have enough solar panels to electrify a small town and a battery large enough to hold the charge. I didn't ask for a dowry. I didn't expect any of this. He's liked me from the start, and I appreciate that, but… I don't know. It's like I missed something."

"You didn't," Lindsay said, cutting in gently. "But I get it. Okay, the first thing, he loved your last name. When I told him over Christmas last year that I was going from being a West to an Eastman, he laughed. Said it sounded like some sort of balance had been achieved."

She smiled softly, then added, "But what really got him was when I told him about your parents. That you were an orphan. That you and your brother were raised by your grandparents."

Martin's mouth opened, but she was already moving forward.

"After years of me bringing home rich boys and mama's boys, I think Dad just latched onto someone real. You weren't polished, and you weren't pretending to be.

"Plus, he's had this land since my grandfather died, and land is his business," she said with a different inflection. "Once he saw that he could finally do something with this section, he got excited. He is looking forward to quadrupling the value of this property as well as telling his friends he owns a ranch."

She paused, while her own mistakes flooded back.

She glanced upward, eyes drifting toward the ceiling.

"You know… I just realized something. Every other guy I dated? They were coasting. Daddy's money. Family name. They belonged to someone else. You? You were running on grit and stubbornness. How many jobs were you working when we met? Two? Three?"

"Three," Martin replied. "Apartment manager. Part time goat wrangler at Brian's ranch. And on weekends either working estate sales or at the auction house. And whatever else I could pick up on the side, like DJ."

"My point exactly," she said. "You were working toward something. Not waiting for someone to give it to you. I saw that from the start. You dropped the noise and kept what mattered."

Martin smiled, sheepish but grateful. "That was just survival."

"That's life," she said. "Dad saw it, too. He saw through all the baloney salesmen. He liked you because you didn't need a stage."

Martin chuckled, and a grin stretched across his face. Lindsay mentioning baloney salesman had left it wide open for some crude humor.

"I've got some baloney to…. "

"Stop it," Lindsay said, rolling her eyes. "Truth is, I love you desperately because you're original. You've played the cards you were dealt and never asked for a cheat. I didn't want r-i-c-h, I found out I wanted r-e-a-l. And honestly? The night we rescued Dumpsy, and you treated that little furball like royalty? That sealed it. Every day I came over for that kitten, I also came to learn more about you. Brian told me you always take care of the animals first. I'm sure it's some sort of compensation by becoming the parent that you wanted and never had, but it makes you unique in a field mostly full of clowns."

She reached across the table and squeezed his hand. "There. That put it to rest? Dad loves you for the same reasons I do. You're already a hit in the son-in-law department. My sisters are gonna have a hard time trying to find someone to measure up. Both Melody and Elise are dating differently now, they see it, too."

Martin glanced down at the floor, not ashamed, just stunned by how plainly she'd said it. Then, as if on cue, Dumpsy strutted through the room, tail high and eyes bright, clearly expecting treats or tribute, maybe both. Martin scooped him up and rubbed his head.

"Thanks," he said. "I'll still feel awkward around your dad."

"Well, don't be."

After a quiet moment, Martin rubbed the back of his neck and said, "Now let me tell you more about the cliff…something about the land out to the west. Like I mentioned earlier. When Brian and your dad and I went to mark that last corner near the canyon, we came across a ledge, sharp drop, sixty feet or more, and just below it was this strange bone pile. Deer, javelina, even a couple of antelopes, all dead in the same spot. Some fresh. Some old. Like they were drawn there and just… fell. Or were driven." He paused, his voice tightening. "And standing there, I swear, I felt something watching us. Not like a mountain lion or buzzards. It was different. Cold. Quiet. Like the land itself had eyes. The wind sounded like it was whispering." He looked at Lindsay, searching her face. "I know how that sounds." She didn't flinch, but she didn't laugh either. Instead, she reached for her water and took a slow sip. "Okay," she said carefully. "I believe that's what you felt. But feelings aren't facts. And the desert plays tricks with shadows, silence, and heat. Let's just say I'm intrigued. " Martin gave a small nod, half in relief, half in resignation. "Fair enough," he said. "But just so you know, it didn't feel like a trick."

And just like that, the mass of skeletons at the canyon's edge faded a little deeper into the backgd. The questions were still there, heavy and strange, but Lindsay had given him something else to carry for a while. His focus had changed, and there was something

grounding in her explanations about his new father-in-law that settled inside.

The house was cool, and it wasn't too late. They weren't too tired. Slowly, the lights inside were turned off, one by one, leaving only the outside lights to pull the night shift.

Somewhere out there, the canyon remained dark and silent. But for now, inside, things were warm, and passionately real, and then… still.

Chapter 6
The Silence That Breathes

Nostalgia was almost unknown to Martin Eastman. He didn't have many pictures of his parents, but he liked to think he could remember them. A laugh. A callused hand brushing his hair. A woman's voice humming over the sound of dishes.

He'd been four when the accident happened. A wreck out on the loop near Temple, Texas. After that, it was just him, his brother, and their grandparents.

His grandfather, a quiet man with a fierce work ethic, passed away when Martin was a sophomore in high school. That left Grandma to anchor the rest of his growing-up years. She had hands like paper and a voice that could cut glass when she needed it to.

She showed him the letter on a winter evening when the heater had gone out again, and they were bundled under three quilts at the kitchen table. It was a worn piece of lined notebook paper, carefully folded and protected in an envelope that smelled faintly of cedar and years.

In it, his mother had written to his grandmother not long before the accident. She wrote about her boys, about how she and Martin's dad never had the chance to go to college, and how they wanted better. She wrote that whatever it took, they would make sure both their sons reached further.

Martin never forgot that letter.

His older brother had enlisted in the Navy straight out of high school, determined to use the GI Bill to earn his degree later. Martin took a different, much harder, route.

Middle school found him pushing a mower from yard to yard, hauling gas cans on a wagon. Winters, he rented a carpet cleaner with his own money and offered steam cleanings around the neighborhood. He didn't mind the work. What he minded was the feeling that he didn't quite belong.

He wasn't built for football, and he knew it. No one said it to his face, but it was obvious. He didn't run drills after school, didn't have practice or playbook meetings. And if you weren't in sports, you weren't anybody.

But he didn't exactly fit with the other kids, either. He didn't play video games. Didn't live on his phone. His hobbies were practical, equipment maintenance and yard design. He liked reading about how things worked. How people worked.

He kept his head down, made his money, and saved.

School itself came easy. He liked learning, especially science. It offered answers, or at least better questions. By the end of high school, he knew he wanted to teach. He wanted other kids, the overlooked ones, the quiet ones, knowing that grit and effort could get you farther than popularity ever would.

Angelo State wasn't a glamorous choice, but it was practical. Affordable. Close enough to home to drive back on weekends if Grandma needed help. He doubled down on classes and odd jobs, tutoring and summer coursework. He worked for anyone presenting him with a fair offer.

That's where Brian found him, through a help wanted sign and a little humor over their shared Ecology class. It was a spontaneous friendship, but one that stuck.

At the time he met Lindsay, Martin had no illusions about charm or luck. What he did have was a sharp eye, a good ear, and a deep belief that work mattered more than polish. She saw it in him before he ever had the nerve to hope for it.

And when her father shook his hand that first time and later asked him to explain what biologists meant by C.H.O.N.P.S., the six essential elements for life - carbon, hydrogen, oxygen, nitrogen, phosphorus, and sulfur - Martin knew he had passed a kind of test. He wasn't handed much, he only asked for a chance. He had no idea the woman he was dating had money, but then he wouldn't care even if she did.

****

The hum of the ceiling fan was the only sound. Outside, the wind had died hours ago, and the desert night had draped itself across the land like a wool blanket, thick, heavy, and absolutely still.

Martin stirred first.

Not from discomfort, or the late summer warmth, or even the unfamiliar creaks of a new house. It was a low, vibrating sound, through the mattress more than traveling through the air. Not a noise exactly. A presence.

Next to him, Lindsay shifted, her breath slowing. He opened his eyes to nothing. Just the feeling of being watched. No porch light bled through the blinds. No digital clocks blinked red from the nightstand. He only knew the hour because it felt like a time when nothing good ever happened, that full-body silence of deep night, where the world felt paused.

And at the foot of the bed, Dumpsy was growling.

It wasn't loud, but it wasn't casual either. The cat's body was tense, head low, tail wrapped close, ears flattened to his skull. His orange fur looked gray in the near darkness. Dumpsy was staring at the open doorway.

"Lindsay," Martin whispered.

She made a soft sound, then propped herself on one elbow. Her other hand reached instinctively to the still smallish swell of her belly.

"What is it?"

"Dumpsy's growling."

She turned slightly and saw him, curled at their feet, eyes locked on the hallway beyond.

"I've never heard him growl like that," she whispered. "He's not playful growling. He's . . . warning something."

Martin sat up slowly, careful not to move too much or too fast. The sheet slipped from his chest.

There it was again, just barely. A sound outside. Faint, distant . . . but close enough to make itself known.

A low whoosh. Then stillness.

Another whoosh, a little louder this time.

"Is that . . . wind?" Lindsay asked, barely audible.

"There's no wind," Martin said. "At least there wasn't when we went to bed."

He crossed the room, moved to the window, and peeled the blind back a little. His truck now sat fully illuminated by the pale light of the gibbous moon, hanging over the ridgeline. He turned and exited into the next room, the one they'd marked for the nursery. This window, already a third of the way open, offered an even better view of the back acres.

The patio light cast its soft glow on a still world. The barn loomed beside the tall black water tank. Nothing stirred, not dust, not leaves, and not shadows.

Then, behind him, there was a sudden noise. Dumpsy had jumped up onto the windowsill.

The cat crouched there, tail flicking, ears twitching. He stared out, not blinking, body frozen except for one slow shift forward, closer to the glass.

Martin knelt beside him. "See something, boy?"

Dumpsy growled, a slow, vibrating rumble that came from deep in his chest. His tail grew slowly into a giant bottle brush shape.

Just then, the moonlight picked out something in the dirt. Not motion exactly, but dust moving. A small puff. Then another.

The moon shifted behind a cloud. And Martin saw it, just a flicker. A shape. Too tall for a person. Too narrow for a tree. There and gone.

Lindsay entered quietly, catching the tension. Then the sound came again.

Not from outside, but all around.

A rhythm. In. Out. In . . . out.

Like wind through a hollow. Or like breathing. . . slow and deliberate.

Low. Steady. Measured. And somewhere deep inside, Martin recognized the pattern.

"Do you hear it?" he asked.

Lindsay peeled her eyes toward the ceiling in the empty room, listening hard.

She nodded. "It's . . . it's like a draft, maybe. A vent?"

"Swamp cooler's off. I shut it down when we went to bed."

The breathing sound came again. This time, Martin felt it in his chest. Like being near a large speaker turned low.

Dumpsy hissed.

Martin turned, nearly knocking over the small stool in the room. Dumpsy leapt from the windowsill and bolted out of the nursery and down the hall toward the living room. Martin and Lindsay followed.

When they arrived in the living room a few seconds later the sound was gone. Only the ceiling fan was making a noise. The only light source was moonlight streaming through the windows and the myriads of kitchen appliances, some with digital clocks.

After a few minutes without any new events or noises, they all returned to the bedroom. Dumpsy resumed his position at the foot of the bed, eyes trained on the gap in the open door, but without growls this time. The house was silent again, but the memory of that breath, of that something, clung to the walls.

"Should I check the outside?" Martin whispered.

"No," Lindsay said. "We're just spooking ourselves in this new house."

They stood there in silence. After a few licks to restore his composure, Dumpsy curled back up to resume sleeping.

Eventually, the feeling passed. Martin left the door slightly ajar and climbed into bed again, the sheets cool now. Lindsay followed, tucking herself in beside him. Dumpsy began to purr.

They didn't speak for a long while.

Then Martin, voice low, said, "Weird night."

Lindsay nodded slowly. "New house noises. That's all."

Martin didn't answer.

Because he wasn't so sure.

He lay there in the dark, listening to the house settle, but a different memory began to surface, one from a dusty Saturday at an estate auction near Sonora. The PA system had failed halfway through the auctioneer's chant, his rhythmic singsong halted by a dying microphone. Martin had wandered over to a bookshelf while they wrestled with the wires and found a faded paperback called *Even More Texas Folklore*. He'd flipped through it, pausing on a section about Native American beliefs tied to the land. One line, circled in blue pen, had lodged in his memory without reason until now: *"Some tribes believed the land itself would breathe when spirits walked upon it."* He hadn't thought of that book in years, but now, lying still in silence, he wasn't so sure the breathing he'd heard was the house at all.

Chapter 7
Earned, Not Given

Despite growing up with every comfort, Lindsay West discovered she really did want something. Summers were pools and popsicles, not summer jobs. Her clothes came from catalogs, and her lunches appeared perfect every time she asked, folded and trimmed neatly by the housekeeper. If someone had asked what her dad did for a living, she might've said something vague about maps or oil wells. He carved out a career as a landman for Transon Oil, part timing, part grit, and a near-mythic instinct for where *not* to drill.

It was when Lindsay reached middle school, she noticed the difference.

Her friends never said anything directly, not at first. But she picked up the cues: the offhand jokes, the hesitation in being invited to sleepovers, the way birthday parties always happened, but she was rarely invited. Only later, through quiet conversations at school, did she realize her friends had been hiding the truth, that they didn't want her to see the humbler circumstances they lived in. Slowly, almost imperceptibly, she came to understand that they were treating her differently.

And by high school, she knew why.

She was the rich girl. Not in a cartoonish, heiress sense, just rich enough to make people think she was gliding through life on a magic carpet of money. There were expectations that came with that, and she hated all of them.

What had once been a blessing now hovered over her like an unspoken rule: don't try too hard, don't take up too much space, don't pretend you're struggling. You got more laughs if you played the ditz.

Volleyball changed that.

When she joined the high school freshman team, something shifted. Her teammates didn't care what car dropped her off after practice or whether she had the latest shoes. What mattered was hustle. Dive for the ball. Show up ready. They admired her for what she *did*, not what she *had*.

And Lindsay loved that feeling, the sweat, the earned praise, the way honest competition made all the other noise fade away.

She never told her parents about this change, and she certainly wasn't going to tell them she was quietly aiming for an athletic scholarship. High school became a quest, not to escape privilege, but to outrun it. To prove, if only to herself, that she was more than a well-dressed passenger on someone else's ride.

Then she fell in love with history.

Twice, by luck or fate, she landed in Mr. Vickers's History classroom, first for U.S. History, then for World. He didn't just teach history; he *painted* it. His lectures had dramas of novels, the punchlines of sitcoms, and the unexpected humanity of family stories. Dates mattered, but so did motives. Lindsay found herself captivated not just by *what* happened, but *why*.

People behaved the way they did for reasons, fear, greed, love, pride. To her, history became a mosaic of human decisions, each tile revealing another piece of the larger picture.

And somewhere along the way, she realized: she was part of that picture, too.

She met Martin at a sorority mixer. He wasn't supposed to be there as a guest, he was the DJ, playing songs off a laptop and reading the room with the quiet precision of someone who had better things to do than flirt. The other girls in her sorority had aimed their charm at boys with money.

She was intrigued before he even said a word.

When they finally did talk, she was struck by how quickly he sized things up, not in a judgy way, just honest. Thoughtful. A man who looked people in the eye and listened. Even with the amplifier humming, he took the time to talk to her, not expecting anything in return.

He was, in every way, honest and unrefined. Definitely not a hick from east Texas, but also not the kind of boy with connections her parents hoped she'd end up with. And that, at first, made her hesitate. Their dates weren't really dates, and that let them connect more deeply, explore feelings, and talk honestly about how they thought the world worked. Dumpsy was the test.

Her parents wouldn't think much of him, but deep down, she knew: Martin would win them over with honesty.

Especially her father. He'd see the curiosity, the backbone, the humor. Maybe, she thought, he'd finally get the son he never had.

And she'd get a partner who didn't care what she had, only who she was.

****

Anticipating another long day, Martin was up before dawn to shower and snag some coffee. As he walked into the living room, he stopped short. "Lindsay?"

She emerged from the hallway with hair still damp from her shower. "What's up?" He stepped aside, revealing the remains of the dreamcatcher by the edge of the couch. The feathers had been ripped loose, the sinew webbing torn clean through. One of the wooden beads had rolled halfway across the floor, and the outer ring was cracked. "I didn't touch the dreamcatcher," he said. "You?"

"No. But I think we both know who did." She glanced toward the kitchen, where Dumpsy sat perched on the windowsill, watching them both.

"He must've gone after it in the middle of the night," Martin said, crouching to gather the pieces. "Or whatever he was growling at," Lindsay murmured.

Martin didn't respond. He was staring at the shredded threads in his hand. "These aren't just torn," he muttered. "They're sliced. Like surgically sliced."

He glanced toward Dumpsy, who was now grooming his tail with deliberate innocence.

"What'd you do, upgrade your claws to razor blades?"

The cat blinked at him.

"Don't try this with the couch," Martin said. "Or you're getting locked in the closet with your litter box." Dumpsy nonchalantly lifted a hind leg to begin cleaning himself.

A "Pfffft," escaped Martin's lips, the cat didn't care in the least.

****

The morning sun was climbing slowly over the eastern ridge, throwing long golden fingers across the pasture and creeping toward the structures behind the house. The heat hadn't fully arrived yet, but it was coming. The air had that still, expectant quality, cool in the shadows, but already dry and tight on the skin. Martin noticed the morning smell was completely different, fragrant and fresh, unlike what he expected from plants roasted daily since June.

Out back, Martin and Mr. West were elbow-deep in lumber, framing out the future goat corral. The railroad ties were already sunk, and now they were setting the corner braces with lag bolts and a level. Mr. West had been the one to suggest placing the corral away from the water tank. With prevailing southwest winds, they'd stay downwind of the smell and flies. Martin hadn't thought of that, he'd only considered proximity to the future skid-tank Brian was bringing in.

"Use the three-two-one rule," Mr. West said, eyeing the diagonal brace. "Three feet up, two feet out, one good whack if it doesn't line up."

The gas-powered auger had made short work of what Martin had dreaded, putting holes into the ground. Only a single rock had caused trouble, throwing off an otherwise straight fence line.

Martin chuckled and tightened the bolt. "Good enough for government work."

While they worked just beyond the tractor-mowed clearing, the double-wide sat quiet and still. Martin's truck was parked between the house and the narrow paved strip where he'd left it the night before, driver's side facing southwest. The windshield and door panel were already warming under the early sun.

Neither of them noticed the faint tick of breeze rolling off the sea of nearby acacia. Gaining traction from uneven ground and morning heat, the breeze swirled into a dust devil, small at first, then

rapidly growing in height and spin. Gravel and trash lifted into the air as it raced toward the truck.

Then it stopped.

Martin noticed it first.

"Who ordered the…." He stopped himself, remembering this was his father-in-law.

"Blow job?" Mr. West finished with a grin. They exchanged smirks. He took off his cowboy hat and wiped his forehead with a folded cloth.

"Kid, I've worked in the oil field most of my life. Where there's crude, there's crude humor. I've heard it all. Mr. Transon's a good man, but he loves a joke from the derrick floor."

The whirlwind twisted in place, sucking dust and bending the tops of nearby brush. Then it began to move directly toward Martin's truck. It stopped at the front bumper and hammered the vehicle for nearly half a minute, rocking it gently. The rattle of pebbles on metal rang out like sleet on a tin roof.

"Free sandblasting? Just what it needs," Martin said dryly.

Under the seat, long forgotten, a dusty can of A/C refrigerant rolled lazily into the light.

It had been there for months, maybe longer, tossed in during a hurried trip to the auto parts store. Unused, it had weathered a West Texas winter and at least one thunderstorm. Yesterday's jostling drive down the ranch road must have dislodged it from its debris nest. Now, it had rolled into the cab's sweltering heat and settled on the black rubber matting like it had a mission.

The dust devil circled the house, then drifted back into the brush with a whispering sound. The vortex dissolved, and the lifted dust drifted toward distant mountains, where puffy clouds loomed above.

By 10:30 a.m., sunlight flooded the truck's floorboards. The cab was sealed. All four windows shut. The interior temperature soared.

Martin didn't hear the hiss. Didn't hear the gas building pressure. But the bang was unmistakable.

A sharp, concussive crack echoed across the property like a muffled rifle shot. Martin's head jerked up. A couple of the truck's windows had shattered. The windshield had turned white with spiderweb cracks.

He and Mr. West both turned toward the noise.

The driver's side window had exploded outward, spraying glass across the gravel like a shattered mirror. On the far side, the passenger window had fractured into tiny facets. The rear window had cracked top to bottom. A faint, gray cloud drifted from the broken glass.

"What the hell?" Martin said, dropping his hammer and jogging forward.

Mr. West followed, wiping sweat from his forehead.

In the sun, the damage was clear. Both side windows were ruined. Glittering fragments littered the ground. Just beyond the mirror, ten feet out, sat the culprit: a small, silver can, half-crushed, the end blown off.

Martin recognized it immediately.

"Refrigerant," he muttered. "A/C recharge. That thing's been under my seat since… hell, since last fall."

He picked up the can fragment carefully. The weld seam had failed, clean off at both ends.

Mr. West gave a low whistle. "You're lucky you weren't driving. Pressurized like that? It'd have turned into a bullet. You'd need stitches after getting hit with that. . . Let me see that."

Martin handed it over. Mr. West turned it over in his hands.

"Look here," he said, pointing to a rust spot on the seam. "It probably failed right there. Weak spot went first, then the whole thing blew."

Martin stared at the rust, barely bigger than a lentil. But it had reached the other side.

He exhaled, shoulders slumping. "I forgot it was even in there. Got beat to hell yesterday, then cooked all morning."

They stood in silence as the breeze stirred the catclaw nearby.

Finally, Mr. West clapped him on the shoulder. "Well, now you've got a reason to replace the windows. Next time don't forget what you're carrying under that seat. Maybe tow it in with the truck I'm leaving for you to borrow?"

Martin looked at the jagged window, then toward the brushy horizon. "That's an option. Thanks." The nearest glass replacement shop was forty miles away, a full-day affair, no doubt.

They had returned to the corral, stretching barbed wire, when the SUV turned off the road and rolled into the yard. It coasted past Martin's truck, paused beside it, then continued to the barn's shade.

By the time either man looked up, the women were already out. Lindsay rounded the front, crossing the 150 feet to the corral, stepping carefully around a flat prickly pear.

"What happened to your truck's windows?" Lindsay called, shading her eyes.

"You wouldn't believe me if I told you twice," Martin said. "Remember last year, when I recharged the A/C in the apartment lot?"

"That was almost a year ago."

Mr. West used the break to remove his hat and mop his face.

"I bought three cans," Martin continued. "Only used two. The third must've rolled under the seat. I meant to return it, but midterms hit, then the deer lease, then student teaching . . . It slipped my mind."

He glanced at Mr. West. "We're guessing a dust devil rocked the truck just enough to roll it into the sun. The cab turned into an oven. The can did the rest."

"Quite a bang, it was," Mr. West said.

"I bet," Lindsay said. "So, what now? Alpine? Pecos?"

"San Angelo," her father answered. "I tell you what…here's an idea. We'll be back in a week or two after y'all start school. I'll borrow a trailer, haul it home. Maybe use the company's dually."

Martin blinked, processing the shift in plans. "Wow. Thank you."

Mr. West shrugged. "We take care of our own."

"Now come on, you two galoots," Lindsay said, heading for the SUV. "Help with the groceries."

"And the new cookware," added Mrs. West, right behind her.

"We'll help if there's lunch," Mr. West called. "Your husbands require sustenance."

"Deal."

Twelve paper bags and one large box later, the kitchen hummed with activity. The swamp cooler had kicked on via timer, filling the house with cool, damp air. Dumpsy napped on the couch, stretched across a throw pillow like he owned it. The pantry was still half-empty, cluttered with unsorted canned goods from San Angelo. The new cookware gleamed, bright stainless steel and pristine glass lids. Too nice for the rest of the house but welcome all the same.

Over sandwiches, conversation bounced between school, unpacking, and the thousand tiny logistics of rural life.

"Anyone got ideas for internet out here?" Martin asked. "I was thinking satellite."

His mother-in-law lit up. "If we hadn't heard from you this week, we were going to get it installed ourselves."

"You've already done so much," Martin said.

"Says the father of my grandbaby," she replied. "Sam and I did our struggling. They say it builds character, well, we have plenty. We promised: if we ever got to help our kids, we would. Didn't think we'd be building a whole new place from scratch, but here we are."

Laughter followed, the good kind, easy and grateful.

"You two earned it," Mr. West added. "Lindsay, you never once asked for money in college. We were proud when you got that volleyball scholarship. I still figured I'd be footing the bill. But you kept your grades up, pulled 18-hour semesters, morning practices, sold plasma for gas money. You didn't touch the account I opened. You two deserve this. You fought to get here."

When the thermometer passed 95°F, they agreed the corral could wait. Stretching wire in the heat wasn't anyone's idea of fun. Instead, they tackled the chaos inside.

Lindsay worked in the master bedroom and bath. Her mother took the guest room, trying to wrangle secondhand furniture into shape. One bed wobbled. The nightstand was scuffed to hell. But the dresser drawers didn't stick, so that was a win.

In the living room, Martin and Mr. West mounted the flat-screen TV and assembled the entertainment center. Dumpsy patrolled the rooms like a quality control officer, offering meows of mild protest whenever he was ignored.

Chapter 8
What the Lightning Found

Repacking wasn't on Martin's to-do list, but Lindsay's voice carried from down the hall: "Martin! I think this is yours. Come look, this isn't bathroom supplies!"

Martin finished with the hole he was drilling and walked back towards the bedroom Lindsay was working in. Mr. West didn't look up, still focused on the TV installation guide.

Martin took the box from Lindsay. He recognized it immediately, marked with the logo from the pool supply company. It had been delivered the day before they moved out, meant for the new apartment manager. Clearly, someone had packed it by mistake.

"Damn. First real screw-up," he said. "This was supposed to stay at the apartment. None of this belongs here."

He pulled out a half-gallon bottle and read the label.

"This one's called Pool Shock Plus. Hydrochloric acid. Stronger than anything I ever used in chemistry. One cup of this stuff will nuke every germ in a hot tub. I used it every Saturday morning at the apartment, on account of the sex that happened there every Friday night."

"People were doing that?" Lindsay asked, her tone halfway between disgusted and fascinated.

"Not 'people,' but that guy in #37. Every Friday. Different girl almost every time. Management put up signs. Cameras. Nothing worked. I suggested we livestream it and sell ad space. Instead, the health department recommended this. It's like biological napalm."

She wrinkled her nose, more at the idea of something possibly living in an apartment hot tub rather than the chemical she was holding and handed the box to Martin. "Well, un-nuke the bathroom and get it out of here."

Martin carried the box into the living room and set it on the coffee table. One of the bottles looked slightly warped near the cap, the plastic discolored. He set it aside and returned to the task at hand, the reasons he had been drilling holes into the wall in the first place.

Recently unpacked and resting nearby was his collection of replica pistols, earned as partial payment from helping with a poorly attended storage unit auction a year earlier. The boss certainly didn't want it and by giving it, and some other boxes to Martin had solved the problem of cleaning the space out. Authentic looking, but non-functional. The case was solid wood with a glass front. Four pistols rested in velvet grooves: a Colt Paterson, a Colt Navy, a Single Action Army, and a tiny Derringer. Behind them, a garish print showed a cavalryman on horseback firing at a Native American warrior, both mid-charge. A banner above them read: **FOUR PISTOLS THAT WON THE WEST.**

That phrasing always made Martin smile. The idea of someone using a single-shot Derringer in a real fight? Gloriously ridiculous.

He took his time mounting it.

Before he drilled the pilot holes for the screws he spent a few moments searching for the "perfect" place to hang the pistol case, somewhere it could be seen easily, but not overbearing. Centered on the living room wall didn't look right. Edge placement felt wrong too. Splitting the difference, off-center but visible from the couch, felt best. He pulled out the stud finder, swept it across the wall, and found two. Two long screws later, it was secure.

Nobody noticed the day had grown dark outside until the thunder cracked it open.

Everyone froze.

They drifted toward the back door and stepped onto the patio. The sky was smothered in storm clouds, flat-bottomed and immense, stretching across the mountains to the southwest. Only a golden rim clung to the far edge of the horizon. In the middle distance, a veiled rain shaft dragged itself across the terrain, wind-smeared and ghostly. Lightning flickered deep in the clouds, silent for now, but stirring.

"Guess the good Lord wants to test your roof," Mr. West said.

Martin stepped down into the yard. The warm air wrapped around him like breath. The wind hadn't arrived yet, but it would.

The first gust came tumbling across the yard in sprints, bending the mesquite and catclaw as it passed. It brought the first trace of rain, humid, sharp, and laced with the rich, earthy perfume of creosote. That smell, sharp and electric, jolted Martin. Unfamiliar, and oddly pungent. Like the land itself was waking up and calling him to witness it. With each gust the catclaw became increasingly animated like line dancers at a honky-tonk. A low bank of clouds was stacking above the ridgeline. Each layer pulsed with flickers of lightning. Thunder rumbled low and long, like something shifting beneath the earth. Beyond the western ridge, streaks of rain shimmered like silver thread.

Behind him, the glass storm door creaked open. Lindsay stepped out, arms crossed over her belly, hair swept back in the rising wind. Her mother stood just inside, eyes on the sky.

"Smells amazing," Lindsay murmured. "I've only heard that desert rains are a feast of smells. Mmm."

"Creosote," Mr. West said. "This smell always shows up before the rain."

Another gust, cooler now, swept the patio. A few droplets spattered the railing, sharp and sudden. The air had changed. The electricity was building, raising hairs, and tightening skin. The world was holding its breath.

Then came the flash. Angled in from the south.

Bright. Immediate. White-hot.

The bolt struck somewhere near the center of the property, not far from the canyon. The thunder followed instantly, like a detonation inside the bones of the house.

KRAK-KA-BOOM!

A second bolt screamed in from the north, striking nearly the same spot. A third crash erupted inside the house, sharp and glassy, like something enormous had been hurled across the floor.

Martin didn't connect it right away, until he remembered the last thing he had mounted on the wall.

He turned and ran up the patio steps through the back door.

The chemical stench hit him like a wall, acrid, metallic, eye-watering. The air shimmered slightly, a low haze rolling across the floor.

The display case had fallen. What shocked him more was what it had landed on.

"Oh shit . . . " he muttered, yanking his shirt over his nose.

The coffee table had shifted several inches. Beneath it, the pistol case lay shattered. The discolored plastic bottle of Pool Shock Plus had tipped, leaking a growing puddle across the glass and velvet interior. The acid was already dissolving through the replica of the Colt Paterson. Its grip bubbled and steamed.

Martin moved without thinking.

He moved the tipped bottle quickly over to the kitchen sink. He returned and grabbed the edge of the display and heaved it upwards, his eyes burning. He dared not breathe, he remembered that much from "fixing" the hot tub back at the Blue Mountain Apartments. The uneven weight of the replicas made it awkward. Broken glass bit his fingers, but he got it up. Sloshing acid streaked the laminate floor as he stumbled to the door. Lungs burning, eyes watering, he burst outside, took three steps into the yard, and hurled the whole thing into the rain.

The case tumbled, pistols clattering, glass shearing free. It slammed into the wet dirt. Rain pounded down, diluting the acid, washing it into the ground.

Behind him, Lindsay tried to charge inside after Dumpsy.

"Wait!" her mother snapped, grabbing her wrist.

Lindsay froze.

Without a word, her mother took a deep breath, yanked her shirt over her face, and darted inside.

Seconds passed.

71

Lindsay gripped the patio post, fingers white.

The screen door burst open. Mrs. West emerged, cradling Dumpsy against her chest. The cat was sneezing but unharmed.

"Got him," she said, voice muffled. She passed the cat to Lindsay and stepped to the edge of the patio, coughing hard.

Martin returned, panting, shirt still over his face.

They all turned toward the open door.

Inside, the air shimmered with chemical haze, but the swamp cooler was running, carrying the fumes out through the partially opened windows at the back of the house. It would take time.

"We leave the door open, let the wind help drive out the fumes." Mr. West said, turning his body away from the approaching storm. He looked from the broken display in the yard then to the trembling cat.

"You all right?" he asked Martin.

Martin nodded. "I think so. Just rattled."

He looked out at the dark yard. The rain was falling now, thick and steady.

"That case," Martin said quietly. "It was heavy. Screwed into the studs. That lightning didn't hit the house. But it still came down."

Lindsay said nothing. She held Dumpsy close, her eyes fixed on the open doorway. This time, Martin noticed her silence, unusual for his new wife, whose thoughts rarely went unspoken. The rain grew heavier.

Chapter 9
Storm Charge

Even as he inspected the cuts, Martin felt no pain, just a dull awareness that it would throb later, probably the moment his head hit the pillow. The storm had begun to fade, its fury trailing off into distant rumbles. After a few minutes of watching the rain ease, Martin retrieved three of the four pistols, avoiding the Colt replica with the still-steaming grip. The stench near the shattered case remained intense, even at a distance.

As he carried the remaining pistols up the steps and into the house. With the fumes gone, the safest place to be was inside.

He placed the dripping, mud-slick pistols gently on the kitchen table, then after retrieving a stack of old towels he went to work on cleaning the pistols from the display. Mr. West stood nearby and examined the remaining screw in the wall before picking up the one that had fallen. The right screw still jutted from the wall, solid as ever. But on the left side, there was only a torn crater in the sheetrock, ripped edges and splintered gypsum told the story. The screw along with a tiny plug of wood, had ripped clean through when the knot gave way. "You hit the lottery," he said, holding up one of the screws Martin had used to hang the case. At the end of it was a perfectly round plug of wood.

It took Martin a moment to realize what he was looking at. He had drilled the screw directly into a knot of wood in the stud. The knot had separated clean from the surrounding wood, like a cork from a bottle. "Of all the luck," he muttered, his eyes returning to where he had just installed the case on the wall. "I picked the spot that felt perfect."

Another peal of thunder vibrated the walls more than it echoed through them.

"That's just your luck," Mr. West said, pressing his palm flat against the wall. "Anywhere else and it probably would've held forever. But you hit the one weak spot that gave way. Like winning the worst kind of lottery, kid."

Still holding Dumpsy, Lindsay stood in the den quietly. Dumpsy began to wriggle in her arms, making it known he was ready to be set free.

Distracted, she let him down. He immediately went under the couch.

Then, without warning, the lights flickered.

The swamp cooler cut out mid-hum. A heartbeat of silence fell across the house.

Another loud peal of thunder struck the house.

Martin froze. So did Lindsay and her mother. Even Dumpsy stopped twitching his tail.

The lights came back on almost immediately, dim for a second, then normal. The cooler restarted with a hesitant groan.

Martin turned and looked at the others. Lindsay had one hand on the back of a chair. Her mother was standing perfectly still.

"Huh," Martin said quietly. "Maybe the barn took a hit."

"Lightning like that, I'd be surprised if it didn't. There is a circuit protecting the battery." Mr. West added, though his voice lacked its usual certainty.

No one said anything for a few seconds.

Then the swamp cooler hummed back to full strength, and the normal sounds of the house resumed.

Martin bent to pick up the towels they'd used to dry the pistols and found his hands were shaking slightly. He clenched them into fists, then released them. Outside, the rain continued to fall, slow and steady now. Inside, the house still felt just a bit too charged.

****

The sky over Highway 17 shimmered with heat as the flat West Texas landscape stretched endlessly in all directions. For a few moments Mrs. West took in the desert landscape they were driving across. Often, she could make out the old concrete irrigation ditches. Abandoned now, they once carried water to the famous cantaloupes that were grown here. Every now and then a derelict cotton gin passed by. There's no escaping the hard reality of the desert. Water is everything.

The storm had lifted out into the upper atmosphere leaving only high cirrus clouds to chase themselves in distorted circles. Mr. West's truck rumbled northbound toward Pecos and IH-20 for the final segment to their home in Big Spring; the Davis Mountains now a blue-gray smudge in the rearview mirror. Beside him, Mrs. West sat with her hands folded, her gaze fixed ahead but unfocused, still replaying the strangeness of the midafternoon.

The acid damage. The shattered display case. The pistol case launched into the rain. It wasn't something you just brushed off with a laugh and a "how 'bout that."

"Well," she said finally, her voice quiet but edged with tension, "if we're being honest… maybe the place is haunted."

Mr. West gave a grunt, not quite agreement, but not denial either.

"All I ever knew about that land," he said after a beat, "was something my great uncle told me. This was back in the early sixties, mind you. He said that sometime in the late twenties, a man came asking to graze cattle up there."

Mrs. West turned her head slightly.

"Did he?"

"He tried. Drove a whole string of them up into that north pasture. But the cows, he said they wanted nothing to do with it. Flat-out refused to cross onto the property."

Mrs. West blinked. "Cattle refusing to graze? That doesn't happen."

Mr. West gave a slow nod. "Not unless they smell something foul. Like water gone bad, or… "

"…or something worse," she finished.

Silence filled the cab for a long moment.

Then Mr. West gave a half-smile, the one he usually reserved for poker nights or moments when he'd slipped one past a defensive coordinator.

"Well, I reckon I've solved the whole mystery," he said, tapping the steering wheel.

Mrs. West narrowed her eyes. "You don't say."

He leaned forward and spoke clearly to the truck's interface.

"Play 'Ghost of a Chance,' by Rush. Album: *Roll the Bones*."

The stereo chirped in acknowledgement, then the unmistakable opening guitars rolled out, a pulsing, rhythm that sounded well enough to work.

Mrs. West closed her eyes and sighed. "You're impossible."

But when she opened them again, she was smiling.

Chapter 10
First to Ride, Last to Fall

Midmorning approached, and the sun was already climbing fast above the Davis Mountains, casting long shadows across the cavalry stables and parade ground of Fort Davis. Open continuously now for some 29 years the morning routines were comfortable and paced, but the men assigned there knew the fort was in its final days in March of 1891. The stone and adobe buildings, bleached pale by years of sunlight, stood weathered but proud against the dusty sweep of the Davis Mountains. The air was already warming fast, though it wasn't yet midmorning, and the scent of horse sweat, leather, and creosote hung faintly on the fading breeze.

Captain Cormac O'Brannach stood at the edge of the drill yard, arms folded behind his back, the hard lines of his face shaded by a broad campaign hat. His was a face carved from flint, angular jaw, strong cheekbones, and a black-and-gray mustache that had weathered as many storms as he had. His eyes, dark and unreadable, carried the weight of someone who had stared down both man and terrain and decided neither would break him. He was forty, perhaps a year older, but the silver threading through his temples and the deep furrow in his brow made him appear older still. His bearing was military to the core: boots polished to a defiant shine, uniform crisp, posture unyielding.

The men of F Troop, 220th U.S. Cavalry Regiment, stood in formation before him, rifles shouldered, sabers gleaming in the angled light. Thirty-five strong, they were among the toughest and most seasoned soldiers left on this edge of the frontier, a mix of Americans, Germans, and Irishmen like himself. O'Brannach's eyes swept the line, sharp and assessing.

He had once thought he'd be a farmer.

When he arrived in America in 1876, fresh from County Galway, he believed what every hopeful fool believed: that land was life, and ownership was freedom. He scraped together every penny earned on dockyards and railroad gangs to buy eighty acres in what the agent swore was prime farmland near the Rio Grande in southern Colorado. Turned out it was dry sand, and at 7,000 feet, much too cold, barely fit for anything a man would want to grow or raise. The agent vanished, the deed turned out to be legal but deceptive, and there was no one to appeal to. No refund. No justice. Just dust.

So, he enlisted.

At first, he was just another immigrant private in a line of sorry souls posted to the far ends of the Republic, expected to die in the heat or rot in some canyon. But he could ride. God help him, he could ride. More importantly, he could teach others to ride. Horses, unlike people, respected firmness and reward in equal measure. O'Brannach made a name for himself training green mounts and greening up recruits. Promotions came slowly, but they came:

sergeant, then first sergeant. A brevet commission after an officer died of heatstroke during patrol. Then a proper commission, signed and sealed. By 1889, he was captain of F Troop.

He never smiled during inspections and today was no exception.

He walked the line slowly, nodding now and then, stopping to tap a boot heel with his riding crop or adjust a rifle sling with quick fingers. The men respected him. More than that, they liked him. He didn't shout unless he meant it. He taught. He drilled. He bought whiskey when drills were flawless and scheduled boxing matches when tempers flared. The troop was lean, hard, and well-prepared. Just the way he liked them.

But none of it filled the empty space left by the failed dream of farming. That gnawed at him, day after day. He was a man of skill, discipline, and strength, yet he'd been conned, reduced to a uniformed laborer in a land he had once hoped to call his own. Even now, with a captain's pay and a troop to command, there were nights he looked at the dirt under his boots and hated it.

He moved past Corporal McKinley, whose boots were poorly shined, and said nothing. Embarrassing soldiers worked with some, but not all men. Sometimes a different tact was needed.

"Captain on the line!" called Sergeant Caleb Voss as O'Brannach neared the end of the row.

O'Brannach stopped in front of the final trooper, nodded once, and turned back to face the troop as a whole. The inspection was done.

"You look ready," he said, voice clipped and dry. "Let's hope the Apache think otherwise."

A ripple of uneasy laughter passed through the line. He let it go. There hadn't been an Apache raid in years. The Apache were gone, or nearly so. But the orders still came. Patrol the edges, keep the line, make a show of force, but most of all make it so that the wagons heading west to El Paso were safe. The Lower Emigrant

Road was vital for mail, freight, and passenger travel by horse and wagon across West Texas. This patrol would sweep the furthest edges of the borderlands to remove, or scare back into Old Mexico, individuals with a score to settle against the white man.

The only highlight of the coming two-week patrol, he realized, was that they might scare off any Apache that dared to move north across the Rio Grande. Only one small band remained, camped at Old Camp Springs some twenty miles north of the fort.

He stepped back.

Sergeant Voss cleared his throat and stepped forward, holding a long cloth-wrapped bundle in both hands. He gave O'Brannach a nervous smile.

"Sir, if I may . . . The men took up a collection. Birthday's tomorrow, but we figured you wouldn't want a fuss then, so . . . here."

O'Brannach's eyes narrowed, but he took the bundle.

He unwrapped it slowly, the cloth falling away to reveal a long, beautifully oiled Whitworth rifle, its hexagonal bore polished to a sheen, the walnut stock dark and clean. An unusual weapon for a cavalryman, but precise. Deadly. British-made, like him in a way.

"This is not regulation. This is stamped with C.S.A. Sergeant Voss, are there Confederates in these parts?" he asked flatly.

Voss grinned. "Sir, with due respect, this fort was occupied by those Johnny Rebs during the war. If you know who to ask in these parts you might be surprised to learn what they traded for food."

Voss took a moment to spit out some chewing tobacco before continuing.

"Every army fights two battles, sir. There's battle with the enemy, of course, and then there's the battle with supply. Like those three inch cannons we got, sir. Ain't no good if they can't be bothered to send us ammo. Why did they send them? So, it turns out Johnny Reb was issued ten Whitworth rifles, and only two were ever requested. If you know who to ask around here, you might find one still boxed and oiled. We also found a crimping tool, for making the bullets."

"Tool? For bullets?" O'Brannach asked, one brow lifting.

"Yes, sir. That rifle takes a hexagonal slug like none other. You can load a soft lead round ball in a pinch, but it takes longer. Gives your target more time to get away."

"I suppose the lesson here is not to miss the first time," he said, voice dry, "it's a muzzle loader. Not many second chances with these."

"First to ride, sir. A killing shot."

It was F Troop's old reply, the first half of their motto, drilled until it came out like breath. The kind of answer he'd trained into them himself.

There was a flicker, just a flicker, of a smile at the corners of O'Brannach's mouth. He lifted the rifle, tested its weight, and sighted down the barrel toward the far edge of the parade ground. In the hands of a trained sharpshooter, this weapon could kill from an impossible distance.

He knew that. Even if he hadn't done it yet.

"Tell the men . . . thank you."

He slung the rifle over his shoulder and walked off the parade ground, the sound of shifting boots fading beneath the weight of a new weapon and the old anger that still clung to his bones like dust.

That rifle would find its mark, someday. Even if he hadn't yet chosen the target.

****

As the sun sank behind the ridgeline, Captain Cormac O'Brannach returned to his quarters. The final bugle call of the day

rang out, its notes drifting on the dry breeze. His barrack was a modest stone structure, cool within its thick walls.

He lit an oil lamp and moved through the room with ritual precision. Hat. Gloves. Saber. Overcoat. Each laid down in turn. He checked and rechecked his gear. Horses. Ammunition. Rations. The patrol would be flawless.

But the rumors could no longer be ignored. Fort Davis would soon close.

The transcontinental rail line had finally connected San Antonio to El Paso through Alpine Station. Supply trains, strategic routes, even cavalry patrols, all rendered obsolete by iron and steam. The frontier was vanishing, not by blood, but by progress.

From his field chest, he retrieved a small wooden box. Inside were his few personal belongings: a leather-bound Bible, a crumpled deed to worthless land near the Rio Grande River in Colorado, and a miniature portrait of his mother, long dead and left behind in County Mayo. The deed mocked him now.

He had tried. And failed.

He turned to the wardrobe and lifted the Whitworth rifle from its case. The wood smelled of oil and oak. In fifteen years of service, he had never killed a native. Not once. Skirmishes, ambushes, raids, yes. But never a confirmed kill.

Other officers told tales of blood and glory. He had none. He looked again at the rifle.

Perhaps this was his tool. His redemption. The mark his legacy still lacked. He set it down beside his uniform, the cold metal catching the lamplight.

It would only take one bullet.

Chapter 11
Thirty-Two Shots

Each man in F Troop, 220th Cavalry Regiment, stood stone-straight beneath the rising sun. Horses shifted along the hitching rails, the thick smell of leather and sweat already hanging in the still morning. Captain O'Brannach paced in front of them, boots raising puffs of dust.

"Men," he began, "what we do today, and in the days to come, is no different than what this unit has always done. Our duty."

He paused, letting it settle.

"Some of you are green as prairie grass. Others have worn this uniform half their lives, but you serve in a regiment that earned its colors the hard way."

He spoke of the Battle of Brandy Station. Of flanks turned and brothers lost, of F Troop holding the line while others broke. Their motto: *First to Ride, Last to Fall.*

There were no cheers as they rode out. No crowds. Only the wind.

Over the remaining morning and into the heat of afternoon, Cormac rode with one hand loose on the reins and the other resting near his holster, eyes half-lidded against the glare. The landscape unfolded around them, brush-covered ridges, wide arroyos that braided and dried and braided again, and the purple rise of distant mountains that never seemed to get closer, only clearer. He'd ridden this country for years now, but today it struck him differently. Not as a barrier to cross or a threat to scout, but as a place a man might *stay.*

He glanced left and saw the taller peaks to the north, the way they held the sky. Not too hot, not yet, and the wind that came down off them felt clean. This wasn't the prickly swelter of Presidio or the choking dust of the Rio Grande's bend. There was space here. Water, if you dug smart and watched the rains. With a good windmill and a clever plan, a man could raise vegetables and goats, maybe even run a few head of cattle.

He swallowed. That had been the dream once, back before the uniform, before the long trail of orders and losses. A few dozen acres and a slow life, something with callouses and fences instead of boots and bugles.

The trouble was that the uniform had a way of clinging. Even now, he sat straight in the saddle because the habit refused to leave him. He could feel the weight of his eyes somewhere behind, could hear the rhythm of hooves like a clock he no longer wound. Duty.

Discipline. Dismount. And after that? Another posting, another march. Or maybe retirement. But to what?

They reached Alpine near midday, the sun high and hard, the horses already blowing from the trail. Cormac watched a Southern Pacific train snake its way east, its whistle thin in the dry air. Somewhere on that train there might be letters, or orders, or maybe just bags of flour. But watching it sparked something: the idea of *stability*. A rail line didn't just bring goods. It brought patterns. Schedules. Employment. He remembered the stationmaster's offer, that the freight office in Alpine might be hiring a permanent clerk or assistant agent come fall. It wasn't the cavalry, but it wasn't plowing rocks either.

He chewed on that as the men took a break near a windmill-supplied stock tank. The idea that maybe you could ranch a little and work part-time for the railroad. Keep your back intact and still put meat on the table. That would've sounded like betrayal to his younger self, *picking up a pen instead of a carbine,* but these days, it felt like insurance. A foothold for something new.

He let his horse drink and took a long pull from his canteen, watching the wind bend the few scattered grasses along the bank. The mountains to the distant south, the objective of this patrol, were steady and bluish gray, like old friends who didn't ask questions. He thought about a simple house. A pair of trees for shade. A dog run porch to pull the summer air from inside. Maybe, someday, a wife who didn't flinch and could tell the difference between a snake's rustle and the wind in the scrub.

He wasn't a fool. He knew the land was harsh, the rains fickle. He knew the Apache were all but gone, wiped from the earth over the previous decades. But something inside him was shifting. Not fast, not loud, but real.

O'Brannach led them five miles south of Alpine before calling a halt for the day. By the map the day's total was twenty-five miles, but with the rugged terrain the journey had been further. Camp was made on dry ranchland. The water was brought from a windmill some few miles away. The tents were pitched in straight lines. Fire pits from previous patrols to the south were reused. The soldiers watered the horses and took care of the other tasks. A signed chit left with a ranch hand ensured no trouble.

Late in the day, he opened the long case near the cook tent. The Whitworth rifle gleamed.

He called for Sergeant Voss.

"Four flags. Put the first one at four hundred yards and place out the others every hundred after. Tie white rags to the tops. I want them fluttering."

The men gathered quietly as Voss rode out.

O'Brannach did not look at them.

"White flags…" he said, loading the rifle with care. "White flags mean surrender. Means cowards, or men turned tail. Miss, and you might as well be one of them."

The first shot missed. The second grazed. By the sixth, the flag twitched. By the tenth, splinters flew. By the thirty-second, a pole snapped clean in half.

The men said nothing. But they watched.

He shifted his weight, settled the Whitworth into the crook of his shoulder, and drew in a slow breath. The sight picture trembled, barely perceptible, as his chest expanded. He let the air out and felt the reticle drop a fraction lower. Fascinated, he did it again, this time holding halfway through the exhale. The barrel hovered steadily. He blinked, realization unfurling in his mind like a map.

Each breath was a tide, lifting and lowering the iron. Even the smallest lungful nudged the rifle's aim enough to miss a man at half a mile. He rolled his shoulders, conscious of only breathing and feeling his own heartbeat. Now he could understand those men who could lie still for hours, watching the rhythm of their own bodies as closely as the target. He tried it once more: a long breath, a gentle exhale, pausing in the slack moment before the next inhale. The front sight froze. He squeezed the trigger, and the crack split the silence. The distant flag snapped in two, cloth fluttering down like surrender. A slow grin crept across his face. He still missed plenty, but now he understood. Breathing was as much a weapon as powder and lead.

He sat back, sweat dripping, breathing slowly. "Now I understand," he said. "How they did it in the Civil War at Spotsylvania, Cold Harbor, and other battlefields. How they took generals off their horses from a distance."

Later, as the others ate, he remained behind cleaning the rifle. Piece by piece: barrel, breech, trigger, stock.

That evening he was restless. He thought of Alpine Station. It was a good job offer. It was a second chance to begin again. He thought of Arizona. He imagined the carnage that would occur when the Indians of the plains found themselves backed into a corner. He knew he was growing too old for that level of battle.

No. He felt it deep inside. He would not go west. He would stay. Here. Where there was still land to try again.

And yet . . .

Fifteen years without a single kill.

He touched the smooth wood of the stock.

Just one kill., He wanted just one kill.

To close the book he had opened when he joined.

The final smear of black wiped clean, he latched the case shut.

Overhead, a sky filled with stars danced, not caring one iota what he, or anyone else, decided.

****

The clock over the whiteboard ticked softly in the hush of the classroom. Morning light streamed through tall windows, slanting golden across rows of empty desks. Dust motes drifted lazily in the beams, as if the room itself represented the calm before the coming storm of students.

Lindsay stood in the center of it all, hands on her hips, slowly turning in a circle to take in her new domain. She was carrying a medium sized plastic storage container that contained her small collection of classroom and teaching supplies.

The walls were a patchwork of history: faded maps of the thirteen colonies, vivid prints of Civil War battle scenes, portraits of presidents, some more dignified than others, and timelines running like vines along the top of the cinderblock walls. The previous teacher, Mr. Cardenas, had retired after nearly three decades, leaving his personality pinned on every bulletin board. Lindsay found most of it acceptable, though she'd already peeled down one poster about "Manifest Destiny" that featured cartoon settlers grinning atop covered wagons like they were on a theme park ride.

She set her supply crate onto her teacher's desk and followed it with her shoulder bag, realizing this was where her career would begin. She felt a combination of excitement and accomplishment. It was one thing to be a student teacher, a guest in some other's classroom, but this felt very real. Robert felt it a good time to give her a kick of approval.

The door creaked open, and Principal Mendez poked his head in. He was a wiry man with a perpetual tan, starched dress shirts, and an air of practiced calm that seemed immune to even the worst teenage drama.

"Morning, Lindsay," he said, stepping inside. "I hope you're settling in."

"I am, thank you," Lindsay said, brushing a strand of hair behind her ear. "The air conditioner even works. That's a minor miracle."

Mendez grinned. "You'd be surprised how often that qualifies as a major miracle around here."

He beckoned someone in from the hallway.

"Lindsay, I'd like to introduce Susan Rusker. She's agreed to be your official mentor this year."

Susan entered with an easy smile, carrying a battered leather tote bulging with folders and a large, insulated cup that read **"World's Okayest English Teacher."**

Lindsay smiled in recognition. She'd met Susan briefly during the all-staff meetings, but only in passing amid coffee urns and clusters of nervous teachers in the cafeteria.

Susan offered her hand. "Hey there, Mrs. Eastman. I can't believe we're finally in our rooms instead of marooned in professional development hell."

Lindsay laughed. "Mrs. Eastman still sounds weird to me. Call me Lindsay. No more acronyms or team-building exercises where I have to catch people falling backward, for now. I'm thrilled to finally be in here."

Mendez clasped his hands together. "I'll let you two chat. Susan knows every trick to surviving your first year. She practically runs the place, even if she pretends she doesn't."

Susan rolled her eyes. "Go. . . shoo. We'll be fine."

Mendez winked and slipped back into the hall.

"Honestly, when I die, I hope it is the middle of one of Mendez's teachers Inservice presentations, because the transition from life to death would be so subtle. I'm surprised no one has thought of loading EpiPens with Adrenaline. . ." Susan smiled and leaned on the edge of a student desk. " So Robert if it is a boy, or Cynthia if it's a girl? Isn't that what you said during introductions?"

"That's right," Lindsay said, her grin softening. "Yes, but I might just name it Pele since it's already kicking hard enough to make me rethink my decision to wear fitted dresses."

Susan snorted. "They say they settle down after they're born. They lie." She tilted her head. "You look good, though. Glowing and all that. So… any wild ideas for how you're starting the year? I remember being a first year teacher and wanting to change the world."

Lindsay hesitated, then leaned closer, dropping her voice to a conspiratorial tone. "Actually… yes. I want to start with a bang. I'm thinking of a field trip to the Fort. Do you know any reenactors?"

Susan's eyebrows rose. "It just so happens I'm married to a reenactor. . . Your plan is ambitious. And brilliant. The kids love it out there. All those reenactors, you'll want those, in wool uniforms sweating bullets for authenticity."

"I know it's early in the year," Lindsay said, "but I thought if we go while it's still mild outside, say maybe October, they'll remember it the rest of the year. Plus, I'd love them to connect the curriculum to the land they live on. Not just memorize names and dates."

Susan slapped her knee. "I love you already. Listen, here's what you do. Call Scott Wilder. He's the main guy for the Union soldier unit. I've got his number somewhere. And talk to Dale Bailey, he's the cavalry reenactor. Used to work at the Historic Site until he retired. He'll let your kids try on the hats and hold the sabers. You'll be a hero, provided the kids keep all their fingers."

Lindsay felt a rush of excitement. "That's perfect. Do you think the principal will sign off on it?"

"Pssh," Susan said. "Mendez loves anything that makes this district look good."

They both laughed.

For the next hour, they sat side by side at Lindsay's new desk, scribbling notes and rifling through Susan's tote bag for contact names. Before Susan had even introduced Lindsay to the basics of classroom routine, they planned logistics, permission slips, bus quotes, which stations at the fort to visit, and which kids might faint if asked to wear a Civil War wool coat if it was a hot day. After that Susan launched into the ways Fort Davis High School worked.

Hearing the lunch bell ringing down the hallway, Lindsay felt the room was hers at last. Not just inherited but claimed.

And her first year suddenly felt less daunting, and full of possibility.

Chapter 12
Storm upon Meadow

Muted starlight still blanketed the hills when Storm upon Meadow opened his eyes. The camp lay quiet, curled in the hush before dawn, and the world around the springs seemed pleasant in the feel. He sat up slowly, drawing his blanket close. The air was cool, not cold. The stream whispered across smooth stones, and a single mourning dove called out from the trees, marking the hour. But it wasn't the sound that woke him. It was the dream. And the knowing it left behind.

Rising, he moved through the low circle of fires, counting the silhouettes he knew by heart. They were fewer than last season. Fewer than he could bear. Still, they endured. Beneath a bent oak, he stood and watched the land brighten. The east ridges sharpened into shape. The tall grass stirred. It was a good place, but not a forever place.

If they stayed, it would be for belief, not abundance. If they moved again, it would be for peace, not war. Peace was not a gift from the land. It was something you chose. He wished for peace over and over again.

He remembered a time before. Before the fences and the wagons, before the thunder of hooves that pulled plows instead of riding into battle. When the white man was rare, a traveler more than a settler, a question instead of a declaration. He and his people had fled west from the land called the Hill Country, driven by relentless army patrols, hoping the Davis Mountains might hide them. His people watched the newcomers from the ridges with wary eyes, never understanding their hunger to divide the land into squares and rows, to tear it with tools and trap it with laws.

They had called their cattle "slow elk" at first, laughing at their docility. Why chase food when it wandered slowly and stupidly into the open? But that laughter did not last. The white men grew like a fire not yet smothered, bright, loud, consuming. And behind their cattle came soldiers, roads, and paper maps with ink that did not match the contours of the hills.

At first, they had wanted them gone. The Apache raided, resisted, spilled blood when they could. But for each man driven out, another came in his place. Like water from a broken pot, they spread, filling the lowlands, rising up the canyons.

He had burned with anger in those days. His arms were strong then. His spirit full of fire. His two sons, brave and eager, had ridden at his side. Until one spring, while scouting near a ranch house west of the Pecos, they had not returned. Days later, he found what was left of them. Bullet-ridden. Bodies left for the buzzards. They hadn't been warriors. Just boys, watching. The ranchers had called it defense.

That day, the fire inside him burned hotter than any council drum.

But with time, and the weight of sorrow, came understanding. They could not fight the river. Only shape the canoe to survive it. It was better to take what could be saved. To remember. To teach. To walk with pride, even if the trail led away.

Behind him, he heard the soft footfalls of his brother, Painted Elk.

"You were restless again," the old warrior said, not asking.

Storm upon Meadow nodded. "The night spoke too much."

"What did it say?"

The chief took a moment before answering. "That the trail to the mountain is not yet gone. But the door is closing."

Painted Elk furrowed his brow. "You speak of New Mexico territory."

"I do." He looked toward the sunrise. "Of the Mescalero lands. The place promised to our kin. It is time to go. Or soon will be."

There was silence between them then, save for the faint crackle of the coals behind them and the continuing sad, plaintive calls of the solitary *xasbidi*. Other shapes stirred within the camp, children stretching, mothers unwrapping dried meat for breakfast, a boy carrying a water jar to the spring's edge. It was life as it had always been. But the weight of that familiarity pressed heavier now.

"I dreamed we were crossing," Storm upon Meadow said quietly. "Westward. Toward the high country. But behind us came smoke, and horses, and men in blue. They did not chase us. They did not speak. They simply came. Like a river that could not turn."

97

Painted Elk stood a little straighter. "We have not raided in many seasons. We have not stolen, not killed. We stayed away from their fences and their wagons. What more do they want?"

Storm upon Meadow gave him a glance that held both sadness and knowing. "To forget us. And we are slow to be forgotten."

The older man folded his arms. "Will you go to the fort?"

"I may. But not today." He glanced back at the sleeping lodges. "I must speak to them. All of them. When the sun is higher. They must hear it from my lips."

"And if they say no?"

"They won't. Not when they hear what I saw. We shall leave this place. They shall trouble us no more."

"They will always trouble us. They have no bonds of brotherhood."

The two men stood for a long moment in silence, watching as the light crept down the ridges and touched the tops of the hills. The world seemed no different than the day before, but something had shifted. Both men were tall and wiry with black hair streaked with gray. Both faces etched with the deep lines of sun and years.

Finally, Storm upon Meadow turned and began walking back toward the camp.

"When I go," he said softly, "it will be alone. If they see many of us, they will see it as defiance. Or a trap. But one man can carry a message. One man can speak peace."

Painted Elk said nothing.

Storm upon Meadow rested a hand on his shoulder and said, not unkindly,

"Díí' naashá."

Painted Elk looked up, questioning.

"Go to the mountain," Storm translated. "It is what our ancestors said before judgment came. Not to flee. Not to hide. To face what must be faced. You remember grandfather speaking of this?"

"Yes," answered Painted Elk, turning his eyes eastward to the rising sun over the ridgeline.

"You must stand there when the wind shifts. And you must know why. Our path has changed, Painted Elk, and we cannot change it back."

As the sun crested the ridge and fell upon the encampment, Storm upon Meadow passed through his people without speaking, returning to his shelter. But the dream lingered behind his eyes.

Even if they were pushed from the land, driven over distant ridges or scattered into government hands, he knew one thing would remain true:

His spirit would never roam far.

He would not leave the green creeks and hidden pools that shimmered in summer. Not from the smell of crushed sage after a passing rain. Not from the hush that came before the wind lifted with a storm. Not from the touch of stars that blanketed the skies above the canyon like a thousand eyes watching silently.

He would not leave the land, at least in spirit.

And the land would not forget him.

In his bones, he knew they could not stay here much longer. Not if they wanted to see the mountain.

Chapter 13
Blue and Black

Being a first-year teacher meant he second-guessed everything, including whether the school's "SUPER" portal had actually submitted his lesson plans. The confirmation banner blinked once, then vanished. It was Saturday. He had no intention of driving to the school just to make sure it went through. If it hadn't gone through, someone would call. Or email. Or text. Probably all three. As a young teacher, he knew the administration would be watching his every move, the state regulations required no less.

The silence in the house was different lately. Not heavy, but taut, like a string pulled just a little too tight. He leaned back into the office chair and stretched, a slight pop echoing from his shoulder. At the far end of the L-shaped desk, Dumpsy was sprawled out like royalty, one leg straight in the air as he cleaned himself with bored precision. The orange tabby had discovered the desk's surface two days ago and now treated it as his personal grooming salon. Martin had given up trying to move him.

The scent of bacon drifted in from the kitchen, wrapping around him like a memory of simpler Saturdays. It mixed with the faint, clean smells of brewed coffee and toast, anchoring him fully in the moment. He pushed away from the desk, letting his fingers trail briefly across Dumpsy's back as he passed. The cat gave a single contented chirp but didn't pause in his efforts.

Out on the back patio, a faint trace of morning cool still lingered in the air. The high desert light was gentle, not yet the piercing brightness it would become, and the land beyond their concrete slab shimmered in pale gold. With the evaporative cooler switched off, the silence deepened, thick and still, save for the occasional rustle of a breeze.

Holding his coffee and cradling it with both hands for the briefest second, Martin eased into a chair as Lindsay handed him a steaming plate piled high with scrambled eggs and an unapologetic mountain of bacon. Even the store-bought biscuits, still warm, released an aroma that tugged a smile from him without effort. A few moments later, Lindsay returned with her own plate and a tub of butter tucked under her arm.

They ate in comfortable silence for a while, watching the sun clear the eastern ridgeline, but only indirectly. They moved from being in the shadow of the ridge to being in the shadow of the house. Its light poured down the slope like honey, golden and slow-moving, touching the yucca stalks and sage clusters with long shadows. As the sun climbed higher Lindsay nudged her coffee mug forward to warm it in the light.

"No birdsong this morning. Why is that Mr. Science Teacher?" Lindsay asked.

"It's late summer, the birds have finished with their broods. Now is the time to finish loading up for the cold weather ahead. Too hungry to sing now."

Martin's gaze lingered on the horizon before drifting skyward. To the southwest, thin lines of cloud had already begun to gather, feathery and white for now, but with the tall, slightly bruised look that often signaled a storm would bloom by late afternoon.

He took another bite of bacon, chewing absently, then said, "Remember the first week? All those weird little things?"

Lindsay arched a brow over her coffee. "You mean the coincidence parade?"

"Exactly. Dumpsy growling at nothing. That weird breathing sound in the middle of the night. The bottle of acid tipping over during the lightning storm. That… wasn't a normal start to country life."

"That bottle of acid didn't tip over. Your pistol display smacked the table it was on when it fell off the wall. And despite that," she said, gesturing with her fork, "no follow-ups since then."

He nodded. "That's what's bugging me. It's like the land, or whatever, flared up for a few days, then just… stopped."

"Maybe it just wanted to see what kind of people we are." Her voice was half-joking, but her eyes held a thoughtful glint.

"Or maybe," Martin said, wiping his hands with a napkin, "it's waiting," he whispered dramatically. Lindsay rolled her eyes in response.

They were quiet for a few moments, the only sound the gentle stir of the breeze and the soft clink of their forks.

"You do need to bury that cable," Lindsay said finally, switching gears. Pointing with her fork to the thick black cable she could plainly see behind Martin and off the porch. "The satellite guy said not to leave it exposed for more than a week, especially with goats arriving soon."

Martin nodded and stood, stretching again. "I can do it after breakfast. Won't take long if I can find the grubbing hoe in all that mess we just piled into the barn corner and forgot." His eyes flicked back toward the clouds. "Assuming the weather holds."

Lindsay followed his gaze. "That's how the last one started. Remember? Clouds like those, then a full-on lightning show."

Martin's mouth tugged sideways. "Let's hope if we get another, it doesn't decide to throw any more of our stuff around."

They both laughed, the sound carried off by the breeze. Somewhere out in the brush, a bird trilled once, then went quiet. The air was warming now, slowly but surely. The day ahead still held work, but for a brief moment longer, they just sat and let the sun find them.

****

Martin leaned the grubbing hoe against the porch rail and straightened up, cracking his neck as he surveyed the shallow trench. The coaxial cable sat neatly in the groove, running cleanly from the antenna post at the edge of the porch to the new wall plate he'd installed beneath the living room window. It wasn't the straightest trench, the buried rocks had seen to that, but it got the job done. Filling it back in was accomplished with ease. He pat the backfill down with his boots until only a trace of darker earth remained. It was even with the sandy loam around it. Another small job done before the sun got serious.

He stepped inside just long enough to wash the dust from his hands and grab another mug of coffee from the pot. The smell of bacon lingered in the house like an invitation. Dumpsy was splayed out on the kitchen floor, stretched long on the cool fabricated wood floor, tail flicking idly.

Two weeks. That's how long they'd lived in the house. Long enough to hang pictures and re-stack boxes that still weren't unpacked. Long enough for the creaks of the trailer to stop sounding like strangers moving in the night. Long enough to finally hear coyotes howl at night. The memory of that strange first night, Dumpsy growling, the whisper of breath or wind outside the wall, had begun to fade. No more strange coincidences since then. No unexplained sounds. No broken glass. Just wind, heat, and the routines of teaching. School started on Monday and both of them were excited.

Coffee in hand he returned outside. Martin sipped his coffee and watched, noting the pops and pings coming from the white metal roof as the temperature began its inexorable climb upward. It hadn't been above 100 during the last week, but mid-90s was still plenty warm. It caught the edge of the water tank and glinted along the top of the Gator's roll bar.

"Beautiful morning," he said.

"For now," Lindsay replied. She pointed with her fork toward the distant southwest, where low clouds were already piling up behind the mountain range. "I give it five hours before that turns into thunder."

Martin squinted. "Yeah, they're forming early."

"That means if you're gonna bury the rest of that line, you better do it now."

"I already did," he said smugly.

"Well look at you. Mr. Accomplished."

"Damn right. I won the trench war."

They sat quietly a little longer, letting the breeze tease the edges of their hair. Then Lindsay broke the silence.

"Today's the day, you know."

He glanced over. "Ultrasound?"

"Yup. They'll tell us the gender, if the little bean cooperates."

Martin smiled. "It's wild, isn't it? We're actually doing this. Oh, it isn't a 'little bean. It's beyond that and has been for some time."

"Yep. We just got things … out of order."

He laughed. "You mean, like, pregnant before the wedding?"

"I mean exactly that," she said, grinning. "We jumped a few steps. But hey, frontier living, frontier priorities."

"Just need some Indians?"

She shot him a look. "Native Americans, please."

"Your parents took it better than I thought they would."

"They've mellowed. Plus, Mom's been itching to be a grandma since Melody graduated high school. Big Spring is just a big, empty nest for her now."

He remembered Lindsay's younger sisters were both in college now. Martin drained the last of his coffee and stood. "Well, I'm ready if you are."

She gathered her cup and followed him back inside. As they moved through the house, quiet except for the hum of the swamp cooler and Dumpsy's faint meow of protest, Lindsay spoke again.

"You remember me talking about my mentor teacher? From the summer Inservice?"

"Yeah. The one you said helped you with the field trip?"

"That's her. Susan, our high school's entire English Department. She's already offered to babysit once the school year kicks off."

Martin blinked. "That's generous."

"She's amazing. Her boys are grown now, but she swears babies are easier than high school juniors. Also, she raised goats for years. Both of her sons did FFA. You'll like her. She's a straight shooter, and she knows the region better than anyone. Like, scary good. She gave me a whole list of things we need to go see before fall: Marfa Lights, the observatory, the Monahans sand dunes, riding the Sunset Limited in a sleeper car, she even knows the guy who runs the feed store in Fort Davis and already warned him that we're 'goat people' now."

Martin shook his head, amused. "You've got a whole secret society going."

"Of course. History teachers don't survive without it."

Martin scooped up Dumpsy and lifted him out in front of him before cradling him in his left arm. "Dumpsy: the Midnight Growler! We'll be back before you finish your fifth nap." With that, he placed him on the back of the sofa and headed toward the front door.

They reached the loaner truck and climbed in, the cool air lingering from the early morning already giving way to the first hints of sweat under the collar.

As they passed the last curve before town, Martin glanced over.

"What's her name again?"

"Susan O'Brannach Rusker," Lindsay replied casually, brushing her braid over her shoulder.

"Sounds Irish."

"She is. Four generations back. Her people came through the area during the land rush. Her great-grandfather was military, I think. Or railroad. Both, now that I think about it."

Martin nodded, but the name meant nothing to him.

"Guess we'll meet her soon enough."

Lindsay smiled as she rested her hand over the small swell of her belly. "Yeah. I think you'll like her. She wants to babysit. She has already invited us over for dinner tomorrow." Martin shot a surprised look across the truck cab, Lindsay was already smiling at him when he did.

"I like secret societies that feed us dinner."

They drove the rest of the way into Alpine beneath the rising sun, the peaks behind them growing darker with clouds, the road ahead still dry, still clear, for now.

Chapter 14
The Ghost in the Wire

Even with the heat rising off the pavement, the drive home from Alpine passed in a golden blur. The air was hot but breezy, and Martin tapped his fingers on the wheel, feeling more relaxed than he had in weeks. About a mile out from the turn onto their land, he stole a glance at Lindsay, who was cradling the black-and-white ultrasound photo against her stomach like it was spun gold.

"So, it's official," he said, breaking the comfortable silence. "Robert Bruce Eastman."

Lindsay smiled, tucking a strand of hair behind her ear. "Robert the Bruce," she corrected softly. "Not just a name. He was one of the greatest kings Scotland ever had. He led a nation at a time when no one believed they could win against the English." She paused, voice growing a little wistful. "He wasn't perfect, he lost a lot before he won. But he never gave up. That's why he mattered. That's why he still matters."

Martin smiled. "Sounds like a good name for our son, then. Maybe he'll live up to it."

"Maybe he already is," Lindsay said, patting her stomach.

They rounded the bend that would lead to their long driveway, the white roof of their double-wide coming into view. The sun was sliding lower behind the mountains, painting everything in long shadows and warm bronze light.

"Oh, hey," Martin said, recalling something. "When we stopped at the ATM in Fort Davis? I thought the account balance flashed up wrong at first. I thought it was a telephone number, like, the machine glitched or something."

Lindsay laughed. "Yeah?"

"I mean, six digits. I had to blink a few times to realize it was real. I'm still convinced it's a typo."

She chuckled and squeezed his hand over the console. "It's not a typo. I told you, I never touched the money my dad set aside for me. Not once, not during college."

Martin raised an eyebrow. "Not even a little?"

"Well… okay. I dipped into it once," Lindsay admitted, grinning. "For my wedding dress. And before you say anything, yes, it was worth every penny."

Martin laughed, easing the truck between the fence posts of their gate. "No arguments here. You in that dress? Best investment ever."

They pulled through the gate and rolled up the drive. It had rained there. The dirt looked darker, helped by a rich scent of creosote. Right away, they noticed something odd: Brian's green truck was parked awkwardly, nose toward the barn, with a flatbed trailer half-jammed through the open gate of the corral they'd worked on building, there were no goats in sight.

Martin frowned and parked between Brian's truck and their house. Dumpsy watched them from the window, his tail flicking lazily.

"Where are the goats?" Lindsay asked, voicing the question on both their minds.

Martin didn't answer. Instead, he stepped out and made for the patio. Brian was sitting at the metal table, elbows on knees, staring across the yard at the borrowed truck they'd used for the Alpine trip.

"Hey, man," Martin called as he approached.

Brian didn't look up right away. When he did, he gave a tired, lopsided grin. "Hey. Congrats on the kid. Boy, right?"

Martin nodded. "Robert Bruce Eastman."

"Good name," Brian said, almost absentmindedly, before rubbing his knee in slow circles. His jeans were dusty and there was a fresh scuff along one thigh.

"You okay?" Martin asked, glancing him over.

Brian shrugged. "Fine. Stupid goats."

"What about the goats?" Lindsay asked from behind Martin.

Brian leaned back in the chair and sighed. "They won't leave the trailer."

Martin blinked. "What do you mean, they won't leave?"

"I mean exactly that. I tried dragging one out by the collar. Soon as I went back for the next, the first one ran back up the ramp. Tried it twice more. Same thing. They won't stay out. It's like they think the trailer's safer than the ground."

Martin frowned. "That's weird."

Brian rubbed his knee, grimacing a little with each pass of his hand. "You know," he said, glancing at Martin with a half-smirk, "I think your land might be haunted."

Martin raised an eyebrow. "Haunted?"

"Yeah. Ghost goats. Or maybe the ancestors are mad you built a goat pen on sacred ground." Brian let out a chuckle, but there was just enough tension behind it to make Martin look twice.

Martin snorted and shook his head. "You realize you sound like a bad campfire story, right?"

Brian shrugged. "I'm just saying. I've moved goats before. A lot of goats. They don't usually cling to the trailer like it's the last lifeboat on the Titanic."

Martin grinned but decided to nip it in the bud. "We are college graduates, remember? You've got your degree in Rangeland Science. I've got mine in Secondary Science Education. Bachelor of Science, both of us. That means," he said, ticking off fingers as he spoke, "we deal with the *natural* world. Not ghosts, not curses, not boogeymen hiding in the catclaw."

Brian rubbed his knee again and gave a half-hearted grin. "Tell that to those goats."

Martin leaned against one of the porch posts, crossing his arms. "Science doesn't even consider the supernatural, because science is about *observables*. Things you can test, measure, reproduce. Supernatural, by definition, means outside the natural world. If you can measure it, it's natural. If you can't, it's not science's problem."

Brian rolled his eyes and gave his knee a few more absent-minded rubs. "Yeah, yeah. Still think it's spooky."

Martin pointed at him. "Stop rubbing your knee and stop trying to summon poltergeists. What happened to your leg, anyway? You get into a wrestling match with a goat?"

Brian winced. "Nah. Tripped over that damn coaxial cable you still haven't buried."

As he said it, Lindsay emerged from the house, smiling, the ultrasound pictures in her hand like they were secret treasures she couldn't wait to share. She didn't hear the last of their conversation, just waved the photos excitedly at Brian.

Martin's eyes followed her . . . turned back to look at Brian. . . .and then paused.

The coaxial cable was no longer buried like he'd left it. It was sprawled across the yard, lying bold and obvious on top of the ground, a black line against the pale dirt, as if someone, or something, had pulled it loose during the day. The rain shower had evened out the backfill. The ground looked as undisturbed as it was before he dug the trench.

He stared at it for a long beat, feeling a slow grin spread across his face.

He turned to Lindsay, his tone as dry as the desert air. "I think we might have a ghost."

Lindsay laughed and shook her head, holding out the pictures for Brian to see.

Brian, still rubbing his knee, muttered under his breath, "Told ya."

****

The goats came out of the trailer, but not without a fight.

Brian grunted, dragging the first stubborn doe down the ramp with her collar. The goat dug in her hooves like a mule, eyes wide, refusing to move an inch voluntarily. Martin crouched by the trailer door, ready to slam it shut.

113

"Go, go, go!" Brian barked, giving the goat a shove. She stumbled out onto the dirt with an indignant bleat just as Martin swung the trailer door closed with a loud clank.

Immediately, two other goats tried to scramble back up the ramp, but Martin darted forward, waving his arms like a madman.

"Back! Stay out! This is a no-goat zone!" he shouted, shooing them with exaggerated sweeps of his hat.

Brian huffed, wiping the sweat from his brow. "They're like teenagers at a pool party, tell 'em the pool's closed, they just want it more."

It took another ten minutes and two more wrestling matches before all six goats were finally out, clustered around the corral, staring mournfully at their precious trailer like it was the last spaceship off a dying world.

Brian dusted off his jeans and limped toward the porch, wincing with every other step. It wasn't a severe pain, just the type to slow you down. "Well," he said, "if this ghost thing is real, at least we know who's first in line to see it. Not us. The goats."

Martin chuckled as he latched the trailer gate. "It'll be a baaa-aad day when that happens."

Brian rolled his eyes and let out a low groan.

****

The scent of roasting garlic and rosemary met them before the screen door even creaked open. Lindsay knocked once, but Susan was already there, wiping her hands on a dishtowel and smiling wide.

"There you are! Come on in, shoes off if you please, I just mopped."

Martin chuckled and obeyed, stepping into a space that felt like a Better Homes & Gardens cover come to life. The living room was cozy and polished, walls painted a soft sage green, with an upright piano in one corner and cross-stitched verses hanging beside family photos in neat, symmetrical clusters. It smelled like comfort.

"I hope you're hungry," Susan said as she ushered them through. "I never learned to cook small, and now that all my kids are grown and out raising little monsters of their own, I miss feeding more than just two mouths."

"Where's your husband tonight?" Lindsay asked, glancing around.

"Omaha. Union Pacific's holding another safety conference, three days of lectures and a fancy dinner I wasn't invited to." She waved the idea off with mock disdain. "So tonight, I get to feed people who actually chew with their mouths closed."

The dining room was already set with mismatched but lovingly polished silverware, cloth napkins folded like lilies, and a roast chicken the color of sunset in the center. There were green beans with shaved almonds, mashed sweet potatoes with toasted pecans, and a lemon tart cooling on the sideboard.

"This looks incredible," Martin said, genuinely impressed.

"Oh, I'm not above bribing people with food. If I feed you two with a good meal maybe you'll come over more often." Susan replied, "Y'all settle in."

Dinner was warm and lively. They talked about everything from school gossip to road construction delays on 118. Susan had a sharp wit and a teacher's timing, quick to listen, quick to quip, and always one story ahead. The conversation drifted to family, and she rose to refill drinks, gesturing toward the wall beside the China cabinet.

"I've kept that photo wall the same since we moved here," she said. "My folks, my kids, my son-in-law who still won't return Tupperware. And that one," she pointed to an older, faded sepia portrait nestled among the frames, "That's my great-great-grandfather, Cormac O'Brannach. He was an officer at Fort Davis way back when. My dad used to say he kept peace and carried a big stick, or was it a long rifle?"

Martin leaned forward slightly. The man in the photo had a strong jaw, a swept-back hairstyle, and dark eyes that stared out with more depth than grainy portraits usually offered.

"Looks like someone you wouldn't want to cross," Martin said.

Susan laughed. "Oh, absolutely not. Family legend says he once shot a coyote from half a mile away. But he's been dead a good while, so we just let him haunt the wall."

Lindsay smiled politely, but her eyes lingered a moment longer than expected.

When dessert was finished and the coffee poured, the conversation dipped into half-laughing stories about classroom mishaps and the time Susan caught a senior trying to Google their way through a short-answer quiz on Shakespeare.

"Well, thank you," Lindsay said as she hugged Susan goodbye on the porch. "That was the best meal we've had since moving in."

"Good," Susan said warmly. "Next time, I'll try and burn something, so you don't get too comfortable."

****

By the fourth day out from Fort Davis, the landscape had fallen into a familiar rhythm, low, broken hills giving way to rising red bluffs, then crumbling into the dry gullies and washes that signaled the approach of the Rio Grande.

Mid-morning, the patrol crested a broad, rocky hill. Before them the desert opened like a wounded hand, the broad, meandering line of the Rio Grande glinting in the distance, and beyond it, the faint silhouettes of the Chisos Mountains clawing at the horizon. Their dark forms rose out of the baked earth, stark and solemn under the hammering sun.

Captain O'Brannach reined his horse to a halt at the summit and shaded his eyes with one hand. The air was dry enough to crack skin, and already the heat waves shimmered off the rocks like ghosts. Dust hung in the air around the men riding behind him, the slow shuffling weight of horseback travel and expectation.

The view was grand, to be sure, but it was a view they'd seen a dozen times before, and he knew it. This patrol was a duplicate of countless others since 1886, each dispatched with urgency, each returning with the same report: no sign of Comanche, no Apache, no anyone. Just dry riverbeds, long abandoned campsites, and the endless, stoic mountains were all that they found.

He shifted in the saddle and made his decision.

Turning to his senior sergeant, he said, "Voss. Break out the wagons and send them ahead to tonight's bivouac. Same site we used last October, down by the cottonwood stand. Assign two squads to guard 'em. No sense dragging them through the canyons."

Voss, tall and wiry, nodded and barked orders. The drivers snapped their reins, and the wagons rattled off at a steady pace, escorted by a cloud of mounted troopers. Soon, only the core of F Troop remained, leaning on their saddles, eager for orders.

O'Brannach shifted his horse toward the canyons, tightening the reins. "We'll ride down, sweep the washes. Stay sharp. If there's sign, I want to know it before sundown."

Voss pulled up beside him, wiping dust from his mustache with a grimy gloved hand. His tone, when he spoke, was low and frank. "You're still hopin' we find sign, Captain?"

O'Brannach didn't answer immediately. He looked south to where the land dropped in tiers toward the river, where brush and mesquite clawed at the canyons like desperate fingers.

"Fort's running on borrowed time," O'Brannach said finally. "New rail lines show the Indians that a human wave is coming. I know it, you know it, and they know it. Like a grass fire on the prairie. The animals in its path have two choices. Outrun the flames or die trying. The Indian is the animal, and we are the flame. Cavalry doesn't need to sit garrisoned anymore. We've burned through here."

Sergeant Voss spat into the dust. "If we don't turn up something soon, Apache, Comanche, hell, a lost bandit, they'll close Fort Davis inside the year. Ship us all west to Arizona. Ain't no Apache here to find, sir. Hasn't been for years. The last real raid was before my third enlistment."

"Maybe they're keeping low," O'Brannach muttered, but there wasn't much conviction behind it.

The sergeant shook his head slowly. "No, sir. Nearest native band left holed up twenty miles north of the Fort, Old Camp Springs way. What's left of 'em, anyway. Ghosts more than men, now. Maybe thirty, forty souls if that. Livin' off what water and meat they can scrape up. Good folks by what the traders say. Haven't raided a soul in years."

O'Brannach said nothing for a while. He leaned forward, resting his arms on the pommel of his saddle.

Old Camp Springs. He knew it. Knowing the name gossiped around the fort like a piece of trivia nobody cared enough to bother with anymore. Not a threat. Not a chance at glory. Remnants.

It gnawed at him.

He glanced at the carbine resting against his stirrup, then thought of the Whitworth Rifle packed carefully in one of the gear wagons ahead. He had practiced with the rifle each evening, sometimes to a crowd of cavalry troopers, but after a few days it was mostly just him and Sergeant Voss. The troopers were either too bored or too tired from the full day of riding to watch anymore.

The world was moving on without him. First there was the bad land deal that killed his dreams of farming. Now it was the Army marching steadily away from men like him, toward rails and wires and policies that didn't need a horseman with dirt under his nails.

If there was no Apache left to fight, then what had it all been for?

"Mount up!" he barked, the thought sliding sour down his throat. "Let's earn our pay today."

The men clicked into motion, boots into stirrups, horses stirring from their patient dust bath.

Voss leaned close enough that only O'Brannach could hear. "It's empty land, Captain. Ghost land. We're just ridin' it so it don't swallow us."

O'Brannach smiled tightly, a slash of white teeth against a sunburned face. "Ghost land or not," he said, "today we ride it because duty demands it."

And with that, he kicked his mount into a slow, determined trot, leading his men down into the waiting canyons, where dust and stone and ancient silence swallowed them up.

****

Dumpsy sat pouting at the door. Dinner that night was casual, patio chairs turned to face the sunset, plates resting on the white outdoor table. The heat of the day was bleeding off, leaving only the low hum of crickets and the sweet, dusty smell of evening.

Brian and Martin recounted the goat battle of the previous weekend in colorful detail, while Lindsay listened, a small, amused smile tugging at her mouth.

When the plates were cleared, and Martin leaned back with a groan, Lindsay finally spoke.

"You two realize you're jumping to the wildest conclusions possible, right?" she said, sipping her sweet tea. "You're skipping past about twenty reasonable explanations."

Martin raised an eyebrow. "Such as?"

"New goats. New smells. New surroundings. Stress. You name it. And as for the trailer thing? Goats like small, enclosed spaces. Safety instinct."

Brian leaned forward, resting his elbows on his knees. "What about the coaxial cable? Reasonable explanation? Wild hogs that were nice enough to pull the line neatly out? Wild hogs will do to the landscape what the Atomic Bomb did to Hiroshima – tear it up."

"Wind," Lindsay said simply. "Or maybe another animal. Jackrabbit. Javelina. They love messing with stuff."

Martin smirked. "You can't tell me javelinas are selectively mining cables."

Brian added, deadpan, "Maybe it's a polterjavelina."

Lindsay laughed despite herself. "Okay, that one's funny."

She let the teasing trail off before getting serious again. "Look, I'm not saying it's *nothing*. I'm saying we don't have evidence yet. No photos. No video. No relics. No weird energy spikes. Just a scared cat, a busted windshield, and a pulled wire."

There was a pause.

"and destroyed pistols…" Martin added.

"What if," she said carefully, "I meet you two halfway? You two can search the property next weekend when you come to help move the panels? North, south, east, west. Check the ravine, every rocky outcrop. If you find anything, anything Native American or odd, or old, you bring it back. Then we'll talk about hauntings. Honestly, I don't even know what you would prove."

Martin and Brian exchanged glances.

"Deal," Martin said.

Brian nodded eagerly. "Gator's full of gas. We'll cover everything from here to El Paso."

Martin added dryly, "Or until we run out of snacks."

****

That night, sometime past two in the morning, Martin awoke to a low, rattling growl.

He blinked into the darkness. Beside him, Lindsay shifted, murmuring half a word before falling still again.

Then the growl came again, closer, steady, guttural.

Dumpsy was upset.

Martin nudged Lindsay. "Linds," he whispered. "Wake up."

She stirred, sitting up slowly. "What's wrong?"

Martin tilted his head. "Listen."

The growl deepened into a full-bodied hiss. Dumpsy's silhouette, puffed-up tail, arched back, standing at the foot of the bed, focused on the dresser beyond.

Then came the sound.

Not a crash. Not a shuffle.

A perfume bottle was sliding.

One perfume bottle moved first, a slow, scraping sound across the wood surface. Then another. Then another. Each moving individually, deliberately, like unseen fingers nudging them forward.

Lindsay inhaled sharply.

Martin was about to throw off the covers when the bedroom door creaked open and Brian stumbled in, cell phone flashlight blazing.

The beam swept the dresser just as four bottles toppled over together, one of them spinning on its base before the cap popped free.

A soft "gluk, gluk" of perfume draining away flooded across the dresser top.

Before Martin could say a word, Brian was shoved sideways, *hard*, into the wall. The thud rattled the pictures hung on the nearby hallway.

All three of them froze.

From the hall came the unmistakable sound of *footsteps*, heavy, fast, retreating into the shadows.

For a moment, the house held its breath.

Then Lindsay flung the covers off and reached for the lamp. Lights flared to life, one after another, chasing the darkness into corners.

Dumpsy bolted under the bed.

They all gathered in the living room within minutes, mugs of hastily brewed coffee steaming on the counter. The clock on the stove read 3:12 AM.

Brian rubbed the back of his neck, still pale. "I heard Dumpsy growling. Figured I'd check it out. Soon as I fully opened the door, boom, bottles everywhere. And something pushed me. Not like I lost my balance. Like shoved me."

Martin stirred his coffee, saying nothing.

Lindsay blew on her mug and set it down firmly. "You slipped. Remember your knee?" she said. "Laminate floors. Bare feet. It happens."

Brian frowned. "I didn't slip."

"And the footsteps?" Martin asked quietly.

"Vibrations," Lindsay said firmly. "When you hit the wall, it knocked the perfume over. Big enough bang could shake the whole house a little."

Martin gave her a look. "Linz. Come on."

She held up a hand. "Look, until you two find something, some pottery shard, some burial marker, anything, this is just a spooky night and a clumsy roommate, not to mention a room with an intense perfume smell to it. It'll take days to get that smell out of there, if ever."

Brian rubbed his palms on his jeans. "Then explain the cold spot. Right before it shoved me, the air felt like ice."

Martin's eyebrows shot upwards in surprise at the mention of the cold air.

Lindsay hesitated, then scoffed. "Cold spots happen. Evaporative coolers can create drafts."

"At three in the morning?" Brian shot back. "With the unit turned off?"

Lindsay opened her mouth, closed it again, and stared into her mug. "There's got to be an explanation."

Martin spoke softly. "Yeah, there is. We just haven't found it yet."

Brian muttered under his breath, "Polterjavelina strikes again."

Martin smirked despite himself.

But when Lindsay wasn't looking, Martin and Brian exchanged a glance.

They didn't say it aloud.

They didn't need to.

Chapter 15
What the Ground Remembers

Rows of school buses stretched along the gravel edge of the fort's parking area, one line from Alpine ISD, another from Marfa, and a dusty yellow Balmorhea bus idling near the entrance, their drivers catching shade under the twisted limbs of a live oak. The crisp fall air, replete with yellow scrub dotting on the hills, held just enough chill to keep the high desert sun from baking the stone, and the re-enactors at Fort Davis were beaming.

"It's been years since we've had a crowd like this," said one, brushing imaginary lint from the sleeve of his dark blue US Army Infantry coat. He wore his kepi low to keep the sun out of his eyes, and a brass belt buckle flashed as he straightened to meet the first wave of students. "A lot of these kids have never seen living history in motion. Lindsay, you've done something special here."

Nearby, a lean man in Confederate gray was fielding questions from a pack of middle schoolers. "You see, the South occupied this fort during the Civil War. Those men from Texas wore this uniform," he said, adjusting the worn leather strap that crossed his chest. "And yes, it's itchy. And yes, it's hot. But it's authentic."

Behind him, two Cavalry reenactors stood beside their horses, yellow piping bright against navy wool. One held a saber in its scabbard; the other explained the evolution of military saddles. A kindergartener pointed at the horse and asked if it had a name.

By ten a.m., the parade ground swelled with students, their chaperones, and teachers guiding them from station to station. The Fort Davis High School principal found Lindsay near the flagpole, where she was handing out laminated scavenger hunt sheets to a group of freshmen. "Lindsay," he said, glancing over the crowd, "I've worked here fifteen years. I don't think I've ever seen this many kids on site at once, not even when the middle school band played here a few years ago. This is something else."

Lindsay smiled, her cheeks already pink from wind and sun. "It was supposed to be smaller," she admitted. "Just Alpine and maybe Marfa. But once Susan floated it to her contacts, the whole thing ballooned."

"Good ballooning," he said. "This, this is how you get them to care. The students are all smiles, but the tape recorders in their heads are going full out."

Kids crowded the Cavalry station, then darted toward the infantrymen discussing daily rations and camp life. One student asked if women ever served. Another wanted to know how many Apache attacks happened during the fort's peak years. Dozens of hands shot up with follow-up questions, some goofy, some insightful, but all earnest.

Susan moved through the crowd like a conductor, steering the younger students in orderly lines toward the museum entrance. Her English teacher instincts kicked in as she pointed out interpretive plaques and artifact tags, encouraging the older students to write down questions or observations for later. A few high schoolers lingered near a rusted field stove, nodding at her commentary.

Inside, the Fort's museum buzzed with new attention. Glass cases that usually earned a glance were now destinations. The antique uniforms, signal flags, field journals, and reconstructed barracks room all took on fresh gravity after seeing their real-world counterparts in motion just outside. For many, this was their first time connecting textbook to terrain.

Lindsay stayed outside, standing in the sun beside a few teachers from Marfa and Balmorhea who had wandered over with thermoses and curious smiles. They asked how she'd pulled it off, how she got three districts to commit to one field day. She laughed and shrugged, then leaned into the moment.

"I've got a dozen more ideas," she said. "What if we recreated a telegraph line demonstration? Or did a Fort-to-Fort mail relay across the Davis Mountains? Or maybe an oral history project with descendants of soldiers and scouts who served here…"

One teacher tapped a pen against her clipboard. "You've got momentum. Don't stop now."

****

Rounded panel joints scraped against each other as the fencing took shape. Martin and Brian worked steadily. The early morning air was still cool, the smell of crushed mesquite and dry dust rising with every bootstep.

Martin hitched the Gator to the makeshift water trough Brian had brought, the old propane tank, cut and welded onto skids made of curved oilfield pipe. Empty, it weighed about fifty pounds. Filled, it was nearly impossible to budge without the Gator's help. Martin groaned as he guided it out from under the main tank's spigot, sloshing water over the side as he dragged it with the Gator toward the temporary corral. Enough spilled to leave a dark trail in the dirt, but not enough to worry about.

The sun was already biting through Martin's long sleeves as they finished anchoring the third panel of fencing. He leaned into the post driver, giving it two solid whacks to seat the T-post, then handed it off to Brian, who took it with a grunt and a wink.

"You know," Brian said as he lined up the next post, "once your goats chew all this scrub down and leave their little round fertilizer gifts behind . . . what's the plan after that?"

Martin wiped his brow with the inside of his elbow. "I figured I'd . . . I don't know. Reseed? Try to keep it from turning back into a thicket?"

Brian smirked. "That's a maintenance plan. Not a future."

Martin took a drink from the water jug. "Didn't really think that far ahead," he admitted.

"Well, I did," Brian said, driving the post with a series of clean strikes. "You've got sandy outwash soil, open sun, and a fifty-gallon-per-minute well, once the goats do their thing, this land's ripe for grapes. Especially if you drip it."

Martin raised an eyebrow. "You a grape expert now?"

Brian chuckled. "Took an elective in Viticulture senior year. Easiest 'A' I ever earned. Homework could give you a killer headache if you forgot to spit, but I paid attention. Hell, I'd love to partner with you. Develop a vineyard. Maybe even breed a new cultivar."

Martin laughed, half in surprise. "What would we even call it?"

Brian grinned and pulled a strand of hay from his pocket, chewing it like he was about to strike gold. "West Slope Red. Or Davis Dust. And hey, even if the grapes suck, we can still slap a label on a bottle and sell cheap wine at a roadside stand to tourists."

Martin looked out across the land, toward the brush-covered gully and distant ridgeline. "From haunted scrubland to hill country knockoff?"

Brian tipped an imaginary glass in salute. "To big dreams and bad wine."

It didn't take long for the sun to climb to high noon over the ridgeline. By then the goats were happily munching on catclaw inside the enclosure, tails flicking contentedly.

Martin latched the panel they were using as a gate and leaned his weight against it, surveying the herd. His brow furrowed.

"Why did you bring me an extra goat?" he asked.

Brian shrugged, brushing dirt from his hands. "It's your father-in-law," he said. "He paid me to bring five more at the last minute. I had six in the pen and didn't feel like fighting the mud to get back to the pasture the rest were at. Figured I'd bring the other four later." He smirked. "Your dad was cool with it."

"That family has more money than, " Martin began.

"Your family," Brian interrupted, grinning wide. "Your family has more money than it knows what to do with."

He clapped Martin on the back hard enough to make him stumble a step.

"You deserve it. Listen," Brian said, his voice dropping into something more genuine, "all that work you did for me a few years back? You're a hell of a good guy. You deserved better even back then. Your grandparents raised you right. Summer help comes and goes, but you… you always did the right thing. Even when me or my dad didn't tell you to."

Martin smiled a little, embarrassed.

Brian wasn't done. "That time you moved the goats out of the dry wash and up the hillside? Man, I thought it was just gonna be a light rain. You didn't even hesitate. Ran right into it. That six-foot wall of water came through not ten minutes later, lightning hitting everywhere, hail the size of apples."

He shook his head, half laughing at the memory.

"Remember? I had to use my drone to fly dinner across the wash to you 'cause you were stuck with the herd overnight. The other summer help? They ran for the house soon as the first thunder rolled. Dad found them hiding inside the barn. You ran the *other way*, straight toward the goats. Risked yourself without blinking."

Martin looked away, pretending to check the latch on the gate again.

"We still talk about that," Brian said, his voice quieter. "Still brag about it."

"Thanks," Martin said simply.

Brian grinned and gave a theatrical stretch. "Okay," he said, rolling his shoulders, "enough sentimental crap. You need to quit talking so much." He grabbed his hat from where it hung on a post and jammed it down on his head. "Let's go look for evidence, Agent Mulder."

Martin laughed. "Does that make you Scully? You need more red in your hair.

Brian pointed a finger at him. "I'm just sayin'. If you find a little green man or a ghost coyote, I'm leaving with the Gator. You're on your own."

Still chuckling, they headed back toward the house to grab the supplies they'd need for their impromptu property search, the goats devouring the thorny shrubs behind them as the morning sun blazed higher over the scrub.

****

The sky was colorless when Storm upon Meadow opened his eyes, the horizon smeared with a thin gray that barely promised a dawn. The dreams had come again, harder this time, jagged with visions of smoke, thunder, and silent mouths stretched in grief. They clung to him now like the morning chill, heavy and unshakable.

Without speaking, he rose and moved through the sleeping camp. Even the dogs barely stirred. The small fires had guttered to embers, and the only sounds were the faint creak of cooling wood and the soft murmur of the spring behind the lodge circle.

At the edge of his shelter, he began to pack. Not much. Just enough to cross the hills and reach the soldiers at Fort Davis. Just enough if he had to run back. Nothing more.

He paused before the final items, the rifle, the pistol. Tools of survival. Tools of death. His fingers brushed the rifle stock, feeling the wear polished into the wood by years of use. He thought of hunts long past, of battles fought when they still believed they could hold this land.

But not today. Not this journey.

With slow, deliberate motions, he laid the weapons on a folded blanket. He would not bring them. A man carrying weapons was a man carrying a challenge. And he wanted no war, not if it could be avoided.

Painted Elk appeared in the gray light, his steps noiseless across the brittle grass. His face was drawn, unreadable.

"You are going," he said.

Storm upon Meadow nodded. "It is time."

The old warrior's eyes fell to the blanket, to the weapons lying still. His mouth tightened. "You go unarmed?"

"I go to speak, not to fight." Storm upon Meadow tightened the leather straps of his pack. "If I do not return by the third sunset, you must lead them to the west. Cross the empty lands. Reach the land promised to all Mescalero."

Painted Elk's hands flexed at his sides, as if trying to grasp something he could not hold. "And if they come for us?"

Storm upon Meadow gestured to the rifle, the pistol. "Then you take these. They are yours now. For the people." He paused, voice dropping. "For the ones who must survive."

Painted Elk bowed his head in silent acceptance. When he spoke again, it was a whisper. "You do not believe you will return."

Storm upon Meadow did not answer right away. He turned his gaze to the east, where the first brittle shard of sun split the ridge line.

"The easy path is not always the right one. Sometimes, we must take the harder trail," he said at last.

Painted Elk stepped forward and unfastened the leather strap from his shoulder. From beneath his cloak, he withdrew a finely crafted water pouch, softened deerskin and darkened with smoke, its seams hand-stitched with sinew. Bands of dyed porcupine quillwork wrapped around its body in patterns that mirrored the distant ridgelines, red and black for the sunset, white for the river trails, a single blue bead at the base where the stopper hung, meant to ward off misfortune.

He pressed it into Storm upon Meadow's hands.

His brother frowned. "You owe me nothing, Painted Elk. I would do this without gift or payment. That is our way."

"This is not payment," Painted Elk said, his voice low. "It will keep you safe. And when it is returned to me… I will know that you are safe."

He tightened his pack across his shoulders, offered Painted Elk a warrior's clasp of the arm, one that spoke of trust, of farewell, and walked away from the camp toward where the horses were.

The land stretched before him, vast and empty. Behind him, the last of the old ways stirred in uneasy sleep. And ahead, the river of history waited to drown him.

****

The column stretched thin under the hard Texas sun, a ragged line of horses and wagons trailing dust over the empty land. Sergeant Caleb Voss rode near the front, one eye on the rails glinting in the distance, the other on his captain, who hadn't said a word in hours.

They were close now. Valentine was no town, just a rail stop, a scattering of weather-beaten buildings and a tall water tower leaning at a tired angle. From there, it was an easy three-day ride east back to Fort Davis, easy if they stayed on the main trail.

Voss edged his mount forward until he was even with Captain O'Brannach. He tipped his hat back and cleared his throat.

133

"Beg your pardon, sir," he said, voice low and easy. "Been thinkin'. Once we hit Valentine, maybe we split. Just after we break camp at the Y6 Hills?"

O'Brannach said nothing at first, just flicked a glance his way. The captain's jaw was set hard, the lines at the corners of his mouth deepening.

Voss went on, smoothing the idea like a card player dealing out a careful hand. "Wagons and the greenhorns could take the straight track east. Safer. Faster. Leave a smaller party, the best riders, to skirt north a bit. Cross through Wild Rose Pass. Show the flag where folk don't see it much no more."

O'Brannach squinted against the sun. "Plenty of dust and mesquite up that way."

"Aye, sir," Voss agreed easily. Then, more carefully: "But also Old Camp Springs country. Ain't been no trouble there, but…" He let the word hang in the air a moment before finishing, "Never hurts to remind the locals that the Cavalry's still ridin'. Might keep 'em honest."

O'Brannach said nothing, but his fingers twitched slightly on the reins.

Voss leaned just a little closer, his voice dropping to a confidential rumble. "Maybe even stretch the Whitworth's legs a bit, sir. Find a nice ridge. Practice some long-range shots. Nothin' hostile, mind. Just . . . preparation."

The bait was laid carefully: no outright suggestion of violence, no direct mention of blood. Just a practice shot, just a reminder of who still ruled these broken hills.

O'Brannach's mouth tugged at the corner, not quite a smile. He looked out over the shimmering waste ahead of them, the empty rails, the dust that never seemed to end.

"Very well," he said at last. "We split tomorrow when we break camp at the Y6 Hills. Have Sergeant Samuel lead the wagons back. Pick a few men for the patrol."

Voss nodded, a quick jerk of satisfaction, and wheeled his horse away to spread the orders.

The Captain watched him go. He reached back, touching the rifle now lashed behind his saddle, feeling the heavy presence of the Whitworth rifle.

Three weeks of dust and failure. No fight, no glory. No mark left on the land.

Perhaps tomorrow, that would change.

****

Brian and Martin spent the better part of the afternoon combing the land.

"Should have packed a frozen lasagna in the glove box," mentioned Martin after a few dozen stops, "It would be done by now."

"Hotter than a stolen tamale, for sure," replied Brian.

"Do that a lot, steal tamales?"

"Did when I was six. I took some off my dad's plate when he wasn't looking. Found out the hard way what habanero pepper means. Tongue didn't grow back until I was eight!"

They took turns driving the Gator in slow, bumpy loops, hopping off when the terrain forced them into the thickets of catclaw and scrub oak. Sweat darkened the backs of their shirts; dust clung to their jeans like a second skin. They carried cheap garden trowels and wore leather gloves to protect against the thorns, but it was a losing battle. Even the Gator's side panels were scratched from where Martin tried, and failed, to push through a stubborn mesquite stand.

During their frequent water breaks, they lounged in the battered utility seats of the Gator, half-shaded by the roll bar and battered straw hats.

"What exactly are we looking for again?" Brian asked, tossing a bottle cap toward the Gator's floorboards.

"Anything native," Martin said, wiping his forehead. "Arrowheads, pottery shards, tools. Even bones."

Brian shifted, eyeing the sea of thorny green stretching around them. "You think this was, like, a burial ground?"

Martin shrugged. "Could've been. Or just a campsite. I don't know. I barely know enough to even guess. We're just trying to find something suggesting maybe there's a ghost. A Native American. I don't know the next step if we find something other than showing it to Lindsay."

"Me either," Brian admitted. He swigged from his water jug and wiped his mouth with the back of his hand. "Most of what I know about Native Americans came from John Wayne movies and Texas History in the seventh grade."

Martin chuckled tiredly. "Not exactly academic."

Brian slipped into a false voice, mimicking a teacher, "Did you know the Karankawa Indians covered themselves with rancid alligator grease to keep mosquitoes away? The Caddo Indians lived inside giant cones. And my favorite factoid, The Comanche played soccer with a priest's head once."

"And what else?"

"Hell, I don't remember…I was too busy staring at Carla Sue's boobs."

They both laughed, a welcome interlude to what was becoming a frustrating endeavor.

"Like I said," repeated Martin "Not exactly academic."

"Nope. Still," Brian said, gesturing toward the rough hills rising beyond their property, "this sure feels like old ground, you know? Not empty. Just . . . waiting."

"At least we're trying," Brian said. Then he grinned. "And hey, I found *something historic.*" He reached into the Gator's little cargo bin and pulled out a crushed, sun-bleached beer can. "Vintage 1977, baby. Pure artifact."

Martin laughed and tossed it into the back of the Gator with a clatter. "Maybe it's ceremonial. Rub it three times and see if a genie appears."

They drove to where they could see over the property but by sunset they admitted defeat. The land was just too rough, every step a fight against thorns and twisting roots. They had barely covered any of it. No relics, no arrowheads, no clues. Just endless scrub and sweat.

****

They ate dinner inside, the kitchen was blessedly cool compared to the stubborn heat outside. The calendar showed October, but it felt closer to August. Lindsay had thrown together grilled cheese sandwiches and a big bowl of cold watermelon slices, a meal that required minimal effort and very little standing over a stove.

Martin and Brian sat slumped at the table, worn out and half-sunburnt, their arms striped with thin red scratches created by too many catclaw encounters.

"Well, gentlemen," Lindsay said, handing each of them a paper towel and a glass of tea, "I'm proud of you for trying. Even if all you found was a beer can."

"Hey," Brian said, mock-defensive, "that can's gonna be in a museum someday. Pull tabs are cool."

"I honestly thought you might at least find a broken arrowhead or something. With this much open space . . . "

She hadn't even finished the sentence when it happened.

THUNK.

A deep, solid impact rattled the back door, hard enough to feel it through the floorboards.

Dumpsy, who had been dozing in a puddle of cool air near the fridge, bolted upright with a yowling hiss. His tail puffed into a bottlebrush as he scrambled into the living room, disappearing under the couch.

All three adults froze.

Brian was the first to move, pushing his chair back with a scraping noise and rising to his feet. "Tell me y'all heard that."

Martin nodded grimly. "Heard it. Felt it."

They approached the back door cautiously. Martin reached it first, flipping the deadbolt and pulling the door open with a tug.

On the landing, in the faint glow of the porch light, lay several objects scattered like offerings.

Martin crouched carefully. He picked up the first item, a small, heavy lump of grey metal, pitted with age. He turned it over between his fingers, feeling the edges protruding from the surface.

"Bullet," he muttered. "Big one. Old, too. Looks like it found its mark, the tip's mushroomed outward a little."

He passed the bullet into Lindsay's outstretched hand before reaching for the next object.

It was a coin, dark with tarnish, but when he rubbed his thumb across the surface, a gleam of silver shone through. He angled it toward the light, squinting.

"Morgan dollar," he said, reading the date aloud. "Eighteen eighty-nine."

He handed it to Brian, who whistled low under his breath.

Brian immediately lifted his cell phone. Now that he could use the satellite internet router, he was back to doing things the normal way.

"Hey Siri," he said, holding the phone close, "what's an 1889 Morgan Silver Dollar worth? It came from the New Orleans Mint and is in at least good condition."

The phone chirped back, "Based on information from the NGC Price Guide, an 1889-O Morgan Silver Dollar in circulated condition is estimated to be worth between $44.50 and $225."

"Thank you, Siri," Brian interrupted cheerfully.

"How the hell do you know it's from New Orleans?" Martin asked, raising an eyebrow.

Brian pointed at the small "O" stamped under the eagle on the coin. "Boy Scout Coin Collector merit badge," he said, flashing a grin.

Martin chuckled once before reaching for the third object, a much darker, corroded coin. He held it up to the porch light.

"Indian Head penny, I think. Date's mostly worn off."

Finally, he picked up the fourth item, a broken shard of rusted metal. It was no longer than his palm, jagged at one end and blunt on the other.

"Knife tip," he said quietly. "Or what's left of one. Looks snapped, not worn."

Brian retrieved each item set it beside the others on the table like assembling evidence at a crime scene.

Martin returned his attention to the lead bullet between his thumb and forefinger. It was heavy, still slightly greasy from old oxidation. He could see a strange hexagonal base and ridges that spiraled up from there. The bullet had a definite twist to it. "What an odd shape for a bullet. It's hexagonal on the undamaged part. Never heard of such a thing." Martin said softly while continuing to look at it. Brian lifted his cell phone up. Now that he could use the satellite internet router, he was back to doing things like normal.

"Hey Siri," he began, "What rifle uses a hexagonal bullet?"

In seconds they had the answer.

"The Whitworth rifle uses a .451 caliber hexagon shaped bullet and was an English-made percussion cap rifled musket used in the latter half of the 19th century. A single-shot muzzleloader with excellent long-range accuracy for its era, especially when used with a telescopic sight, the Whitworth rifle is widely regarded as the world's first sniper rifle."

All three of them stood there, the kitchen pressing in around them, filled with the heavy quiet of realization. Outside, the last of the daylight bled away.

Lindsay finally broke the silence, rubbing her hands over her face.

"I don't know if I believe in ghosts," she said, voice tight, "but I *do* know you don't just stumble across things like this on a clean porch. Not all at once. Not like this."

Martin looked at her, his face drawn and serious.

"Someone's trying to tell us something," he said quietly.

"Or warn you," Brian added under his breath.

They stood a few moments longer, the artifacts glinting quietly in the porch light. No one needed to say it out loud.

Everything had already changed.

Under the couch, still tucked deep into the shadows, Dumpsy let out a soft, uncertain meow.

****

Sunday came and went. The sun was already tilting low over the hills when Martin and Lindsay clustered near the driver's side window of Brian's battered pickup. The air still baked off the gravel, but the worst of the day's heat had finally begun to bleed away.

Brian leaned one arm casually out the open window, tapping the steering wheel with a dusty finger. Martin stood beside him, arms crossed loosely, while Lindsay shifted her weight between one foot and the other, her hands tucked in the pockets of her new "stretchy" jeans.

Brian blew out a low whistle. "Two weekends in a row. First one, your house smells like a funeral home because of that perfume bottle. This weekend, you've got projectiles launching themselves at the back door. I'm starting to feel like a target."

Martin snorted. "Give it time, next weekend we're installing a dunk tank over the septic tank."

"I want hazard pay," Brian said. "Or at least a freakin' helmet."

Lindsay gave a half-smile, though her brow was still faintly furrowed. "There's probably a rational explanation for everything. The bottle could've been knocked over by heat expansion or something. And the back door, maybe pressure changes, wind patterns, renegade crows. . . I don't know."

Brian raised an eyebrow. "Sure. Normal West Texas wind. The kind that throws things *into* your house."

"I said *maybe*," Lindsay replied. "Still, I might do some digging tonight. Online stuff. See if anyone else around here's had similar… incidents over the years. Local history, you know?"

Brian gave her a sideways grin. "You're always the History teacher."

"History hides a lot in plain sight," Lindsay said, glancing past them toward the horizon. "And sometimes the worst things leave the faintest scars. You just have to know where to look. I think it's time to do some looking, too."

Brian nodded, serious now. He turned the key and the old engine rumbled to life. "I'll leave you two lovebirds to the haunted homestead," he said lightly, though the weight of the conversation still clung to his voice. "Call me when you're ready for another date with the goats. Preferably with less shit hitting the fan… I mean back door."

"You could bring some more goats?" Martin hinted.

"Well," Brian said, stretching the word out like taffy, "next trip I'll make sure only to bring goats with a death wish. Easier to unload. Maybe rig the trailer with a diving board or something."

Martin chuckled, but Lindsay's smile was faint, distracted.

She pulled her hands from her pockets and straightened a little. "Actually, before you go planning goat rodeos . . . we need to talk."

That got both men's attention.

"I'm serious," she continued, lowering her voice a notch. "This whole… ghost thing? It's on shaky ground. And if word gets around, it could cause real problems."

Brian grinned. "Oh, don't worry. I'm already in talks with a guy in San Angelo to put up a billboard. Big flashing lights, *Come See a*

Real Ghost! Family Discounts Available! Make that sacrifice for the ones you love!" He made a jazz-hands motion out the window.

Lindsay gave him a look that could have withered fresh paint. "I'm not joking, Brian."

The humor slipped from his face, leaving something closer to sheepishness.

"We are both in our first year of teaching," she said, turning to include both. "It's the most critical year. Everything we do until next May is under a microscope. If parents start calling the principal saying we're seeing ghosts or acting strange…" she broke off, shaking her head. "It could wreck things before we even get a foothold."

Martin shifted uncomfortably but didn't argue. Deep down, he knew she was right.

"There are so many gates to be opened, so many boxes to be checked before we can even *think* about chasing this further in public," Lindsay went on. "We have to be smart. Careful. This land…this history…whatever's going on here, it isn't going anywhere."

Brian leaned his head back against the seat, exhaling slowly. "Yeah. You're right."

Lindsay softened a little. "I'm not saying we ignore it. I'll start looking into the history of this property, the surrounding area. Official records, news archives, whatever I can find. Real facts. Real paper trails."

He waved and pulled away in a cloud of dust, the truck and attached trailer rattling down the drive.

Martin watched him go, then turned to Lindsay. "You're right," he said quietly. "We gotta keep this close."

Lindsay nodded. "You move the goats back where they belong. I'll start digging into the records. Maybe you can feed Dumpsy before he decides to haunt *us*."

Martin smiled faintly and headed toward the portable fencing, already planning how long to allow them to graze before herding the goats back to the permanent corral. Lindsay disappeared inside, the screen door clattering softly shut behind her.

For a moment, the land fell quiet again, just the low whisper of wind across dry grass, the sharp, clean smell of creosote rising as the evening cooled.

But somewhere just beyond the reach of the porch light, something unseen waited. Watching.

The hunt for the truth had begun.

Inside, the house was dim and cool, the last light of the day slanting low across the wood floor. Lindsay set her phone and keys on the counter, kicked off her boots with a practiced nudge, and headed for the battered desk in the corner of the living room.

Dumpsy emerged from one of the back bedrooms. He gave a soft, grumbly meow as he padded over, bumping his head against her calf.

"I know, buddy," Lindsay murmured, scooping him up with one arm. "This weekend was weird."

She scratched him absently behind the ears as she sat down at the office cubby tucked away into the corner of the living room. The fan whirred a little louder than it should have, but the screen flickered to life.

Setting Dumpsy in her lap, Lindsay opened a search window and typed in **Jeff Davis County Land Grants 1880s**.

It was a start. If there was something hidden out here, some deed, some long-forgotten survey line, some sliver of ugly history, she'd find it. "Let's knock off the low hanging fruit first," she told the cat.

She already had half a clue with the date of the Morgan Silver Dollar sitting nearby on the kitchen sink windowsill. History didn't vanish.

The first few results loaded slowly over the satellite connection, and Lindsay leaned in, eyes sharp, fingertips already poised to chase the past down rabbit holes.

Outside, Martin's faint voice carried through the cooling air as he coaxed the goats, his laughter mixing with the restless shuffle of hooves.

For now, everything was normal again.

But for how long.

Chapter 16
A Man Who Carried No War

Strapped to a willow pole, the white cloth fluttered in Storm upon Meadow's hand as he rode slowly toward Fort Davis, his horse moving at a measured, steady pace. Dust rose in slow, lazy clouds from each hoofbeat.

There were no walls to block his way, only the spread of low, sun-deep red stone and adobe buildings, arranged around the broad, empty parade ground. Soldiers in blue emerged from the mess hall and the barracks, pausing mid-step to stare as the solitary rider approached.

From a doorway near the headquarters, an officer stepped out and narrowed his eyes against the glare. Tall, broad-shouldered, and weathered by decades on frontier posts, Colonel William Hall stood a moment with his gloved hands folded behind his back before striding toward the parade ground.

He raised one hand, deliberate and slow, a signal etched in discipline, The few soldiers nearby, rifles in hand, relaxed their stances but stayed alert.

Storm upon Meadow guided his mount directly into the heart of the fort, weaving between the assembled buildings until he drew up before the Commander's quarters. He dismounted with quiet grace, tying his horse to a rail outside.

Colonel Hall met him there with a respectful nod, wary.

"You come under a white flag," Hall said, his voice even. "You are welcome under it. Come inside. We'll talk."

He led Storm upon Meadow into the building, a modest adobe building with a wide porch, functional rather than grand. Inside, the commander's office was plain: a heavy wooden desk, maps pinned to the walls, a battered field chest tucked neatly against one side. The air smelled of dust, old leather, and the faint bite of lamp oil.

Hall gestured to a chair opposite his desk. Storm upon Meadow took it without hesitation.

For a long moment, neither spoke.

Finally, Hall broke the silence, settled back into his own seat with a small creak of leather.

"I was a young officer in the Red River War," Hall said slowly. "My commander told me once that winning peace is harder than winning battles. Takes a different kind of backbone."

Storm upon Meadow inclined his head slightly. "There were wrongs," he said in a deep, rough voice. "Yours. Mine. Blood for blood."

Hall's mouth tightened. "Aye. Good men buried on both sides. Good boys, too."

The Apache gave a short nod, his dark eyes steady. "We will leave this place. No more fight. No more blood. Yours is a river with no end, carried by ribbons of iron. My people will go to New Mexico. To Mescalero lands."

Hall exhaled slowly, a long breath that seemed to carry the weight of years.

"You make a wise choice," he said at last. "Better for your people. Better for ours."

Storm upon Meadow was silent for a long moment, eyes lowered as though studying the polished grain of the table between them. When he finally spoke, his voice carried the weight of old wounds and distant horizons.

"When the soldiers came before, I thought only of war. Of blood for blood. Two of my sons were killed by white men's bullets." He paused, the muscles in his jaw working as he drew a careful breath. "My heart was fire. My mind was full of killing. I dreamed of riding at night, burning cabins, hearing your people cry as ours have cried."

He lifted his gaze and held Hall's eyes. "But fire burns itself out, Colonel. I have seen too many graves. Death visits all men in time. There is no need to hasten its arrival in the name of not understanding."

Hall swallowed hard but said nothing. As a father he understood, losing a son would be devastating.

Storm upon Meadow went on, his voice softer now, almost weary. "The land grows smaller each year. Fences come where open grass once lay. Soldiers watch trails where my people used to hunt. We are pushed, always pushed, and yet… I have no more sons to bury."

He tilted his head. "If there is to be dying, let it be for something greater than vengeance. Let it mean a future for those who remain."

Hall exhaled slowly. "I wish your words carried farther than this room, Chief."

Storm upon Meadow's eyes glimmered in the lantern light. "So do I. But wind carries words only so far. It is men who choose what they hear. Díí' naashá. It means to go to the mountain to be judged."

He rose from his chair and crossed to the door, where a young enlisted private waited, hat in hand.

"Fetch three sacks of flour and five pounds of tobacco from the Commissary," Hall ordered quietly. "And bring them here."

The young man nodded and hurried away at a trot.

Hall turned back to Storm upon Meadow. From a leather pouch at his belt, he drew out three shiny silver coins and placed them carefully on the desk between them, Morgan silver dollars, heavy and bright in the morning light.

"These are yours," Hall said. "For supplies at the trading post. Or whatever you need for the journey. It's not enough, I know, but I am giving them to you man to man. I am giving you all that I have with me. A symbol, if nothing else."

Storm upon Meadow reached out, gathering the coins with slow, deliberate fingers. He tucked them away without ceremony.

When the supplies arrived, flour in rough canvas sacks, tobacco tied in tight twists of brown paper, Hall had them loaded by hand onto Storm upon Meadow's horse. Several of the soldiers from the 3rd Cavalry stood nearby, watching in silence.

As Storm upon Meadow mounted again, Colonel Hall stepped closer, raising an open hand in farewell, not a salute, but a gesture of respect between two old survivors.

Storm upon Meadow returned the gesture, a small nod accompanying it, then turned his horse northward, riding at an easy pace through the open fort and back towards Wild Rose Pass, sunlit land beyond.

The dust from his passage rose lazily in the still air, the only evidence he had been there at all.

Colonel Hall stood watching until the rider became no more than a flicker against the stone and mesquite. Only then did he turn back toward his office, the heavy burden of old wars pressing just a little harder on his shoulders.

The dust from Storm upon Meadow's departure lingered long after he had vanished into the dry morning light. Colonel Hall remained on the porch, watching the space where horse and rider had faded into the wilderness.

Behind him, the officers of the 3rd Cavalry and a scattered few from 5th Infantry stood silent, respectful. But not all expressions were easy.

Second Lieutenant Franklin, barely a year out of West Point, shifted his weight awkwardly, a crease of confusion pulling at his brow. He leaned slightly toward Major Hall and muttered under his breath, "Sir, letting them go without terms? Without papers?"

"And with my three silver dollars, too." Hall, a veteran of two decades of frontier duty, answered without looking away from the empty parade ground. "Sometimes the best treaty's the one you don't write, Lieutenant. They're leaving."

Franklin pressed his lips into a thin line but said no more. He was young yet, and men like Hall had learned that not every victory needed signing ceremonies or brass bands.

Colonel Hall finally turned, his spurs jingling lightly as he stepped down onto the hard-packed earth. His boots crunched across the parade ground as he made for his office, shoulders squared beneath the old sun-faded coat.

Before he could reach the steps, a voice called out crisply: "Colonel Hall, sir!"

A Private in Quartermaster Corps uniform jogged toward him, one hand clutching a yellow envelope, the other balancing his hat. He skidded to a stop, snapped a salute, and thrust the envelope forward.

"Telegraph just in from El Paso."

Hall returned the salute briskly, plucking the envelope from the young soldier's hand. "Thank you, Private."

The soldier hesitated for a moment, as if curious, then turned smartly on his heel and retreated.

Hall broke the seal with a practiced thumb, unfolding the thin paper. His eyes scanned the brief, blocky lines.

The senior officers gathered near the steps watched the change in his expression, the slight tightening around his mouth, the shift of his jaw as he finished reading.

Hall lowered the paper, pinching it between two fingers, and addressed the assembled men.

"Gentlemen, the date of the fort's closure has arrived," he said, voice steady, "we are ordered to close Fort Davis on the thirtieth of June. The garrison is to be abandoned within ninety days. We've known this day was coming for months, well here it is."

A murmur rippled through the group, surprise, disbelief, resignation.

Hall continued, unshaken. "The 220th Regiment is reassigned to Fort Verde, Arizona Territory. The 5th Infantry Regiment will report to Fort Sam Houston and 3rd Cavalry are to report to Foot Hood. Final orders, signed by Secretary of War Redfield Proctor himself."

He folded the telegraph neatly and tucked it into his breast pocket. He knew other orders would be forthcoming, orders about the land and disposition of the buildings. There would be orders for transport by train as well and would require dealing with the Southern Pacific in Alpine to secure passage. The Fort may be closing, but an entirely new world of paperwork and planning was just opening.

No one spoke. The sky, brilliant and immense, offered no comfort. The fort's stone walls throwing long shadows onto the empty parade ground. The buildings, built with such effort, guarded with such blood, seemed suddenly brittle, as if they too sensed their days were numbered.

Hall glanced once more toward the horizon where Storm upon Meadow had disappeared.

"Times are changing," he said softly, almost to himself. "The old wars are over. And the frontier . . . is closing."

Without waiting for a reply, he climbed the steps back to his office, leaving the others to absorb the weight of the morning, a morning when two very different nations had both taken their first, reluctant steps into a future they could not yet see.

That evening, as the sun bled itself into the rugged teeth of the Davis Mountains, the bugler sounded retreat. The notes drifted thin and lonely across the parade ground, weaving through the cottonwoods and adobe walls like a farewell too proud to speak aloud.

As one, the officers and enlisted men of the fort paused in their tasks, turning to face the flagstaff.

The colors descended slowly, the fabric snapping once in the restless breeze before drooping like a tired soldier at the end of a long march. From his office window, Colonel Hall watched the ceremony in silence, the folded telegraph still resting on his desk.

153

The flag came down with practiced precision, but to every man who stood witness, it felt heavier tonight.

Heavier than any of them dared admit.

Chapter 17
The Silence Knows

With October settling in and the first true chill whispering through the nights, the rhythm of school life had begun to take hold, early alarms, packed lunches, tired dinners, and lesson plan updates scrawled on scrap paper, then forgotten in jacket pockets.

Inside the house, Martin and Lindsay clung to a small but necessary ritual: dinner together, no grading, no laptops, no student talk, at least not for the first fifteen minutes.

Lindsay set down two plates of leftover meatloaf and kicked off her shoes under the table. "We made it," she said, lifting her glass of iced Cinamon Chai tea. "Another Monday down."

Martin slumped into his chair with a groan and raised his own mug in return. "Only a hundred sixty something days to go."

They tapped rims and ate in companionable silence. Outside, the wind stirred dry leaves across the gravel yard, a whisper of cooler weather pushing in from the northwest.

Martin set his fork down, meatloaf mostly demolished, and let out a long sigh. "That may have been the best meal I've had since… last Tuesday."

Lindsay grinned. "High praise."

He nodded solemnly, pushing his plate forward. "It had structural integrity, flavor, and temperature. All the classic food groups."

She raised an eyebrow. "It's Meatloaf. You're just listing nouns again, aren't you?"

Martin smirked but didn't deny it. A wink brought a smile to her face as she reached for her glass.

After a few moments, Lindsay broke the silence. "I found something interesting today, researched it on my break."

Martin looked up, mid-chew.

"About the fort," she said, leaning back in her chair. "I was going through some of the digital archives for Fort Davis, Army records, troop logs, patrol summaries. All of it's available through the state historical site. You'd be amazed how much of that stuff is scanned."

Martin wiped his mouth. "So, what did you find?"

"The 220th Cavalry," she said. "The ones stationed there in the final months before closure. They were still running mounted patrols through the spring of 1891, despite the fact that everyone knew the fort was about to be decommissioned. They performed the last patrol, and it might be, based on the Morgan Silver Dollar date, the only long patrol that occurred after the coin was minted. The 5th and 23rd Infantry stopped patrolling in 1888. "

He raised an eyebrow. "That sounds like a waste of time. I guess the native's had vamoosed?"

"Exactly," Lindsay replied. "The paperwork shows it, too. You can see how things start breaking down. For most of the 1880s, everything's clockwork: detailed reports, neat signatures, supply requisitions filed weekly. But once you get into the spring of '90? Gaps. Handwriting goes sloppy. Some entries don't have any signatures at all. I never found out who replaced Colonel Hall in May of 1891, there's no record of his replacement."

"Like they stopped caring," Martin said.

"Or like they knew it didn't matter anymore," Lindsay answered.

She stood and carried their empty plates to the sink, rinsing them while she talked. "There's a noticeable drop in effort. Like, the men were still doing the work, riding out, checking trails, escorting supply wagons, but the paperwork's just… going through the motions."

Martin leaned back in his chair. "Can you track where they went?"

"Sometimes," she said. "Some of the 220th patrols were afternoon-long local training, just out toward Wild Rose Pass or down to Alpine Station. But others were longer. There's one route noted in late March that sweeps north toward what would've been open ranchland back then. It doesn't give exact coordinates, but it lines up with the general direction of our place, but the record is incomplete."

Martin blinked. "Wait. Are you saying they rode through this land?"

"I don't know for sure," she said. "But maybe. That's what I'm trying to figure out."

157

She drank her iced tea. "And here's the odd part: there's a short field entry, no heading, no formal report, just a line on a supplemental form that reads, *'One hostile encountered. Not recovered. No friendly casualties. Marked and logged.'* That's all it says."

Martin's face tightened. "That's vague."

"It's almost nothing," she agreed. "And the date is smudged. There's no attached report. No follow-up. It's like someone jotted it down so they could say they did and moved on. How is it that the patrols from 1886 till 1891 find nothing and then viola! A dead native on the final patrol sent from the fort?"

They sat for a moment, tea glasses between their hands.

Martin finally said, "And this isn't unusual for that time?"

"Not in the last months. You can see how the standards start to fall apart. It's like the Army had already shifted its focus elsewhere. Fort Davis was winding down, and everyone knew it. They just wanted out. Some of the officers probably had their next assignments lined up. Others probably didn't care anymore."

Martin ran a hand over his face. "This guy, whoever he was, 'one hostile', just ends up as a footnote."

Lindsay nodded. "No name, but that's exactly what I need. No tribe. No details. Just a checkmark on a form. And if the body wasn't recovered, it's entirely possible the man was left where he fell."

Neither of them spoke for a moment.

Then Martin asked, "Does the location line up with that ravine?"

Lindsay shrugged. "Not conclusively. But it's not impossible. The Army had loose maps back then, based more on local ranch trails than surveyed roads. They'd name a ridge or a spring and call it good. Our property could have easily been part of an old route north."

Martin leaned back and stared out the kitchen window, where the last of the dusk had faded into night. "The canyon. The bullet. It's like all the clues are spread out, but none of them point clearly to anything."

"History's not a straight line," Lindsay said. "Especially not at a time like that. These things, margins, footnotes, omissions, they're where the truth hides. I can't really see those online."

Martin stood and refilled both their mugs. "So what's next?"

She took a sip and set the glass down. "I'm going to keep reading. There's still a lot of the 220th's logs I haven't gone through yet. They're inconsistent, but I might find a name. Or at least a pattern."

He nodded. "Let me know if you find anything… compelling."

"I will."

Martin gave a tired half-smile. "You always were the researcher."

She smiled back. "After all, you were the one who got spooked when the cat growled at the shadows."

Later, Martin sat on the recliner with Dumpsy curled up on his lap, both purring and like a small furnace. Lindsay took up her usual spot on the corner of the couch, laptop open, the screen casting a soft glow on her face.

She scrolled through a list of transcribed entries: grain orders, patrol records, maintenance logs for mules and wagons. But her eyes kept returning to that single entry:

"One hostile encountered. Not recovered. No friendly casualties. Marked and logged."

That dehumanizing word, "hostile", had a weight to it. Not a name. Not a person. Just a label. Just enough to disappear someone.

The cursor blinked below the line like it wanted to say more but didn't know how.

Outside, the wind stirred again, rattling the screens on the windows. Lindsay barely noticed. Her fingers hovered over the keyboard, uncertain.

Chapter 18
The Weight of a Bullet

Heat shimmered across the ridges as Captain O'Brannach paused his horse atop a rise, scanning the broken landscape below. The patrol had cut eastward after crossing the Southern Pacific tracks at Valentine, pushing through the jagged folds of the central range with the dry determination of men who wanted to finish strong, even if their mission had yielded nothing but silence and heat.

Behind him, Sergeant Samual led the wagons in a separate arc, trailing southeast toward Fort Davis via the longer, safer canyon route. There was no sense in dragging heavy wheels through uncertain stone and scrub. His orders had been clear: rendezvous at the parade grounds.

That left O'Brannach and his handpicked group of seven men edging along a high ridge line overlooking the basin beyond. Wild Rose Pass loomed off to their south, not yet visible but O'Brannach knew it was there, a scar of stone and shadow. From here, the ridgeline dropped sharply into the folds of Little Aguja Canyon. The land, harsh and raw, flattened beyond that as both Little and Big Aguja washes combined. Cutting up the side of a ridge that nearly extended to Star Mountain, their view increased tremendously with each step of their steeds.

Sergeant Voss eased his mount to a halt at the crest of a rocky fold in the ridge, leaning forward in the saddle as he peered across the shimmering grassland below. A few seconds later, he turned, urgency in his voice.

"Captain!" he called out, beckoning with a gloved hand. "Got movement!"

Captain O'Brannach rode up beside him, dust swirling around the horses' hooves. Voss extended his arm, offering up the battered binoculars. O'Brannach took them without a word and raised them to his eyes.

Across the distant flats, no more than a single figure rode in the morning glare. An Apache man on a chestnut horse, moving at a steady, deliberate pace. Even at this range, he noted bundles tied across the back of the horse, large canvas sacks.

O'Brannach adjusted the focus ring, lips pressed into a thin line. "He rides alone. Confident. No sign of others. But the distance… he's still too far for any shot worth taking."

He lowered the binoculars and exhaled. Sunlight glinted off the Whitworth rifle slung across his saddle, the hexagonal barrel catching tiny sparks of light.

Voss cleared his throat. "Sir, I'll say it plain. He's drifting close to that cut over there." He pointed to a low fold of earth, half-hidden by scrub and shadow. "There's an earthen rampart at the far end. If he slips into it, he'll be gone. And if he sees us and gets back to camp. . .blows the alarm. . ."

"We'll have a whole hornet's nest coming for us," O'Brannach finished.

Voss nodded. "Seven men can do damage, sir. Plenty of it. But against a whole camp, one we don't know the first thing about in size, ready for a fight? That's another story, Custer's story."

The captain sat silent for a few seconds, studying the ridgeline and the path of retreat the Apache might take. Finally, he drew a long breath.

"We hold the high ground," he said. "No rash moves. He doesn't see us. Tell the others to conceal themselves. And I'd rather know why he's riding alone than leave seven men dead for no reason."

Voss gave a short nod. "Aye, Captain."

O'Brannach dismounted, rifle in hand. The Whitworth was already loaded, he had done so without conscious thought at the last place they had watered the horses. He lay prone now on the warm stone at the top of the ridge, peering through the crude scope and watching the land below with the patient precision of a predator.

****

Storm upon Meadow felt the familiar looseness of the reins as his horse picked its way down a long slope toward the dry creek bed. The ramp had formed over generations of floods, a gentle descent of earth and packed gravel that allowed access to the flat below. He would cross the arroyo and turn south toward the springs, where the scattered lodges and low smoke of the camp would soon come into view.

The meeting at the fort had gone better than he had hoped. Words had been spoken. Old wounds named but not opened. A promise had been made and a gesture of goodwill given. Three sacks of flour, a pouch of tobacco, and silver coins now nestled in his pouch at his waist. He had not expected warmth, but he had not expected violence either. And in these times, that counted as hope.

He rode loosely, scanning the horizon without tension. The sun warmed his back, and the wind carried the faint scent of dry cedar. For the first time in many weeks, he allowed his thoughts to drift. Perhaps the time for running was done.

Storm upon Meadow slowed his horse in the tall grass, where the land leveled briefly before giving way to the dry wash ahead. He sat quietly in the saddle, the morning sun warming his shoulders, the wind dry but gentle across the chaparral. Only a short ride remained before he would reach his home of the last several seasons, and the familiar voices of his people.

He uncorked the water pouch thinking of Painted Elk's gift, and took a long, quiet sip. The water carried a faint taste of smoke and cedar, and as it settled on his tongue, so too did a feeling of peace.

He smiled.

With his other hand he removed one of the large coins given to him back at the fort. Money was still mostly a mystery. He turned it over with his fingers. In the other hand he held the water pouch and these two completely different items somehow being equal. He knew when he returned this pouch, whole and dry, it would be a signal to his brother. A wordless way of saying: *I am safe*, but the coin would never be able to convey that feeling. He had four pieces of money because the white man made these as common as raindrops in a rain shower, but only the pouch meant something.

He re-corked the pouch and decided not to tie it down, maybe another sip once he was down into the wash? He held onto the coin.

Storm upon Meadow fixed his eyes towards the steep dirt ramp just ahead, it was a pale scar, covered in dirt and rocks sloping down into the deep wash below. The trail was narrow but familiar, a twisting descent used by generations of hooves and rain. To him, this ramp was the final challenge of his long journey, the last obstacle before he could reach safety. Once he rode down into the wash, it would be only a short distance to the camp at the springs where Painted Elk and the others waited, sheltered among the Cottonwoods and red boulders. He felt the weariness in his bones, but also a flicker of relief, he was nearly home. He guided his horse forward, thinking about how the tricky passage ahead and the relief of this journey to find peace.

****

Captain O'Brannach had dropped to the rocky earth, settling into a prone position with practiced ease. Beside him, Sergeant Voss remained on his horse, binoculars lifted to his eyes, scanning the shimmering distance where the solitary rider moved across the sun-blasted flats. The Whitworth rifle, cradled against O'Brannach's shoulder, gleamed dully under the brutal afternoon sun.

"Long shot, sir," Voss muttered, his voice tight with a mix of doubt and admiration. "He's damn near a thousand yards."

O'Brannach said nothing. His jaw was set, a bead of sweat sliding from his temple into the corner of his eye. He blinked it away and focused through the primitive scope. The Apache rode at a relaxed gait, unaware of the eyes fixed upon him, unaware that he had been judged. Bags tied down behind the rider, he noted.

O'Brannach exhaled slowly, the way he'd discovered at the beginning of the patrol. He adjusted the rifle's elevation slightly, compensating for the range, observing the motion of the Davidson telescopic sight, and adjusting. The slightest movement on his part caused the view in the sight to move wildly. The crosshairs drifted over the moving target's head, no larger than a pin head held at arm's length at this distance. O'Brannach settled the sight onto the target.

He squeezed the trigger.

CLICK! The Whitworth's hammer struck the percussion cap.

The Whitworth cracked like a whip, the report rolling out across the empty landscape.

The recoil slammed into O'Brannach's shoulder, but he rode it out, lowering the barrel slightly as he and Voss both strained to watch.

For a moment…a long, aching moment…nothing happened.

"Missed," Voss said grimly, lowering the binoculars a fraction. "Too far. He's still…"

The Apache lurched violently. His legs jerked awkwardly, spasming once before going limp. For several heartbeats, the horse continued its steady course, rider slumped but still mounted, hands instinctively clinging to the reins.

Finally, as if the strings holding him upright had been cut, Storm upon Meadow pitched sideways and tumbled from the horse, landing hard against the earth in a puff of dust.

"Hah!" Voss breathed out, half in shock. "Sir, you hit 'im! I'll be damned!"

Through the binoculars, Voss watched as the figure lay motionless, arms twitching weakly but legs unmoving.

"He's not getting back up," Voss confirmed after another long look. "You dropped 'im clean."

O'Brannach remained prone for a moment longer, staring through the empty scope, the faint tang of burned powder curling in his nostrils. His hands tightened once on the rifle stock before he forced himself to move.

He rose stiffly, dusting grit from his trousers. The other troopers, a small knot of hard men handpicked for this final sweep, were already mounting up, sensing that the moment had passed.

O'Brannach slung the Whitworth back across his shoulder. No words of celebration passed his lips. No smiles cracked his weathered face. This was what it was, a clean shot, a job done. Nothing more. Nothing less.

"Sir, it's time your rifle earned it's death mark, a tradition of the 220th since it first saw battle. May I see your rifle, sir?"

Voss wiped his hands on his coat, then pulled the offered weapon toward him. Inspecting the long barrel and finely tuned scope. Without asking, he took out his knife and scraped the tip carefully across the topside of the wooden stock, so that it went on both sides of the cheekpiece ….a slow, deliberate motion that cut deep.

O'Brannach looked up. "The mark of death?

Voss didn't answer right away. He finished the line and ran his thumb over it.

"One mark," he said at last. "For today. A tradition. Our tradition. Ten or more years ago, we scratched them into our stocks near daily."

O'Brannach stared at him realizing he had only been posted here for two of those years.

Voss set the rifle back down. "This mark shows every member that you have joined the true ranks of 220th Regiment soldiers. This mark can only be given by someone that already has it, and we never do this around soldiers who haven't killed. This is from one killer to another, sir."

The Captain said nothing.

The scratch would remain there, a raw groove in the wood, darker than the rest, stained over time by oil and handling.

"Mount up," he ordered curtly, voice low and flat. "We ride for Wild Rose Pass. If we want supper tonight, then we're going to need to move."

The troopers clicked into motion, spurring their horses back into a weary trot. They had no desire to spend another night rough in the canyons. The sun was already bleeding across the western sky, and they had miles to cover before darkness fell.

As they rode eastward, dust pluming from their passage, the fallen figure of the Apache grew smaller and smaller behind them, swallowed by the vast, unfeeling desert.

O'Brannach didn't look back.

But Voss did.

And for a moment, squinting into the heat-haze, he thought, just for a heartbeat, that he saw the fallen Indian raise his hand slightly toward the sky.

****

The sun stood high when the bullet struck, an invisible thread snapping across the land. Storm upon Meadow did not hear the report of the rifle but felt the crack of bone as lead met spine. He simply felt his legs vanish. Both the water pouch and coin slipped from his hands with the jolt. One moment he was seated upon his horse, thoughts turned to his people, to the hope that perhaps the path forward was no longer bristling with war . . . and then, nothing. His thighs slumped like sacks of meat, and the muscles in his lower back gave way.

His horse, sensing the shift in weight, hesitated. For several heartbeats it walked on, Storm upon Meadow swaying, his hands steady against the horse, more out of instinct more than control. Then he slipped. His body slid sideways and collapsed into the hard soil, a dull thud muffled by brittle grass and dust. He did not cry out. Pain knifed through him, but deeper still was the awareness that something sacred had been stolen.

He lay still at first, shocked by the suddenness of it. When he tried to move his legs, they refused. He clawed at the earth and tried to sit up, tried to rise, but the body below his waist answered with silence. With horror.

His horse lingered, circling back once, whickering in confusion. Storm upon Meadow reached out, gripping the reins just long enough to meet its eyes. In a language older than words, he asked it to go.

Go. Let them know. Bring them to me. I am so close.

The animal hesitated. Then, with a snort, it turned and galloped westward, mane catching the wind like a torn banner. Dust rose behind it, trailing toward the ramp to the wash and toward the springs.

Storm upon Meadow was alone.

****

The sun beat down like a smith's hammer on the back of Captain Cormac O'Brannach's neck as he rode through Wild Rose Pass. The walls of the narrow canyon blazed in colors of rust and blood, the rhyolite cliffs holding the heat long past midday. It was like riding through the throat of a furnace, no breeze, no shade, only the rhythmic scrape of hooves against dry stone and the slow creep of sweat down his spine.

The pass was short, but brutal. A natural choke point flanked by ancient volcanic ridges, steep and unyielding, but it was also like an oven.

The Apache hadn't even stood against him. Hadn't raised a weapon. Hadn't known he was being hunted. The shot had been clean, by the army's standard. Long distance, unflinching execution. But O'Brannach had aimed high, the reticle above the head. The bullet had dropped sooner than expected.

It hit low.

In the back.

He saw that much through the scope, even though Voss had announced otherwise.

He swallowed. The pass closed around him, a narrow constriction on what had already been a hard ride.

He shifted in the saddle, gripping the reins harder than necessary, as if the leather might ground him.

Murderer.

The word came unbidden, unspoken, but it echoed in his mind with a weight the army couldn't measure.

Not war. Not victory. Not duty.

Just one man, and one shot, and a hollow space in his back that hadn't been there yesterday.

He didn't slow the horse. Didn't look back. But something in the way the shadows clung to the stone made him wonder if the pass would ever let him leave. The events of this day merged with others

. .

****

It was Ireland in 1860 . The air smelled of peat smoke and wet stone. The tiny town of Furbo, small, whitewashed, scattered houses mostly with the sea never far off. He'd been just a boy, barely ten, sent out in the gray hour before dinner to fetch his father from the pub before the rain hit full. The clouds to the west were dark and threatening, a sure sign he needed to be quick in his errand.

He pushed open the door and stepped inside. The warmth was stale with whiskey and boiled meat. His father stood near the hearth, voice low but taut, jaw working under the weight of some quiet argument with another man. Not fists yet. But close.

Cormac had crept forward and tugged at the thick wool sleeve. "Da. Mam says come home."

The old man looked down, smile blooming like spring despite the dark behind his eyes. He nodded, hand resting firm and warm on Brian's shoulder. They turned.

Then froze.

There was no warning. No shout. Just a jolt.

Brian felt it before he saw it, the sharp intake of breath, the way his father's grip faltered. Then the warm spatter of blood across his shoes. His father staggered forward one step, looked at him again with eyes wide and already losing light. A knife buried in his back.

171

The other man, face slack, stunned by what he had done, didn't flee.

****

The first hour passed in a haze of grit and disbelief. The heat bore down like a slow fire. He dragged himself a few feet into the shade of a narrow scrub oak tree, his elbows torn and bloodied from the sharp rocks hidden in the grass. The wound in his back wept steadily. Blood soaked into the waistband of his trousers. Flies found him quickly. He waved them off with one hand while the other clutched his knife, his only defense.

By nightfall, his mouth was cracked and dry. No one came. No one had seen. In the dying light, the shadows danced longer, and coyotes called from the far hills. They knew the scent of blood. He gripped his blade tighter.

The stars emerged one by one, dispassionate witnesses to the slow ruin of a man. He slept in fits, jerking awake to distant howls, to the rustling of something near his feet. At one point a coyote crept close, eyes gleaming. He slashed with his knife and caught it across the snout, sending it yelping into the dark. The blade snapped in the strike, just the tip, but enough.

He wept then, not from fear, but from the knowledge that it was not a clean death. The white men had always told stories of noble warriors dying in battle, surrounded by enemies or at the climax of a raid. But this was a forgotten place. A place of slow endings.

In the morning, ravens came.

They circled at first, wings silent. Then one landed on a nearby branch. Storm upon Meadow stared at it, unblinking. Its black eyes regarded him with a curiosity that bordered on judgment.

"You see me," he whispered through parched lips.

The raven did not answer.

****

The horse returned just before sunset, her steps sure and slow as she came down the wash alone. A heavy breeze stirred the trees around the camp, rustling the cottonwood like voices just out of reach. The older children were the first to notice, their play forgotten as they stood frozen, watching the mare approach the camp without a rider. One of them called a name. Painted Elk heard it and rose to his feet.

He met the horse near the edge of camp, saying nothing at first. She wasn't lathered or panicked, only windblown and alert, as if she had been released from duty rather than driven off. Her reins dangled loose. A soft blanket was still tied down along with bags of flour and tobacco. Painted Elk laid a hand on her neck, feeling the warm breath of her nostrils fan his sleeve.

"He is not coming back," he said at last, low and steady. Behind him, the others had begun to gather, one by one, drawn by instinct and silence. He didn't turn to face them. His eyes remained on the empty saddle, on the dust that clung to the mare's flanks, on the bags of flour tied down. A lone gust swept down through the trees, and somewhere in it was the shape of a name that none of them spoke aloud.

Painted Elk straightened. "We leave tonight," he said. "Before the stars rise."

****

By the second day, the wound had gone bad. The air around his hips buzzed with the scent of infection. His skin had turned clammy, and the edges of his vision pulsed. He drank water from a shallow pool left by a passing storm, dragging himself inch by inch to reach it. Each sip was agony and salvation.

In the heat of the afternoon his sons and daughters joined him. They danced about the area, telling tales of brave deeds, evaporating from one side of his body only to instantly appear somewhere else.

He lost his pouch, he never saw it fall.

Storms passed overhead each evening, pounding the distant cliffs with rain and brilliant light. He lay exposed beneath them, body trembling from fever, listening to the booming sky. When lightning struck a nearby ridge, he thought he saw shapes within it, men in old uniforms, their rifles pointed at the heavens.

By the third night, he no longer feared the coyotes.

He saw them in his dreams, painted like warriors, standing upright, faces masked in war paint. They danced around him, sang in broken Apache, and whispered truths he could not grasp. One coyote leaned close and spoke with a woman's voice:

"You are not forgotten. But they will not remember on their own. You must remind them."

When he woke, the ravens were closer. One sat atop his leg, pecking at the fabric. He did not move.

****

On the fourth day, his voice was gone. His strength, too. He could no longer pull himself forward. He simply lay there, the earth slowly claiming him. The sun blistered his face, the insects chewed at his arms.

Each breath rattled through a throat lined with dust. Even blinking felt distant, like something remembered rather than done. His tongue had cracked open in the heat. Every movement came with a cost, until movement itself slipped from the world of choices.

But in his mind, a storm was building.

It churned behind his eyes. Not a storm of clouds, but of memory, of fury, of things undone. The kind passed down in blood.

He saw his people. He saw the children who would grow up never knowing the names of the hills around them. He saw Painted Elk, stoic and faithful, leading the tribe north toward the Mescalero lands.

He saw them leaving, footsteps soft in dry soil, shoulders hunched not from burden, but from surrender. They were not defeated, only scattered. Torn from the roots that had named them. The hills behind them would forget their names if no one stayed to speak to them.

He began to whisper, not to himself, but to the sky.

"Let it not end in silence.

Let it be remembered.

Let the land speak with my voice."

The sky did not answer, but it listened.

On the evening of the fifth day, the final storm came.

It did not roll in with warning. It arrived like a reckoning, black clouds stacking over the ridgelines as if the mountains themselves had called them.

Thunder shook the mountains. Lightning lit the grasslands. Rain poured in great sheets, drenching the earth. Storm upon Meadow lay beneath it all, eyes wide to the sky, lips barely moving.

The drops fell into his mouth, bitter and cold, and he drank them like a man reborn. Just for a moment. A single flicker of something close to life.

When he awoke again Storm upon Meadow knew death was close. Even with the approaching sunrise he wouldn't see it. It saddened him. He heard the sound of coyotes eating his legs, tugging and tearing at his flesh, yet no pain.

"Coyote, you take what I no longer need, but I will walk upon this land….soon."

He could no longer feel their teeth. Only the stillness that followed. The stillness of the land, watching, waiting to remember.

And with his last breath, carried by the morning wind between small gusts, he spoke:

"Remember me."

The raven flew.

The land listened.

****

The morning had started to cool for once, with a lazy breeze sweeping across the ridge and the scent of juniper hanging in the air. Martin stood at the edge of the goat pen, one hand resting on the panel gate, the other gripping a travel mug of now-lukewarm coffee. October in the Davis Mountains had finally remembered it was supposed to feel like fall.

Brian's diesel truck growled into the drive with a familiar rattle. The old livestock trailer behind it swayed slightly as it bounced across the gravel, and Martin gave a lazy wave as the truck coasted to a stop.

Brian hopped out, hoodie sleeves shoved to the elbows. "Morning, sunshine. I brought your goat death squad."

Martin chuckled. "How many this time?"

"Four. The rest of your father-in-law's contribution to west Texas desertification." He popped the latch on the trailer and peered inside. "They're in a better mood than the last bunch. Think they like this place. This will make it fifteen now."

It took only a few minutes to lead the goats into the permanent pen, a far cry from the swearing match that had been their first unloading. The animals ambled out willingly, hooves clacking on the plywood ramp as they stepped into their new grazing zone.

Brian leaned on the fence post and scanned the sky. "It was forty-three when I left San Angelo this morning. That front is moving fast. Bet you feel it before lunch."

Martin followed his gaze. Low scud clouds were already galloping in from the north, flat and gray and mean-looking. "Yeah, we'll want the new panels up quick."

They began pulling the temporary fencing apart, dragging it out and reconfiguring it toward the untouched section. What had once been a tangle was now bare and silent.; the goats had stripped the underbrush with terrifying efficiency. What had been a tangle of mesquite, catclaw, and scrub was now open earth, scraped clean.

They worked for nearly an hour, joking and complaining about the wind, the dirt, and the single goat that had already decided to be a problem. It was during the tugging of a particularly stubborn panel near a thicket of scrub oak that Martin stopped dead.

His hand, reaching out for a branch to shove aside, froze in place. Something pale, bleached and round, peeked from beneath the leaf litter just beyond the root ball of the oak.

It took him a second to register what he was looking at.

Then he took a step back. "Brian," he said, his voice flat. "Come here."

Brian strolled over, still holding a small sledge he was using to pound the stakes. "What, snake?"

Martin pointed.

Brian's brow furrowed, then deepened. He dropped the hammer without a word and stepped closer, crouching low.

Underneath the curled brown leaves and plant debris was the unmistakable curve of a human skull.

"Jesus," Brian said. He reached carefully with a stick, brushing away the leaves. More bones showed, ribs, a forearm, partially collapsed and tangled in roots.

They stood in silence for a long moment. The wind whipped around them, stirring the dry scrub and tugging at the tarp over the empty trailer.

"We need to call the sheriff," Martin said.

"Yeah," Brian replied quietly. "Now."

Chapter 19
Where the Bones Lie

Eddying wind swept ahead of the front carrying a stinging sprinkle of raindrops and the first taste of cooler air just as the sheriff arrived. Martin stood with his hands tucked into his jacket pockets, watching as the county-issued Suburban rumbled through the gate and rolled to a stop beside the Gator. Dust danced around the tires before being flattened by the vehicle's weight.

Sheriff Armando Villareal stepped out, tall and broad, with a gray mustache and the kind of steady gait you only got after decades in West Texas law enforcement. He introduced himself to both Martin and Brian, shaking hands quickly before ducking his head against the wind and following them toward the makeshift corral.

The clouds overhead were heavy and low, streaking across the sky like bruises. The drizzle wasn't enough to soak through yet, but it added a chill to the air and left a sheen across the scrub and grass.

"Well, I'm missing the Tech game, but duty calls, maybe I can get back before the fourth quarter. You're the one who found it?" Villareal asked, glancing at Martin. In his left hand he held a roll of bright yellow "CRIME SCENE" tape and a dozen or so tiny surveyor's flags.

"Yeah. We were moving temporary fence panels and… saw the skull first," Brian nodded in agreement, confirming it.

"Well, let's take a look."

They walked out to near the newly placed fence panels, still not completely set into the pen shape in which the goats might soon buffet. Beyond it lay the scrub oak thicket. Martin pointed to the location. Villareal took several steps then crouched slowly, resting one hand on his thigh as he examined the partially uncovered bones. He didn't say anything for a moment, just studied what lay there in the dust and sparse yellow leaves.

After a while, he exhaled through his nose and stood up. His right hand reaching for the first tiny yellow surveyor flag.

"All right. Here's the situation," he said, glancing between them. "I can't say for sure what we've got yet, but if I had to guess, and I'm just guessing, it's probably Native. Maybe historic, maybe older. Either way, it's a big deal."

Martin nodded slowly. "So… what happens now?"

"I'm declaring it a possible crime scene," the sheriff said plainly. "Not because I think foul play happened last week, but because that's the protocol when human remains are found on private property and there's no prior record. Until a qualified professional can say it's archaeological, not forensic, we treat it like a potential homicide."

He waved them back a few steps and began marking the perimeter with caution tape pulled from a pouch at his hip. "I'll call Sul Ross. See if I can get Professor Ostertag out here, she's their senior archaeologist. Smart professor. If she agrees this is Native and old enough, we'll bring in the Texas Historical Commission and notify NAGPRA too."

"NAGPRA?" Brian asked.

The sheriff switched to poking the tiny flags into the ground, careful to watch his step. Some of the flags barely cleared the tops of the scrub oaks.

Both Brian and Martin watched the sheriff. The sheriff noticed much more than they had. There, half-buried in the soil, was a scrap of leather. Like the bones scattered around it, it also gained a flag. Something glinted faintly near it, too. Both Martin and Brian noted the sheriff had found many more items than they originally had.

"Native American Graves Protection and Repatriation Act," Villareal replied. "It governs what happens when tribal remains or cultural items are found. Long process. Lots of red tape. The Sheriff before me had to deal with an Indian body found in a cave near Mount Livermore. It was the body of a young boy, and he told me all about it. See that? That's Star Mountain to the south," he added, pointing toward the broad rise behind them. "Now imagine a stack of paperwork that large. That's what I'm in for."

Martin let out a breath. "So… you found more than just bones?"

Villareal was already finishing placing small flags beside additional fragments barely visible in the brush. "You saw three, I see about a dozen. Scattered like this, I doubt it was a proper burial.

Either it was shallow, or the body was exposed and scavenged. Coyotes, probably."

Brian winced, shifting uncomfortably.

"Still," Villareal added, "that's just a preliminary call. DPS will send a forensics team. But it's Saturday, and I wouldn't expect them until Monday."

"Should I take the day off when they come out?" Martin asked.

"Not unless you want to be professionally bored," the sheriff said. "As long as we have your consent to investigate and collect remains, you're good. You own the land?"

Martin hesitated. "It's my father-in-law's place, but I'm sure he wouldn't have a problem with it."

Villareal nodded. "Have him call my office or meet me out here, just to square things up. Shouldn't be an issue."

The sound of a diesel engine behind them drew their attention. A blue pickup truck rolled up behind the Suburban, slowing near the gate. Martin recognized it instantly.

"That's them now," he said. "Mr. and Mrs. West."

Villareal tipped his hat. "Perfect timing."

As the sheriff walked back to his truck Martin stood watching the yellow caution tape fluttering in the wind. Brian didn't speak, just stood with his arms crossed, staring down at the patch of disturbed earth where so many questions now waited. Glancing over his shoulder he watched as the Sheriff introduced himself to the West's.

"You think this is our ghost?" asked Brian in an unnecessarily quiet voice.

"Yep. Let's get him gone and buried. Lindsay will be relieved," answered Martin.

For a few moments they listened to the occasional raindrop collide with their hats with gentle pops.

"Well, it sucks," said Brian objectively.

"Why?"

"Because your goats need to eat and our best weather literally went south about two hours ago. We still gotta get the temp pen up. The goats need their vittles."

And above them, the clouds continued to roll in from the north, low and fast, like they were trying to catch up to something that had already happened.

The West's truck had rolled to a halt beside the house, the bed overflowing with a tarp peeled back enough by the trip down that both Martin and Brian could see a tall white box with the image of a child's highchair on it. The two of them walked the short distance back to the house as the in-laws worked in unison to remove and fold the tarp, which exposed even more boxes of various sizes. Some were brightly colored, but others were of the standard brown corrugated type. "Y'all better have cleared a spot, I've got enough baby stuff to supply a maternity ward."

Martin laughed, and by coincidence met Lindsay coming down from the front porch wearing a light jacket. The idea of having a skeleton on the land hadn't surprised her near as much as Martin thought it would. "Anywhere inside the baby's room and be careful of the bassinet!" Lindsay said as she noticed Martin and Brian walking up.

Mr. West walked around the truck's driver's side and gave a quick nod to the sky before turning toward the field. "That front's nearly here. Won't be long now."

Along with another round of introductions, Martin informed Mr. West about the skeletal remains. Sheriff Villareal also helped to

bring a couple of boxes inside while they talked and worked to empty the truck. Martin sometimes walked alongside Lindsay or Mrs. West to brief them on what they had found and why the Sheriff was there.

Job finished the crowd walked out in the field. The wind had only turned colder, and the occasional raindrops seemed a little larger. They stopped near the edge of the permanent goat pen, and Martin brought the others up to speed on the new goats. Even the sheriff asked a few questions. They then covered the field and approached the taped off area.

The wind scraped across the field, bending the dense catclaw mostly emptied of leaves, and whispering through the taped-off rectangle of flagged ground like it carried secrets. Dust shifted around the crowd standing in a loose semicircle just outside the yellow crime scene tape. Sheriff Villareal adjusted his hat against the gust, eyes scanning the disturbed earth one more time before turning back to Mr. West.

"Like I told Martin," he said, voice firm but not unkind, "this looks like a historical burial, not a recent crime. Most likely Apache since they were the last group here in the Davis Mountains, but you never know, it could be older. I'm not an expert, I can't rule out Comanche or Kiowa. No signs of a formal grave shaft, just a body left out, maybe shallowly covered, maybe not. Whatever the case, scavengers took their toll. I found some bones over there…" The Sheriff pointing to the farthest corner of the yellow taped box.

Mr. West nodded slowly, his hands shoved into the pockets of his canvas jacket. "And you're sure it's some sort of Native American?"

"Likely, but there's no telling till the forensics team gets a look at it. Unlike television investigators I can't just assume my guess is correct from the get-go."

Martin stood off to the side, arms crossed, his jaw set but silent. Brian hunched his shoulders against the wind and kept his hands clasped behind his back, his usual easy manner gone.

Mr. West looked out across the tape again, then back to the sheriff. "And this… removal and relocation… this is gonna take a while, isn't it?"

Villareal nodded. "Yes, sir. A while. This is a probable Native American burial and that puts it under federal protection. That means everything's going to move slower than you'd expect. We've got to coordinate with the Texas Historical Commission, the State Archaeologist, and NAGPRA out of D.C. There'll be tribal consultations, a formal permit for excavation and removal, and likely a rep from one of the Reservations brought in to witness or approve the handoff."

He shifted his weight. "Best case? We might see the skeleton out in a week, and the paperwork wrapped up before Christmas. Realistically, this could go into January."

Mr. West's face didn't shift much, but his fingers flexed once at his sides.

"And you need my permission," he said.

"Yes, sir. You're the legal landowner. Without your consent, we can only move forward with a court order, that I am required to get anyway. I've flagged the area, and I'll call for the permit applications. But we need your formal okay to allow this investigation to continue and for any human remains or cultural materials to be relocated."

Mr. West nodded again, then reached into the inside pocket of his coat and pulled out a business card to hand to the sheriff. "You have my permission and here's my contact information."

Villareal took the card, gave it a quick glance, then tipped his head respectfully. "Appreciate that, Mr. West. Saves time, and time matters."

There was a long silence. The wind moved again, lifting the edge of the sheriff's coat and rattling the tape slightly. A raven called in the distance from a scrub oak, harsh and solitary.

Villareal stepped back and gave them all a quick look. "We'll secure the site as best we can. No one's gonna touch anything until the right teams arrive. In the meantime, I'd advise keeping your fencing efforts a few yards clear. Just in case."

Brian nodded. "We'll give it space."

Martin looked up. "Anything else we need to do?"

Villareal shook his head. "You've done right by it. Just keep your head down and the fewer people know about this right now, the better. Knuckleheaded artifact collectors...." The Sheriff didn't finish the sentence, "Might put up a few more 'No Trespassing' signs if the forensics team can't make it out here on Monday."

With that, he offered a final nod and turned toward his parked SUV and covered the distance a little faster than when he first arrived. The door shut with a hollow sounding **thunk,** and moments later, the vehicle crunched over gravel and rolled back down the property entrance road, a small amount of dust trailing behind it.

For a long time, they stood watching the tape ripple faintly in the wind.

Then Mr. West spoke, voice quiet.

"Well. Looks like history's still breathing. . .still here."

Martin glanced sideways. "Yeah," he said. "And it wants to be remembered."

****

Together, the three men began setting up the new temporary enclosure, well away from the fluttering yellow crime scene tape. The goats had chewed the original section bare, and the new panels Brian had hauled in made expanding the grazing area easier than expected. Using the north fence line, they set up the new temporary pen, taking advantage of the barbed wire fence already there, they were able to stretch the pen into a much longer shaped one.

"Second time's a charm," Brian muttered as he hammered in a ground stake. "These goats barely even argued."

Martin grinned. "I think they remember the trailer now."

"or maybe it's because it was away from the grave," Brian finished.

They worked quickly, hands moving without much talk. The wind was sharpening, skimming across the flats and catching on the high brush. Overhead, thick low waves of clouds scudded fast from the north, racing ahead of cold, possibly wet, late afternoon.

Once the final panel was locked in place and the gate secured, Mr. West leaned against the Gator and removed his leather work gloves and flexed his fingers on both hands a few times. "We'll call that a job well done. Let's get the goats along with the portable water trough and let them start munching."

****

187

The coffee was good, even if it was from the morning and reheated in the microwave. Mr. West reached into his jean pocket and pulled out his phone, thumbing through images before turning the screen toward the others.

"I was going through some old records earlier this week. Transon Oil does some work with the company that runs the pipeline just down the road from here. Here, look at this pipeline survey flight from '74. And this one, mid-'80s. Same area, different year."

Both Brian and Martin put down their mugs of coffee. The women were talking in the background. The photos were grainy but clear enough to reveal a wide ramp leading down from the north rim into the dry wash below.

"Natural grade," Mr. West explained. "It was the only way down into the wash for miles. Soft slope, good footing. Not ideal for wagons, I'd bet, but for people, and animals? It was that route or be forced to walk a lot further."

Brian leaned in for a closer look. "What happened to it?"

"Flood of '78," Mr. West said, swiping to the next image. "The pipeline manager for that section said it chewed the whole thing out like a backhoe. You can't see the ramp now, it's just jagged rock and brush. That ramp was probably the result of the water washing out the limestone under the rhyolite. The water made it happen and then it made it gone. Weathering at its best. It can happen overnight in these parts."

Martin studied the photos and gave a slow nod. "That's why the fourth corner is lower. . .down in the wash. It didn't just get knocked down, it got erased."

Mr. West gave a half-smile. "I talked to Mr. Miller, the man that owns the land to the north of you on Tuesday. He's fine with us crossing his land tomorrow. We can use the east ranch gate and take the Gator down to where the ramp used to be, see if we can find the original corner stake or at least flag the site."

Brian was already nodding. "That's perfect. Tomorrow after the baby shower?"

"Nope. Tomorrow *before* the shower," Mr. West said firmly. "I've seen what happens when I miss a baby shower. Your mother doesn't forget. Sun sets early these days, and the baby shower might go past sunset knowing my wife, so let's do it early rather than late."

Martin checked the light outside. The clouds were rolling in fast, the light level slowly dimming and painting the house windows with a deep grey. "Yeah… we're losing the day."

"We roll at dawn. We'll be back before noon," Mr. West said, folding the phone back into his pocket. "Got a room this time at the hotel in the state park so we're not too far away. If we're lucky tomorrow, we'll get it all marked before the wind really starts kicking. Supposed to be cold."

Inside, Lindsay entered the room almost dancing. "You three making plans again?" she called, slowing down to normal walk.

"Just old man stuff," Mr. West replied. "Maps, boundaries, missing corners."

"Well don't forget who's supposed to be the center of attention tomorrow," she said, patting her belly.

"Wouldn't dream of it," Martin said, wrapping an arm around her briefly as she came over to hug Martin seated in the chair. "We're all done out there, but let's not go out of the way to point out to the people coming for the shower that there's an active crime scene out back?"

"Great idea," replied Lindsay.

Mr. West poured himself another mug of microwave-warmed coffee and sat back at the table, gazing absently at the scuffed boots of his son-in-law and Brian, drying near the back door.

"Tomorrow morning," he said again. "We'll finally see what's at that fourth corner."

The wind scratched softly at the windowpanes, and in the distance, the yellow tape danced across the ridge….waiting.

****

The next morning dawned cold and clear, the sky washed pale blue behind twisted, but fast-drifting high cirrus clouds. Frost still clung to the grass in the shade of the barn, but the sun was already working to melt it off. Before the crowd arrived, Martin busied himself by burying the coax cable with the growing morning light.

With their travel mugs steaming and gloves pulled tight, Martin, Brian, and Mr. West loaded into the Gator and rumbled away from the house. The engine clatter smoothed to a steady hum as they surged into the sunlight as they set out toward the gate leading to the Miller Ranch, a few miles north. Now that the Sun was closer to its winter track, the house spent much of the morning now in the shade of the ridge located to the east.

It took them the better part of twenty minutes, the road bouncing between patches of gravel and rutted earth. When they reached the gate, Mr. West dismounted with a knowing grin and walked to the fourth fencepost on the left. He reached into a narrow crack in the wood upright that faced away from the road and pulled out a shiny key from a deep crack in the wooded fencepost that was invisible to anyone actually at the gate or on the road.

"Gentlemen," he said, holding the key aloft, "you're now partners in a crime of trust. Mr. Miller told me this hiding spot on Tuesday and made me swear I'd never tell a soul."

"We'll take it to our graves," Brian replied solemnly. "Unless there's a goat emergency, in which case all bets are off."

They passed through the gate and re-locked it behind them, continuing another mile down into the dry wash. In the wash, the road split near a clump of mesquite. Mr. West gestured to the north fork. "The downstream trail leads to Old Camp Springs. It shows up in every picture from aircraft or satellite I've seen."

At best they could see the tall cottonwood trees that had proudly staked their claim on the area around the spring. Some in the wash, but most scattered up the proper hillside the scene was a perfect landscape painting captured in the low light. The sharp yellow leaves of fall contrasted dramatically against the cold sky beyond. A scene that looked like it was stolen from an art museum.

Nobody answered Martin. The Gator turned south into the gravel-choked wash, bouncing and sliding gently as the terrain narrowed. Dust rose behind them, curling into the bright morning air. An easy journey, but still a cold one.

When the GPS chirped and Mr. West called, "This should be it," they all dismounted. At first, the wash looked like any other, dried mud, loose cobble, scattered brush. Half the wash was still in the shadow of the cliff that towered above. The red rhyolite cliff in stark contrast of the limestone beneath it. Then the bones began to appear.

Old animal bones, ribs, vertebrae, what looked like a jaw. Martin counted at least three clusters just in the open.

Then Brian, who had climbed onto the third bench above the wash, froze. "Uh, Martin, up here."

Martin joined him and felt the chill even before he saw it.

The goat lay on its side, one front leg stretched unnaturally, the numbered yellow ear tag still attached. Blood had pooled beside it in a dark, wet halo, still glossy.

"This happened recently," Martin said quietly. "Like… maybe an hour or two ago."

The three men stood in silence, surveying the brush, scanning for other signs of movement. Nothing. Just that one goat. But the message felt deliberate.

"Should we take it back with us?" asked Martin.

"And pull up to the house with a dead goat as the guests are arriving?" asked Mr. West.

"We could pass it off as a sacrifice. You know, for the health of the baby, biblical style," intoned Brian.

All three men smirked at that thought.

"I would rather remain unknown, than be known for that," stated Martin, grinning at Brian with his mood breaking joke.

"Let's just mark the corner and go," Mr. West said grimly, "they found a way out of the pen maybe. You'll need to check regardless."

They quickly found the GPS location for the fourth property stake and drove the stake at the edge of the bone pile, the goat not more than ten feet away. None of them spoke much as they climbed back into the Gator and turned for home.

It wasn't until the house came into view, its white siding bright against the dry land when Brian finally broke the silence.

"Maybe it's good the skeleton's getting moved tomorrow," he said. "Maybe it'll take this bad luck with it."

Martin didn't reply, but his knuckles whitened on the steering wheel.

Mr. West sighed. "You know, I've been wondering the same thing. About what might be buried out there."

He paused, waiting for the other two to glance over, then continued.

"Back in the early '00s, I was out near Andrews, working at solving a new lease since the owner had sold half of his land without telling us. Wouldn't have been an issue except Transon Oil had a rig that was hugging the new property line. The geologist's trailer, a portable, sat on a little rise next to the pad. Turns out it was on top of three unmarked Indian graves. No one knew 'til things started happening....strange noises, shrieks, stuff flying off shelves. Geologist damn near quit the site. Only settled down when we moved the shack because it was located on the wrong side of the line. The graves were only discovered by the fencing crew that came through later."

He shook his head as they pulled up to the house.

"You don't have to believe it. But I saw the way he left. Didn't even take his coffee mug."

"That is serious," said Brian with a grin.

As they rolled up the driveway, they were met with a different kind of commotion. In front of them was a yard full of cars and voices carrying in the crisp fall air. A new record for people on the property just looking at the people walking toward the stairs. Martin imagined standing room only.

The baby shower had begun.

"Brian, come with me out to check the pen. I may have more than one goat out. Mr. West, you get in there and fly the flag for us? Remember not to mention the goat or the crime scene." With that he pointed toward the yellow tape in the distance.

"Will do," he replied touching the tip of his cowboy hat with a nod.

And somewhere to the west, back in the dry wash, the blood of a freshly killed goat darkened the ground beneath the mesquite.

Chapter 20
The Parade Ground Waits

Ribbons of heat shimmered ahead when he returned to the fort under a cloudless sky, the heat crawling out of the dry ground and shimmering against the ruins like ghosts in the sun. What remained of Fort Davis in 1895 wasn't much anymore. Some of the buildings remained upright and cared for. The landowner had found tenants willing to rent.

A few buildings' walls still stood, facades without backs, crumbling slowly into the silence. Time had worked its slow magic here, turning sharp angles into softened mounds, parade routes into weed-choked lanes. The old cavalry barracks had collapsed on themselves, save one corner where a rusted stovepipe jutted out defiantly. The officers' quarters, once whitewashed and trimmed, were little more than rubble and shadows.

O'Brannach paused at the edge of what had once been the parade ground, boots sinking slightly into the cracked earth. The wild grass had reclaimed it. What had once been a flat, raked expanse of order and rhythm now bristled with knee-high weeds and scattered clumps of mesquite. The flags were gone. So were the men. But the ghosts remained. He could feel them.

A wind stirred the long grasses, whispering through the skeletal remains of the fort like breath through teeth. He shifted slightly on his feet, then took a slow, measured step forward, as if expecting to hear a bugle call or a shouted order echo off the stones.

The air here was heavy with memory. Not nostalgia, not the kind that softened pain into something warm, but the kind of memory that wore grooves into the soul. He didn't come to reminisce. He came to understand why the weight had never left his shoulders. Why sleep never came easy. Why silence always seemed to bring voices.

He crossed the edge of the ground and moved into the center, his eyes scanning the weathered horizon. And then he saw it.

Half-buried in a drift of windblown sand and prickly pear lay the Whitworth.

It hadn't been there last time.

He didn't bring it.

O'Brannach stopped cold. The rifle lay as if placed deliberately. No case. No wrap. The walnut stock was dulled with dust, but the barrel still caught the sun in places.

He felt the breath leave his lungs in a short, staggered exhale.

He knew what it meant.

Kneeling slowly, he reached for it but did not touch. The sight of the rifle dredged up the weight of too many years. The precise geometry of its bore, the foreign elegance of its form, they all came rushing back. He remembered the day the men had given it to him, Voss laughing, the others clapping him on the back. He had thought it a kindness then.

But it was not a gift. It was a ghostly burden.

He closed his eyes. He remembered the saddle blanket, the rise above the canyon, the way Storm upon Meadow had moved into view, unaware. He had waited for the wind to die. He had wanted it to be a clean kill. And then he had fired.

It had been a beautiful day.

The kind that made you forget what this land had taken from men. A soft breeze, warm sun, the faint buzz of insects returning to life after winter. The ocotillo had been blooming. Bright red tips on naked spines, vibrant against the pale sky.

He remembered how the saddle creaked beneath him as he eased down, whispering to the horse to stay, stay, good girl, just a little longer. The scent of juniper and dust. He had licked his thumb and tested the wind. It carried nothing.

Below, Storm upon Meadow walked slowly across a clearing, head high, not hurried. There was a calmness in his stride, a rhythm as old as the land itself. O'Brannach had

wondered, just for a moment, what the man might be thinking. He would never know.

He had sighted in. Finger ready. The trigger broke like a snapped twig.

And the world changed.

The sound echoed across the canyon like thunder with no storm. Birds erupted from the brush. The target fell like a sack of stones, and still the dust from his footfalls had not settled.

O'Brannach hadn't moved. Couldn't. For the briefest instant, the day stilled. And in that stillness, he felt something leave him. Something vital. He had thought it would feel like duty. Like service. But all it felt like was loss.

He opened his eyes again. The rifle hadn't moved. But the light had shifted, and now the shadows beneath the nearby rubble looked deeper than before.

O'Brannach rose and stepped back. He would not touch it. Not now. Not again. The rifle evaporated from in front of him, leaving only dirt and weeds in its wake. He knew the rifle wasn't really there. He wanted it gone for forever, but the weight hadn't left.

Instead, he turned slowly and let his eyes trace the outline of the parade ground. In his mind, the troop assembled. Young faces, sun-reddened and unafraid. Boots struck in time. Leather and metal gleamed. He heard the cadence again, echoing off walls that no longer stood.

He had come back to erase the demons. But all he had done was wake them up.

A raven watched him from the bent remains of the flagpole. Its eyes were dark and silent.

The parade ground waited. The officer turned railman turned away.

Chapter 21
Gathering Storms

Engines idled up the gravel drive as dusty pickups and mismatched sedans arrived, each one bringing another familiar face to the celebration. What began as a baby shower quickly became a full-blown celebration. Teachers from Fort Davis High made the trek, along with half a dozen townsfolk who had met Lindsay at the fort reenactment. The front yard and drive filled with dusty pickups and a few mismatched sedans, their bumpers shining in the cold autumn sun. Inside the house, warm conversation and the scent of sweet pastries filled the air.

The spread on the table groaned with offerings of casseroles, dips, platters of cookies, and a towering punch bowl filled with something that tasted like lime sherbet and ginger ale. Most of the drinks were non-alcoholic, though Martin caught sight of someone discreetly slipping a splash of bourbon into their coffee. The consensus was this was because Thanksgiving wasn't far away. This was practice for the upcoming holiday season.

Lindsay's principal, Arturo Mendez, stood near the fireplace with a coffee mug in one hand and a wide grin on his face. A second-generation Texan with roots in Presidio and a voice that could still command a classroom, he had thick black hair just beginning to silver at the temples and wore his usual sport coat over jeans and boots. A former history teacher himself, he had a way of making everyone feel like they belonged in the room, even if it was their first time in it.

He quieted the crowd by tapping the rim of his coffee mug with a spoon. When the room hushed, he raised his voice with the rhythm of a seasoned storyteller.

"I have it on good authority," he said, glancing toward Lindsay, "that baby Robert Bruce Eastman already has a bank account at the Fort Davis Community Bank, no less, and it's sitting at just over five hundred dollars. Not bad for a kid who hasn't even been born yet."

Someone shouted, "The kid's a future mayor!" The room erupted in laughter and applause.

Principal Mendez covered all the bases with his speech. Recalling how surprised he was when she had first interviewed at the job fair at Angelo State, pointing out that unlike the other applicants she incorporated historical events into almost every answer. After several more minutes of talking the gift opening commenced.

The present opening was a predictable mix of adorable chaos, tiny socks, blankets, diapers, and books with pastel illustrations. Lindsay beamed with gratitude, her hand resting instinctively on her stomach as she carefully opened each card and passed the contents to a small pile on the couch.

Susan Rusker excused herself quietly and stepped into the kitchen for a glass of water. The house was full of laughter and conversation, but the kitchen had grown momentarily quiet. She opened the cabinet, grabbed a glass, and turned on the tap. As she waited for it to run cold, her eyes drifted to a small ceramic bowl near the sink.

Inside it were three objects: a Morgan silver dollar, worn but still legible; a slightly deformed bullet, tarnished with age; and the tip of what looked like an old, rusted knife. They weren't labeled or displayed, just sitting there like paperclips or lost buttons.

She reached out and gently nudged the silver dollar with her finger.

A few minutes later, after rejoining the group, Susan found a quiet moment to lean toward Lindsay. "Hey," she said in a low voice, "do you collect coins? That Morgan dollar near your sink… pretty unusual thing to leave out."

Lindsay blinked, surprised. "Oh. No, not really. We found it on the property. Along with a few other things."

Susan tilted her head, sensing there was more. "Find it recently?"

Lindsay hesitated. "Yeah. Just a few weeks ago, actually. We were looking for something else."

Susan waited, but Lindsay didn't offer more. Instead, she turned to accept another baby book from a laughing coworker. The conversation moved on.

Two hours after it began, the shower wound down.

Susan Rusker lingered near the front door as the last guests trickled out. She was halfway down the steps when she suddenly

lurched forward and went down with a gasp, landing hard on the ground.

Several people rushed toward her. Principal Mendez got there first.

"Susan! Are you okay?"

She groaned, wincing as she sat up with help. "I think I sprained my damn ankle," she said through clenched teeth. "And I swear, I swear, it felt like I was pushed. Like someone shoved me right in the back."

The few adults swarmed outside. Concern flickered across a few faces. A couple of guests laughed awkwardly, but the unease was real. Martin and Arturo Mendez helped her hobble toward her car after she sat on the porch steps to investigate the wound. Brian and Mr. West fetched an ice pack from the kitchen. She walked to her car slowly with half a dozen offers of help and a few jokes about needing a walker for the next school day.

After the crowd cleared and the last of the folding chairs were stacked, Martin, Lindsay, Mr. and Mrs. West, and Brian gathered around the table again, sipping what was left of the coffee.

Martin leaned forward and spoke quietly. "We found a goat dead this morning. I didn't even know it was missing. Had all ten when I put them in the temp pen earlier. Blood still pooled nearby, it beat us out there to the cliff by an hour."

Lindsay sat back, eyes narrowing. "Was it attacked?"

"Hard to say," Martin replied. "No signs of a predator, no broken fence. I checked the temp pen during the party, nothing's out of place, and the other goats are fine. No holes, no tracks. Just gone."

Mrs. West pursed her lips. "You know, I'm not usually one for ghost stories… but I'll be honest. I'm glad that skeleton is getting moved soon."

Brian nodded, setting down his mug. "It's not just the skeleton. It's the timing. The way things happen. The goats, the storm, that bullet, the coin. Hell, even Susan falling down."

"What bullet? What coins?" asked Mrs. West.

Brian fetched the items that had arrived at the back door on that night. Martin told them the story of the fruitless artifact search. Both parents closely examined the four items carefully.

Lindsay looked around the table and let out a long breath. "It's all too much to be nothing. Still doesn't mean we know what it is."

Mr. West scratched at his jaw. "That has to be the oddest shaped bullet I have ever seen," he began with a low voice before returning to normal volume, "We don't have to know what it is. Just that it's not finished yet."

He turned the hexagonal shaped bullet over in his hands. "This might be the bullet that killed the Indian they dug up," he contemplated out loud.

"If it means anything, I noticed earlier the coax wire is pulled up again," mentioned Lindsay.

Martin rolled his eyes and let out a soft sigh without adding anything else.

They fell quiet. Outside, the wind tugged gently at the corners of the house, and the last of the afternoon sun was just starting to turn the sky pale gold. Dumpsy padded softly across the floor and leapt into Lindsay's lap, curling up with a satisfied chirp.

Martin stared past the window toward the taped-off stretch of land between them and the distant canyon where the goat was becoming a feast of another type.

Whatever it was, coincidence or not, he hoped it was going away with the skeleton leaving.

****

The sun had only just begun to shine through the windows when Lindsay unlocked her classroom door. The hallway lights flickered overhead, buzzing faintly, the way they always did on chilly mornings when the building revealed its age grudgingly.

Her classroom, Room 107, still smelled faintly of floor wax and printer toner. She dropped her tote onto the desk, slid off her coat, and powered on the computer. Her coffee thermos steamed beside her open gradebook, and she took a long sip, grateful for the quiet before the day's usual din.

A soft knock came from the door, and then it opened. Susan Rusker stepped inside, limping slightly but still upright, her usual warm smile firmly in place.

"Well look at you," Lindsay said, standing. "You're walking."

"Barely," Susan chuckled. "It's more of a shuffle with ambition and taking a lot of ski candy."

"Ski candy?"

"Ibuprofen, I use to water ski…. a lot."

They exchanged quick hugs, and Susan made her way slowly to the side desk she sometimes used when she needed a quieter space before first period. She lowered herself with care and exhaled slowly.

"I've got ibuprofen, a compression bandage, and a prayer holding me together," she said. "But I didn't want to miss any school."

"Glad you're here," Lindsay said sincerely. "That fall scared the hell out of everyone."

"Tell me about it. Embarrassing, too. Getting pushed off a porch by a ghost" she smiled, "or the wind. Still haven't decided."

Lindsay raised her brows. "Funny that you should say 'ghost', because I've been thinking about it, a ghost, more seriously than I'd like to admit."

Susan tilted her head. "Oh?"

Lindsay leaned back against her desk and folded her arms. "You ever had a stretch where too many weird things stack up to call coincidence? Objects falling, noises, animals acting up. My husband swears something's going on out there. And after what happened to you and a goat also died….and that skeleton they found…"

Susan's brow lifted. "goat dead? skeleton?"

"Yes. Since you mentioned ghost first, allow me to bring you up to speed, but keep this under your hat. Martin found a skeleton on Saturday. The Sheriff and a big crowd from Odessa and Sul Ross are going to remove it starting today. Indian skeleton. Martin says it will take a few weeks to finish since we have all kinds of paperwork and agency coordination, but the skeleton should be gone before Wednesday. Enough weird things have happened since August to even make me skeptical and question my beliefs. The skeleton just makes me uncomfortable," Lindsay admitted. "But it's not just that. I've been digging into the Fort Davis online archives in the evenings, trying to find out if it made the news. Newspaper searches. I wanted to know if something happened near our land, like something bad. But the records around 1891? They're… patchy. Like someone yanked a page right out of the story."

Susan leaned forward, her interest piqued. "Did you say 1891?"

"Yeah. The year the fort closed."

Susan nodded slowly, then her expression shifted into something more animated. "Lindsay, I might have something for you. Not 1891, at least I don't think it's 1891, but close."

Lindsay blinked. "Really?"

"One of my cousins in Marfa…she's sort of the accidental family historian…she inherited a pile of old belongings from our side of the O'Brannach family. The man who started our branch was a cavalry officer. Cormac O'Brannach. I remember because we used to joke about how serious he looked in the old tintypes. Scowl like you wouldn't believe."

Lindsay's breath caught, the name clicking like a door latch. She had seen the name in online research, but knew little else. "Wait. O'Brannach? That's your middle name."

"Yep," Susan said. "He was stationed at Fort Davis. Married fast after it closed. Bought land, worked for the railroad. For a while, he did well. But…" she trailed off, her expression dimming. "Toward the end of his life, things got darker. Drinking. Isolating. He died in 1916. The family donated most of his military things to the Fort's preservation committee, uniform, saber, rifle, even his field chest. Actually, it's mostly on display in the Fort's museum."

"What about personal papers?" Lindsay asked, voice sharp with sudden hope.

"That's the thing," Susan said. "The family kept one thing back. A journal. Supposedly it's not cheerful reading. I've heard bitterness, regret, not the kind of thing you frame under glass. But I remember my cousin saying she still had it. I'll call her tonight."

Lindsay couldn't help the grin that bloomed across her face. "Susan, that could be-"

The shrill ring of the first bell cut her off. Students' footsteps echoed in the halls beyond the door. Susan pushed herself up with a grunt.

"I'll bring it to you," she said with a wink. "Around Thanksgiving, or better yet, when you're on maternity leave. Let's see what old Captain O'Brannach had to get off his chest."

Then she was out the door, hobbling down the hall with slow, determined steps, leaving Lindsay standing by her desk. Coffee forgotten or no longer needed, her mind racing.

****

Lindsay carved another piece of baked chicken for her plate, steam curling upward between them at the table. Outside, a soft wind rattled the porch screen, carrying a few dry scrub oak leaves across the steps.

Martin reached for the pepper shaker. "You're quiet. Planning your next great teaching scheme, or just enjoying the chicken?"

She smiled faintly. "Both, probably. But mostly… Susan is going to loan us the journal from her great-grandfather, the man who led the last patrol of the 220th from the Fort."

Martin paused mid-shake. "Susan Rusker? The woman that invited us over for dinner?"

"That's the one," Lindsay said, poking her fork into a buttery wedge of potato. "A journal. From O'Brannach."

Martin blinked. "And this will help?"

"Mm-hm." She laid her fork down. "Apparently, Susan's family has been holding onto it for decades. She figured since we've been digging into Fort Davis stuff… and since, well, the other day happened… it might help answer a few questions."

Martin leaned forward, brushing his elbows against his plate. "Like what kind of questions?"

"She didn't say everything. But she hinted it's… kind of depressing. Like O'Brannach might have done something wrong. And maybe he knew it."

Martin frowned. "You mean wrong as in military politics… or wrong like something worse?"

"I don't know yet." Lindsay's voice dropped. "Susan said it's a little tough to read. She made it sound like a confession at a Catholic church without forgiveness."

Martin chewed that over for a moment. "Well. We're in deep enough already. Might as well see what ghosts the good Captain left behind."

Lindsay gave a small laugh, though worry tugged at her mouth. "I just hope reading it doesn't make me hate him."

Martin reached across and squeezed her hand. "Knowing the truth's better than guessing. Whatever it is, we'll figure it out."

Outside, a gust rattled the windows, as if reminding them that secrets had a way of finding daylight.

Chapter 22
The Unearthing

By the time Martin pulled through the front gate on Monday afternoon, the landscape beyond the house looked completely different. What had been a patch of dusty goat pasture and yellow crime scene tape now resembled a small field camp, bustling with quiet purpose. Several pickup trucks were parked in the area, along with two marked DPS vehicles, a sheriff's SUV, a white enclosed trailer hitched to a dual-wheeled dually, and somewhat incongruously a brush cutter and front-end loader parked just off the fresh dirt trail that led past the permanent goat corral. A large tent was now sitting on top of the location that was taped off only two days earlier.

Martin slowed the truck to a crawl, taking it all in. The yellow tape was mostly gone, but the stakes still dotted the area around the tent, including a few new ones of various colors. The remnant tape fluttered lightly in the afternoon wind, reminding him of when the neighbors in Temple, and home of a high school quarterback, had their house toilet papered before each football game. Martin assumed the front end loader was used to scrape the new dirt parking lot, and not to launch an assault on the skeleton.

As he stepped out, one hand holding a 32-ounce Styrofoam cup filled earlier in Balmorhea, he spotted the sheriff from Saturday striding toward him. The man was dressed in the same plain brown jeans, starched khaki shirt, windbreaker, and the same wide-brimmed hat that hadn't budged since they first met. He looked tired.

Martin covered the hundred plus yards to the edge of the spacious new dirt parking lot that had appeared.

"Mr. Eastman," the sheriff called, offering a short nod as he reached him. "Appreciate you comin' over. Figured you'd be curious."

Martin shook his hand and matched his pace as they walked back toward the excavation site.

"What'd you find?" Martin asked.

"Quite a bit, actually. I'll walk you through it, but first things first, this is old. Real old. We had Professor Ostertag out from Sul Ross this morning, and she's confident we're not dealing with anything recent. No grave, no coffin. Body was left above ground or in a shallow scrape and scattered by scavengers. Left arm's about ten feet from the main skeleton. Right hand's missing entirely."

They reached the edge of the tent, inside where several kneeling researchers and techs were carefully working around what looked like an honest hole, shallow and wide. Martin kept to the perimeter, watching as small flags marked items waiting to be removed.

"We found a knife," the sheriff continued, "broken at the tip. Rusted, heavy. Nearby was a pouch, pretty far gone, but the beadwork they recovered is Apache. Lipan Apache, most likely. There was a coin inside, an 1888 Morgan silver dollar, a few sewing needles, and an unused clay pipe, too."

Martin glanced down at the grid of flags. "That's incredible. Tragic, but incredible."

The sheriff gave a small grunt. "Two things I thought you'd find interesting. First, we found the twelfth thoracic vertebrae shattered. The DPS forensics team says that kind of bone damage is consistent with a low kinetic energy gunshot wound."

Martin felt a chill creep along the back of his neck, remembering that a bullet was among the items that had slammed into his back door recently. "Did you recover a bullet?"

"No," the sheriff said, shaking his head. "We looked, even used a metal detector, but nothing turned up save for the coins and a knife missing a fair bit of its tip. The bullet could've passed through, but the vertebrae isn't completely shattered. The DPS lead here thinks it's either a bullet that didn't have a lot of kinetic energy remaining or a spear puncture. Hard to say after all this time. It's around here somewhere, I bet," He paused. "Second thing… we keep finding fulgurite."

Martin blinked. "What's that?"

"Lightning glass. When a lightning bolt strikes sand or rocky soil, it can fuse it into glass. Weird-looking stuff made of tubes or branches, real fragile. Looks like there've been a lot of strikes in this area over the years. Enough that some of the folks joked this place must be a lightning magnet."

Martin looked past the flags to the exposed bones, then up to the sky, where clouds had begun to rebuild behind the mountains again.

"What happens next?"

"Well," the sheriff said, glancing toward a woman in a DPS jacket talking into a satellite phone, "we've submitted for a court order to hand the remains over to NAGPRA, the federal repatriation program. But that takes a few days. We're treating the site as a protected historical scene until then. Professor Ostertag's team is cataloging everything the DPS team digs up."

He turned back to Martin. "The fulgurites, though, they're not part of the body or burial. Those are yours. If you want to keep 'em or sell 'em, up to you. Collectors pay good money, apparently. Hell, someone already asked me if I'd part with a sample."

Martin let out a low exhale. "Thanks for the update. I didn't expect all this."

The sheriff gave him a sympathetic nod. "Didn't figure you would. But you've been cooperative, and I'll make sure the paperwork reflects that."

He adjusted his hat. "One more thing, just between us. Professor Ostertag said she's never seen this kind of scatter with this kind of trauma. It's not a typical battlefield burial. Someone left this man behind. Maybe intentionally. Abandoned? There weren't many Apache left in this area at the dates on those coins."

Martin nodded slowly, the words settling heavy in his chest.

As the sheriff turned to return to his crew, Martin remained a moment longer, staring into the tangle of flags, bones, and time. Above them, a hawk wheeled once in the air, riding the thermals. The land was quiet again, but it didn't feel the same.

Chapter 23
A Report Without Truth

Late afternoon light spilled through the office windows of the Fort Davis headquarters, casting long golden bars across the oiled floorboards and maps. Captain Cormac O'Brannach stood at ease, his uniform pressed and clean despite the long patrol, while Colonel Hall leaned back in his chair, idly thumbing a worn pencil between his fingers.

"So, Captain," Hall said, his voice low and even, "I see your discharge papers came through from the department." He gestured at a thick folder near the edge of his desk. "Looks like it's official. Fifteen years… gone in one last thunderclap, but you led the last full patrol from Fort Davis. That's something to be proud of."

O'Brannach nodded once. "Aye, sir. I am proud of that," he said, but feeling uncomfortable doing so, "It's time." His voice was steady, almost relieved. "I wouldn't trade the years I served. Wouldn't undo a single day. But remaining in the Army only slows down my dream of owning a home."

Hall allowed himself a half-smile. "Sensible. You sound like a man who's seen through the romance of cavalry life."

"I've seen through the pay scale, sir," O'Brannach said dryly. "And the sleeping on rocks. And the cooking on coals in wind that stings the eyes. I've had my fill of empty horizons. I think I'm ready to try something with walls. And maybe try to do this with a woman who's tired of waiting."

The colonel chuckled and leaned forward. "Railroad job still waiting for you down in Alpine?"

"It is," O'Brannach confirmed. "Shipping clerk. Steady work. And I've got enough saved for a small bit of land. Maybe a wee cottage, one I can add to. A garden and some crops, even."

"From sabers to seedlings," Hall mused. "That's a journey."

O'Brannach offered a faint smile. "Seems appropriate."

The colonel gestured toward a thin stack of papers. "You've yet to turn in your final patrol report, Captain."

"Yes, sir. I'll have it on your desk tomorrow. It's already started."

Hall nodded but waved a hand as if brushing away a fly. "Don't fuss over it. If I'm being honest, with the wires buzzing every hour and the post closing in only weeks, I may not read it as closely as I ought to. Hell, I doubt anyone will. Headquarters already has one boot in the next decade. I've been posted to Fort Logan in Colorado."

O'Brannach nodded again, but something about Hall's tone made him pause. The colonel leaned back, folding his hands across his chest, eyes wandering to the window where the shadows of the flagpole stretched long across the parade yard.

"You know the irony of it, Captain?" Hall said slowly. "While you were off chasing shadows in the canyons, we had a visitor."

O'Brannach tilted his head, not quite puzzled, not yet concerned. "Sir?"

"Apache," Hall said simply. "Name was Storm upon Meadow. Came in alone, white flag and all. Rode straight through the center of the fort like it was still 1870."

O'Brannach's hands tightened slightly behind his back. He didn't speak.

Hall continued, "Told me his people, what's left of them, are leaving Old Camp Springs. Heading to the reservation in New Mexico. Said it was time. Said the mountain was calling. Díí' naashá"

The colonel looked at O'Brannach then and saw nothing but polite interest in the Captain's expression.

"Seemed changed, that man," Hall said. "Not broken. Not scared. Just… resolved. Like the war was long over and we'd all missed the ending."

O'Brannach nodded once. "And you believed him, sir?"

"I did." Hall's eyes narrowed slightly. "You know what else I believe? That we're done out here. The country's changing, and we either keep up or we grow roots and get buried in our boots. I sent him out with a couple of bags of flour and some tobacco. Imagine that? I spent most of my career killing those men in every blank spot on a map, but they know. . . he knew, that all things change if you give it time. It may not be the change you want, but change is inevitable."

O'Brannach blinked hard. In his mind he saw the Apache on the horse, he saw the bags of flour, too.

The silence between them stretched.

Finally, O'Brannach stepped forward, snapped a crisp salute, and said, "If there's nothing else, sir, I'll begin packing my quarters."

Hall returned the salute, slower. "Go on then, Captain. Thank you for your service."

O'Brannach turned and left without another word, his boots echoing faintly on the wood.

Only once he had cleared the building and stepped into the lengthening shadows of the late-day sun did the weight settle on him. The Apache he had seen through a rifle scope. He had been riding peacefully, unaware, was the same man who had come in peace, not war.

And he shot him in the back. He was no better than the man that killed his father in Ireland.

O'Brannach's jaw tightened, but his face remained unreadable. No one saw the flicker of guilt behind his eyes, or the way his shoulders stiffened as he turned toward the barracks.

There was nothing more to say.

Only a rifle remaining to be packed. And a past that would never quite stay buried.

Chapter 24
The Child and the Storm

Over the hiss of the maternity wing doors, Martin stepped out, his grin impossibly wide and his hair still tousled from hours of waiting. The group seated in mismatched chairs stood up in unison, conversations dying mid-sentence as they turned to him, eyes filled with expectation.

"Well?" Brian called, hands on his hips.

Martin raised both arms like a victorious quarterback. "Robert Bruce Eastman has officially arrived!"

A wave of cheers and laughter swept through the room. Mr. and Mrs. West hugged each other tightly, both misty-eyed. Elise joined in seconds later. Brian let out a low whistle and gave Martin a firm pat on the back.

"Seven pounds, fifteen ounces," Martin continued, barely able to contain himself. "Twenty inches long. All fingers, all toes. A healthy set of lungs, too. He's already tested them out."

Everyone laughed.

"And Lindsay?" Mrs. West asked quickly.

"Doing great," Martin assured her. "Delivery went smooth, no complications. She's resting now. Honestly, she made it look easy."

Susan Rusker, leaning on her cane and standing beside Mr. Mendez from the high school, gave a wide smile. "Knew that girl had grit."

Arturo Mendez stepped forward and shook Martin's hand. "Congratulations, Mr. Eastman. This is going to be one well-educated baby."

Martin chuckled. "I hope so. He's already got a faculty fan club."

As the excitement settled into murmurs and phone calls to friends and family began, Martin glanced around at the group gathered. "Hospital policy says only immediate family gets in today. But tomorrow, tomorrow you can all meet him at home. We'll be discharged first thing tomorrow."

Brian leaned in, mock serious. "I expect to see that kid in a onesie with a goat on it."

"You think you're joking, but Elise already brought three," Martin said, laughing.

He looked back through the maternity ward doors for a moment, then back at the group. "He's perfect. Just . . . perfect."

There were nods and smiles all around. The hard weeks, the strange happenings, the fatigue of first-year teaching, all of it faded in the glow of the moment. For now, there was only joy, warmth, and the promise of a new beginning.

As the excitement in the waiting room gave way to softer conversations and the buzz of text notifications, Mr. Mendez quietly motioned Martin to step aside. The two men moved toward a quieter corner near the vending machines, out of earshot of the others.

For a moment, Martin's heart skipped. The principal's expression was calm, serious, but not grave. "Is everything all right?" Martin asked.

Mr. Mendez gave a quick, reassuring smile. "Relax. Nothing's wrong; quite the opposite actually."

Martin raised an eyebrow, still on edge.

Mendez folded his hands. "I just wanted a quiet moment to talk to you, away from the celebration. I've been meaning to say something since Halloween and now felt like the right time. Your wife… she's a miracle worker."

Martin let out a breath and smiled. "That's not news to me."

"No, I mean it. The kids love her. Staff do too. That AP U.S. History section was a challenge before she stepped in, but she's transformed it. And her stepping up to help with the volleyball team? That wasn't just a favor. She's got those girls believing they can win. They're one game away from clinching the district title."

Martin blinked. "She hadn't mentioned that."

Mendez chuckled. "She's modest. But that's not all. The senior class and some of the juniors wrote and submitted a nomination on her behalf for the United States History Teachers Association's Rookie Teacher of the Year Award."

Martin straightened. "They what?"

"It's national," Mendez continued. "And I just got word last week that she made the finalist list. They're sending a representative

in late January to interview her, the students, and some of us on staff."

Martin rubbed the back of his neck, stunned. "She's going to freak out, but in a good way."

"She deserves it. If she wins, there's a substantial classroom grant, enough to change how she teaches. And she'll be given the right to nominate one student per year for a scholarship that covers nearly any tuition, any college. I mean there's an asterisk to that line on their webpage but let's not worry about those details just yet."

Martin let out a slow whistle. "That's… incredible."

Mendez nodded. "I'll need her to give me a call sometime during her maternity leave. We'll have to coordinate a few things and make sure her sub is looped in. But I wanted you to hear it first. Let her enjoy these first few days before you tell her, if you think she'd appreciate that."

Martin looked back toward the waiting room, where Lindsay's sisters were still laughing with Mrs. West.

"I think she'll cry when she hears it," he said quietly. "But the good kind of cry."

Mendez clapped him on the shoulder. "Then you'll be the one to deliver the second-best news of her week."

The two men shared a quiet laugh, the kind that comes from mutual respect and hope for good things ahead. Then they turned back toward the waiting room, where a new life, and a new chapter, were just beginning.

Chapter 25
The Horse That Knew

On the quiet drive home from Alpine, the backseat was full of soft cooing and the occasional rustle of a swaddled blanket. Martin kept both hands on the wheel uncharacteristically, aware that there were more lives to be concerned with. Their silence filled with something deeper than words, the kind of calm that only came when a new life was safely in your arms.

But as they crested the final rise before the gate, Martin's brow furrowed.

The yard was packed.

Trucks, sedans, and a few SUVs crowded close to the house. The crowd from the hospital seemed to have migrated. More notable, though, was the quarter horse standing in the goat pen. The last time he'd seen that pen, it was holding exactly fourteen goats and zero horses.

He slowed the truck and blinked again.

The quarter horse was definitely in there. And she didn't look thrilled about the company.

"Huh," Martin said, leaning forward slightly. "Is that… Jobella?"

Lindsay craned her neck from the backseat to look. "That's Melody's mare. What the heck is she doing in the goat pen?"

Martin put the truck in park and stepped out, careful to shield the car seat from the low afternoon breeze as he pulled it gently from the back seat.

He barely got two steps before someone shouted, "They're here!"

A small wave of cheers and whistles rippled through the yard. Mrs. West stood on the porch like a commander inspecting returning troops, already wiping her hands on a dish towel. Brian leaned against the railing with a paper plate in one hand and a smirk in the other. One of the attendees raised a plastic cup in salute.

Martin grinned sheepishly, lifting the car seat a little like a trophy. "No autographs today," he said.

"You're on camera, son," Mr. West called, holding up his cell phone with exaggerated care. "I've been ordered to document this exact moment for future blackmail and scrapbooking."

"Does he still have all his fingers and toes?" someone asked.

"Check the wristbands," another voice chimed in. "See that they match. Make sure they didn't trade him at the hospital."

Martin laughed. "No trades. Not unless you've got a horse that stays out of the goat pen."

That got a round of chuckles. Someone said, "You should see the goats. One of them is trying to ride that horse like a rodeo bronc."

"Good luck with that," Martin muttered as he climbed the steps and slipped through the front door.

He set the car seat down beside the crib and gently lifted Robert Bruce Eastman into his new home. The boy didn't fuss. He just sighed and shifted slightly in his sleep, fists clenched like he was already preparing to wrestle life.

Martin barely had time to turn around when Lindsay's phone buzzed in her pocket. She glanced at the screen and answered on speaker.

"Melody! You're supposed to be in Japan right now. Why is Jobella here?" Lindsay said.

Melody's voice crackled through the speaker, bright despite the distance. "I am in Japan! It's two in the morning and I'm downstairs and surrounded by vending machines because I didn't want to wake the other girl in my dorm room. Listen, I swear I told you about Jobella at the wedding. I told you that I was heading to Japan for this yearlong intensive exchange program. You even smiled and said, 'Sounds cool.' Jobella can't stay alone at the Co-op barn, and Mom said it was fine. So… there she is. I told dad to bring her once the baby arrived."

Martin blinked. "At the reception?"

"Just after the first dance," Melody said. "I was wearing heels and holding champagne. You both were a little distracted."

Lindsay tilted her head slightly. "You're lucky I believe you."

Melody laughed. "I figured having Jobella there might give you something to do while you're on maternity leave and keep you from losing your mind. Besides, she'll like your pasture better than the boarding barn. Mountains and all."

Lindsay sighed, shaking her head. "Only you would send me a horse from halfway around the world."

"Love you too. Now send me baby pictures or I'm hacking your cloud storage."

The conversation continued, but Martin retreated to the front of the house and the small crowd waiting there.

****

After a quick lunch and a round of visitors cooing over Robert, the crowd thinned. The driveway cleared out. The last of the cold cuts and deviled eggs were tucked away. Mr. West, Brian, and Martin pulled on their jackets and stepped outside into the thin, chilled sunlight.

They walked without talking, boots crunching over the gravel as they passed the goat pen and Jobella who watched them warily from behind the pen fencing, her ears flicking like she wasn't quite sure about this new assignment.

The taped-off excavation site now looked . . . ordinary. The tent and crew were gone. Only a scraped patch of bare earth and a makeshift parking area remained, gouged into the soil by tire tracks.

"It's like the circus left town," Brian muttered, kicking at a loose clump of dried mud. "Think they found enough of that guy to calm things down around here?"

Martin shrugged, eyes on the now-quiet spot where the bones had once lain. "I don't know. Maybe. Or maybe this was just part of it."

Mr. West remained silent for a moment, watching a distant buzzard circle high above the ridgeline. Finally, he spoke. "I didn't have the heart to tell Melody 'No'. She was so excited. She comes back from Japan in the spring, and she says she trusts us with Jobella. I wasn't about to crush that."

"You weren't going to tell her, 'Plenty heap big evil spirits. You no bring horse," Brian laughed.

They all laughed at that.

Martin nodded slowly. "No harm in that. Just… strange timing, is all."

As they turned back toward the house, Jobella gave a sharp snort and danced to the far corner of the pen, eyeing something in the brush. Martin glanced at her and raised an eyebrow.

"She seems jumpy," Brian said, watching the mare with concern. "Maybe she's never seen a goat before. Might've thought she'd landed in a petting zoo," added Mr. West.

Martin chuckled and crouched by the edge of the concrete slab patio, brushing his hand over the dirt and rocks. Then he checked the side of the house, following the gentle curve of buried cable. The coaxial line was still there, still buried. Untouched.

He exhaled through his nose. "Well . . . small miracles."

Mr. West was already heading inside. Brian lingered on the porch for a moment longer, then gave Jobella one last glance and followed.

Martin stood alone for a beat, staring out over the scrub and the ridge beyond, the wind tugging lightly at his shirt. The winter shadows were long, but the silence was complete.

He wasn't sure what that meant.

But he'd take it.

Chapter 26
The Weight of What Remains

Dust stirred as Susan Rusker's aging sedan pulled into the Eastmans' drive, just as the cold wind found its edge. The sun was long gone behind the mountains when she arrived. The porch light was already on, casting a cone onto the dusty front yard. Jobella whinnied softly from the newly erected metal barn, her silhouette shifting in the pen as she pawed at straw.

Inside the house, Martin had just finished burping Robert and was handing him gently to Lindsay when the knock came.

He opened the door to find Susan clutching a tote bag tight against her coat. She smiled, a little windblown, a little tired, but warm as ever. "Thought I better deliver this before the week carries us off again."

"Come in," Martin said, stepping aside. "You didn't have to bring it all the way out here tonight."

Susan entered with a nod, glancing around the cozy living room. "If I didn't, I might've just talked myself out of it. This thing's more fragile than I remembered."

She handed Martin the canvas bag with great care. He opened it and carefully removed a leather-bound journal, the cover cracked with age and the pages inside browned and brittle. Several loose sheets fluttered slightly in the air current as Lindsay leaned in for a closer look.

"This was passed down through the family," Susan explained. "It belonged to Captain Cormac O'Brannach. My cousin in Marfa let me borrow it. It's old, I know, and she's a little possessive, but I told her you two were trustworthy. Probably the first time in decades anyone has bothered to look at it."

Martin turned the book gently, flipping past the first few pages filled with stiff, formal handwriting. There were dates in the corners of those few pages he scanned ranging from 1890 to 1893. Mentions of patrols. A bitter note about a denied transfer. And many, many empty pages. He paused, noting a line about thunder rolling through the mountains and the desert swallowing up "what men forget."

"There's more," Susan said, retrieving her phone and tapping through her photo gallery. "This is the headstone. The family replaced it after the Second World War, gave him a proper military stone. But this was the original."

She turned the phone to show them a grainy but legible image of a worn granite marker. The name was barely readable: **Cormac O'Brannach**, with a birth year of 1850 and a death date: 1916.

Below it, a simple phrase had been carved: *No man is forgotten who served with honor.*

The next picture was sharper.

It showed a glass display case inside the Fort Davis National Historic Site Museum. Behind the glare of lighting was a long rifle, distinctive, elegant, and unmistakable. "That's his Whitworth," Susan said. "It's one of their centerpieces. They don't let visitors touch it. The placard says it was donated by the O'Brannach family in the 1930s, and it's believed to be the same one he carried during his service. All the other rifles on display are replicas."

Martin leaned in, zooming the photo with a pinch of his fingers. His eyes narrowed.

"There," he said. "Right there. What is that long scratch over the stock?"

Susan watched their reactions, then tucked her phone away and reached for her coat. "I'll leave the journal with you for a while. Maybe it'll help make some sense of this."

"Thanks, Susan," Lindsay said. "This… this is more than we expected."

As Susan reached the door, she paused. "Could I trouble you, Martin? Just down the steps. My ankle's better, but I'm not taking any chances on these metal treads."

"Of course." Martin pulled on his coat and stepped out with her, keeping one hand gently beneath her elbow as they descended.

At the bottom of the steps, Susan looked back at the softly lit house and faint glow from the livestock barn.

"You've got something special here," she said. "History runs deep in these hills. Sometimes it wants to stay buried. And sometimes…" She trailed off, thoughtful. "Sometimes, it just wants to be seen. I hope the journal helps. I'll pick it up before New Year."

Martin stood at the edge of the drive, listening to the fading hum of Susan's car as it disappeared down the highway. The taillights shrank to twin red specks and finally winked out behind the curve of the distant bend.

For a moment, the night felt impossibly quiet.

He turned and looked out toward the corral, where the wind worried the grass and Jobella shifted in her pen. The mare tossed her head, ears flicking, as if trying to decide whether to call out or settle. Martin walked the short distance to the corral's edge, resting a hand on the fence rail.

"Easy, girl," he murmured. "It's all gone now."

Jobella snorted softly and dropped her head toward the hay.

Martin exhaled, trying to shake off the chill gathering along his shoulders. His mind kept drifting back to the journal now resting with Lindsay. He thought of Lindsay, inside the house, determined to piece together a story the Army had tried to erase.

And he thought of the skeleton formerly hidden under their soil.

He swept his eyes across the darkness beyond the barn. Somewhere out there lay the dry wash, the scrub oaks, the reddish loam turned by a recent shovel. The wind gusted harder, rattling a piece of tin on the barn roof.

He glanced down and noticed a few scraps of straw caught in his coat sleeve. He brushed them off absently, mind buzzing with questions.

Finally, he turned and headed back toward the back patio, boots crunching over the grit.

****

Lindsay was surprised by him entering through the back door. Martin stepped inside, the door clicked shut behind him, and he exhaled sharply.

"Cold out there," he muttered, stamping his boots once against the entry mat. "It's the kind of chill that gets into your fingers. Not wind. Just still. Like the air's waiting for something."

Lindsay looked up from the couch, a blanket draped across her legs, her laptop perched on a pillow with the journal next to it.

Lindsay took it carefully, fingers running over the frayed spine. "You think it's real?"

"I don't know. But it smells like dust and linseed oil, so either it's legit or somebody's a hell of a forger," Martin suggested. "Who would pass a forgery off? It's from a forgotten soldier in a remote outpost. No one."

She smiled faintly, but her eyes stayed on the cover. Martin sat back into the recliner, rubbing his palms together to warm them.

"Remind me again," he said, "why is the personal journal more useful than what you've already found? You've got the patrol report already. The government version."

Lindsay opened the book gently, stopping just past the title page. "Because the official version isn't going to tell us what really happened. That last patrol, it's listed as routine. Nothing significant. Just one hostile killed. No detail, no witness accounts. But this journal? It might tell us if they wound up on our side of the Davis Mountains. The patrol was supposed to be returning from Big Bend. That route runs south and west of Fort Davis. Not through our land here on the northside."

Martin frowned. "So, either they got lost . . . or they were chasing something."

She nodded slowly. "Or someone. It's only a hunch that the last patrol split."

Martin glanced toward the windows, now dark with early evening. "And that someone might be why he wrote things down he didn't dare report."

Lindsay looked up. "Exactly. I think something happened on that return leg of the patrol. Something not meant for the record. And this journal… it might be the only place where the truth survived."

She turned a few pages in silence, eyes scanning the cramped script. Dumpsy found Martin's lap and began rubbing on Martin's hand hoping to earn some head scritches.

****

Later that evening as Martin drifted off to sleep in his favorite recliner, Lindsay reached forward and pulled the slim, leatherbound field journal off the coffee table, where she'd left it earlier after transcribing a few sections onto her laptop. The leather was cracked, the pages brittle, but legible. The title page read simply: "Journal of Cormac O'Brannach. 1888 - "with the final date never written. She realized the dates in the upper corners of each page would be critical and made a mental note.

While Martin slept and Dumpsy purred, Lindsay kept digging.

She skimmed the passages until she found something that stopped her. Tucked between two routine entries about weather and patrol times was an unsettling note, dated just two weeks before the fort's closure:

"I told myself the bullet was meant for the back of his head. The mountain ridge I shot from was hard to judge the angle from. The shot dropped lower. I

witnessed that I hit him lower down. The spine or close to it. I took from him not only his life but his dignity, and worst of all, his voice. I killed a peacemaker. Against all I find holy I destroyed the very thing I wanted… peace. He did not face me. He did not raise a weapon. I turned a messenger into a ghost that haunts me every waking moment. Every train whistle I hear becomes his scream…"

She swallowed hard and turned the page. Another entry, written in darker ink, followed a few days later:

"There is weight in my sleep. I feel it sitting on my chest each night. I see his eyes, but realize I never saw the body. I see his broken back, but never the wound. Not accusing. Not angry. Just . . . waiting. That is my nightly burden. That is the sin."

And one more, half a page later, in slanted handwriting that shook slightly:

"The storms linger longer these days. I don't mean in the sky. I mean in me. The rain begins and it's as if some forgotten gear within me starts to grind. Joints ache. Breathing tightens. And the rifle… it seems heavier, louder, more alive. I clean it often, but it resists now. The oil won't hold. The metal steams in the cold like it knows it's back where it doesn't belong. When the thunder rolls, I sometimes find myself staring at the sky for too long. When it happens I forget where I am. I have the strangest feeling the rifle remembers something I've tried to forget."

She sat back on the couch, the weight of the journal across her lap, the silence broken only by wind blowing past the house.

"He's the one." She spoke softly to Dumpsy, "He murdered the Native American on that last patrol, but is it the skeleton on our land?"

A soft click sounded behind her.

The flat panel TV, untouched, glowed to life.

Lindsay stiffened. The screen remained dark but lit at the edges, as if a signal was trying to form.

She didn't move for a moment, heart beating fast. Then she spoke aloud, slowly, as if testing the theory in her mind. Dumpsy flopped on his back in a completely "I am peace" position, leaving only the tip of his tail twitching in slow movements.

"That final patrol report. The official one I found online. It says nothing about the rifle. Nothing about the circumstances. Just a one-line mention: 'One hostile killed. No further action taken.' But this journal . . . " said Lindsay as she looked at Dumpsy. She tapped the cracked cover with one finger. " . . . says everything. Not just guilt. Detail. The terrain, the shot, the silence afterward. And the guilt. It was real. He knew what he did." The TV flickered once again. Then shut off.

Lindsay didn't sleep that night.

Chapter 27
Patterns in the Dust

Files and ungraded assignments waited for Martin beneath the steady flicker of classroom lights, but the hallway still brought nods and soft congratulations from the other teachers. His classroom greeted him with the familiar stacks of ungraded work, and a few knowing nods from fellow teachers in the hallway who offered quiet congratulations between bells.

Returning home that evening, the warmth of the trailer hit him before he even stepped inside, both in temperature and aroma. The air fryer's steady hum mixed with the unmistakable scent of roasted garlic and thyme. As he closed the door behind him, Lindsay's voice called out from the kitchen.

"Your son is a prodigy," she said dryly, cradling a dozing infant in one arm and Mrs. West stirring a pot on the stovetop. "He can eat, sleep, and crap. Sometimes all at the same time."

Martin laughed, dropped his bag by the door, and kissed her on the cheek. "Truly gifted."

He found Mr. West on the patio, seated in one of the folding camp chairs with a blanket across his lap and a travel mug steaming in his hands. Beyond the railing, the new barn glowed in the night, ringed with solar-powered LED spotlights that threw long, angular shadows across the wide pen.

"Evening," Martin said, easing into the other chair.

Mr. West nodded, still staring toward the barn. "She's been acting strange."

"Jobella?"

"Yeah. Started this evening." He took a sip from his mug, eyes still locked on the paddock. "She does what horses do, eats, stands around, swishes her tail, but then out of nowhere she bolts across the pen like something's chasing her. She always stops just before the fence on the west side. Turns and does it all again a few minutes, maybe tens of minutes later. The goats don't know what to make of it."

Martin frowned. "Could it be coyotes?"

"I thought that at first. Even went down to check. But it's not like that. It's like…" He hesitated, then sighed. "It's like something's on her back. Not just chasing her. Ridden. That's the best way I can describe it."

Martin felt the hair on the back of his neck stand up.

"Four times since I've been sitting here," Mr. West added, voice low. "Almost like she's following a pattern."

As if summoned by the words, Jobella suddenly tossed her head in the corral, turned hard, and galloped from the eastern edge straight toward the western fence. She halted again, hooves skidding slightly in the dirt. A snort, then silence.

Martin stood. "Let's get her in the barn."

Together, the two men crossed the dim yard, the goats shifting restlessly into their corner. Jobella seemed reluctant at first, then fell into line beside them. Inside the barn, they latched the door and checked the feed, both men silent in their thoughts.

****

Later, over dinner, Martin kept glancing out the kitchen window. The roast was perfect, Lindsay's smile was tired but content, and Robert Bruce let out a heroic belch from his bassinet beside the table. But outside, in the dark beyond the barn's lights, something old was stirring again.

****

The first Saturday of Christmas break dawned cold but bright, the kind of crisp winter morning that made coffee taste better and silence feel like a gift. With Lindsay's parents and baby Robert still sleeping, Martin and Lindsay finally found a quiet moment together at the breakfast table. A plate of waffles and bacon steamed between them, and the smell of cinnamon syrup mixed with dark roast coffee hung in the air.

The Christmas tree stood in the corner of the living room, nearly hidden beneath a growing pile of presents, most of them for Robert. Martin smirked as he sipped his coffee.

"I think he has more gifts under that tree than I've had in the last five years combined," he said.

Lindsay grinned. "He's their first grandchild. We'll be lucky if we can see the tree by Christmas Day."

As she speared a bite of waffle, Lindsay stretched one leg under the table. "Thinking I might try a short jog today. Just down to the pressure station and back."

Martin raised an eyebrow. "You just gave birth."

"I didn't say sprint. Just a light jog. Gotta start somewhere."

Before he could reply, a sudden *crack*, sharp, clean, and close, ripped through the quiet. Both of them jumped. Lindsay's fork clattered onto her plate.

"That was a rifle," Martin said, already pushing away from the table.

He rushed to the front door, throwing it open and stepping out cautiously, scanning the ridgeline east of the house. The low winter sun made long shadows out of scrub and rock, but nothing moved. Not a single deer or hunter in sight.

Pulling on his boots and grabbing his jacket from the hook, Martin climbed up into the bed of the loaner truck parked near the house. From the elevated view, the entire landscape lay open before him in amber silence.

Still nothing.

He spent the next thirty minutes searching the property, checking around the equipment barn, the horse barn, and the water tank. He opened the gate to the pen and let Jobella and the goats stretch their legs, guiding the latter into the temporary enclosure. The only thing he noticed was the coax wire above the ground again.

Returning inside, chilled and puzzled, he shrugged out of his jacket.

"Found nothing," he told Lindsay. "Might've been a trick of the atmosphere. Sound carries funny on mornings like this. It's also deer season."

Lindsay, now in warm-ups and stretching in the living room, frowned. "But we've never seen deer hunters near this property. I mean, not once."

"No," Martin agreed. "Not here. Not this close."

Mrs. West shuffled in, still in her robe, just as Martin started frying more bacon. Lindsay greeted her with a smile and announced her jogging plans again.

"Just down to the pipeline station and back. A couple of miles. Easy."

Martin chuckled as he plated food. "Shoot, you should run all the way to the old Boy Scout camp at the end of the road. Only eight miles or so."

"I'll pass," she said, tying her hair back.

The first stretch of her jog was peaceful, the sun warming her face and her lungs appreciating the cool air. Then, without warning, a massive buck erupted from the ridgeline brush and thundered across the road just feet in front of her.

She skidded to a stop, heart pounding.

Two hundred yards farther, a doe did the same, darting across her path with barely a second to spare.

Still catching her breath, Lindsay shook her head. "Y'all need to slow down," she muttered. "There's a handsome buck looking for you."

But the third close encounter with a panicked deer finally made up her mind. "That's it," she huffed, turning back.

As she neared the house, flushed and annoyed, she saw Martin holding the screen door open.

"Deer are everywhere today," she announced. "Three nearly flattened me."

Martin opened his mouth to reply when Lindsay stiffened, eyes fixed on the backyard.

Jobella was standing on the patio, head tilted, ears forward and staring through the glass like a curious houseguest.

"What the…" he muttered.

Martin grabbed an apple from the counter and stepped out cautiously. The horse turned and trotted off across the yard toward the old gravesite, stopping there once she arrived.

He followed, heart pounding again, but for a different reason.

"Hey girl," he said softly, holding out the apple. He realized that she could bolt into the brush and join the goat that was decaying at the base of the cliff not more than a half mile away. By the time he could get the Gator going and give chase, if that's what you call driving "pell-mell going to hell" through catclaw and scrub oak, the horse would be at the heavenly equal to the Kentucky Derby long before.

After a tense moment, Jobella approached and let him slip a lead rope over her halter. Martin walked her back to the pen, checked the gate latch twice, and leaned on the fence as she settled in.

"Hope you weren't running from anything," he said quietly.

But the horse didn't answer. She only stood there, breathing steam into the cold morning air, ears flicking looking to the Northwest.

****

The smell of strong coffee and reheated cinnamon rolls filled the kitchen as Saturday morning sunlight poured through the east-facing windows. Mrs. West had gotten up earlier and changed Robert before putting the coffee on. Her presence at the house was deeply appreciated by them both. For now and the next few weeks leading up to Christmas she was settled into the guest bedroom.

Lindsay rocked Robert gently in one arm, cradling him with practiced ease, while Martin poured more coffee into mismatched mugs and slid a plate of bacon between them.

"He finally slept through the night," Lindsay said with cautious pride, glancing at Robert's sleepy face. "Almost five hours straight."

"This explains why we're functional adults today," Martin said, passing her a napkin. "So… I've been thinking. We should go see the rifle."

Lindsay raised an eyebrow. "The *rifle?*"

"The one from the journal. The Whitworth. The one in the museum display case at the Fort."

Lindsay blinked, then nodded. "Yeah. That rifle." She shifted Robert to her other arm and smiled. "Seems fitting, doesn't it? His first big trip, our son, the child of a history teacher, going to a National Historic Site."

Martin grinned. "There's symbolism in there somewhere."

A knock on the front door interrupted them. A second later, Brian let himself in with the usual absence of ceremony. He carried a crinkled gift bag in one hand and a stuffed goat plushie in the other.

"Special delivery!" he called, stepping into the kitchen. "I come bearing gifts for the future livestock overlord."

Martin gestured to the empty chair and motioned for the coffeepot. "You're just in time. We're planning a field trip."

Brian's eyes narrowed. "Field trip?"

"To the fort," Lindsay said, patting Robert's back. "We're going to look at the rifle. The Whitworth. The one from the journal."

Brian blinked. "Wait, wait; so, baby's first day out is to go look at a rifle, one that may contain the soul of an Apache? It makes perfect sense. Really checks all the boxes. Did y'all at least pack his holy water rattle and silver-plated teething ring?"

Martin chuckled. "You're welcome to come. Do you have a Latin to Apache dictionary we can borrow? All the movies use Latin to communicate with the dead."

"Knew I forgot something. It's on my dresser back home."

They both turned as Mrs. West entered the room, dressed in jeans, boots, and a thick fleece jacket. She'd clearly overheard the conversation. "You, too. Mrs. West. Want to go on baby's first trip out? Or stay here?"

"Oh no," she replied nearly instantly, already reaching for her coat. "You're not leaving me here in the funhouse. If things start flying off walls again, I'll be the one that gets blamed. Plus, you're going to need my SUV for this crowd."

"Fair enough," Martin said. "Field trip just got bigger."

The next hour passed in a whirlwind of preparation. Lindsay was calm and methodical; the others… not so much.

"Why does he need *two* blankets?" Brian asked, holding them up like mismatched flags.

"One's for warmth," Lindsay said, adjusting the diaper bag, "the other's for when he spits up all over the first."

"Diaper bag, bottle bag, changing pad…" Martin ticked the items off on his fingers. "This is like deploying a platoon."

Brian clicked the SUV's baby seat receiver from "lock" to "open" and back again, observing the mechanism swing up and down. Martin set the baby seat with Robert into the custom shaped void and moved the tiny handle to "lock" position. Brian sat upright and reached for his seatbelt, "Operation Baby Thunderbolt is a go. . . does it have an ejection seat, too?"

Martin smiled and backed away. Lindsay piled in and sat next to the child's seat. Brian waved a tiny wave at Lindsay from the other side of the baby seat.

Slowly they loaded into the vehicle, Robert snoozing peacefully in his carrier, the back seat was a chaotic masterpiece of bags, blankets, wipes, and emergency pacifiers.

Martin started the engine, looking over at Lindsay with a sideways smile.

"First trip out. Fort Davis National Historic Site."

She nodded. "History, mystery, and possibly haunted artillery."

Brian leaned forward from the back. "What could *possibly* go wrong?"

They drove off into the crisp winter light, unaware that the answers to that question were already waiting behind the glass in the museum's quietest room.

Chapter 28
A Weapon That Waits

Exhibits lined the walls of the cool, quiet museum hall, where the air smelled faintly of varnish and old creosote. The main hall of the Fort Davis National Historic Site Museum was cool, quiet, and smelled faintly of old varnish and creosote. Fluorescent lights buzzed overhead, and the worn linoleum floor clicked under their steps as the group meandered past dioramas of cavalry barracks, faded photographs, and meticulously arranged uniforms behind scratched plexiglass.

This was not the Smithsonian. It wasn't even the Midland Petroleum Museum. But in its modest way, the place preserved the old feel of the frontier.

The Fort Davis Historical Museum was quiet, save for the soft creak of the old floorboards under Martin's and Brian's feet. A few ceiling fans stirred the air. The building itself felt like it remembered too much, stone walls and timber beams that had seen over a century of history drift by, even if it was less than a few years old. They wandered past glass cases filled with rusted tools, faded photographs, and handwritten journals, their edges curled with age.

They passed a rack of old cavalry uniforms, yellowed maps of survey routes, and shelves lined with arrowheads grouped by region and date. For a while, they didn't speak, simply absorbing the curated fragments of a land that had never really forgotten its scars.

Then, as they turned the corner near the back of the museum, they stopped short.

Before them stood a full-scale diorama, taking up nearly the entire length of one wall. A prehistoric scene had been reconstructed in frozen drama from ten thousand years ago, by the plaque's reckoning. A Native American man, mouth open in a scream, was captured mid-lunge, a long spear braced in both hands as he drove it toward the flank of a towering bear. The beast, reared up on its hind legs, was massive. Glass eyes glinted from the dim display light, and its mouth gaped in a snarl, teeth as long as a man's fingers. Dust hung in the air, caught in the slats of angled sunlight from the high windows.

Martin squinted at the display. "Jesus. That takes some serious huevos."

Brian smirked, arms crossed as he stared up at the frozen combat. "You think that guy had a backup plan?"

"Probably not one that worked." Martin tilted his head. "Man with pointed stick versus bear. That's not bravery. That's mythology with a death wish."

The spear in the hunter's hands was long, maybe seven feet, the flint point still sharp and gleaming under the layer of dust. Its shaft was thick, weathered, but solid. Whoever made the diorama had gone to real effort.

Brian leaned closer, eyes narrowing. "You know, I think that's real wood. Not a replica. Look at the grain."

Martin grinned. "You want to tap the bear? See if the bear flinches?"

"Only if you're standing closer."

They shared a laugh and moved on.

They found the rifle in a low-lit corner behind a glass case labeled *Special Exhibits: Arms of the Frontier*. The plaque beneath it had clearly been printed sometime in the mid-1980s, the font slightly faded and curled at the edges.

Martin leaned forward to read aloud: **"Whitworth Rifle, c. 1860. English-made percussion rifle, .451 caliber, hexagonal bore. Known for exceptional range and accuracy. This particular rifle is believed to have been used during the Confederate occupation of Fort Davis (1861–62) and later came into the possession of Captain Cormac O'Brannach of the 220th Cavalry Regiment. Donated by the O'Brannach family in 1929."**

"That's it," Lindsay said quietly, shifting Robert in her arms. "The one from the journal."

Martin leaned closer, squinting through the reflection on the glass. "There," he pointed. "The scratch. Just like Susan's picture."

Brian folded his arms. "If he's the one that killed the Apache buried on your land then this is the rifle he did it with. The rifle is real, the murder is real… and the museum glosses over how this

Confederate rifle ended up being used by a Union officer who wasn't here during the Civil war."

"History has its blind spots," Lindsay murmured.

Behind them, a voice said, "Afternoon, folks."

They turned to see a middle-aged woman in a forest-green Parks Service uniform, holding a clipboard and offering a polite smile. Her name tag read *Harris.*

"Just us in here?" Martin asked.

She nodded. "Short holiday hours, and most folks don't come out here unless they're already lost." Her eyes went to the baby. "But y'all picked a good day, weather's holding."

Brian gestured toward the case. "Got any idea how Captain O'Brannach ended up with this?"

"Not officially," she said, stepping up beside them. "That plaque's old. Supposedly the rifle stayed in the family, and they eventually donated it to the site when we opened as a National Historic Landmark. They still technically retain ownership, though, it's on permanent loan. Legal quirks."

Lindsay's brow furrowed. "Do you know anything about a man named Storm upon Meadow?"

The woman blinked. "That's… not a name I've heard before. Apache?"

"Yes," Lindsay said, stepping forward. "We think he was Lipan Apache, possibly connected to this area, maybe someplace called Old Camp?"

The woman's expression shifted, more curious than surprised. "Wait… if he was here in the Davis Mountains, then there's a good chance he is in a book. There was a book, printed way back, 1906, I think. Some government ethnography project. Researchers went to the Mescalero Reservation and collected oral histories from the Apache who had arrived in the 1890s."

She paused. "Your Apache might be in that, especially if he made the journey to the reservation. Some of the stories are vague, but I don't remember that name. The problem is that the book is rare. They only printed a few hundred copies. Shows up at auction sometimes, usually goes for four, five hundred dollars or more. The museum doesn't have the budget to buy one."

Martin exhaled. "That's a dead end, then."

"Maybe not," she said. "Sul Ross State might have a copy in the Borderlands archives. If anyone does, it's them. Try their library, ask for Special Collections."

Lindsay knew she needed more than the museum cases displayed. She extended her hand to the nearby park ranger.

"I'm Lindsay Eastman. I teach history over at Fort Davis High," she said, offering a friendly smile. "My conference period falls in the middle of the school day, so I have a little time most afternoons. I was hoping I might get a look at any primary documents you might have about the last days of the fort, the weeks just before it was closed."

The ranger introduced herself as she shook hands, nodded thoughtfully. "That's good timing, actually. We have some of the original logs, final duty rosters, even a few handwritten orders from that period. They're not organized too well, but accessible."

"Would I need to fill anything out in advance?"

"Not if you're with Fort Davis ISD. We've got a Letter of Agreement on file with the district. There should be no problem. You'll just need to sign in and grab a pair of document gloves from the bin."

She paused, then added with a knowing smile, "And bring a cushion if you plan to stay long. The chairs in the records room are . . . historically accurate. I've sat on softer concrete."

Lindsay laughed. "Thanks for the heads-up. I'll plan accordingly."

They chatted a few minutes longer, arranging a time for her to return during the weeks ahead. As she turned back to rejoin Martin and Brian, her eyes lingered briefly on the rifle in the case. She didn't say anything, but something in her posture straightened, excited at the research chances.

They thanked the Ranger and stepped back into the sunshine, where the wind cut colder than it had an hour earlier.

"Ghost rifles, lost books, buried Apache," Brian muttered as they loaded Robert back into the truck. "We really know how to show a baby a good time."

Lindsay laughed. "He's got to learn early."

Martin leaned on the hood. "Okay. No haunted museums. Let's go get a soda. There's still a historic soda fountain in the town, want to meet a real soda jerk? The last one I saw was pretty cute."

"Now *that* is history I can get behind," Brian said, climbing into the back seat. "Lead the way, Dr. Eastman."

The truck rolled down the quiet road toward town, the fort shrinking behind them, silent under the pale winter sky.

****

Twenty miles beyond Fort Davis, the sign at the Sul Ross State University library read *Closed for Winter Break* in blocky red letters taped to the inside of the glass. Martin sighed and jiggled the locked door out of habit, though he already knew it wouldn't budge.

"Figures," Brian said, bouncing Robert's car seat gently on one hip while the baby slept soundly through the motion. "Take the kid to see a cursed gun, then drive twenty miles to a closed library. Hell of a Monday."

Lindsay smiled and tugged her scarf tighter. "We're teaching him that history's full of delays and disappointment."

They turned back toward the truck, resigning themselves to one more research dead end. The air was sharp with winter chill, and the clouds, thin, wind-whipped, galloped above them like banners.

When they were about ten minutes from home, Martin noticed the headlights in the rearview mirror. A white sheriff's SUV, following with polite distance. When he signaled for the turn onto the Ranch road the SUV mirrored him. "Sheriff's following us."

Brian leaned forward from the back seat, holding up Robert's rattle and giving it a soft shake. "Well, look at that, kid. First trip to the museum, first brush with the law. You grow up fast out here."

Martin chuckled but kept his eye on the road. "I guess he's tracking us down with news."

When they turned through the gate and pulled up the long gravel drive to park between the corral and the house, the sheriff's SUV eased in behind them. Sheriff Villareal stepped out, his hat pulled low, and his jacket zipped against the breeze.

"Afternoon, folks," he said as they got out. "Figured I'd catch you here rather than call."

"Bad news?" Martin asked, shifting Robert's car seat protectively.

"Not at all." Villareal glanced at the baby and smiled. "Congratulations, by the way."

He rocked back on his boots. "Just wanted to let you know the remains we recovered, well, they cleared through Professor

Ostertag's lab over at Sul Ross last week. Based on everything, including the clothing scraps, beadwork, and that pouch, she's confident it was Lipan Apache. Rare in these parts, but not unheard of either. The case is no longer classified as a potential homicide."

Martin nodded slowly. "What happens next?"

Villareal folded his arms. "As per NAGPRA, the remains and associated artifacts were formally handed over to a representative from the Mescalero Apache tribe. All paperwork's filed, everyone's in the loop. But there's more."

He paused and looked at Lindsay.

"One of the elders, a man named Chayton, from the tribe asked if he might visit you to deliver a small thank you gift, something to acknowledge y'all did the right thing. No pressure. Just let me know if that's okay."

Lindsay blinked, clearly moved. "Yes. Absolutely."

Martin gave a small nod. "That's the least we can do."

Villareal smiled. "Didn't think it'd be a problem. Oh, and if you find anything else, bones or otherwise, just call me directly. No need to go through dispatch. Everything after this will be done by Sul Ross, the DPS forensics team is off the case with the status change."

Villareal reached into his breast pocket and extracted a calling card.

Martin raised an eyebrow. "You think we will?"

Villareal looked thoughtful. "Let's just say . . . these kinds of stories tend to have layers. If this land's been holding secrets this long, there might be more buried."

Just then, his eyes drifted past Martin's shoulder.

"And speaking of strange things, did y'all leave that horse standing in the middle of the old dig site?"

Martin turned, following the sheriff's gaze.

Out near where the forensic tent had once stood, where the ground still showed signs of disturbance and tracked tires, Jobella stood motionless, her body framed by the orange-tinged sun and her ears twitching like radar dishes.

"I'll go get the harness," Said Mrs. West as she walked to towards the door.

She wasn't grazing. She wasn't wandering. She was just . . . standing there.

Looking to the northwest.

Martin's stomach dropped slightly.

"No," he said softly. "She was in the pen when we left."

Villareal exhaled through his nose. "You sure that fence gate was latched?"

"I'm sure."

The group stood in silence for a moment, the wind brushing past them, carrying the distant rustle of dry oak leaves.

Robert stirred in his car seat but did not cry.

"Well," Brian said, finally breaking the silence. "Guess we're not done yet."

****

The stars grudgingly gave way to the winter sun that came up bright and gold on Christmas morning, casting long, warm light across the Davis Mountains. It was the kind of day that made winter feel like a rumor. Mid-seventies, clear skies, and just enough cool breeze to remind everyone that summer was in full retreat.

The rest of the West family, Melody not included, arrived mid-morning in a convoy of SUVs, the kind of entrance only possible

253

with a full cooler, an overflowing bag of even more presents, and at least three different opinions on how to season a steak.

Elise wasted no time saddling up Jobella and riding her out across that bit of pasture leveled by the goats, reins loose, boots light in the stirrups. Meanwhile, Martin and Mr. West fired up the outdoor grill and laid thick, marbled steaks across the hot iron, letting the smoke curl into the blue sky. It reminded Martin of the August cookout, but without the fierce heat.

Beside the white expanded metal table, Mrs. West had set up a folding table under the shade of the house awning, humming to herself as she arranged napkins, soda cans, and a wrapped gift bag with a ribbon that had survived a three-hour drive mostly intact.

When lunch was winding down, and the last few bites of steak were being traded for sips of sweet tea and beer, Mrs. West stood and held out a small envelope.

"Merry Christmas, you two," she said, handing it to Lindsay and Martin. "It's not just a card."

Inside were two Amtrak tickets: **Alpine to Seattle**, with words "Sleeper Roomette," printed just below, and tucked behind them, two airline tickets: Seattle to Midland, connecting through Denver.

Lindsay blinked. "You planned a trip?"

Mrs. West smiled. "I planned a break. For you. And for me. I want to enjoy my grandson, not just help raise him. And yes," she added with a wink, "I'll take Dumpsy, too."

Martin laughed. "We'll need someone to check in on the goats. I bet Brian could be bribed with smoked brisket, pork loin, and wild-caught salmon. Maybe you could pick some up in the big city?"

From across the pasture, Elise suddenly called out, her voice amused. "Uh, I think this horse is broken!"

Everyone turned.

"She's not responding to anything!"

Elise was riding Jobella, tugging at the reins. The horse plodded along, not fast, not wild, but deliberate, and came to a gentle stop at the exact place she always stood at. Elise sat astride the mare, reins loose in her lap, looking perplexed.

Martin and Mr. West stepped away from the group.

"Did you ever tell the other girls about… the visitor?" Martin asked quietly.

Mr. West shook his head. "Nope. Both me and the Missus talked about this back in August and agreed neither of us wanted the deluxe padded room at the funny farm. Neither of the other girls know. Thought it best to let Christmas be Christmas, so I didn't talk about it last night when she came to stay at the house."

Jobella shifted, then turned slowly away from the spot. Elise nudged her into motion and guided her calmly back toward the barn. The mare didn't resist.

As the sun dipped lower in the sky, dinner was served. Plates piled with mashed potatoes, biscuits, and pecan pie filled the outside table, laughter echoing through the rooms. When the time came to leave, all of the Wests packed up quickly, anxious to make it back to San Angelo and Big Spring before what Mr. West called "stupid o'clock in the morning."

The porch light burned above them as they waved goodbye. In the silence that followed, Martin and Lindsay looked at each other, baby in her arms. Dumpsy sat inside rubbing his head on the door, waiting for attention.

It had been a perfect day.

Almost.

Chapter 29
Small Hands, Heavy Shadows

Life settled into a rhythm, gentle, surprising, and shaped now by the needs of a squirming, curious, increasingly vocal infant. Robert Eastman had grown impossibly fast, filling out his cheeks, his gaze already hinting at expressions too old for his age.

Mornings came earlier. Lindsay was often up before sunrise, balancing a thermos of coffee, a folder of lesson plans, and a bundled baby on one hip as she stepped into the chilled morning air. Her drive to Fort Davis included a daily drop-off at the new day care center, tucked behind the post office near the old stone church. She claimed it was good for Robert to see other babies.

By the first Thursday in January, dinner felt like a small victory. Lindsay stirred a pot of venison chili while Martin set the table and recounted how many students had forgotten their laptops again. After a few bites, Martin leaned back in his chair and said, "I've been thinking about cameras."

Lindsay looked up. "For the barn?"

"For everywhere. House, barns, back fence, where the coax cable keeps getting dug up." He paused. "Maybe even up by the trail near the gully."

"You think our ghost friend will pose for the camera? If he's still here, that is."

Martin grinned. "Only one way to find out."

As if summoned, something clattered onto the roof with a hard *tock*. It wasn't loud, but solid enough to make them both pause, eyes drawn to the ceiling.

"That sounded like hail," Lindsay said.

Martin was already standing. "It's fifty degrees outside."

He grabbed the flashlight by the door and stepped out into the dark. The stars overhead were clear and hard, the chill just sharp enough to sting the back of his neck. On the porch lay a smooth stone, no bigger than a walnut.

Then he heard the faint rustle of feathers and aimed the flashlight up.

A raven stood perched at the apex of the roof, eyes glinting back at him like coals. It didn't caw or flinch, just watched.

"Well, look at that," Martin muttered.

Lindsay stepped outside, arms folded. "Is that a raven?"

"Could be. They all look alike in the dark."

"It dropped a rock on our house."

They stood there for a moment, the bird unmoving, the quiet absolute.

Eventually, Martin laughed. "It's just being a raven."

"I guess," Lindsay said, although she didn't sound convinced.

Inside, the warmth felt deeper by comparison. While Lindsay loaded the dishwasher, Martin cracked open his laptop and began scrolling through listings for outdoor cameras. Solar-powered, motion-triggered, some with night vision. He made a shortlist, even picked a spot on the bookshelf for the DVR base station.

That night, the wind picked up. Not a storm, just a few stiff gusts funneling down from the hills. Around two in the morning, the clatter of hooves jolted Martin awake.

He lay still for a moment, then rose, slipping on his boots and jacket. Outside, the barn lights flickered under motion sensors. Jobella's stall was empty. Again.

He found her pacing the small paddock, ears back, and nostrils flared. The stall door stood wide open. He *knew* he had latched it.

Martin calmed the mare, walked her back inside, and latched it again, double-checked it, even gave it a tug. Jobella snorted once but didn't resist.

Back in bed, Martin didn't tell Lindsay. Not yet. Let her sleep.

But he lay awake for a while, staring at the ceiling, thinking about ravens. And cameras. And open doors.

****

The clouds hung low over Fort Davis, their bellies heavy and gray, blotting out all but the bases of the mountains. From the parking lot of the high school, Lindsay could barely make out the rocky silhouettes beyond the football field. She zipped her coat

259

higher and stepped into the cold, her breath fogging slightly as she crossed to her car.

She always took lunch during her conference hour, thanks to the scheduling gods who'd placed it in the middle of the day. It gave her just enough time to drive to the museum, scan a few documents or exhibits, and return in time to wrangle her fifth-hour Texas History class, a group she privately referred to as the "Seven Samurai of Sass and Snacking."

The Fort Davis National Historic Site sat quiet in the midweek lull, the tourist surge of summer long gone. Lindsay parked in her usual spot, near the back where the gravel lot gave way to dirt. She checked in at the front desk with a quick nod, exchanged pleasantries with the same Park Ranger who'd waved her in on past visits, and made her way into the records room. It was only the third week of January, but going to the museum now was a daily habit since returning from maternity leave.

Her "usual" seat was a padded wooden chair beside the long table in the corner, just under the high window that rarely let in more than a sliver of light. She retrieved her makeshift cushion, a couch pillow from the Fort Davis High School teachers' lounge, discreetly borrowed and now unofficially repurposed for research.

The room smelled faintly of old paper, dry insulation, and varnished wood. Lindsay sighed and settled in, flipping through the metal tabs of the file cabinet. She was searching for letters, late 1880s correspondence from officers stationed at the fort. But the bottom drawer of the second cabinet stuck halfway. With a grunt, she yanked it.

The metal drawer gave way with a metallic shriek. Lindsay rifled through a bundle of fragile papers labeled "Correspondence of

March 1891." A thin report slipped free, typed but signed in precise script: *Colonel W.A. Hall, Commanding Officer.*

She read the opening lines, curiosity sharpening with each word:

"March 14, 1891: This morning, Storm upon Meadow, leader of a small Lipan band encamped near Old Camp Springs, presented himself at the fort. He declared his people could no longer endure the conditions in Texas and would leave immediately for Mescalero lands in New Mexico. He requests no pursuit, stating his band seeks only peace and safe passage. No hostilities observed. Telegraphed intentions to Fort Bliss with request to alert other forts."

Lindsay's lips moved silently over the name. "Storm upon Meadow..." It pulsed through her mind like a drumbeat. She couldn't explain why, but the name felt tied to everything strange simmering around their land.

She reread the passage and jotted a few notes down before returning her attention back to the still open drawer.

There, wedged between a stack of pamphlets and duplicate maps, sat an old issue of *History Alive!* magazine. The cover was worn, corners bent, the masthead faded. She recognized the style instantly. It had been a favorite during her undergraduate days at ASU, filled with thoughtful essays, oral histories, and rare regional accounts.

This copy was filed incorrectly, out of order and out of place. She almost pushed it aside, but something stopped her. An impulse. A nudge. She pulled it free.

The pages crinkled softly as she turned them, skipping past stories she already knew, a piece on the Butterfield Overland Mail, an article on adobe brickmaking in Northern Mexico. Then she stopped.

The cover picture showed a Mississippi steamboat, but it was a side bar headline that piqued her interest. The headline read:

"When the Land Remembers: A Lipan Tradition"

She turned the pages to the story as she seated herself at the table. At the top of the page below the headline, a black-and-white photo of a weathered man sitting cross-legged under a cottonwood tree. No name in the caption. Just the words: *Oral testimony recorded near Fort Davis, Jeff Davis County, 1971.*

The article was short, just three columns long, but it hit her like a whisper in a quiet room. The man being interviewed wanted to see Fort Davis and this was his only chance, a trip sponsored by the magazine.

"In a soft voice nearly lost to the breeze, the elder spoke of a place his grandfather had visited, a sacred spring called Old Camp by the white man, north of Fort Davis. 'The wind circles there,' he said, 'even when the air is still.' When the interviewer asked if the place was haunted, the elder shook his head. 'It is not haunted. That is not the term we use,' he said. 'It is remembering. That is different. But when a warrior is murdered, his spirit is not quiet unless balance is found. If the land breathes, someone is still walking.'"

Lindsay read it twice, then a third time.

A footnote at the bottom of the column noted that the elder had passed away before the magazine had gone to press.

She sat back in her chair, the cushion sighing beneath her. The clouds outside still loomed low, but the room felt even more still to her, as if the story had soaked into the air. That last line: *If the land breathes, someone is still walking,* felt more like a warning than folklore.

She checked the time and cursed softly. Lunch was over. She carefully slipped the magazine into the "To Be Refiled" bin and rose, stretching. As she stepped back into the cold, she glanced once more toward the cloud-choked horizon. The wind had picked up, but only in fitful gusts. It tugged at her coat, then vanished.

Back in her car, she turned the heater up and pulled onto the highway.

As she drove, she couldn't shake the feeling that the story had been waiting for her.

In the few minutes it took to drive less than a mile back to school, the clouds had darkened even further. She smiled anyway. Her fifth hour, her beloved pack of seventh-grade history hooligans, was waiting. And Lord help them, today they were going to learn about the Comanche and Quanah Parker.

"Settle down," she'd say. "History breathes too."

****

The cameras arrived on the first Friday afternoon after school had started, packed into a pair of heavy boxes that barely fit in the backseat of Martin's car. He picked them up from the Toyahvale Post Office Box on the way home, resisting the urge to open them right there in the gravel lot. Before he pulled into the driveway, the sun was already sliding behind the ridgeline, casting long, golden shadows across the house and barn.

Saturday morning broke bright and crisp, the air still holding winter's bite despite the clear sky. Martin had just finished his coffee when the crunch of tires announced a visitor. He stepped outside to see Mr. West pulling up with a flatbed trailer hitched to his truck, and sitting on that trailer was Martin's old pickup.

Only now, it gleamed.

Mrs. West stepped down from the passenger seat and gave a theatrical sigh as she walked past. "Boys and their toys," she muttered, heading straight inside to see her grandson.

Martin walked around the truck slowly, blinking. The windows had all been replaced. The faded, sun-scoured paint was gone, replaced with a glossy blue slate color that caught the light like water. Every dent had been pulled, every scar smoothed. When Mr. West popped the hood, Martin let out a low whistle.

"New crate motor," the older man said, visibly proud. "Put it in myself."

"You're serious?"

"As a snakebite. Took me back to when Mr. Transon and I were keeping the company fleet together with coat hangers and borrowed parts. That was back when oil prices were down, and we knew to stretch every dime or go belly up. I had bet my truck against a two-percent payout."

"Two percent bet?"

"The company was on its last legs. We knew it. I asked Transon if he would be willing to try one last time. I knew a landowner that didn't have an active lease on his land….land that turned out to have one 200-barrel-a-day well after another on it when we drilled it. I bet my truck against a two percent payout with him. Even though I'm not a geologist, I suspected a fault trap when the majors didn't. At that point we were broke, but not broken, both of us, Ramen Noodles were exotic cuisine, and a single can of discount beer made for an exciting Friday Night. Lindsay was on the way at that time…my next stop would have been working as a deck hand on someone else's drilling rig, probably have sold this place off, as well."

Martin pondered the information. It explained a lot about Mr. West's character.

Martin ran a hand along the fender. "I don't even know what to say. Thank you. For this, and for everything else."

Mr. West gave a modest shrug. "You're doing good out here. That matters."

He clapped his hands together, then pointed a thumb at the sky. "We better get moving. Weather says we're due for our first snow tomorrow afternoon."

Martin looked up at the clear sky. "Seriously?"

"Big Spring forecast for six inches, can you believe that? If it hits out here, even half that would be a mess."

He grinned, settling into a familiar rhythm. "Rule number one: Texans don't know how to drive on snow. Rule number two: If you think you do… go read rule number one again."

Martin laughed. "I'll keep that in mind."

Later that morning, with the women and Robert headed off to Fort Davis and Alpine for groceries, baby wipes, and "just a peek" at the consignment shops, Martin and Mr. West got to work.

They started with the patio camera, then mounted two at the barn, one angled at Jobella's stall and another at the paddock. A solar unit faced the fence line where the coax cable kept getting mysteriously dug up. The final camera, their highest, they mounted to a cedar post on the slope that overlooked the narrow path to the gully.

Martin ran cable while Mr. West adjusted the small antenna dish they'd installed the week prior. The wind picked up around midday, flinging bits of grit and hay across the yard, but both men worked through it with quiet satisfaction.

During a sandwich break on the porch, Martin said, "Honestly… it's been quiet lately. No smells, no noises. Jobella did stand over where we found the bones again, and there was that weird raven with the rock, but… I don't know. Maybe the spirit's settled."

Mr. West chewed for a moment, then said, "Or maybe it's just watching."

Martin snorted. "Thanks for that."

When the women returned, arms full of groceries and cheeks pink from the wind, the cameras were online, and the fire had been lit inside. The house didn't have an honest fireplace, but what the potbelly stove lost in atmosphere it more than made up with heat. Martin and Mr. West sat on the couch with a couple of beers and the Cowboys game murmuring from the TV.

The warmth in the house was thick and pleasant. Outside, the breeze calmed.

Then came the knock.

Three firm raps. Not hurried. Not hesitant.

Martin muted the game. Mr. West looked at the door.

Neither moved at first.

Then Martin stood. "I'll get it."

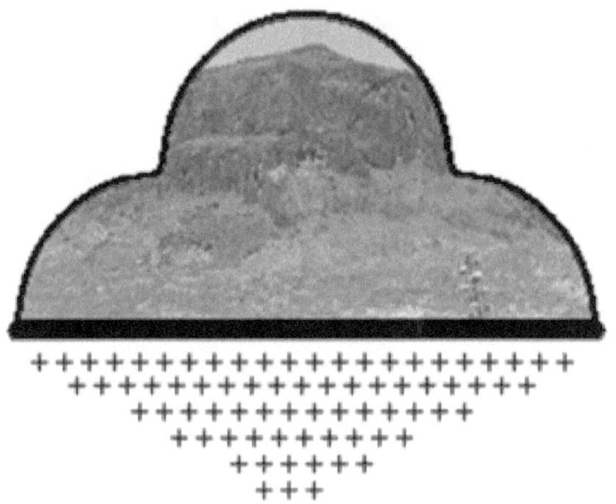

Chapter 30
A Veil of Stones

Leaving the hinges to creak open, Martin stepped back from the door as Sheriff Villareal appeared, hat in hand, and beside him, a tall man in a dark wool coat. His hair was long and streaked with silver, tied back neatly at the neck. His face bore the quiet gravity of age and memory, creased not just by time but by weather, wisdom, and grief.

"Afternoon, Martin," the sheriff said. "Sorry to drop by unannounced."

Martin stepped aside. "Come in. It's cold out."

The stranger offered his hand. "My name is Chayton Altaha. I've come from the Mescalero Reservation. My mother's people were Lipan Apache. My father's, Mescalero. I serve both now."

Mr. West stood from the couch, shaking hands with a curious smile. "Pleasure to meet you."

Martin gestured toward the kitchen. "Coffee?"

"Gladly," Chayton said. "It's a long drive from New Mexico when the weather worries you."

While the coffee brewed, Mr. West pulled out an extra chair. The room fell quiet, filled only with the subtle hiss of the heater and the low tick of the wall clock. Laughter and conversation came from the back of the house. Mrs. West and Lindsay were having a good time together with Robert.

Chayton broke the silence with grace. "You did something good, Martin. Both of you. Most people would've turned their back on those bones. Or taken something. You called the sheriff. You waited. You returned what was never yours. That matters to my people."

He reached into his coat and removed a small deerskin pouch bound with a strip of red cloth. "Sweetgrass, cedar, and ash from our last ceremony. Keep it in your home."

Martin accepted it, since he sat closer, with quiet reverence. The scent was earthy, foreign, but oddly comforting.

Before he could speak, a sudden *crack* jolted the room. Something hit the roof, a sharp, solid strike, loud enough to make them all freeze.

"That wasn't the wind," Mr. West said.

Martin was already heading for the door.

Out on the porch, the air was colder, heavier. A lone raven stood at the peak of the roof, black feathers glossy under the sunlight. At its feet, a smooth, rounded stone rolled slowly toward the gutter.

Martin exhaled, half a laugh. "I swear, if that bird's trying to pay rent in rocks, it's going to need a whole lot more."

Chayton stepped up beside him and raised a hand. He began speaking softly in Apache, the words fluid and rhythmic, half chant, half conversation.

The raven tilted its head but didn't flee. It cawed once, sharp and harsh, and flapped its wings without leaving.

When Chayton finished, he turned to the others. "Ravens are not just birds. In our traditions, they are watchers, tricksters, messengers. They cross between the worlds. They bring warnings… or guidance."

Martin looked up at the roof again, suddenly aware of the weight of the land around them.

Chayton continued, "This land is trying to tell you something. The spirit found here may still have a message."

They lingered outside for a moment longer before retreating to the warmth of the house.

Back inside, Martin poured another cup of coffee and asked, "Do you think… is there any chance the man we found had a name? Something recorded somewhere? Looking for information about an Apache named Storm upon Meadow."

Chayton nodded slowly. "It's possible. I don't recognize that name. I know of a book, written in 1906 by a man sent by the government to record us, our stories, our arrival on the lands given to us. It mentions several Lipan families who fled these mountains. Oral histories, written in his words. I'll look through it."

Martin nodded, grateful. "Even a name would be something."

A moment later, Sheriff Villareal stood, glancing at his phone. "We've gotta get moving. If that snow really rolls in early, I don't want to be on the roads past sundown."

Moments later, the four men stepped down off the porch. The cold had deepened, and clouds were stacking on the northern horizon.

Chayton clasped Martin's shoulder once, firm and meaningful. "Listen to your land. It remembers."

As the two visitors stepped into the sheriff's truck and pulled away, Martin and Mr. West stood watching until the taillights vanished down the dirt road.

From above, the raven cawed again, this time louder, more urgent, wings flaring as it hopped along the peak of the roof. Not flying away. Watching.

Martin looked up at it and felt the hair on his arms rise despite the cold.

"Yeah," he muttered, "we're listening."

A brief pause allowed the two remaining men to hear the silence. "Well we'd best be getting down the road. The forecast says the snow starts in Big Spring after midnight," said Mr. West as both turned to go back inside.

****

The snow began drifting into the goat corral just after breakfast on Sunday, soft at first with just a few lazy flakes drifting past the kitchen window. By late that evening, it was falling in thick curtains, blanketing the scrub and catclaw in soft white silence. Martin and Lindsay stood outside under the patio light, breath rising in clouds, watching in awe.

"I feel like a kid again," Lindsay whispered.

Martin scooped up a handful and tossed it skyward. "You *are* a kid. I'm a kid. We just don't get snow often enough to treat it like adults."

It was true. Out here in the Davis Mountains, snow like this was rare, *this much* snow almost unheard of. San Angelo had already reported six inches. At their house in the Davis Mountains were soon pushing eight, and it was still coming down. Martin spent the afternoon moving the goats back to the livestock barn, a challenge on a dry day made even more difficult with the thick, white blanket now covering the ground.

Lindsay disappeared into the kitchen and reappeared a few minutes later with a bowl, carefully gathering clean snow from the back railing. A splash of milk, a little sugar, and a touch of vanilla later, she handed Martin a spoon.

"Snow cream," she said, smiling. "Only the second time I've ever had it."

They stood barefoot just inside the door, eating dessert from winter's hand, giggling between bites. The school district alert came in around nine that night. Classes canceled across Jeff Davis County. They cheered like students.

****

Monday morning, the world was still. The storm had passed overnight, leaving behind a pale new world. Snow coated the ground in every direction, a soft silence pressing against the windows.

Lindsay padded to the nursery and lifted the curtain. Her breath caught.

"Martin."

He stirred from bed. "Hmm?"

"Jobella's out."

Martin sat up. "What?"

"She's just standing there… in that same spot."

He joined her at the window. Sure enough, the mare stood motionless in the exact area where the dirt had been scraped away during the skeleton's removal. Snow outlined her hooves. The gate to the pen was closed, but the livestock barn door wasn't. Goats enjoyed frolicking in the snow covered corral.

Martin dressed quickly, kissed Lindsay and Robert, and headed out. Dumpsy the cat watched from the windowsill, tail flicking as if puzzled by this frozen new world.

Once dressed Martin grabbed the harness on his way out the door. Jobella kept doing the same thing for so long it was almost a habit to keep a harness inside. Outside, Martin trudged through eight inches of powder, boots crunching softly. The air was sharp and blue with cold, the sky pale with cloud-filtered light.

As he approached, he froze.

There, on Jobella's broad back, rested a raven.

It stood calmly, feathers puffed slightly against the cold. The mare didn't flinch.

Martin narrowed his eyes. The horse… she was just standing still, she was facing northwest, toward the far corner of the property. Toward the dry wash. Toward where the natural ramp had been before the 1978 flood.

And then he saw it.

Rocks.

A ring of them….no, a box around the horse, a rectangular box with somewhat rounded corners. Maybe five or six feet wide. Dozens of smooth, red rhyolite stones, each roughly the same size and shape, arranged with eerie care around the mare. Martin blinked, stepped back, pulled his phone from his pocket, and snapped a picture.

Jobella turned her head. So did the raven.

He approached slowly. As he drew close enough to touch her, the raven gave a single, harsh caw and burst into the sky, banking westward on slow wings.

Martin slipped a lead around Jobella's neck and guided her back to the pen. The latch clicked shut behind her this time, and he gave it an extra tug. He was now confident that Jobella was playing steeplechase with the shorter fence meant to hold the goats. Still stunned, he turned back to the oblong rectangle of stones.

It was a message. He returned to it.

He stepped inside the formation and slowly turned in place.

Facing northwest, he looked toward the dry wash, where they'd marked the final corner stake. Then he turned southeast. There, rising in the distance, was the tallest point of the ridgeline. Farther than the stake and outside the property boundary.

The angles connected. He looked back behind him now, to where the skeleton had been found.

And it clicked.

The shot.

The bullet had come from that ridge. Fired from above, across the flats. It was a sniper's perch. A military shot. The circle of rocks is where the bullet had struck but not killed the Apache.

Suddenly, as if memory itself surged through the earth, a vision overtook him. The sound came first, not a gunshot, but a distant, suppressed *pop*. Then the crack of the bullet hitting flesh, louder than the report. He saw a Lipan Apache warrior, riding tall amid this pasture strangely devoid of everything except grasses . . . and silence

when a bullet struck him in the back. Then he saw the Whitworth. The vision focused on the rifle and this land.

The land never forgot. And that rifle . . .it wasn't just a weapon . . .it was the keystone. Without it, the act never would've been committed. Without it, maybe the ghost wouldn't linger. The shot that killed the Apache didn't just end a life, it anchored something here.

Martin gasped, staggered slightly in the snow.

The rocks. The horse. The raven. All pointing him to this.

Chapter 31
A Raven and a Horse

A blast of warm air hit Martin as he stepped inside, boots heavy with snow and his mind still reeling from what he'd seen. Lindsay looked up from the kitchen, where Robert gurgled happily in his bassinet near the heater.

"Well?" she asked.

Martin shook his head slowly. "You're not going to believe this."

She listened quietly as he recounted everything, the horse standing in the same spot again, the raven perched on her back, the oblong rectangle of carefully arranged stones. Then, the way both animals turned to look at him… and how the raven flew off only when he was close enough to touch them. He described stepping inside the ring and realizing it pointed northwest to the old ramp site, and if you turned 180, southeast, toward the high ridge beyond the stake. And then, the vision. The shot.

Lindsay blinked slowly, processing. "Martin…" she began gently, "you didn't eat any of that snow cream before I added the milk, did you? I don't remember Vanilla flavoring having that much alcohol in it."

He smiled faintly but didn't answer.

She leaned against the counter. "Okay. First of all, you know ravens are in almost every native culture I've studied. They're *tricksters*, Martin, just like Chayton said. Mischief-makers. Story-stealers. They're not spirits of vengeance or destiny. Pick any tribe from the plains and the stories are all similar."

Martin opened his mouth, but she held up a hand, continuing.

"And Jobella? She's not some oracle. She probably likes that spot because there's no catclaw there, and she's away from the goats. She's a horse, not a compass. Maybe she likes the sun on her back?"

"Chayton also said they were messengers," Martin answered. After a few minutes Martin sat down at the computer. He clicked open the footage from the southwest camera they'd mounted on the equipment barn and the scrape site. It wasn't close but it was closer than the house. Lindsay wandered over, still mulling over the events.

"I'm not trying to dismiss what you felt, babe," she said more softly. "But all of this can have other……"

"Just watch," Martin said.

He hit play.

The video was crisp despite the snow flurries. At first, nothing moved. Then, from the left side of the frame, the raven appeared, hopping deliberately across the snowy ground. It stopped and dropped a stone. Then another. Then a third. With eerie precision, it arranged a line. Then a curve. It worked with quick, purposeful movements, stepping back, and even adjusting the shape.

Lindsay leaned in as he gave her the computer mouse.

Minutes passed. The shape took form. The raven paced once around it, wings flaring briefly, and then it hopped up onto the fence rail and sat.

And then, out of the trees at the edge of the frame… came Jobella.

Alone.

She walked straight to the oval and stood inside it.

Lindsay inhaled sharply.

On screen, the raven hopped lightly onto the horse's back and settled, perfectly still.

He saw Lindsay's hand freeze on the mouse. For a long moment, she didn't say a word.

Then, quietly, "Forget everything I just said."

Martin turned toward her. "It's not just me?"

She shook her head. "No. It's not just you. It's too weird."

Outside, snow still clung to every branch, but something deeper had settled inside their home, a sense of something watching, guiding, and perhaps, demanding to be heard.

****

The house was quiet except for the hum of the DVD player and the soft dialogue of the film drifting through the living room. Martin sat with his feet propped on the coffee table, cradling a mug of tea, half-watching the movie. Lindsay curled up at the other end of the couch, the soft light from a reading lamp illuminating the worn leather journal in her lap. Mrs. West sat between them, knitting needles clicking faintly in the rhythm of habit while the baby monitor glowed on the end table beside her.

Robert had gone down easily that evening, finally settled into something like a routine. Martin didn't dare jinx it by saying so aloud.

Lindsay flipped another page, brow furrowed, trailing a finger under the tight, cramped script. Her lips moved silently as she read. Then she stopped, eyes narrowing. The room's warmth and comfort seemed to vanish around her.

Martin noticed immediately. "What?"

She didn't answer at first. Instead, she turned the journal, reading a short poem scratched across the page in heavy, slanted script. Then, she said, softly but clearly, "He admits it here."

Mrs. West lowered her knitting. "Admits what, dear?"

"O'Brannach. He killed someone. Says it plain as day. Says he killed a man who only wanted peace. He was tormented before, but this is a confession. A man with honor. Then he writes that the rifle is cursed, he sees the spirit in the gun. He says a man's soul was bound to the weapon. That he can't be free of it."

Martin muted the television and turned to face her. "Does he say who? A name perhaps?"

Lindsay sighed, flipping back a few pages. "That's the part that's confusing. The end of the journal is messy. He was clearly drinking. There are sections where the writing devolves into gibberish. One whole page looks like he spilled liquor on it."

She tapped a line with her finger. "But here, this is legible. He says the man's name was *Storm upon Meadow*. That happened just south of a place called 'Old Camp.' Said the Apache there had agreed to stay peaceful, stay out of trouble, and the fort left them alone. As long as they didn't steal cattle or raid settlers."

Martin leaned forward, hands clasped. "Then that's not the skeleton on our land."

"What makes you say that?" asked Mrs. West, sitting up.

He looked between them. "You think he shot this man while he was riding away. From a ridge. You don't shoot a man in the back and then go introduce yourself. He wouldn't have known the guy's name unless . . ."

"Unless he knew him already," Lindsay said.

"Exactly. If he didn't know him, how'd he learn his name? And how would he know it was him from a shot half-way across the county?" Martin stood and began to pace slowly. "Our skeleton? If it's Storm upon Meadow, then how did O'Brannach know? He didn't exactly shoot first and asked questions later. He just shot."

Lindsay looked back down at the page and slowly closed the journal. "Then Storm upon Meadow *isn't* the man buried here…was buried here" she corrected quickly.

Martin stopped mid-step. "That means…"

He didn't get to finish the sentence.

A rapid-fire staccato *THUMP-THUMP-THUMP* rattled the walls of the house, starting at the east side and circling around like footsteps slamming into siding in quick succession. The walls seemed to vibrate with each hit.

Mrs. West screamed, her knitting tumbling to the floor. From the monitor, a shrill wail pierced the room, Robert was crying.

Martin bolted for the back door, wrenching it open and stepping into the cold night. The wind had picked up again. A few high clouds skidded across a half-moon sky. But no one was there.

He looked toward the animal pen.

All the goats were huddled in a tight cluster at the west end of the enclosure. Jobella stood pressed against the fence, ears back,

eyes fixed on the house, her breath made visible by condensation, but coming in short, hard bursts. All of them stared at the house like an audience waiting for the curtain to rise.

Martin stepped out onto the back patio and immediately spotted it.

The coaxial cable. The one he'd buried repeatedly was back on the surface, snaked along the dirt in a single, exposed line, leading from the satellite receiver toward the middle of the house.

Something had pulled it up again.

He bent slowly, touching it, feeling the cold of it under his fingers. It wasn't from a recent rain or erosion.

Chapter 32
What the Glass Holds

Night had finally lost its grip. February was the month the days grew longer by leaps and bounds. The wind moved softly now, and the pale blue sky hinted at a season long delayed. A new season, a new day. With each sunrise, the sun crept a little farther north, a quiet reminder that everything changes. Cold winds had given way to cooler whispers, and the land seemed to exhale.

Lindsay stirred before the alarm and eased out of bed quietly. She stood at the edge of the mattress for a moment, listening to the baby monitor's soft hiss, then glanced at Martin. He was still out cold, one arm thrown over his head, the other curled toward the pillow like a man who hadn't slept well in days.

She tiptoed to the dresser, pulling her robe loose and letting it drop away, careful not to bump the end table where Dumpsy was already awake and in full play mode.

The cat had found a tube of lipstick, an older tube she thought she'd lost, and was now batting it across the floor like a hockey puck. She had last used it at Angelo State during her senior year. It was called "Cochineal Red" which she had found hilarious, since Cochineal insects were definitely not that color. The purple liquid that came from those bugs was a favorite of the southwest Indians for war paint she remembered from Mr. Vicker's high school history class.

Lindsay rolled her eyes, then decided to leave it be. "I'll get it after the shower, gremlin, have your fun," she whispered, disappearing into the master bathroom with a soft click of the door.

Martin grunted and turned over at the sound of plastic skittering across wood. "Dumpsy . . . " he mumbled groggily for a few more minutes of sleep.

The cat was relentless. With a few more enthusiastic swats, he sent the lipstick tube bouncing once, twice, and then it vanished. Right under the bathroom door.

Martin sat up, blinking.

"You little weirdo," he muttered, yawning. "Leave her alone."

Dumpsy had stopped moving. He stood frozen, staring at the bathroom door with his tail fluffed and twitching, like something had startled him. He backed away with deliberate, stiff-legged steps.

Martin rubbed his face. "Silly cat," he said, swinging his legs over the side of the bed. He proceeded to dress.

The house was quiet except for the soft whisper of the shower and the baby monitor's faint buzz.

Then came the scream.

Sharp. Human. Lindsay.

Martin lunged to his feet, heart punching into his throat as he crashed through the door of the bathroom, the handle slamming into the drywall.

Lindsay stood there, clutching a towel to her chest, water dripping from her hair, eyes wide and locked on the mirror above the sink.

"Look!" she gasped, one hand shaking as she pointed.

Across the fogged mirror was a single drawing, perfectly scrawled in red lipstick.

A rifle.

But not just any rifle.

The long barrel, the distinct thinness, and etched into the stock in uneven lines a familiar jagged scratch.

Martin didn't need to ask what it was.

The lipstick tube lay below in the sink, uncapped, empty, the last of its color used to draw that impossible image.

No smudges. No fingerprints. No signs that it had been touched by human hands.

Just the unmistakable image.

The Whitworth rifle.

Complete with the scar across the cheek plates of the wooden stock.

Martin's breath left him in a rush. Lindsay didn't speak again. Neither did he.

Dumpsy meowed once, low and strange, from the bedroom beyond.

The room was silent except for the dripping water and the soft taps of the cooling pipes behind the wall.

The haunting was back, or maybe it had never departed.

****

By the following weekend, the snow was nothing more than a memory.

West Texas had shrugged off winter with its usual disregard for transition . . . ninety degrees and bone-dry, the snowmelt long gone, the hills baked in dust and sun.

Brian rolled into the yard Saturday morning, his truck rattling with more fencing panels and a trailer in tow. Five new goats clattered nervously inside the mobile pen.

"Figured if y'all are going to play ghost detective, someone better keep the herd growing," he joked, stepping down in his worn hat and mirrored sunglasses. "Also, I missed Jobella." He tipped his hat toward the nearby horse.

The plan was simple: move the temporary pen to a new area, let the goats clear more brush, and then spend the afternoon checking on the cameras and revisiting the ridgeline. The sun was already punishing by midday when they finished wrestling the panels into place, but both men agreed that there was one more thing they needed to do.

As they climbed into the Gator with cold water bottles retrieved from the refrigerator and the 30.06 rifle bag in tow, Martin explained how he got permission from Mr. Miller to drive high up the ridge.

First stop: the first stake. Just to say hello. Then they wound uphill, the tires scrabbling over sun-bleached rock and scattered dead agave leaves as they ascended the ridgeline northeast of the property. No fences up here. No signs. Just land, old and wide.

They turned almost ninety degrees to the south once they arrived at the NE property stake. Travelling to the southeast took them quickly onto the Miller's property. The Gator UTV never struggled, but the steepness of the climb up the ridge was unsettling to both passengers, especially when one of the wheels slipped on the loose rocks that covered most of the ridge.

Noticing the fresh evidence left by a cow near their path, Brian thought out loud. "How did Miller's cattle get up here? Fly?"

Martin considered the question and was just a s baffled as Brian, "Don't know, the Jumping Cows of Jeff Davis County mystery? See the Marfa Lights and then see the levitating cows that made them… At least they're not going down that slope we just climbed and getting on the property."

Brian smiled at the reply and wiped the sweat from his forehead.

Within a few minutes they had climbed hundreds of feet higher and were well off the property. They parked near a stunted cedar tree and walked until Martin found the spot. He checked his phone's GPS for the marker he'd pinned the week it snowed: the rough center of the stone oval in the snow. There was no trace of it now. Just dirt, grass, and red rhyolite poking up everywhere else.

Martin unzipped the soft case and pulled out his bolt-action .30-06. "Besides being three thousand feet away, let's see what the ghost's location looks like from here. I brought some steel jacket rounds."

Down below, they'd stacked an old tire and a few rusted oil cans where the oval had been. A distant makeshift target, if nothing else.

With the scope dialed in, Martin took the first shot while Brian used the binoculars kept with the Gator. The rifle cracked, echoing across the field below. Dust puffed behind the target, wide right.

Brian took the next shot. Miss, but without a confirming cloud of dust it was exceptionally hard to tell.

"Even with the scope, this is guessing," Martin admitted. "We're shooting blind."

Brian agreed. "This is an impossible shot without practice, lots and lots of practice. Windage and drop play a much larger role here."

Martin nodded and cycled the bolt.

They alternated shooter and spotter position with each shot.

Then Brian shouted, "*Cease fire!*"

Martin froze, finger straight off the trigger. "What?"

"Look, down there. It's Jobella, she's out again."

Sure enough, the mare had somehow escaped again. She stood just beyond the target zone, picking her way calmly across the clearing. They watched, stunned, as she reached the spot where the oval had once been.

And then, impossibly, she began to *nudge* the tires. One at a time. Gently, deliberately.

In the time it took the men to race back down the hill, she had scattered every object away from near where the skeleton was recovered.

When Jobella saw them, she gave one short huff, circled once, and resumed her silent vigil standing exactly where she'd stood during the snow. Facing northwest. Toward the former grave of the Apache. Toward the dry wash.

They didn't speak. Not at first.

They guided her back to the barn, secured the pen latch twice, and then stood in the heat, staring at the empty patch of dirt she'd returned to over and over again.

Finally, Martin said, "She's not standing where they dug up the skeleton . . .That's thirty feet over there," he said as he pointed to the northwest. "Let's dig here. Not where the body was removed. Let's dig here where Jobella keeps standing."

****

It took less than twenty minutes. About a foot down, Brian's shovel clanged against a rock. After a few more attempts he brought the rock up and a mass next to it. Martin knelt and brushed away the dirt and dust.

A water pouch. Deerskin, stitched with sinew, its shape still intact. It was much larger than the pouch he remembered the sheriff showing him. Except for the missing wooden plug, it was preserved by the rock above it and protected from scavengers. Carefully, Martin lifted it out and set it aside.

Something else gleamed at the bottom of the hole.

Brian reached in and came up with another Morgan Silver Dollar. He brushed at the coin with his hand as well as blowing on it. The date was 1887.

"That's three Morgan silver dollars now, total," Martin exhaled slowly. "This was someone's cache. Maybe what they carried to trade. Or to escape?"

Brian looked toward the ridge. "Or what got him killed."

Neither said what they were both thinking.

Chapter 33
The Sky Returned Fire

Despite the hum of the air conditioner, heat pressed against the windows as Martin assembled lunch, while Lindsay fed the baby. Martin layered thick slices of turkey on bread while Lindsay cradled Robert in one arm, feeding him from a bottle. The baby kicked lightly at the table leg, sucking greedily and making contented little snorts.

"He's all in," Martin grinned, watching his son.

"Doesn't even know there's a sandwich three feet away," Brian said, taking a bite of his own. "Tragic."

Lindsay shifted Robert upright to burp him. "He'll get there. We'll corrupt him with grilled cheese soon enough."

They retold the events from that morning, setting up their makeshift target, driving up the ridge, firing from the elevation. When Martin described Jobella nudging the tires out of the ghostly oval, Lindsay went still.

"She cleared the circle?" she asked.

"Cleaned it," Brian confirmed. "Like it offended her."

Martin nodded. "And stood right in the middle, just like last time. Same direction. Same posture."

Brian added with a laugh, "We don't even know where the shots went now. For all we know, one hit a boulder.... in Marfa someone's blaming aliens."

Just then, a sharp *clink* sounded on the metal roof above them.

They froze.

Unlike the earlier rock strikes, this one rolled. A clear metallic sound skidded down the incline and dropped somewhere near the front of the house.

Brian was on his feet instantly.

He reached the porch just in time to see the object bounce once and land in the dirt with a dull *thud*. The raven, if it had been there, was already gone, no trace of movement, no dark shadow.

He crouched, picked it up, and stared.

Then he looked up slowly and called out, "Martin? You need to see this."

Martin stepped outside, Lindsay right behind him with Robert still in her arms.

Brian held out his hand.

In his palm lay a clean, shiny steel .30-06 round. Still new looking. Identical to the ones they'd fired from Martin's rifle just hours ago.

Martin stared at it. "That's impossible."

"I know," Brian said. "And yet…here it is. Just like that."

The three of them stood on the porch and looked at the round intensively, as if they expected it to begin moving.

The raven appeared from the other side of the roof, in flight. Flaring its wings it alighted near the peak of the roof, something clearly in its mouth. With a toss of its head followed by a release the next round began its journey rolling down toward them. The raven cawed and flapped its wings before settling down and tucking in its wings. The bird had landed nearly where the first bullet had come from, only moments earlier. The bullet rolled off the edge of the roof where Martin simply caught it before striking the ground. What mass it lacked was more than compensated for by surprise.

"Two bullets," Lindsay whispered. "No way."

"How would a raven even *find* that?" Martin muttered. "Even if it could smell the brass or, hell, I don't know, track heat, it would be buried. I bet the bullets weren't landing anywhere near where the horse moved stuff."

Another loud caw from the jet black raven and it launched off the roof to fly away toward the other side of the house. The three adults entered back inside, sharing ideas.

"Okay," Brian said, rubbing his forehead, "hear me out, what if we spread out pieces of paper numbered one to sixty-seven across the yard and see what six come back? Then we just have to buy a ticket with those numbers and change the bonus ball, one for each bonus and we're in the money!"

Martin chuckled despite himself. "Fair enough. We might win the lottery."

"Only brought two back," Lindsay stated.

"With about the same odds as lightning striking twice," answered Brian as he sat down to resume his sandwich eating. Lindsay placed the two bullets on a folded kitchen towel and placed in on the counter that separated the kitchen from the living room.

Then came the knock.

Sheriff Villareal stood at the door, dusty hat in hand. "Afternoon. Came to pick up that water pouch y'all called about. You three were just outside."

Martin opened the door and allowed the Sheriff inside.

As Martin stepped aside to let him in, *clang*, a third round rolled down the roof and landed with a dull *tap* on the ground the raven caw-cawing as it flew off towards the former gravesite and was out of sight from the front side. Sheriff Villareal heard the noise and watched as it fell off the roof, near the expanded metal porch. A few steps later, he picked it up, looking back toward the roof with a puzzled expression.

"Sheriff, I'm not sure how to start with this," began Martin, who was now on the porch as the Sheriff walked over to enter.

Lindsay met them in the living room as she stepped around from the counter.

"This is the third one," Lindsay said, holding out the towel like evidence. Villareal picked one up slowly, as if it might vanish in his fingers.

"We shot those this morning and that Raven has found three of them! Time to call in world records people!" said Brian.

"Uh huh," he said finally. "That's impossible."

"No kidding," Martin replied, "We shot five rounds from the ridge east of here down to near where the skeleton had been. I think the body that was found on our land was sniped from the ridge to our southeast."

"Right," the sheriff murmured. "Makes sense. And the raven is returning the bullets?"

"Ravens. It appears so, and we missed the target wide. Half-mile shots are tricky," answered Martin. Sheriff Villareal wanted to ask why, but the question wasn't developing quickly. In a tribute to all of the Star Trek reruns he watched growing up, he raised a single eyebrow.

"We were seeing how difficult that shot would be," Brian spoke before biting into his lunch.

"That's the darndest thing I've seen," replied Villareal as he returned the bullet to the towel and added the third, "I'm here for the artifact?"

Martin retrieved the item and the Morgan Silver dollar as well and showed him. He examined the beadwork with care, nodding slowly. "This is the real deal. Intact, intricate. Best-preserved one I've ever seen. I'll get it to the tribe. But the coin, you can keep that. Not an artifact under the law."

As he stepped back onto the porch with the pouch in hand, a fourth bullet began its journey and rolled off the roof to land just to his left a few feet.

He repeated his earlier motions. Looked at it.

"How many rounds did you shoot?" he asked still looking at where the Raven had been.

"Five, sir."

A puzzled look crossed Villareal's face.

"Can I see the others again? The one inside?"

Brian disappeared inside and came out a few moments later with the other rounds delivered by the raven.

Sheriff Villareal looked at each carefully.

"Well," he began, "all of these rounds were shot by the same gun. I have heard of ravens and crows delivering items to people that fed them...Ya'll aren't feeding it are you?"

Martin shook his head.

"Many rounds? I mean, Have you been shooting a lot of targets out here?"

"Just five this morning. My 30.06 with a seven mag scope." Answered Martin.

Then, as if on cue, the raven arrived and the fifth and final round fell, rolling and clinking against the metal and landing squarely in the same area where the others landed.

"That was fast. Is there more than one raven?" asked the sheriff, contemplating every possible angle. The sheriff took a deep breath and looked back toward the ridge, then down at the bullets, then up at Martin. "I'm not writing any of this in my report," he said.

"Just the artifact?" Martin asked.

"Just the artifact," he confirmed. "And even that feels like I'm tempting fate. Weirdest thing I've seen."

He walked over and opened the truck door, the pouch carefully wrapped in a clean towel on the passenger seat.

As he climbed in, he paused, one hand on the steering wheel, the other resting on the door.

Something about this place. About these people. Something *deep*. He couldn't explain it, and he'd learned long ago not to try.

The law required reports. Logic demanded evidence.

But this?

This was different.

He shook his head once, put the truck in gear, and rolled down the long gravel drive, the sun throwing long shadows across the porch.

Sheriff Villareal steered the cruiser along the dark ribbon of Highway 17, the not too distant peaks of the Davis Mountains bruised purple against the sinking sun playing against the orange

Cirrus clouds in a beautiful symphony of colors. The deer skin pouch lay on the passenger seat, its weight small but troubling. Five spent bullets, each accounted for, yet somehow returned like a message sent from a hand unseen. He rubbed a thumb across his jaw, feeling the bristle of a day's tension.

None of it made sense. Ravens dropping ammunition. And that the ranch kept turning up in the middle of things. How would he write this incident up? Another strange event tacked onto a growing list of things he'd rather not explain to Austin.

Villareal let out a slow breath.

No. He wasn't putting any of this in writing, not the ravens, not the bullets, not the possibility that something older than any of them still prowled those rocks. The only thing he'd document was the retrieval of the artifact. Beyond that, this was one of those times a man kept his own counsel.

As the rooftops of Fort Davis appeared ahead, Villareal tightened his grip on the wheel. Some truths, he decided, were better left unpenned.

****

After a snack and some time with Robert, they sat at the kitchen table with the laptop open between them, the footage looping quietly.

"It's the same bird, right?" Brian said.

Martin nodded. "Pretty sure. I only see the one flying in from near the gravesite. I can't see exactly where it settles each time, but it flies to a particular area, sometimes twenty feet away, and recovers something from the ground."

"Twenty feet off? Must be your bullets," quipped Brian.

Martin exchanged grins along with sharing an eye roll with Brian.

Brian leaned in, his brow furrowed. "Okay, but why? What's it doing? It's not random. It's not just flying in and dropping shiny stuff. That's a bullet. That's intentional."

Martin hesitated. "Maybe it's trying to warn us."

Brian shook his head. "No. Warnings come with urgency. This thing is . . . steady. Precise. It drops one, then flies right back out there."

He sat back, crossing his arms. "Animals don't act like that unless something's guiding them. Not unless they're part of something."

Martin looked down at the five bullets still on the table. They hadn't rolled or moved. Just sat there, heavy and quiet.

Brian spoke again, softer this time. "You ever think it's not trying to scare us? Maybe it's trying to make us understand. Whatever it is . . . it's choosing the raven. And that raven's choosing us."

Outside, the wind stirred the porch light in a slow, steady rhythm.

Neither man moved.

Chapter 34
The Lesson Remembered

Sitting at her desk, Lindsay enjoyed the morning spring-scented breeze through the window. The scent of early spring drifted through light, dry, and sweet with sun-warmed mesquite. Outside, birds chirped busily in the courtyard, building nests in the crevices under the eaves like nothing had ever been wrong with the world.

It had been weeks since the last bullet had rolled off the roof.

Since then, nothing. Several weeks of nothing.

No strange noises, no phantom scents, no tools going missing or coax cable yanked from the ground. Even Jobella had stopped her midnight excursions to near the old burial site. She'd gone nowhere near it since winter faded. Not once.

Lindsay had promised Melody she'd keep the mare exercised and trail-ready, but she'd yet to climb in the saddle. And she reminded herself with a wry smile, it was starting to show in both of them.

She flipped through a stack of quizzes and scribbled a few comments, her red pen moving with automatic ease. *Manifest Destiny* this, *Sherman's March* that. Her thoughts drifted to the ridge, to the hidden violence that still slept in their land. Peace had begun to feel like forgetting. How quickly peace began to feel like forgetting. A soft knock at the door broke the stillness.

She looked up.

Principal Arturo Mendez poked his head into the room. "Mrs. Eastman, got a minute?"

"Of course. Come in."

He stepped in with a smile stretched wide across his face, the kind he usually reserved for graduation day or Friday afternoon football wins.

"I just got off the phone with the United States History Teachers Association," he said, almost reverent. "Lindsay, you won. United States History Teachers Association's Rookie Teacher of the Year!"

She blinked, stunned. "What?"

"You *won*," he said again, practically bouncing. "You beat out high school teachers from Boston, Chicago, even one from the Smithsonian-affiliated charter in D.C. It's official. You'll be honored at the conference out at the State Park in April."

Before she could speak, a sudden *blast* of music erupted in the hallway. Horns. Drums. Someone in the percussion section was slightly off, but it didn't matter, her students had learned Queen's *We Are the Champions* just well enough for the moment.

Lindsay stood, half-laughing, half-teary.

Then came the PTA president, Mr. Casarez, bursting through the door like a sitcom entrance. He held out a vibrant bouquet of wildflowers, sunflowers, Indian blanket, even a few bluebonnets just starting to bloom.

"For the best history teacher we've ever had," he said, proudly.

Behind him came the other teachers, Mrs. Hartman from English, Coach Reyes, even the shy algebra sub with the cracked glasses. Applause erupted. Someone popped one of those mini confetti cannons with questionable results.

Lindsay clutched the bouquet to her chest as confetti drifted lazily to the floor. Someone handed her a soda. A student from the band wheezed into a trumpet with more enthusiasm than pitch, but the spirit of it was impossible not to love. Smiling faces filled her classroom, students peeking in, teachers crowding the doorway, everyone talking at once.

She turned back to Principal Mendez, blinking past tears and laughter.

"Wait, when did they call you?"

He grinned, unapologetic. "Yeah… just off the phone…" Then, with a slight shrug and a smirk: "Yesterday, but it was Susan that did a lot of the footwork. She submitted pictures of that day you took your classes to meet the reenactors at the fort. You didn't know it, but half those reenactors are on the school board, the city council, or both. Susan did you a favor when she invited Marfa and Alpine out, too. Turns out those teachers wrote recommendations as well."

She looked shocked as the music hit another key change.

He leaned in to speak over the din. "They'll present it at the lodge in the state park, late April. Big banquet we will put together. Plenty of people flying into Midland or El Paso to be here."

Then he added, more sincerely, "We're proud of you, Lindsay. You earned it."

The crowd cheered louder, and Lindsay laughed again, heart full, throat tight.

For now, everything felt… right.

Chapter 35
Framed in Light

Turning off the county road, Martin rolled down the long gravel drive, mentally debating whether it was a pasta or taco kind of evening. The goats were grazing contentedly in the temp pen, and the house looked peaceful, at least from a distance.

Then he saw it.

A white van was parked beside the house, gleaming in the afternoon sun. On its side, emblazoned in bright vinyl graphics, was the unmistakable logo of the regional TV news station out of Alpine. Satellite dish raised, camera tripod set up nearby.

Martin hit the brakes halfway up the drive.

"Oh… my *God*," he muttered.

His first thought, no, his *certainty*, was that something had leaked. The bullets. The raven. The grave. The Apache elder's visit. Somehow, the supernatural chain of events had reached the news, and now they were parked on *his* land, ready to film ghost-hunting B-roll.

He stared at the truck a moment longer, stomach tightening. Indian remains? Some internet theory gone viral?

Then he remembered the telephone call that had occurred in the middle of sixth hour. Then he heard the confirmation he needed to hear, the soft buzz of a reporter's voice carried faintly on the breeze.

"…local teacher of the year, a rising star in the field of public education…"

Martin blinked. He stepped out of the car slowly, moving with deliberate care, as if approaching someone else's house instead of his own. He kept low, circling wide through the gravel, and paused at the corner of the double-wide, heart ticking in his throat. "…award to be presented in April in Fort Davis…"

He risked a peek.

There was Lindsay, standing on the front porch with Robert in her arms, smiling politely as a young reporter with aggressively styled hair nodded along. A camerawoman adjusted a mic on Lindsay's collar while the PTA president hovered awkwardly nearby, clearly thrilled to be part of the scene.

Martin exhaled in relief and amusement. It had nothing to do with bullets or ravens.

It was just Lindsay. Being brilliant. Being recognized.

Still, rather than insert himself into the middle of the lights and cameras, he circled quietly around the side of the house, stepped through the back door, and opened the fridge.

"Tacos," he said to no one. "Definitely tacos."

He pulled out the ground beef and set a pan on the stove, the sizzle of onion in oil soon replacing the muffled questions and answers coming from out front.

And as the sun slid low across the Davis Mountains, Martin chopped tomatoes with a quiet smile, his home, for the moment, just a little more normal than it had been in weeks.

****

The room was quiet now, the only sound the soft ticking from the mantle clock in the front living room and the gentle hum of the heater cycling air overhead. Outside, the gibbous moon was dodging fast moving clouds. It was waning but still produced enough light that shadows were still real, still brightening and darkening the house windows. The shadows in the room were long and soft, pooling around the edges of the furniture like forgotten questions.

Martin lay beside Lindsay, one hand resting on her stomach, fingers idly tracing the hem of her tank top. The sheets were tangled around their legs, neither of them bothering to fix it. The air held the faint scent of sage and skin and hints of moisture.

"I keep wondering," Martin said, his voice low, "if leaving our jobs, that little apartment… the college life, was the right call."

Lindsay turned toward him, one arm tucked under her cheek. "You mean moving out here?"

He nodded. "Yeah. I mean, I love the quiet, I do. And I love the land, even the parts of it that are a damn tangle of thorns and boulders. But lately, I've been thinking… what if we're wrong? What if we're trying to live a life that doesn't want us here?"

She didn't answer at first.

"But I have these ideas," Martin went on, his words gathering like small stones. "Things I want to do with this place. Not just goats. Brian got me thinking about vineyards. I've looked into it, you know, on slow days at school. Turns out there are wineries just east of Marfa and up past Fort Stockton. Real ones. People make a living at it."

"You want to grow grapes?" Lindsay asked, not mocking, just surprised.

"Maybe. Maybe not. But it's an idea that doesn't go away. Something with roots. Something to leave behind."

"Ideas that don't go away are called dreams, sweetie. You know you have a thing for the land and being outdoors, right?"

"I do?" Martin sounded half-surprised.

"You didn't mow lawns just to save for college. You used to talk about the challenge of it. You wanted to battle the weeds. A vineyard makes sense, I think you would love it, and I bet my father would love to help you do it, Brian, too."

Lindsay reached out and brushed a finger along his jaw. "It's a beautiful dream, Martin. Really. But maybe… maybe we don't have to *live* here full-time for that to happen. Maybe we manage it from a safer distance."

She hesitated, her voice softening. "Jobella possessed. Animals found at the base of that cliff. Bullets, roofs. There's something here, and it doesn't feel done with us. I was a skeptic, but we know there was a murder here…on this property."

Martin exhaled. "Yeah."

They lay in silence for a few minutes, letting the weight of that truth settle in the room. Then Lindsay stirred, rising slowly from the bed and tugging the sheet around her shoulders. "Come on," she whispered. "Let's go look at him."

Martin followed her barefoot into the nursery. The floor was cool against their feet. A soft orange glow spilled from the baby monitor night light, painting the crib and wall in a warm, quiet hue.

Robert Bruce Eastman lay sleeping on his back, one tiny fist curled near his cheek, his breath steady and slow.

A faint draft from the floor vent stirred the curtain. It lifted just slightly, like something unseen had entered and exited without pause. But the room held only stillness.

The heat had finally kicked on.

Martin reached down and touched the edge of the crib rail with two fingers.

Lindsay leaned her head on his shoulder.

"Whatever happens," she said, "I think we're exactly where we're supposed to be, with him."

Martin looked down at their son, bathed in the amber cast of the night light, the soft curve of his cheek catching the glow. A cloud slid off the moon, and moonlight poured across the crib.

Framed in light.

He closed his eyes and held the moment.

Chapter 36
Brian's Overwatch

Oddly enough, riding the train, it turned out, made Lindsay emotional, even on her first trip. "I didn't think this would be hard," she said softly, still holding Martin's hand as the SUV turned down the gravel drive. "I mean, it's just five days."

"Six, technically," Martin replied, trying to smile but not quite pulling it off.

She elbowed him gently. "You're not helping."

Mrs. West waved from the window; Robert's little face was barely visible behind her as she turned out of sight. Dumpsy's carrier meowed once, faint but clear.

"Do you think he'll remember us?"

"Dumpsy?"

She rolled her eyes. "Robert."

Martin looked toward the sunrise edging over the Davis Mountains. "I think he's going to sleep through most of it and give your mom hell the rest of the time."

Lindsay laughed, wiped the corner of her eye. "Good. I want him to miss me just enough to cry."

Spring Break had arrived like a balm, unexpected and needed. The platform was quiet except for the distant whistle. Somewhere between exhaustion and anticipation, they stood side by side, waiting not to leave something behind, but to find something they'd nearly forgotten how to hold: time together.

Then the train came, and the earth shook gently beneath their feet.

The *Sunset Limited* pulled them west through El Paso, along the fringe of the desert. At Los Angeles, they transferred to the *Coast Starlight*, heading north through green hills and wide beaches, past cliffs that looked like they belonged in another world entirely. Time stretched.

Once the sun cleared the ridge, Brian led Jobella from the barn, the morning light catching on her flanks like brushed gold. The sun had just cleared the eastern ridge, a soft, slanted light cutting across the high desert and pushing the long shadows back toward the canyon. Brian cinched Jobella's saddle straps tight, then patted her neck as he led her from the permanent corral. The spring morning was quiet, still heavy from the storm that had rolled through the night before.

****

Having departed for their spring break trip days earlier, Martin and Lindsay were halfway up the California coast, riding the Coastal

Starlight. Brian had volunteered to house-sit, feed the animals, keep an eye on things, not because he loved chores, but because Lindsay had looked anxious about leaving Jobella. After everything they'd been through that winter, she didn't want to come home to another mess.

Jobella snorted softly and pawed at the ground, ears forward. She was alert, but placid.

Brian mounted up and guided her toward the ridge trail, steep and narrow, the kind of rocky terrain Martin half-joked was only fit for goats and fools. The air still carried the earthy sharpness of acacia and damp soil, punctuated with mesquite and the clean edge of receding storm.

They climbed in silence. At the crest, Brian spotted the white flutter of ribbon tied to the first stake, still in place after the wind. A good sign. He turned Jobella to the west, toward the house and temporary goat pen.

The panels glinted in the sun, but the enclosure itself was still.

Too still.

No goats.

Brian narrowed his eyes, adjusting his posture in the saddle as he scanned the brush. The pen was intact. No broken panels. No loose gates. No disturbed soil. Just… empty.

He muttered under his breath and nudged Jobella into a trot. They cut back down the ridge trail, crossed the Ranch road, and skirted around the back side of the house. Within minutes he was at the pen.

Still no goats.

He dismounted and went inside the pen, circled it once, checking for signs of a breakout, drag marks, chewed fence, hoof prints, but found nothing. The gate at the other end was still latched. The field beyond was undisturbed.

His stomach tightened.

He remounted and turned Jobella towards the west, toward the gully. It was a mile away, but the sickening feeling that swept over him wasn't due to the vicious wall of catclaw that lay ahead.

The trail narrowed, acacia thickened. Spring green clung to the branches like brittle lace. Jobella started resisting, her ears flicking sideways, then flat. She stepped high, nostrils flaring. Her smooth gait grew jittery.

"Easy, girl," Brian said, gripping the reins tighter. "We're just going to take a look."

After nearly an hour of riding slowly through the rough terrain, it was apparent Jobella didn't like the look of anything. Not the path, not the sky, not whatever scent lingered on the breeze. She slowed, then stopped cold. Her muscles twitched beneath the saddle.

And then she started backing up.

"Whoa, easy there girl," Brian said with a reassuring pat on her neck. He brought her to a stop.

Brian dismounted, noticing Jobella's legs were quivering.

"All right, I get it," he muttered, patting her neck. "You're not going any further and I don't blame you. I'll walk from here. "

He walked her to the neighbor's fence line, tied the reins to a post, and gave her a moment to settle.

Then he started forward alone, boots crunching over rock and wet grass, pushing past low limbs and thorny brush.

He walked the remaining fifty feet to the cliff.

And saw them.

All of the goats, scattered like fallen debris in the dry wash below, crumpled against rocks and twisted branches. Some lay together. Others had landed apart, limbs askew. The cliff's shadow still fell across the ravine, keeping the morning sun off their bodies.

He stumbled backward, the edge too close, and sat down hard on the packed earth.

Dead. All of them.

Wind rolled up the gully wall, carrying a smell sharp as iron, tinged with dust and something sour. It curled around Brian's shoulders like a living thing, pressing into his throat. Far below, a piece of a goat hung from a dead mesquite stump that stuck into the air like a dagger, snagged there as though the canyon itself were trying to hold on to the dead. The goat corpse nearest to it void of a back leg and some hide along with showing exposed muscle.

A dark stain spread beneath one of the bodies, soaking into pale gravel. Brian blinked, trying to focus, but his eyes struggled to comprehend the grotesque scene below in the shade.

Somewhere further downstream in the canyon, a raven croaked once, the sound bouncing against the stone wall like a question. Then silence swallowed it whole.

Brian scrubbed a hand over his face. He felt small up there on the rim, as though the land itself was leaning closer to see what he'd do next.

He forced himself to look again. A breeze twisted through the canyon and sent dust spiraling over the goats' still forms. One had fallen in such a way its front legs were folded beneath it, caught like it was kneeling for prayer.

Brian's chest tightened. He crouched lower, squinting into the sun's harsh glare. Here and there, small white glints showed amid the rocks, fragments of horn, or bone, or maybe even teeth. The dry wash smelled wrong, like singed hair and wet goats.

He shivered despite the heat gathering on the ridge.

Below, the canyon walls seemed to breathe, exhaling warm gusts that carried whispers he couldn't quite hear. The silence was pressing now.

"De nashaaa" whispered through the brush. The same thing he had heard back on that first day in August.

Brian wiped sweat from his brow and forced himself upright. His knees wobbled as he stepped back from the cliff's edge. He kept his eyes averted from the drop as he turned toward Jobella.

He had to tell Martin, but he had to get the hell away from this place first.

He gathered the reins, threw one last glance toward the canyon, and swore under his breath.

Chapter 37
The Edge of Enough

Riding the rails in a private bedroom proved to be one of the most enjoyable journeys either had experienced. It gave them room enough to rediscover all the things they loved about each other. Shared headphones. Quiet handholding. Movies on the laptop. Cards in the observation car, laughing like teenagers. Conversations that felt like unburdening. The kind you didn't have time for in the thick of daily life.

They barely mentioned the ranch.

Instead, they talked about the past, the future, silly dreams they hadn't voiced in years. They watched surfers from the windows as the train wound up the Pacific coast and drifted to sleep listening to the rhythmic song of the rails.

But peace, as ever, proved temporary.

It was nearly sunset when Martin's phone vibrated on the fold-out table. Lindsay was deep into a nap, curled up beside him beneath the thin train blanket. The train was climbing into Oregon, trees black against deep orange sky.

The caller ID read *Brian Millrick*.

Martin stepped into the vestibule between cars and answered quietly.

"Hey," he said. "Everything okay?"

"Uh… no, man," Brian replied, his voice serious but calm. "I came down to check on things yesterday, doing my part of the house sitting. Figured I'd make a run to town today, refill the troughs, maybe give Jobella a treat."

Martin leaned against the wall. "And?"

"I found them this morning when I exercised Jobella. All the goats are dead."

The words hit like a jolt. "What?"

"They're at the bottom of the cliff. Every one of them. Same place, same cliff. Like they were herded off it. But the temporary pen was secure. No break, no struggle. The goats were just . . . gone."

Martin ran a hand through his hair. "And Jobella?"

"She's fine. In her stall now. Hadn't seemed worked up until we went near the cliff. She refused to get any closer than about fifty feet. I was riding her when I discovered the goats were missing. Maybe she knew, but I didn't until I looked."

Martin exhaled. "Damn it."

"I'll call a friend in Ozona next week, he's always got extras. But Martin…" Brian hesitated. "I think it's time to call Ghostbusters. I mean it. Hell, I'll pay for the proton packs myself."

Martin barked out a tired laugh. "I'll grab the number next time it's on cable."

"I'm serious, man. This land is cursed or haunted or both. I don't care how many cameras you've got, you can't fence in whatever's doing this."

Martin nodded slowly. "We're flying back Saturday night. The Wests are picking us up, driving us home."

"I'll stick around 'till then. Keep an eye on the place."

"Thanks," Martin said quietly. "When I get there, I'll pull up the video and maybe we can see what happened to the goats. I appreciate it, even if it's bad news."

They hung up.

Back in the roomette, Lindsay stirred when he slipped under the blanket. She blinked sleepily. "Was that Brian?"

Martin nodded. "Yes. Goats are gone. Same spot. Cliff."

Lindsay's brow furrowed. "What about Jobella?"

"She's fine. Still in her stall."

For a long moment they lay in silence, the train rumbling northward under them.

Finally, Lindsay whispered, "We can't keep doing this."

Martin looked over.

She added, "Maybe when we get back… we should ask dad how upset he'd be if we just… moved into town. Fort Davis. Somewhere with sidewalks. Somewhere away from whatever that thing is."

Martin stared at the ceiling, watching the faint shadows slide across the curve of the roof.

He didn't answer.

But in the stillness between them, he was already wondering how to ask the same thing.

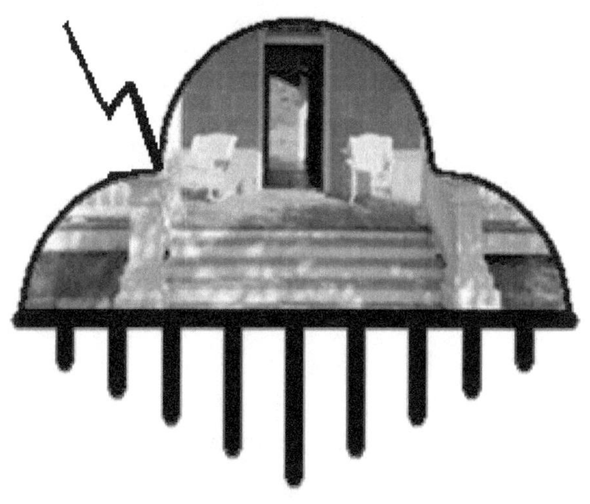

Chapter 38
Not Safe Anymore

Mrs. West was the first to spot them, Martin and Lindsay, stepping out of the jet bridge at Midland International Airport with travel-weary shoulders and smiles that spoke more of gratitude than rest. Robert continued sleeping in his portable car seat. Luggage retrieved, they walked the short distance to the short term parking. Dumpsy greeted them the moment they opened the door. Sealed in his carrier on the SUV's third-row seat, let out one sharp, offended meow and immediately turned his back to the world.

Martin ducked into the backseat and reached through the bars of the carrier. "Miss me, you little tyrant?"

Dumpsy flicked his tail in response. Then he turned for head scritches.

It had been warmer in Seattle than here. A late cold front had pushed through. Lindsay climbed in beside him, sliding her bag over her lap as Mrs. West shut the SUV door. Cold air rushed in before the door latched, and Martin could already see the cloudbank stacking to the north, maybe snow flurries in Lubbock by sundown.

"How close was it in Seattle?" asked Mrs. West as Mr. West eased the SUV out of the terminal loop road. "Did the train actually arrive on time?"

"Not quite," Lindsay said. "We caught a shuttle from the King Street Station and barely made it to the airport. The airline was an hour late, too. Our three hour layover in Denver was only an hour and some change. Tailwind from there with this cold front."

Mr. West gave a small nod from the passenger seat. "Good. I brought tacos in the cooler. Some drinks, too."

Lindsay leaned forward between the seats. "You're a saint."

Martin, still rubbing behind Dumpsy's ears, glanced sideways at her. "It wasn't a relaxing trip, exactly. But it was what we needed."

The SUV rumbled onto the loop and picked up speed.

Mrs. West looked at them in the mirror. "Did the train ride live up to expectations?"

Lindsay nodded. "More than. And not just the views. The people. The quiet. We'll tell you everything later."

Martin smiled faintly. "We even saw Mt. Rainier. The observation car attendant said that was a rare sight since it hides in clouds most days."

Mrs. West smiled. "You picked the right time of year."

Outside, the oil field rolled by in winter gray, along with the rotten egg smells of money. Inside the SUV, the warmth slowly returned, and so did the sense that, despite whatever waited back home, they weren't alone in it.

The Suburban put Odessa behind it just before sunset, easing west into the two-hour haul toward the mountains. Martin had expected an awkward conversation, perhaps starting by making an apology, or maybe resistance to the idea he and Lindsay had discussed on the train.

Instead, Mr. West surprised him.

"You're thinking about moving," he said flatly, after a few minutes of silence on the highway, "Brian told us about the goats."

Lindsay hesitated. "Just . . . maybe into Fort Davis. For a while. A break."

Mr. West nodded, eyes forward. "Good."

Martin blinked. "You're okay with it?"

"Son," Mr. West said, voice gravelly but calm, "we've lost a lot of goats. That's not bad luck, that's something else."

"I thought maybe, " Martin started.

"No. Skeleton's gone, but not all of it. Sheriff told me they didn't find it all. I think he said the bottom half of the left leg and the right ulna, wrist, and hand were all missing."

The car went quiet.

"Whatever's there," he said at last, "isn't going away. Not just because we want it to."

Before they reached the house, the plan had mostly taken shape. They'd finish out the school year. Over the summer, the Eastmans would move into a house in Fort Davis, Mr. West would help find one. He'd then sell the house and have it removed from the land. The barns, the permanent corral, and the well would stay.

When they arrived home, they found Brian waiting on the patio, hands in his jacket pockets, face hard. It was surprisingly warm compared to what they had left. The cold front had made it no further than south of Pecos.

With a cordless spotlight Mr. West had borrowed from his work truck before leaving Big Spring, the three men climbed into the Gator without a word, and they drove out toward the cliff.

The bodies of all of the goats lay scattered and bloated along the rocks below, broken and still, just like the last time. No signs of claw marks. No blood. Just fall trauma. Like they'd been driven off deliberately.

"This ends where it started," Mr. West said quietly, staring out over the land.

No one argued.

Back at the house the group split, Martin rode with Brian into Alpine to retrieve his old pickup from the train station. The West's returned east, headed back to Big Spring. Lindsay, Robert, and Dumpsy remained inside.

When the two men returned to the ranch the winter constellation of Orion was diving below the horizon. They grabbed beers, kicked off their boots, and opened the computer in the kitchen.

"Let's see what happened," Martin said.

They scrubbed through the outdoor footage from the last week. Monday night, there it was. The goats were calm inside the panel fence. The wind was high, the cameras shaking, and flashes of lightning lit up the frames.

Then came the storm, fast-moving and fierce. Gusts shoved against the temporary fence until it collapsed inward in a gust of wind and maybe hail.

The goats scrambled, panicking in their movements.

But then… the panel stood back up.

Not slowly. Not pushed. It just . . . stood. On its own.

Brian leaned forward. "No way."

Martin rewound it. Watched again. Same result. The second the last goat slipped through the gap, the panel snapped upright like a switch had been thrown.

Then the goats turned and bolted. Not scattered, *ran*. All in the same direction. Toward the old dirt ramp. Toward the place where the land broke.

"Like they were being herded," Brian whispered.

Neither of them spoke for a long time. The glow of the monitor reflected in their eyes. Outside, the land was dark and quiet again.

Martin swallowed. "How does a metal fence panel stand up by itself in the middle of a windstorm?"

Brian sat back, exhaling hard through his nose. "I don't know, man. But that's not wind. That's not physics. That's…" He gestured vaguely at the screen. "That's something else."

Martin shut the laptop gently, as though afraid to disturb the darkness crowding the kitchen. A faint hum from the refrigerator was the only sound between them.

Brian rubbed his palms over his jeans, leaving streaks of dust. "I used to think it was just one ghost. Now I'm not sure. Feels like… like it's the land itself. Like it's sick of secrets."

Martin stared at the table. "I thought moving to Fort Davis would fix it. Distance. Walls. Neighbors close by. But what if it follows us?"

Brian didn't answer. He was looking past Martin, out the kitchen window into the dark. The porch light cast a pale cone over the yard, picking out the edges of the empty goat pen.

"Do you ever feel like it's watching?" Brian murmured.

Martin nodded, throat dry. "Yeah. Like it's waiting for the right moment."

A gust rattled the window glass. Both men flinched, then shared a nervous laugh.

Brian drained the last of his beer and set the bottle down with a soft clink. "Well. This place is like a loaded mouse trap. It feels like it gets serious given the opportunity. Snap, it goes off."

Martin offered a wan smile. "Yeah. I feel the same way, too; but I'm the mouse."

Outside, the land lay silent, the canyon unseen, hiding whatever waited below.

Chapter 39
Chayton Returns

Spring break was over, school was now nearing its conclusion. Shadow stretched across the yard as the last light of day slipped behind the distant ridges to the west. The knock came just at dusk.

Martin opened the front door to find Chayton beneath the porchlight, shoulders hunched in a windbreaker, eyes sweeping the horizon like he hadn't yet decided to stay.

"I hope this isn't a bad time," Chayton said quietly.

"Not at all," Martin said. "Come in. We're both just grading papers."

Lindsay was already in the kitchen, and when Chayton sat down at the table, a ceramic mug of coffee was set in front of him.

He wrapped his hands around it and stayed quiet for a long moment. "I'm not here officially," he said at last. "The other elders would frown on this kind of visit. They believe the matter's been resolved now that the remains are in tribal ground."

"But you don't," Lindsay said.

He didn't answer immediately. "There've been… problems," he said. "Small things. But strange."

Martin leaned in.

"When we last met the reservation hadn't received the bones sent from here, but I was sent once the tribal office had the package tracking number from the Sheriff. The remains arrived a few weeks ago. I am also still trying to find the book you mentioned . . .Storm upon Meadow is still with my thoughts."

"And that's why you're here?" asked Martin just before sipping his coffee.

"Yes and no, but you need to know this. The transport truck caught fire at a gas station on our reservation just after the box arrived. Total loss. It happened after the delivery, while the driver was getting lunch. No clear cause."

"That's awful," Lindsay murmured.

Chayton nodded. "The secretary who signed for the remains lost feeling in her right hand that same afternoon. Probably unrelated, but sudden, and odd. She never had a problem like this before."

He sipped his coffee, eyes distant. "The elder who performed the ceremony for the remains fell down the entry stairs the next morning. Said he felt lightheaded."

Martin rubbed his jaw. "You think these things are connected."

"I don't know," Chayton said. "But I know enough not to dismiss patterns too quickly. We Apache believe disturbed warriors don't rest until justice is done."

"What if I told you I had a vision in which I saw the rifle being fired at the man whose skeleton you now have?" Martin asked.

"That would be a powerful vision. That would be a call to action, His spirit clings to the place where blood cried loudest." answered Chayton.

With that he sipped his coffee again as Martin injected his update about the dead goats. Chayton offered his condolences and then spoke again, almost as a follow on to Martin's announcement.

"A raven arrived and sat on the reservation administration building, and it did not leave for some time, not until well after all the other events took place. It wasn't aggressive. Just… watching."

He glanced toward the window. "I remember seeing the Raven here. I talked to it. I asked what message it had."

A light *tap-tap-tap* came from the front door. Then a pause. Another tap.

Martin stiffened. "You hear that?"

Chayton didn't move. "It's the black one. He knows I am telling you. He knows I am listening to him. He was on your roof when I arrived."

The sound stopped.

"The black one still tries to tell me, tell you, the spirit is not settled here.

Tap tap tap.

A low caw rang out, muffled by the walls.

No one spoke. Dumpsy jumped into the window frame closest to the front door, curious to see outside, maybe smart enough to know something was outside.

Finally, Chayton stood and zipped his jacket. "I wanted you to know this. I must leave now. I am on my way to see family in San Antonio, and I need to get down the road."

Martin followed him to the door. "Is staying here dangerous?"

Chayton considered that for a long moment.

"Some things feel heavier than they should," he said. "But there's a chance… now that the remains are home… maybe that

weight will lift. Sheriff Villareal informs me he has another package coming to the reservation. A pouch in good condition. Maybe that will end this. Only the raven will know."

He paused on the porch. "Either way, be careful. Even coincidences can turn sharp if you brush up against them wrong."

****

Chayton's hands rested lightly on the wheel as mile markers flicked by. He was eastbound on Interstate 10, bound for San Antonio to visit his daughter, but his thoughts stayed behind in the West Texas mountains.

He'd seen strange things in his life, signs, dreams, events that defied explanation, but nothing compared to what he'd felt on the Eastmans' land. The air there seemed to breathe, carrying a threat he couldn't name.

He kept wondering: what injustice had occurred to the man buried there? Murder alone couldn't explain such unrest. It felt deeper, more personal.

Was the man betrayed, humiliated, left to die stripped of dignity?

Chayton sensed pain still clinging to that canyon. Maybe more than one spirit cried out from beneath the silence.

The truck's tires hummed as moonlight broke through scattered clouds, spilling over distant hills. Wind rocked the cab, rattling the mirror.

He glanced into the rearview, half expecting shadows to follow.

A thought pressed hard in his chest: this wasn't just one spirit, it was the land itself remembering a wound too deep to heal.

Whatever the truth was, he would face it. For the Eastmans. For the dead. For the land that had waited too long.

Chapter 40
What Comes Next

With the sun slipping low, golden light filtered through the kitchen window and pooled across the dinner table, still cluttered with crumbs, glass rings, and the streaks of a well-earned meal. The evening light filtered through the kitchen window, soft and golden, casting long shadows over the wooden table. Saturday had been a busy day with routines, but the end of the school year was now in sight. Six more weeks sat between them and moving away.

Robert sat in his highchair at the end of the table, kicking his legs lazily as Lindsay coaxed a spoonful of rice cereal into his mouth. Every third attempt landed with success. The others ended up as abstract art on his bib.

Martin leaned back in his chair, arms crossed, watching his son with distracted affection. The story about the reappearance of Chayton had sparked a long discussion over the meal, but now it was quiet and reflective. The silence stretched, Lindsay still feeding Robert, Mr. West frowning slightly, and Mrs. West staring at her folded hands.

Mr. West broke the silence. "We need to talk about what comes next."

Lindsay looked up, then passed the spoon to Martin, who took over with practiced ease.

Mrs. West folded her hands. "I think we're all thinking the same thing."

Martin nodded. "Losing the goats the way we did . . . it changed things. It was eerie before, sure, but now . . . it's not just weird coincidences anymore. It's loss. Real loss."

"All the goats, dead," Mr. West said grimly. "That's not mischief. That's targeted. And I'm not about to let it spread to people."

He glanced toward the window, where Jobella stood in her pen, quiet and still, "Jobella. She goes back to the Co-op barn in San Angelo. This week. I want to get her away from this place."

Lindsay nodded slowly. "I agree. She's not to blame, but something's drawn to her . . ."

Martin spooned another bite into Robert's mouth. The baby gave a satisfied grunt.

Mrs. West cleared her throat gently. "And the two of you? What do you want to do?"

Lindsay exchanged a glance with Martin. "It's time to move like we talked about after the train ride. Not far. Fort Davis. Rent first. Then see what comes up."

Mr. West looked relieved. "That makes sense. You're still close to the school. And out of reach of . . . whatever this is."

He hesitated. "I was thinking of putting the property on the market as well. Just get rid of it."

Mrs. West raised a hand. "Not so fast."

He raised an eyebrow.

She continued. "You said as much on the drive back at Spring Break, but you spent all last summer talking about gas potential. The geology. How the Delaware Basin slides right under here and nobody bothered to look until ten years ago. It looked promising, you said that over and over. You really want to throw that away now? Since when have you walked away from land that might have money parked underneath it?"

He frowned. "It's not worth keeping if it's cursed."

"Maybe it's not cursed. Maybe it's just not meant to be a home."

Martin tilted his head. "What do you mean?"

Martin noticed Mrs. West's slight smile. "Hunting lodge. Weekend retreat. Rent it out to some oil execs who want to pretend they're ranchers. You already have the barns, the corral, the well. Fix up a cabin, maybe build a second. Maybe the ghost spirit power is split in half, or haunts only one."

Martin wanted to grin but decided not to after scanning the other looks.

Lindsay added, "When I was jogging in December, I saw three deer in twenty minutes. I had to dodge them. This place is alive with wildlife."

Mr. West leaned back, thinking.

After a moment, he gave a quiet grunt of agreement.

"We wait until after the awards ceremony," Lindsay said, wiping cereal from Robert's chin. "Then start packing. Move after the school year ends."

Everyone nodded.

Outside, the wind stirred faintly. Jobella lifted her head.

Inside, the plan, finally, was beginning to take shape.

Chapter 41
Saying Goodbye

April had just begun when Mr. West arrived with the horse trailer. The air was mild with spring smells, but only by a thread. The mesquite trees stood bare, though the breeze hinted at green returning to the hills. The acacia, always first, was already in bloom. He came inside without knocking, waving off the morning chill and stomping the dust from his boots.

"Just got off the phone with Melody," he said, setting his coffee down on the counter.

Martin looked up from where he was reviewing grades. "How's Japan?"

"Confusing. Beautiful, apparently. She's already eaten several somethings she can't pronounce and got lost in a train station the size of a shopping mall. She made the mistake of climbing Mt. Fuji and then looking into the crater. Sounds like she would scoff at the pile of bones at the fourth stake because of it. And yes, she agrees Jobella should come back to San Angelo, even if she doesn't know why."

He scratched his jaw. "I told her the mare was lonely now that the goats are gone. That was about all I let on."

Lindsay smiled, carrying Robert on one hip. "You always were good at saying a lot without saying too much."

"Yeah, well," he said, stretching. "We'll see what my cell phone bill looks like after calling *into tomorrow.*"

They all stepped outside together, but Jobella wasn't in her pen.

Martin spotted her first. It was habit to look there now. "There."

The mare was standing in the same place again, the worn patch near where the skeleton had been unearthed. Just standing in the same place again. Watching something no one else could see.

They approached quietly. Mr. West took the lead rope, clipped it to her halter, and gently coaxed her forward.

She followed without resistance, until they reached the trailer.

Then she stopped.

And turned.

Her gaze locked on the patch of dirt she had stood in all winter. The same direction. The same posture. She didn't whinny or shift. She just stared.

It felt like goodbye.

Mr. West gave her a soft pat, then led her up into the trailer and latched the gate. He dusted his hands off and turned to Martin and Lindsay, who stood with Robert under one arm and the other hand shading their eyes.

"You two," he said, "are about to have a lot on your plate. Moving, working, finding a house. So let me say something while I have the chance."

He took a breath.

"I'm retiring. End of this year. Maybe sooner. I've got more money coming in from well royalties than I know what to do with, and I've finally figured out I don't have anything left to prove to Transon Oil."

Lindsay raised her eyebrows. "Really?"

Martin blinked. "Wow. That's . . . big."

"I figure it's time to spend less energy chasing more energy. And," he added, "when y'all find that house in Fort Davis, I want to help."

Martin shook his head. "We've got two incomes. We can manage."

"We appreciate the offer," Lindsay added, shifting Robert in her arms.

"Appreciate it or not, I'm helping," Mr. West said. "Let me be part of it. I want to build something with you, even if it's just painting the trim. I feel kind of bad I put you here…"

They hesitated, then nodded.

"Fifty-fifty?" Martin said.

"Fifty-fifty," Mr. West agreed.

He climbed into the cab of his truck and rolled down the window.

As the trailer pulled away, Lindsay lifted Robert's arm and waved it gently saying, "Bye-bye, Jobella."

The baby cooed softly, eyes following the shape of the trailer until it vanished behind the bend of the road.

Martin put his arm around her waist.

The land was quiet again.

But it wasn't over yet.

****

The lunchroom at Fort Davis High was unusually quiet for a Thursday. She only noticed because she stayed back from her near-daily trip to the museum. Lindsay had retreated to her classroom with a Tupperware of leftover brisket, grading papers with one hand and texting Martin with the other when her phone rang.

It was her father.

She wiped her fingers quickly and answered. "Hey, everything okay?"

"Not exactly," Mr. West said. His voice was calm, but there was an edge beneath it. "Wanted to give you a heads up before you hear it from anyone else."

Lindsay sat up straighter. "What happened?"

"Jobella's gone."

She froze. "Gone? As in stolen?"

"That's what the Co-op barn thought at first. Called the sheriff and everything. But they've got cameras. Turns out she wasn't taken. She left."

"Left?" Lindsay blinked. "How does a horse just . . . leave?"

"Broke loose from the walker. Someone stepped inside to take a call. When they looked up, she was tearing down the fence line. Cleared the gate like it wasn't even there."

Lindsay pressed her fingers to her temple. "She's never done anything like that before."

"No," Mr. West said. "That is why I've got help. I called in a favor with one of the pipeline guys from Transon Oil. He's flying around in his helicopter, sweeping the area."

"You think she could find her way back?"

He hesitated. "Honestly, I don't know what to think."

"Martin and I can come help," she offered quickly. "We can help. Just say the word."

Chapter 42
The Quiet Line

In the sheriff's office, the ceiling fan spun lazy circles against a morning already too warm for April. The sun hadn't just risen, it had pushed its way into the sky, bright and overconfident, as if daring someone to argue with it. Sheriff Villareal leaned back in his chair, watching the blades rotate, the weight of his restless night still dragging at his body. He checked his watch, recalculated for New Mexico time, and frowned. The unease from the restless sleep still clung to him, sharper than any hangover.

He tried coffee, at least several trips to the coffee pot, to take his mind off whether he would be bothering Chayton or not. If it was early in Texas, it was still an ungodly hour in New Mexico. Thirty years earlier, his Army drill sergeant would have reminded him that the "O" at the beginning of any army time really meant *Oh my God it's early.*

He waited until he couldn't stand it anymore. Then he reached for his phone.

The contact read: **Chayton – Apache Repatriation Office**.

He stared at it for a long moment before hitting "Call."

It rang three times.

"Villareal?" Chayton's voice came through alert but cautious. "Didn't expect to hear from you this early."

"Didn't expect to be making this kind of call," the sheriff replied, rubbing the back of his neck. "You got a minute?"

"Always," Chayton said. "What's going on?"

Villareal leaned forward and closed his office door. "When I was at the Eastmans' place to pick up that water pouch artifact, something happened that I can't make sense of. To a rational man, the odds are impossible. When I was leaving, a raven dropped five thirty-ought-six hunting rounds on their roof. One at a time. Neatly. Spaced out like a damn parade.

"They had a friend with them, and the four of us watched this. I was there for three of the five bullets. But the two men had shot a 30-06 that morning from a nearby ridge at the place their horse keeps standing. They fired five rounds. And that raven dropped all five on the roof."

Nothing but silence on the other end.

"I can't make sense of it," Villareal continued awkwardly. "This has never happened, I mean, this never happens. Ravens don't just... ya know... clink, clink, clink, clink, clink. It's like the damn thing was delivering a message."

Chayton collected his thoughts for a brief moment of silence.

"Sheriff, in our way, the raven is a powerful messenger. It uses magic, and very few are selected to hear its message. Never the white man. No offense." Chayton's tone held no mockery.

"I read that on the internet, Apache beliefs. Could a message be so powerful that the raven..." He stopped, trying to frame the thought.

"That the raven brought the message to a white man?"

"Yeah. My mind is playing hopscotch here. It's like another world."

Another pause.

Then Chayton said, "You think this has to do with the bones?"

"I don't know what to think," Villareal admitted. "All I know is it isn't something I can write up or put in a report. Not something I can go around talking about either."

"No," Chayton said quietly. "You can't. Yours is a world of observable and testable things. My daughter is a medical doctor, and she's about the ways of the real. But there is another realm. All Native Americans know this. It's not that we are blessed with a gift of vision, we just accept the earth knows things we do not."

There was a rustling on the line, like Chayton was moving to stand or pace.

"The things that happened before we buried him..." Chayton continued, his voice lower now. "The truck that burned. The secretary's loss of feeling. The elder that fell down the stairs after the bones arrived here... The other realm is speaking."

Sheriff Villareal rolled his eyes to the ceiling while switching the phone to his other ear. Chayton had mentioned the strange occurrences at the reservation.

"I need your advice," Villareal said. "And maybe something more."

Chayton didn't respond right away.

"Is there something you can do? Something to settle the other realm?" Villareal asked. "The wife, Lindsay, is receiving a national award for her teaching ability. We need to keep people like that here."

"I'm not asking you to spook the family," he added. "But maybe, maybe talk with them. Maybe see if there's something to be done."

"Sheriff, I live on a reservation. We are haunted daily by those who leave to go somewhere else. Our talent pool shrinks too. I know the battle you face. I can leave shortly," Chayton replied. "If they're open to it, I'd like to offer a purification ceremony. Not a show. Just what our tradition allows, if they want it. No cameras. Perhaps the spirit may be settled this way."

"They won't be home this evening," Villareal said. "Lindsay's receiving her award tonight. Big deal. Town's proud of her. But I'll get you a discount at the new Adobe Rose Hotel, and we can meet later. I can give you directions to see the award ceremony tonight if you call me when you get here."

"That'll work," Chayton said. "I'll pack my kit and be there mid-afternoon. Between Interstate 25 and Interstate 10, it's an easy drive."

"Appreciate it."

Villareal lingered a beat before ending the call. Then he stared out the small window of his office, past the patrol cars parked in crooked lines, toward the long ribbon of highway that stretched out of town and into the hills.

Whatever this was, it had started a long time ago. Maybe now, finally, it was trying to finish.

Chapter 43
The Birding Call

Tugged by a warm spring breeze, Saturday morning rolled in bright and quiet, the Davis Mountains framed by clouds that couldn't decide whether to stay or break, but the ranch was bathed in light.

Lindsay poured a second cup of coffee and sat at the kitchen table, Robert bouncing gently in his bouncer seat nearby. Martin joined her, shirt damp from moving panels out by the barn, dust streaking his forearms.

"It's going to be a good day," Lindsay said, smiling faintly. "Feels like it, anyway."

Martin nodded, glancing at the mountains. "Still no sign of Jobella?"

She shook her head. "Not in over a week. Melody texted again yesterday. Co-op barn hasn't heard a word. It's like she vanished."

He sighed. "Brian and your dad have checked every back road from here to Sterling City. Nothing."

They let the silence sit for a moment, broken only by Robert's rhythmic leg kicks and the soft tick of the kitchen clock.

"I have a couple of errands in Alpine," Lindsay said at last. "I found a real salon, not just a haircut, but actual color and styling. Gotta be stage ready. I'll take Robbie since you have outside work."

Martin grinned. "Rookie, you'll look amazing."

Lindsay smiled.

"I better. I'm sharing a stage with people from actual national institutions."

She sipped her coffee. "Martin . . . Susan's going to babysit Robert during the ceremony."

He raised an eyebrow. "Susan Rusker? She doesn't want to be at the ceremony?"

"Yes. She actually asked to do this. Said she didn't just want to get gussied up and clap. She wanted to do something useful. Wouldn't even let me offer to pay her."

Martin considered that. "Huh."

"She'll stop by later this afternoon to pick him up."

"Okay."

"Also," Lindsay added, standing and grabbing her purse, "there's a rehearsal I have to be at. I didn't know about it until last night, some sort of lineup and tech check. So I'll be back later than I thought."

Martin stood with her, brushing dust from his hands. "That changes things, but we'll work around it. Brian and I will get the panels loaded. Should be done before Susan arrives."

Outside, the clouds over the mountains hadn't moved.

Inside, everything felt settled.

Almost.

****

The office had grown quiet again, the nearby highway seemed devoid of cars and their accompanying doppler shift noises. Sheriff Villareal poured himself a cup of coffee and sat heavily at the office desk. He stared for a moment at the legal pad he'd fished out of a nearby filing cabinet to take notes, the pen resting across the top line.

With a sigh, he reached for the phone and scrolled through his contacts until he landed on one labeled simply "Greg - Lions Club/Birds." He tapped the name and waited.

Two rings.

"Sheriff!" came the cheerful voice. "Was just thinking' about you the other day. How you been?"

Villareal leaned back in the chair, cradling the phone. "Hey, Greg. I'm all right. Coffee's bad and the paper's late, but otherwise I can't complain. How's your boy doing up at Tech?"

"Oh, Weston's thriving. Joined some wind turbine design club, believe it or not. Said Lubbock finally got interesting once he stopped trying to get out of it."

Villareal chuckled. "That sounds about right. You still doing those Saturday hikes at Point of Rocks?"

"Every weekend I can. Got a nesting pair of Chihuahuan ravens I'm keeping an eye on. Smart birds. Too smart sometimes."

"Funny you should mention that," the sheriff said, taking a sip. "I've got a question that's gonna sound . . . odd."

There was a pause. "Okay, you've got my attention."

Villareal rubbed his temple. "You ever heard of a raven finding bullets? Spent rounds. Like, from a rifle. Not just picking 'em up off

the ground, *finding* them after they've been fired, when they are possibly buried. Like the bird knows where they are."

Greg gave a contemplative "hmm" before answering. "No, sir. I mean, ravens will grab shiny things, sure. Coins, earrings, bottle caps. I've seen 'em stash stuff in gutters and even trade food with hikers. But tracking down bullets under the ground? No. That's not just unusual…that's impossible."

Villareal didn't answer immediately. His eyes drifted to the map pinned beside his desk. Somewhere out past the Aguja draw, something was watching. He remembered his grandmother once told him, *"The desert keeps receipts, and you can't always read 'em."* At the time, it sounded like superstition. Now, he wasn't so sure.

Villareal stared at the window. "What if I told you it happened five times?"

"Five?"

"Five rounds fired into the dirt, long-range shots, half a mile at least. Within a few hours, those same bullets show up back at the house of the shooter. One at a time. Dropped right on the porch roof."

Greg laughed once, then went quiet. "You're serious."

"I watched it myself," Villareal said. "Rolled right off the metal. Picked it up with my own hand."

A pause. Then Greg cleared his throat. "You'd have better odds getting struck by lightning. . . while buying the winning lottery ticket. At the same time."

"That's about what I figured."

Another silence, this one longer.

"Sheriff," Greg said finally, "you think someone's messing with you? A prank?"

Villareal let out a long breath. "Not in a way that makes any sense."

"Well, if you ever see a raven reading a ballistics chart, give me a call. Listen, I gotta fly. See you at the next Lion's meeting. . ."

Villareal chuckled, but it didn't reach his eyes. "Will do, Greg. Appreciate it."

"Always."

The call ended with a soft click. Villareal set the phone down beside the legal pad, picked up the pen.

He hesitated with the pen hovering. Then slowly, deliberately, he wrote:

HAUNTED

Not because he believed it. Because nothing else made sense.

Just as he capped his pen, a *tap-tap-tap* sounded at the window behind him. He turned. Nothing there. Just the high limb of the live oak swaying, empty. He stood and pulled the blind shut.

****

Before Chayton reached Interstate 25 to begin the long drive south toward the Texas border, he saw it…a raven perched on a weathered billboard advertising a nearby diner. It wasn't the sort of thing he usually noticed while driving, but something about the bird caught his eye. In the passenger-side mirror, he watched as it launched itself into the air, wings spread, veering off toward a nearby field.

A few miles later, another raven landed on a telephone pole ahead. Then it, too, took flight, gliding back into the fields beyond the road. It kept happening. One bird after another, appearing on a

343

signpost or powerline, always just ahead. Sometimes there were two, sometimes more. But never long between sightings.

Each time, they watched. Then they turned away.

Chayton squinted toward the open stretch of highway and murmured softly, "What are you telling me, raven?"

He eased off the gas slightly, feeling the vibration of the road through the steering wheel. Memories drifted in, his grandfather telling stories of ravens as messengers, guides between the seen and unseen. A warning, or an invitation.

Wind buffeted the truck as he passed a broad plain dotted with dry grass and scrub. The sky seemed enormous, clouds rolling like dark water overhead.

Ahead, a raven rose from the shoulder, black wings stark against the pale sky, circling once before drifting southeast, the same direction Chayton was headed.

He couldn't shake the feeling they wanted him to follow, or maybe to turn back.

His fingers tightened on the wheel. "I'm listening," he said under his breath, voice low, as though afraid the birds might actually answer.

A mile marker flashed past, the numbers suddenly looking unfamiliar, as if the road itself had shifted under the weight of unseen things.

Chapter 44
The Air Holds Its Breath

Fence panels clanged against the trailer as Martin and Brian worked through the humid afternoon, their shirts soaked and the air heavy with waiting. The clouds above the Davis Mountains had thickened, turning dull gunmetal gray, though the breeze hadn't yet broken into a wind.

"You sure you want to leave that big battery in the barn?" Brian inquired, "Feels like it's begging to be stolen."

Martin grunted and glanced at the bank of deep-cycle batteries near the generator wall. "The 500-foot well doesn't run on unicorn farts. That pump pulls serious amperage. Back in January, with those short days, the battery never got to full charge."

Brian laughed. "Fair. Still, if it disappears, don't come crying to me."

"I'll invoice the ghost."

After wrestling the last panel onto the stack, they stepped back to inspect their work, only to realize they'd packed the panels too far forward. The hay bales meant for Jobella sat waiting near the barn, but there was no way to fit them without rebalancing the load.

"Of course," Brian muttered. "We load first, think later."

An hour later, with the panels nudged back and the hay finally secured, they both leaned on the tailgate, breathing heavily.

"You ever think about how far a horse could go?" Brian asked. "How long it'd take to sneak across the state, dodge traffic on I-10, and find water before giving up?"

Martin stared out at the road, an unreadable expression. "Best not to think about it."

They were so focused they didn't realize how much time had passed until a car crunched up the drive.

Susan.

Martin checked his watch. "Lindsay's not back yet."

Concern flickered between them.

Susan climbed out of her car with a polite wave, dressed in casual but neatly pressed clothes. "I figured I'd come a little early. Maybe beat the storm. This one's going to be a dandy."

"She should be back soon," Martin said, ushering her into the house. "Help yourself to some iced tea."

While Susan settled into the living room, Martin and Brian changed into their best clothes. Just as they emerged from their respective bedrooms, their phones buzzed in unison.

Severe Thunderstorm Watch - National Weather Service

No doubt now that the storm over the mountains wasn't going to become an average garden variety raincloud.

Before they could speak, Lindsay burst in, breathless and wide-eyed. Even Robert was wide-eyed in his car seat, having just been awakened by several jolts and tugs. Lindsay set the car seat down by the door. "She was late, the salon owner. Didn't get back from lunch until nearly two! I missed some of the rehearsal."

She disappeared down the hall to change, and Martin and Brian exchanged a look.

They stepped outside.

The sky had changed.

A massive thunderstorm loomed over the mountain range. The base of the cloud was dark and ragged, but it was the structure above that made Martin pause.

"See that overshooting top?" Martin asked, pointing. "And that anvil spreading out to the east? That's a monster."

"Looks like a spaceship."

"Meteorology lab at ASU was my favorite. We had one trip where we saw a wall cloud over Sterling County. Took shelter in a ditch, but it never touched down. That class is how I knew to get your goats to higher ground when I worked for you."

Brian squinted at the horizon. "Let's hope this one doesn't make a flash flood."

Lindsay stepped out, dressed and ready, still fastening her earrings.

"I need to go. They're expecting me."

Martin gave her a kiss. "Be careful, beautiful."

"I will. I'll see you both there."

They watched her car disappear down the long drive, the sky darkening as it came rolling in from the southwest.

****

Ten minutes later, Martin and Brian were straightening their ties and checking their watches. Susan was giving Dumpsy a good full belly rub while talking with them about the award. The sky outside

had dimmed just enough to suggest that the storm was drawing closer.

Robert stirred awake in his car seat near the door and made a low, unmistakable sound.

Martin winced. "That was definitely a mess."

Susan laughed. "Go on, I'll take care of it."

Martin hesitated. "You sure?"

"It's what needs to be done. You two have enough to worry about tonight. I'm a grandma, remember? Got seven grandkids under ten. I've changed more diapers than you've had cups of coffee."

"Thank you again, Susan," Martin said, reaching for his keys.

"Go," she waved him off. "Just be proud."

Martin and Brian stepped onto the porch. Brian eyed the truck and raised an eyebrow. "Wait a minute. This isn't the loaner truck."

Martin grinned. "Just noticing this now? Nope. It's the one my father-in-law rebuilt. Better engine, new tires, and an AC that doesn't smell like mildew."

"Fancy."

They climbed in and drove off, tires crunching over the gravel, taillights disappearing toward Fort Davis.

Inside, Susan cleaned Robert up efficiently, cooing to him and wiping his cheeks. "You're a good boy," she murmured. "We'll have you fed and in pajamas before the sun goes down."

She secured him back in the car seat and grabbed the baby bag, slinging it over her shoulder as she stepped out onto the porch. She locked the door behind her.

A sudden rustle made her jump.

A raven, jet-black and too large for comfort, flapped its wings and took off from the top of her car with a throaty caw.

Susan exclaimed "Shoo!" as she carefully navigated her way safely down the front porch steps.

She loaded Robert into the back seat and dropped the bag beside him. Something in the back of her mind was telling her something was off with what she was doing. Settling into the driver's seat, she started the car and shifted into gear and immediately noticed something was definitely wrong.

The car leaned noticeably to the right. The passenger seat was lower down, in fact the whole car was tilted.

Putting it into park she stepped out again and rounded the front to the passenger side.

Both tires on the right side were flat.

Susan stood there for a long moment, the first cool breath of wind lifting her hair, and the scent of rain in the air. She pulled out her phone, happy that she had access to the nearby Wi-Fi router.

"Hey," she said when her husband picked up. "Yeah, both tires are out. No clue why. I haven't driven over anything. I'm here down the scout camp road. It's the first house on the right about two miles in…wait it's the only house on the right."

She paused. "No, it's fine. I'll take him back inside. Just annoying."

With Robert back on her hip, she tried the front door. Locked.

Around the side of the house, the back door was still unlatched. She stepped inside as the wind picked up behind her, easing the door shut with her heel.

Somewhere nearby, thunder murmured low and long, like something waking up.

****

The turn from Highway 17 onto 118 took them right past the stone buildings and long parade field of the Fort Davis National Historic Site. The storm loomed in the mirror, high and slow-

moving, its anvil head expanding like a mushroom cloud thrown high into the atmosphere.

Brian glanced toward the northwest. "It's sliding northeast, toward the ranch."

Martin nodded. "Yeah. It looks like it split around the mountains and drifted northeast. We might miss it completely here, but no observing at the observatory tonight."

A few miles farther and they pulled into the Davis Mountains State Park, the road winding gently uphill toward the adobe lodge built during the Depression. Its smooth white walls and flat roof seemed to glow beneath the dimming sky.

They parked near the conference center and stepped out, adjusting their collars.

"You ever feel underdressed the second your feet hit the ground?" Brian asked.

Martin gave a crooked smile. "Every time someone else wears a tie."

Around them, guests moved toward the entrance in tailored suits and evening dresses. Inside coats were pressed, shoes shined. The occasion felt elevated, not just a school award, but a national one.

Martin paused before entering, drawn to the skyline. A thick grey rain shaft was descending from the far edge of the storm, a heavy column slicing across the horizon. Lightning jabbed down through it in stark white forks, stabbing the ground with silent violence.

Both of their phones buzzed again.

Severe Thunderstorm Warning – NWS

Martin silenced his alarm with a sigh. "Well, someone is getting plastered."

Inside, the conference room was already half full. Mr. and Mrs. West stood among a crowd near the center of the room, waving them over with polite excitement. Round tables draped in white linens filled the space, each set with real China, polished silverware, and glinting crystal glasses. No plastic in sight.

"This is . . . a whole thing," Brian murmured.

Martin nodded, eyes drawn to the two camera setups in opposite corners. Each was manned by an operator wearing a headset and murmuring into a mic headset. He couldn't make out the words, but the tone was upbeat.

The event menu rested atop each plate, printed in embossed lettering. A full three-course dinner, served by uniformed hotel staff.

Martin looked around.

The lodge's charm was unmistakable. The cedar-trunk ceiling gave the room depth and warmth, while the tile floors echoed softly with footsteps. Stone archways and wrought iron accents completed the atmosphere. It felt less like a school ceremony and more like a banquet hosted in an old-world manor.

He took a breath, one hand in his pocket, and finally smiled.

"She deserves this," he said.

Brian nodded. "Yeah. She's earned every bit of it." He swept his eyes over the crowd. "I feel out of place. I'm not a teacher."

Martin chuckled. "Relax. Nobody's looking at us."

Brian leaned in conspiratorially. "Except that one lady over there who keeps side-eyeing my boots."

Martin followed his gaze, spotting a woman in a pearl necklace and satin dress casting a faintly scandalized look downward. He laughed under his breath. "Well, too late to change now."

The murmur of conversation filled the room, underscored by the clink of glassware and the soft shuffle of servers moving with silent efficiency. Light glowed warm across polished wood beams, catching reflections off the crystal centerpieces at every table.

A man in a dark suit stepped onto a small stage near the front, tapping the microphone gently. His voice rose above the crowd,

welcoming everyone, his vowels rounded in a precise, professional cadence.

Brian looked around. "Kind of feels like a wedding reception. Except I'm not obligated to dance."

Martin smirked. "Don't get too comfortable. Lindsay might still drag you out there."

Near the windows, the mountains loomed black against a sky streaked with fading purple. Lightning flashed on the horizon, silent and white, turning the glass panes into brief mirrors.

Martin exhaled, feeling a curious calm. For the first time in months, the weight pressing on his chest seemed lighter.

He turned to Brian. "Let's go find our table."

Brian grinned. "Amen to that."

They started across the room as a waiter passed carrying a silver tray of champagne flutes, the bubbles catching the chandelier light like tiny stars.

Martin glanced toward Lindsay again, her laughter bright as a bell. Whatever storms waited outside, for this one evening, they belonged somewhere else.

Chapter 45
The Storm Talks

Ominous clouds had stacked deep and dark by the time the first raindrops tapped at the roof. A moment later, the storm arrived in full, sweeping across the house in long, rustling waves. Susan sat with Robert in her lap, the blanket rising and falling with his breath. He wasn't fussy. Just wide-eyed, his little head swiveling toward each rumble and gust. Attentive, but calm.

Susan ran a hand gently over his hair. "You've got your daddy's eyes," she whispered, brushing his curls. The house creaked as wind pushed against the side. Outside, the first streak of lightning landed near the western horizon, bold and white. A few seconds later, another flash sliced through the clouds, this one jagged in the opposite direction, like nature had crossed its arms.

Thunder rolled over the house in long, uneven waves. The walls seemed to flex with the sound, as if breathing. The last of the thunder faded, leaving only the sound of the rain.

Then Susan heard it.

A low growl.

She turned slowly.

Dumpsy was crouched beneath the couch, ears flattened, tail tucked. The sound in his throat was guttural and constant, vibrating against the laminate floor.

Susan rose carefully, lifting Robert into the crook of her arm. She looked again at the back window.

There was nothing outside. Only the dark and the storm remained.

****

Dinner was winding down. Plates cleared, glasses refilled with fresh coffee or sparkling water, and quiet conversations dimmed as the lights above the stage brightened slightly. There was no audible thunder, but the windows facing northward strobed brightly with each bolt of lightning cranked out by the nearby storm.

A tall man in a charcoal blazer stepped to the podium, a wireless mic clipped neatly to his lapel.

"Good evening, ladies and gentlemen. I'm Dr. Allen Brewster, current president of the United States History Teachers Association, even if I now currently teach University of British Columbia in Vancouver, where I recently relocated. It's an honor to welcome you to tonight's ceremony." Muffled laughter passed through the audience.

He gestured to a table to his right. "Please join me in welcoming our selection committee: Dr. Sandra Hobbs of Chicago, Illinois; Professor Elaine Singh from Bloomington, Indiana; Mr. Thomas

Reede of Milwaukee, Wisconsin; and Ms. Marjorie Lane from Las Vegas, Nevada."

Martin and Mr. West exchanged glances. Lindsay's eyes went slightly wide. Brian leaned closer to the table and whispered, "That's quite the group. Not a one from Texas."

Martin smirked. "Not even close."

Dr. Brewster continued. "Tonight's award recognizes outstanding dedication to historical education at the secondary level. This year, we mark a historic first. The last Texan to receive this award was in 1977. And never before has it been awarded to a teacher working in a school district with fewer than ten thousand students."

Brian grinned, leaning back in his chair. "This whole *county* doesn't have ten thousand people. Living or dead."

The others at the table chuckled quietly as the speaker went on, but Martin's phone buzzed in his jacket pocket.

He pulled it free, intending to silence it, but stopped cold when he saw the name: **Chayton Altaha**.

The message was simple: *Check your voicemail.*

Martin excused himself quietly and stepped toward the back of the room, finding a quiet corner near the double doors. Cell service was strong, a rarity in the mountains.

He tapped to play the message.

Chayton's voice came through, low and urgent.

"Martin. I have just arrived in Fort Davis to visit you later. The water pouch arrived yesterday, and it reminded me to locate and read the book I mentioned to you and your wife. I've been reading *Our Stories*, the 1906 collection. There is a mention of a group of Lipan Apache who came to the Mescalero reservation from the Davis Mountains. They were led by an Apache named Painted Elk. He tells of leaving the mountains in haste, without ceremony, because only the horse of Storm upon Meadow returned to camp.

That was March of 1891. The tribe was camped at Old Camp Springs."

There was a pause.

"They took it as a sign, a warning from the fort. Storm upon Meadow had gone to deliver word of their departure. He never returned. The tribe fled that day. The body on your land, the one we buried a few weeks ago on our reservation, can only be that of Storm upon Meadow. May he be at peace now. It would be the rifle that ties the spirit to the land. It needs to be destroyed . . .it needs to be destroyed *there*. I felt I needed to call you when I got here…I was watched by ravens all the way here."

Before the message ended Martin heard the distinct caw of a raven along with road noise. Chayton hadn't bothered to step inside once he got out of his vehicle.

The message ended.

Martin stood frozen.

Mr. West, now standing behind him, asked quietly, "Everything all right?"

Before Martin could answer, his phone rang.

Susan.

Martin answered the call, heart already sinking. Her voice was barely coherent, shaky, and strange.

"The man is here now," she said, over the roar of wind and rain. "And I am going with him . . . "

Susan hung up.

Martin stared at the screen, stunned. "That made no sense . . . "

"What happened?" Mr. West asked.

"That was Susan. She said someone is there, and she's supposed to go with him. But how can it be pouring in Fort Davis when it's not even raining here? Fort Davis is further from the storm than we are."

"She never left your house?" Mr. West asked.

Martin pulled up his phone again and quickly remoted into the house's camera system. It was pouring at the house.

He moved from camera to camera, scrutinizing each frame. The award ceremony faded away. . . Lightning flashed on screen. Camera four revealed Susan's car was still parked in front of the house, noticeably tilted to one side. Other cameras revealed no other vehicle. Martin hazarded a guess it wasn't Chayton, making this unbelievably serious now. 'The man' she mentioned must have either walked there or parked away from the cameras.

Mr. West leaned in. "That's not good. Storms bring that . . . thing . . . out."

"You got that right," Martin muttered, cycling through feeds. The camera six image came up on his phone. His breath caught when motion appeared on the back door camera.

Susan, holding Robert, walked slowly down the steps and into the rain. The back door remained open. Her movement was deliberate. Stiff. Methodical. And then she disappeared from frame.

Martin switched to the barn camera, it was focused on the empty goat corral, but the top of the screen showed the back of the house, too. Rain streaked the lens, but the pasture between the corral and the house lit up with each lightning strike. In one brilliant flash, Susan could be seen moving out into the open field, arms cradling Robert, her steps slow and dreamlike.

"She's going to the cliff!" Brian's voice came from behind them. He had just arrived at the back of the room and was now staring at the screen over Martin's shoulder.

His words were louder than he meant.

The back tables turned. A few people rose to see what was going on.

At the front of the room, Lindsay stood at the edge of the stage, just about to be introduced.

She heard the words clearly.

The ceremony halted.

Martin bolted for the exit, Brian right behind him.

Mr. West looked at the room full of confused faces, the MC now frozen mid-sentence.

Mr. West opened his mouth, struggling, for once in his life, to find the words.

"Babysitter problems . . . baby problems . . . My God, my grandson . . . "

Then he, too, ran for the door.

Onstage, Lindsay was rooted in place.

She had never seen her father lose composure like that. Panic surged through her.

Without thinking, she bolted offstage and ran for the back of the room, guests gasping and murmuring in her wake. The Master of Ceremonies stood there with the plaque while a well-dressed lady stood behind him carrying a large check made out to Lindsay.

Somewhere inside the storm, the ghost had come home.

Chapter 46
Into the Rain

Rain hammered the pasture in long, soaking sheets, relentless but not yet wild, as if the storm was holding its breath, waiting for the exact moment to break. Susan walked forward one step at a time, her boots squelching in the soft earth. Her arms cradled Robert against her chest, his small fists occasionally flailing as droplets peppered his face. He squirmed, made a few grunting noises of irritation, but didn't cry.

Lightning split the sky behind them. In the flash, Susan saw movement in the distance, just shadows at first, scattered between the mesquites, then the outline of figures. Men. Riding. Marching. Watching.

She blinked, and they were gone.

Thunder cracked above, and it wasn't just sound. It was a voice. A command.

"Close it up! Keep your spacing, boys! Keep it tight!"

She didn't stop. Her pace was slow, even, unwavering. Her mind was no longer her own.

Another step. Another flash. This time the pasture looked like a parade ground. Figures turned their heads as she passed, faces vague but uniforms sharp. A rider nodded at her from horseback, hand resting on the butt of a long rifle slung across his chest.

Thunder rolled again.

"Sir, you hit 'im! I'll be damned!" said the voice. It sounded like it came from behind her, or within her, or from the sky.

She whispered back, lips barely moving, though she didn't seem aware she had.

"Yes, Sergeant."

Robert shifted again. Rain trickled into the side of his eye. He blinked furiously, shook his head, and let out a whine of protest. But still, no tears.

The back of the house was gone from view now. The corral vanished behind the curtain of water. Each bolt of lightning painted a ghostly white edge along the rise ahead, the cliffs, the gully, the place where the earth fell away.

"This is from one killer to another, sir."

She nodded again.

Ahead, somewhere in the storm, something waited. Not a presence she could name. Not even a shape. But the direction was fixed. The path was known. The catclaw branches peeled back from the path.

Susan walked on.

The thunder kept time like a funeral drum.

****

The tires howled on the pavement as Martin's truck surged down the highway, pushing 90, maybe 95. Headlights of oncoming cars veered to the shoulder, horns blaring as the gust of displaced air shoved them aside from a bothered semi.

Inside Martin's cab, the air was as tight as the storm clouds hanging overhead.

Martin gripped the wheel with both hands. "It's not Storm upon Meadow. Not exactly. It's the rifle. That damned Whitworth rifle. It's . . . possessed. Somehow. I've felt this ever since I stood outside in that rectangle of rocks laid out by the raven."

Brian looked over, face pale but focused. "You think the spirit is inside the rifle? Like, the ghost isn't free, it's *bound?*"

Martin nodded sharply. "O'Brannach wrote about visions. Wrote like a man trying to confess without admitting it. I think when he killed Storm upon Meadow, something happened. The Indian's spirit didn't move on. The rifle held it."

Brian shook his head. "But the skeleton, the bones were buried. Mostly. Some bones were never found. Maybe still in the ground?"

Martin swore under his breath. "Then that's the tie-in. The bullet's still there, the bullet is sitting on the windowsill above the kitchen sink. It's like two halves of a chain. The spirit is still bound to the weapon."

Brian pointed up the road. "Museum's just ahead. But it'll be closed by now."

Martin didn't even blink. "Then I'm driving through the doors. I have to get that rifle. And I have to destroy it. *On my land where the ghost is.* The ghost needs to see it, or feel it, or whatever ghost sense with."

Brian stared ahead for a long moment as they hit a straightaway near the edge of town. Then he smirked. "Think we can get the same jail cell? I play a mean tic-tac-toe."

Martin didn't smile. "This is my fight. My land. My son. You don't need to do this."

"And miss three hots and cot?"

The truck veered off the highway and into the museum parking lot without slowing much. The building loomed ahead, dark behind the soft floodlights. The double glass doors flashed once in the headlights and then shattered in a bloom of glittering shards as Martin slammed through.

Metal shrieked. Glass rained down. The truck thudded over the curb and stopped just shy of a display wall. One headlight flickered and died.

Martin threw it into reverse and backed out fast, leaving behind a wrecked entryway and the rising wail of an alarm.

They ran. Feet pounding against polished concrete, red strobe lights flaring. Sirens inside and out.

They found the display.

The Whitworth rifle rested inside a tall case, angled perfectly beneath a museum light.

Brian turned and yanked a spear from the nearby life-sized Bear vs. Native American diorama, leaving the manikin to face the monstrous bear without his spear.

"Good luck!" he said to the plastic man standing in the diorama, "You're on your own." He slammed it through the glass. Alarms shrieked louder. The rifle fell into Martin's hands, surprisingly heavy.

They ran again. The truck idled outside, the new dents and scratches on it in stark contrast to the repairs that were done.

Martin climbed in, sticking the rifle into the footwell of the passenger seat so that the barrel was up in the cab with them. Brian slammed the passenger door and buckled in.

They turned back onto the highway. The Balmorhea road opened ahead, slick black under the lights. The rain shaft loomed ahead like a wall of smoke, streaked with angry forks of lightning.

They didn't slow down.

They couldn't. Not now.

Chapter 47
Teeth of It

Pressure built with every mile. Wind howled, and rain mixed with sharp hail hammered the windshield in thick, wind-driven sheets. The wipers fought to keep up as Martin and Brian tore down the highway. With only one headlight working, he was driving more from memory than seeing the road. Heavy *thunks* against the truck's side made it clear not all the hail was small. Lightning flashed close enough to light the cab like a camera flash, each burst casting the storm in stark, skeletal frames.

Brian leaned forward slightly, eyes locked on the rifle resting at Martin's side, the butt planted against the floorboard, the barrel rising within a few inches of the ceiling. The vehicle jostled, and the rifle shifted slightly, humming faintly.

"It's getting warm," Brian said.

Martin didn't take his eyes off the road. "What?"

"The barrel. Feel it. It was cool a minute ago. Now it's . . . warm."

Martin reached over and brushed his fingers along the barrel. It was subtle, but real…like something simmering from the inside out.

"Is that a good sign? Or a bad one?" Brian asked, his voice quieter now.

Martin shook his head. "I don't know."

The words had barely left his mouth when the world outside turned pure white.

A bolt of lightning struck just off the shoulder, a searing flash accompanied by an instant, window-rattling boom. The truck swerved half a lane before Martin corrected. Both men shouted, instinct and adrenaline firing at once.

Inside the cab, for a split second, the rifle glowed, a clean, brilliant white light pulsing from the barrel and down through the stock, casting long, unnatural shadows across the dashboard.

Silence reclaimed the cab in the aftermath.

Brian stared at the rifle. "Tell me you saw that."

Martin nodded, eyes wide, jaw tight. "Yeah. I saw it."

"What the hell was that?"

Martin swallowed, then forced a half-breath. "Maybe it was St. Elmo's fire."

Brian looked at him. "You ever seen St. Elmo's fire?"

Martin shook his head once. "No. But maybe that's what it was." He paused. "Hopefully, it wasn't something else."

Brian stared out the windshield for a long moment. "Hopefully," he repeated.

They hit the turn onto the Ranch road, tires sliding just slightly before catching the gravel and mud. Rainwater rushed across the low dips in the road, running six inches deep in places, but the truck powered through, sending sprays up in both directions.

Brian pointed ahead. "We'll never get this truck through the catclaw behind the house. Even with the lift."

Martin nodded. "We switch to the Gator. Run it down along the north fence line. The goats cleared a lot of that growth out before they died."

Brian grunted. "We can find the spot. But we can't find her. Not in that field. Not in this storm."

Martin's grip on the wheel tightened. "Then we stop her before she gets there. We have to."

"Just remember there's a cliff with a body count, and Gators don't fly."

Outside, lightning struck again, this time so close it left the smell of ozone in the truck cab.

The storm wasn't behind them anymore.

They were driving into the heart of it.

Another blast of wind rocked the truck sideways, and for a moment, the tires skated across the mud-slicked road. Martin fought the wheel, jaw locked, knuckles pale. Water poured off the windshield faster than the wipers could shove it aside, turning the headlight into a pale beam swallowed by a moving wall of rain.

Thunder cracked overhead again, so loud it seemed to punch through the roof. A tremor passed through the truck's frame. Brian twisted in his seat, as though expecting the storm itself to come clawing into the cab.

"Look at the gauges," Brian said suddenly, voice tight.

Martin flicked his eyes to the dashboard. The battery light glowed red, flickering in time with the lightning outside. The oil pressure needle danced close to low.

Martin hissed a breath through his teeth. "Not now, come on…"

The engine grumbled, coughing once, then caught again.

Brian's voice dropped, a near whisper. "Martin…if that thing dies out here…we're two miles out."

Martin's face was pale, but his eyes stayed on the twisting road ahead. "Then we run."

The gun still glowed faintly, as if holding the echo of the lightning flash inside its barrel. A low vibration thrummed from the steel, like a tuning fork struck and still humming.

Brian reached out and touched the rifle's stock again. He jerked his hand back instantly. "It's hotter now. Like a heating pad left on high."

Martin didn't answer right away. He could feel it too, the warmth, a tremor beneath the wood, like something alive. The knowledge crawled over his skin, leaving goosebumps in its wake.

Turning onto the ranch road Martin powered it through the first few low water crossings. Lightning forked across the sky, revealing the slope of the mountain ridge ahead, briefly silver-white. Sheets of rain fell like steel chains, hammering the hood. Only the tight bend in the road forced him to slow the truck.

He cleared his throat, voice low. "We've come this far. We finish it."

The truck roared forward, splashing through another flooded dip, headlights flickering as the storm swallowed them whole.

Chapter 48
The Edge of the Storm

Every inch of Susan was soaked, but she didn't seem to notice. Rain clung to her hair, her clothes, her skin, flattening everything but her resolve. She moved steadily, eyes distant, as if called by something only she could hear. Her grip on Robert was firm but gentle, cradling him like something sacred.

The baby whined again, not in fear, but discomfort. Rain ran into his eyes, and he turned into her chest, seeking shelter.

She didn't react. She just kept walking.

Lightning struck somewhere behind her. The brief flash revealed the land ahead, the rise, the low scraggle of brush, and the thinning stretch of rocky soil that led to the cliff.

Another flash.

The ground beyond the edge gleamed like silver, the distant wash a dark vein through the desert.

Thunder cracked, close and sharp.

"Sir, you hit 'im! I'll be damned!"

The words were clearer now. Louder. Not imagined. Not dreamlike. They rolled across the pasture in rhythm with the storm.

"His name was Storm upon Meadow."

Her lips moved, silently mimicking the cadence.

Robert kicked once, then fell still again.

Susan stepped over a washout rut, her foot sinking slightly into the softened ground. She didn't adjust. Didn't even glance down.

As she walked, the acacia before her pulled back their branches, like a soldier's saber line, only to fall back into position after her and the child's passage. The ground rose beneath her feet, just a shallow swell before the drop.

One more flash.

And this time, she saw them.

Figures ahead. Watching. Silent.

"His name was Storm upon Meadow," she repeated.

She kept walking.

The wind pushed back her soaked blouse. Robert made a sudden, sharp sound, a short cry, like a hiccup of protest.

Susan's head tilted.

Behind her, she heard voices.

But she didn't turn.

Not even when another thunderclap landed like a command:

"First to Ride, Last to Fall!'

She stepped forward.

And the cliff edge rose before her…not ten yards away.

Chapter 49
Into the Storm

A wall of wind slammed against the truck, jarring the frame and cutting Lindsay's breath short. The Transon Oil pickup roared down the darkened road, tires slicing through sheets of runoff as the storm bore down harder with every mile. Rain hammered the windshield, relentless, and lightning flashed in rapid succession, so bright it felt like the sky was stuttering.

Lindsay sat between her parents, shaking. Her hands were balled in her lap, knuckles pale, her heartbeat loud enough to drown out the storm. She couldn't stop thinking of Robert… his blanket, his bottle, the way he curled against her chest. He would be crying now, confused. Or worse.

"Faster," she said, her voice barely above the wipers.

Mr. West didn't answer, but the truck picked up speed.

"Thank you," she said, voice barely rising above the roar of the rain on the windshield. "For driving. I couldn't . . . I couldn't do it."

Mr. West gave a brief nod, eyes forward, both hands gripping the wheel.

Mrs. West leaned closer. "You did the right thing."

Lindsay looked down. "I keep thinking… there were signs. All those months. The bones, the artifacts, the strange weather, the dreams. I should have seen the connection. I teach historical connections like this. I should've put it together. We gave it what it wanted… It wants Susan, because unlike other descendants of O'Brannach she had actually returned to the killing ground."

Mrs. West shook her head. "Everything was circumstantial until Chayton from the reservation contacted Martin. No one could have known what was really happening . . . not like this."

The truck jolted as it crossed a shallow dip in the road. Lightning flashed sideways across the sky, illuminating the clouds in layers. Short of a tornado dropping, the storm was an entity all its own. It walked upon the land with a vengeful spite.

"Still," Lindsay whispered. "Susan. I trusted her with Robert. And she is a descendent of the man that killed Storm upon Meadow."

Lindsay stared ahead. This wasn't just strange anymore, it was a supernatural force.

"Maybe that's what gave it leverage over her," Mrs. West continued. "A thread to pull on. Blood and guilt. That old rifle. It's tied to the family."

Lindsay swallowed hard. "Then she never stood a chance."

Thunder boomed so loudly it rattled the truck windows.

Mr. West kept driving, eyes hard on the road, rain whipping sideways now. The storm was no longer something they were heading toward.

****

They were in it.

****

Rain streamed down Susan's face as she stepped to the very edge of the cliff, toes inches from nothingness. Lightning peeled across the sky behind her, illuminating the drop, a sheer, black void carved into the earth. The next step was death.

The wind howled. Thunder rolled.

The voices came again, louder now, and layered: clipped commands in English, shouts in Apache. Two languages, one intention.

"One step forward!"

"Díí' naashá!"

"Deliver the justice!"

"Díí' naashá!"

"Maintain formation!"

"Díí' naashá!"

"Restore balance!"

She stopped at the edge. The lightning illuminating the dead below. Her foot lifted slowly, trembling, extending into the air over the abyss.

"STOP! Susan, don't do it!"

The shout cut through the storm.

She froze.

The Gator UTV skidded to a halt behind her, tires gouging the mud. Headlights locked on her silhouette, catching her soaked clothes, her pale face, and the baby clutched to her chest. Robert squinted and turned his head away from the glare, miserable but silent.

Martin stumbled out, breath heaving. Brian was right behind him.

"Please!" Martin cried. "For the love of God, don't do it. Don't kill my child! Don't take that next step!"

Susan turned slowly to face them. The wind twisted her hair across her face. Her eyes burned with something ancient and unwavering.

Her voice, when it came, wasn't hers.

"This white man has no honor. There is no brotherhood with murderers."

Her feet remained planted at the very lip of the cliff.

"You came with peace in your mouth and a rifle in your hands," the voice continued. *"You killed what you could not understand."*

Martin stepped closer. "I didn't do this. None of us did. That wrong wasn't ours."

"A man was given a weapon built for death. He did not know what it meant to carry that power."

Martin's voice cracked. "I do. I see it. But this isn't the way. My son should not pay for that man's sin."

Susan wavered. Her foot dropped back to solid ground. But her eyes never left Martin.

"The weapon remembers. The wound does not heal."

Brian, wordless, reached into the Gator bed and passed Martin the Whitworth rifle.

Susan's gaze locked onto it instantly.

"It is still here," she said. Her voice was rigid. Cold. *"Still whole. Still proud. Still waiting."*

Martin looked at the rifle, the rain now running down its barrel. It was heavy in his hands and the warmth from earlier was still there.

As Martin raised the rifle above his head, the voice in Susan rose, louder, unrecognizable in its tone. He could hear her and someone, or something else, blended in.

"Break the skin, and the wound shall heal. Break the peace… and carry the weight forever. There is no honor in destroying peace."

He raised it higher, and swung it down with all his strength.

The stock split, but not randomly. It divided precisely along the fine carved line scratched deep into the cheek plates, the old mark that had been cut there long ago by Sergeant Voss. And from that break, a sudden burst of brilliant white light flared outward, blinding and clean, a flash that radiated across the clearing like a ripple spreading across still water. A loud and low hum exploded into the air, then faded like a bell rung for the final time.

He swung again, and again, until the metal frame bent and the scope cracked loose.

The rifle lay broken in several large pieces in the storm.

Susan gasped, a full-bodied, ragged sound, and staggered backward.

She was slipping.

Martin and Brian lunged forward. Mud flew. Hands grasped.

They caught her and the child.

Her foot had just started to slip, heel dragging over the muddy edge.

Martin yanked her back with everything he had, Brian grabbing the baby in the same motion.

The three of them collapsed into the mud as the wind died for the first time in hours.

The storm still raged.

But the haunting had ended.

Then, behind them, far off and unseen across the canyon, a blue-white flash arced up from the gravesite.

The clouds above absorbed the bolt, glowing in response.

Once.

Then again.

And again.

Three bolts in quick succession, more than coincidence. Each one lit the landscape like noon, momentarily exposing a skeletal tree line and the craggy stones near the burial trench where the Apache remains had once been disturbed.

A fourth strike split an acacia tree, and even in the rain, it burned. Flame climbed the twisted bark as if to mark the place.

The fire hissed but did not go out.

The storm pressed on, but something beneath it had changed.

The air no longer hummed with unseen judgment.

The silence wasn't a threat now, it was an absence.

Robert began to cry, loud and strong, the first sound since the rifle shattered.

It was just a baby's cry again. Nothing more.

Chapter 50
The Rider of Light

Clouds thinned as the Gator rumbled across the wet pasture, its one remaining headlight flickering through the lifting mist. Rain still fell in light sheets, but the worst of the storm had begun to retreat, dragging its fury northeast into the dark horizon.

Martin drove with one hand on the wheel, the other arm around Susan to keep her steady. Brian sat beside them, soaked and silent, cradling Robert. They crested the final rise and saw the house, still standing, porch light glowing faintly through the haze.

A crowd had gathered. The Wests. Sheriff Villareal. Lindsay. The high school principal, Arturo Mendez stood nearby. Several well-dressed guests from the ceremony, some in heels, others in evening coats, all standing awkwardly in the churned-up mud. Flashlights flickered. Raincoats flapped.

Susan was crying. Silently at first. She couldn't process what had just happened , it was like she was there, but not there at the same time. Her actions felt almost remote and robotic as she walked across the field. When she saw her husband in the gathered crowd the tears began to stream down her face. Then suddenly and fully, the emotion took over.

Lindsay ran forward, arms out. She was closest to the Gator and with his hands shaking, Brian handed over the child.

Lindsay took the baby and held him to her chest, her own tears falling freely. Mrs. West wrapped her arms around Lindsay, weeping softly.

Martin killed the engine and stepped out of the Gator. He and Brian walked directly toward Sheriff Villareal.

The sheriff looked tired and wet, but resolute. He pulled out a set of handcuffs.

"I have to know," he asked Martin, "did you break into the museum. Drive your truck through the doors?"

Martin nodded, "Sir, I had to save my son here. I had to save Susan. I can't explain it to you in a way you will understand, or believe, either. No one here would believe it."

Sheriff Villareal shook his head slightly. Everything was surreal. "After the raven dropped those five rounds a few weeks back?" he spoke quietly, "I saw an impossible thing and you three treated it like just another day. I don't understand what happened then or just happened now. I'm positive you boys did the right thing," he said. "But the museum's still broken into. And the calls have already been made."

The first handcuff clicked onto Martin's right hand. Sheriff Villareal began to recall the Miranda Warning in his mind. He wanted to say it smoothly. He also realized about a dozen people were watching his every move, some recording with their cell phones.

Mr. West stepped up. "You won't face this alone, Martin. I'll get you two the best lawyers in the state, even if I have to work past retirement."

Those few people that were recording the scene with their cell phones all jumped in unison as their tiny screens blinked off.

Everyone turned as a nearby horse whinnied.

At Jobella's favorite spot in the pasture, a soft, white light shimmered above the ground. It pulsed, formless, then began to shift. After twenty seconds, arms and legs formed. The contour of a human form. Then another shape was illuminated: broader, quadruped.

A horse.

Jobella.

But she wasn't glowing. She was real. Mud splattered, ears flicking, breathing heavy. It was Jobella, unmistakably.

Mounted now with a fully formed rider, Jobella turned toward the house and began to walk toward it, picking up speed as the apparition spurred her forward. No one blinked and several jaws opened. Many of the people standing there were mesmerized.

The ghost riding her shimmered now in its full form, not the broken, drunken man from the journal entries, but a proud cavalry officer in crisp uniform: Captain Cormac O'Brannach of the 220th Regiment. Muted colors filled the apparition.

Gasps turned into silence. Some continued to stare open-mouthed.

Near the back of the group, just beyond the last flickering tendrils of the porch light, Chayton stood with his arms crossed, the wind tugging gently at the collar of his jacket. He hadn't said a word since arriving, and no one had asked him to. His eyes remained fixed on the spot where the bones had been found, as if trying to see through the earth itself.

To him, it felt familiar, not the place, but the weight of it. He had heard stories all his life, some half-whispered over fires, others passed with sober eyes and the firm warning not to tell them lightly. But this… this was different. Older. Heavier. Even his uncle's war tales and the records held by the tribal elders hadn't prepared him for the feel of the ground here.

This land didn't just carry memory, it remembered back.

Chayton shifted his stance but didn't move closer. He didn't need to. What lingered in the air wasn't waiting for him. It was watching someone else.

That was when more gasps came.

O'Brannach dismounted. The saddle faded as he touched the ground. Jobella stood steady. O'Brannach walked toward the crowd. Sheriff Villareal, Brian, and Mr. West stepped back instinctively.

He stopped in front of Martin.

The ghost extended his right hand.

Martin, confused but steady, reached out. The hand passed through his, and the handcuff clicked loose, falling into the mud in two distinct pieces like the rifle had done, very much broken.

Both man and ghost looked down at it.

O'Brannach stepped back, touched the brim of his hat. Not a salute.

It was a thank you.

He turned and walked away, mounted Jobella, whose saddle now reappeared and shimmered into place beneath him. She trotted away, slowly, back toward her spot.

As they reached it, O'Brannach's shape began to blur, light folding inward. Jobella turned to the northwest one last time, then the glowing orb vanished in a flash of light.

And the field was still. The storm faded.

****

The broken cuff lay in the mud like a question mark, but the question had been answered by Martin, except for one item.

Martin pivoted slowly, still breathing hard, staring at the warped metal. Then he turned to Chayton.

"Díí' naashá," he said quietly. "What does it mean?"

Chayton paused. The briefest flicker of surprise crossed his face before he nodded.

"It means, 'Go to the mountain,'" he said. "It's what we say when the truth must be faced. When a man walks toward judgment and cannot carry lies, or pain, any longer."

Martin looked back toward the cliff. The storm had shifted direction.

Chapter 51
The Human Aftermath

Evening came slowly now, stretching golden and warm across the West Texas hills. School was out, and the days unfolded like pages left unmarked. Thunderstorms came and went like visitors, never staying long, never arriving with fanfare.

If there was lightning, Martin noticed, it busied itself striking elsewhere.

Martin, Lindsay, Brian, Susan, and little Robert sat outside beneath the awning of their house, the one they had nearly abandoned but chose to stay in after everything settled. The grill had gone cold, and the plates from dinner still rested on the folding table nearby. Several large fulgurites sat as showpieces in the center of the table. Robert sat in his highchair gnawing on a piece of watermelon, sticky-fingered and content. Dumpsy sat behind the glass of the closest window, enjoying the last rays of sunlight softly warming him. The evaporative cooler hummed nearby.

The distant rumble of thunder rolled off the mountains, but no one flinched. The storm had peaked earlier, and the thick grey stripe of the rain shaft was thinning visibly with every glance. The storm was in the distance and for all purposes looked likely to remain that way. Maybe the Scout camp at the end of the road was getting rain, but Martin doubted the storm would last much longer.

Melody was back from Japan, already telling tales of Tokyo ramen and 12-story bookstores. Jobella went back to the Co-op Barn near San Angelo, but in her place now grazed ten new goats in a temporary pen on the edge of the yard. They seemed content enough with the brushy acacia and the quiet company.

The trial that had once seemed inevitable never happened. The lawyer Mr. West brought in was sharp, connected, and persuasive. Martin had pled guilty to a misdemeanor, reckless driving and operating an unsafe vehicle. He paid full restitution to the museum, including the installation of a brand-new, replica-standard issue Winchester rifle to replace the shattered Whitworth. All other charges vanished at the drop of the gavel.

In the weeks that followed, they had reconsidered the plan to move to Fort Davis. And in the end, they stayed. Not out of stubbornness or denial, but because the land no longer felt angry. The ghost was gone. The bones had been buried. And their home, for better or worse, was here. Plus, the new goats were eagerly leveling the acacia in record time.

From inside the house came the sound of a door opening and a young woman stepped out onto the patio. She was in her twenties, her boots dusty and her laugh light. She walked straight to Brian and slid onto the bench beside him with the comfort of someone already welcomed. Brian smiled. Seated nearby Susan couldn't help but smile. Her experience told her the newest couple at the table were more than just friends.

"Thanks again for letting me use your bathroom," she said to Martin and Lindsay. "Your new guest house has everything but water to the plumbing."

Lindsay smiled. "Anytime, and it won't be an issue next time. They tie in the septic later next week. It's going to be different with a second house, a guest house, for friends and family. We had all but decided to move away from here. Now my father has added a second house so my parents can stay and enjoy Robert. Free daycare when they're here!"

The young woman glanced at the fading sky, then looked back at Martin.

"So," she said. "Is it true? You really broke into a museum and stole a haunted rifle to stop a ghost from killing a woman and Robert here?"

Brian smirked and leaned back with a lazy grin.

Martin wiped his hands on a napkin and took a long drink of tea.

"Well," he said. "That depends. Do you want the sunset or the sunrise version?"

"What do you mean?"

"One version will have us inside before the sun sets," he lifted his hand and pointed to the west, " and the other version will keep us out here until the sun rises tomorrow. Which one?"

The young woman grinned. "You know which one."

And just like that, the story began again.

Only this time, with everyone still here to tell it.

And no plans to leave.

The End

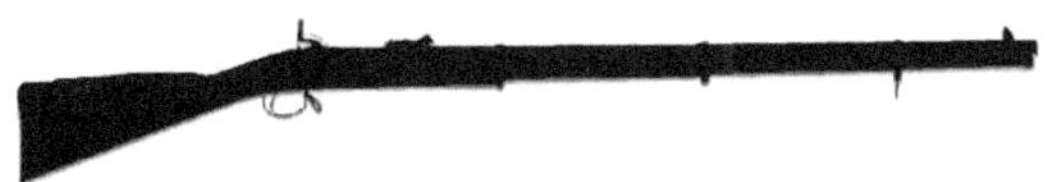

About the Author

Kyle Vernon grew up in Midland, Texas, but his teenage heart belongs to the Davis Mountains, where he spent most of his summers working. It was there, beneath thunderheads and starlight, that he first learned the weight of silence, the shape of old stories, and the kind of stillness that never fully leaves you.

Now based in Lubbock, Texas he teaches astronomy at Frenship High School, helping students discover wonder in the skies above West Texas. His teaching career has taken him across four nations and even into a combat zone, but the high desert remains his compass point.

A Davis Mountains Ghost Story marks a return to that land and its long memory, a novel about place, guilt, weather, and the things that echo.

He lives with his wife, Teri, and continues to write, teach, and listen closely when the wind changes.

Addendum: Picture Locations

Each chapter in *A Davis Mountains Ghost Story* begins with a visual flourish drawn from the land itself. Many of the images are taken from real locations across West Texas, places where the sky, stone, and wind shape memory and mood. Unless noted, all pictures were taken in June of 2025. Below is a list of the chapter flourishes and their corresponding locations:

Chapter 1 - **Ranch Road 1832, Jeff Davis County**

Chapter 2 - **Balmorhea, Texas**

Chapter 3 - **Fort Davis National Historic Site**

Chapter 4 - **Sul Ross University, Alpine, Texas**

Chapter 5 - **Fire Truck Display, Balmorhea, Texas**

Chapter 6 - **Fort Davis Courthouse, Fort Davis, Texas**

Chapter 7 - **Fort Davis National Historic Site**

Chapter 8 - **BTSR, Davis Mountains (Oct 2020)**

Chapter 9 - **Sawtooth Mountain, Jeff Davis County**

Chapter 10 - **Fort Davis National Historic Site**

Chapter 11 - **Indian Lodge, Davis Mountains State Park**

Chapter 12 - **Indian Lodge, Davis Mountains State Park**

Chapter 13 - **Wild Rose Pass, Jeff Davis County**

Chapter 14 - **(AI Generated)**

Chapter 15 - **BTSR, Davis Mountains (Oct 2020)**

Chapter 16 - **Wildflowers, Marfa Lights Viewing Area**

Chapter 17 - **VLBA Station, Jeff Davis County**

Chapter 18 - **Storm upon Meadow, AI Generated**

Chapter 19 - **(AI Generated)**

Chapter 20 - **Star Mountain, Jeff Davis County**

Chapter 21 - **Indian Lodge, Davis Mountains State Park**

Chapter 22 - **Marfa Lights Viewing Area, Marfa, Texas**

Chapter 23 - **Fort Davis National Historic Site**

Chapter 24 - **Scenic Drive, Davis Mountains State Park**

Chapter 25 - **Balmorhea HS Stadium, Balmorhea, Texas**

Chapter 26 - **Valentine, Texas**

(Note: Though called "O'Brannach's Ridge" in this work, the landform remains unnamed on all official USGS topographic maps. It can be seen from Ranch Road 1832, and it also displays contact metamorphism at the base. Do not trespass.)

". . .Until we meet again."

www.ingramcontent.com/pod-product-compliance
Lightning Source LLC
Chambersburg PA
CBHW020526110726
47899CB00004B/1265